This book is a work of fiction. The characters, dialog, and events portrayed herein are not to be construed as real. Any resemblance to actual incidents or persons, living or dead, is coincidental.

No part of this book may be reproduced, stored in a retrieval system, or transmitted in any form by any means without written permission of the publisher.

AuthorThomasEmry@Gmail.com

Cover art completed by Kelsey Halka | HalkaDesign.com

Shrapnel and Avalanches. Copyright © 2023 by Thomas Emry.

Second Edition

All rights reserved.

ISBN-13: 979-8-9883136-0-1 (paperback)

ISBN-13: 979-8-9883136-1-8 (e-book)

This book is dedicated to Courtney, Colin, and Nolan. Thank you so much for your encouragement and support. As well as your feedback when I bombarded you with question after question about out-of-context scenarios. I could never have done this without you.

Shrapnel and Avalanches

Thomas Emry

This page intentionally left blank.

CHAPTER ONE

Up and down. Up and down. First blue velvet, then it would change to red rose or matte coal black. Up and down, and up and down again. Seth Roberts watched in a hypnotic state as the robots painted the automobile door panels. So much technology behind performing such a mundane task. Simply going through the motions they were programmed, no variance or conscious thought. He could relate. Hovering somewhere between mesmerizing and mind-numbing, the robots themselves looked bored as they sprayed. He wondered what would happen if, instead of killing Sarah Connor, the T-800's prime directive was to go back to 1840's St. Petersberg and help Tom Sawyer whitewash a picket fence?

Seth thought to himself often, actually. His wandering mind was where the best conversations took place. Much of his life these days felt like one run-on internal monologue. Like Dexter minus all the murder.

He didn't hate his job, unfulfilling as it was. But it had transitioned into a "you scratch my back, I'll scratch yours" situation. He would come in daily and do no more than asked of him, if Torcon allowed him to pay bills and keep his one-bedroom apartment from getting an eviction notice on the door. They held a silent understanding. He hadn't confirmed with anyone, but he assumed Torcon had that same understanding with numerous others employed for as long as him. That was the issue he found himself in. How long he had been there.

What the hell happened? Seth thought as he stared down at the card in his hand.

He began working at Torcon at eighteen years old. Right out of high school, the entire world ripe for the taking. His father, Simon, worked there, and got him the job. Now, pushing thirty, Seth was no longer the kid making good money while figuring out what to do with his life. This was his life, and it had slowly been falling apart as of late. Not solely because of his job, but it wasn't helping in any case.

Seth didn't even program the robots. He monitored them. The product moved autonomously down the line, while he and the rest of his team ensured everything moved along without issue. If a door panel fell off or a robot caught fire or any other numerous disasters occurred, it was his responsibility to radio maintenance. They would troubleshoot and fix the issue. Boring was an understatement, but it was certainly a step up from some of the other basic labor jobs in the facility. Last week, one of the robots got their wires crossed, spun around, and punched a hole in the protective window behind it. Immediately afterward, the thing fell unresponsive. Shattered glass and a broken robot stopped production for the rest of the day. It also gave everyone something to talk about the rest of the week.

He was what they referred to as an operator. A floor grunt if he were blunt about it. But that wasn't the Torcon way. Here, "Every Person is an Equal Piece to the Torcon Puzzle." He couldn't even say the slogan out loud without feeling like a complete douchebag. Framed posters with that quote hung all over the plant, coupled with a capital T sectioned out like a completed jigsaw puzzle. Each piece of the puzzle had a smiling Torcon employee to really drive the point home. It appeared in the break rooms, the front hallway, and above the time clocks. For a brief time, it was written in black Sharpie on the middle stall wall of the men's bathroom, changed fittingly to: "Every piece of shit is an equal piece to the Torcon puzzle."

Seth again read the card he received in the pre-shift team

meeting.

**10 Years of Service!
Congratulations on reaching this important
milestone in your Torcon career.
Thank you for your continued commitment
to our company's success.**

"Hey, Seth! How's it going today?" Paul Musgrave asked as he walked by.

Paul smiled grandly at Seth. Paul always smiled. He'd be the first to greet workers in the morning and made sure to tell them to have a great day before they left. He also towered over almost everyone. Paul stood easily over six feet six inches. His stomach protruded over his belt line like the overhang roof of an old barn, but it paired with the skinniest legs one could allow without snapping under the weight of the rest of his frame.

"Ugh. Tuesdays, amirite?!" Seth replied.

Fuck, was it Tuesday? he thought to himself. He didn't even know anymore. It didn't matter though.

"I hear ya!" Paul said. He chuckled and slapped his giant midsection before the snowman on stilts teetered away.

For Seth, the days have blurred together for quite a while now. Business was good for Torcon, and he worked eleven hour shifts six days a week going on eight months now. While most were happy to have the overtime, it was starting to take its toll on him. The more he worked, though, the less he sat alone in his apartment. Thinking about how it used to be their apartment.

He swore it still smelled like Lauryn sometimes. He also was smart enough to know it was all in his head. She'd been gone for over a month. No goodbye. No note. No fight even. She just left. She remained highly active on Instagram though, and he'd talked to mutual friends to check on her. So, while he sat there after work, marinating in the darkness and silence, all his mistakes projected themselves from his brain onto the wall. Like a low-budget movie made from regret and isolation. Every sign, every hint that something wasn't going right. Every silence that should have been a wakeup call for him. But they were all just ghosts. None of it mattered. This was what he did rather than sleep at night. Thought of all the signs that were missed. Thought back on the turning points that led them to end up this way. And the closure he never got.

He was owed that much at least, right? Eleven years together. For what? For her to walk out with barely even a goodbye. He still loved her, and he knew he wasn't perfect. But to go from talking to someone every day for eleven years, knowing them inside and out, to having them not even return a text or phone call? He deserved better. Deserved answers. Was it one sided? Did she think about him? Still love him deep down? Had she already moved on? Was she dating again? She didn't even take a lot of her things. Mainly just her clothes and some jewelry, which made it appear to Seth she needed space and would return. That felt like ages ago. He felt stupid looking back on it. He often sat alone, floating atop the thick sludge of his past. He thought about what she was doing at that same moment. Was she with a new guy? Was she as alone as him? No, of course not. She had people. They gravitated toward her. It was Seth who always felt like the "and guest" of life.

And so it went every night. Repeating into every day. Overworked and unrested.

"Seth! Time for break!" Albert yelled out to him.

Seth looked up to a black man in his early sixties creeping toward him. Within the last three years, Albert Harold had had both knees replaced, and a hip operation. Otherwise in good health, he got around slowly. Albert made it a point to yell out to anyone as he headed their way, casting a heads up as he reeled in his body, shuffling to his destination.

"C'mon, man," Seth said. "I'd think with all that metal in you you'd be damn near bionic by now. Should be moving around this whole factory like Inspector Gadget."

"Yeah, you'd think so," Albert chuckled. "I sure paid enough. Hell, I'm just glad to not be in pain anymore. Now get out of here, smart ass."

Albert mimed punching Seth in the shoulder, which he leaned into mainly so Albert didn't whiff and fall over.

He made his way down to the small break room closest to his work area. It was a fifteen by twenty-foot room with a single door to enter and exit. Three rectangular folding tables sat spaced apart with enough chairs that, when full, everyone sat just slightly uncomfortably. Along the wall stood three machines filled with standard snacks and drinks. The coffee machine bragged about containing the world's finest coffee- it didn't. The 32-inch television on the side wall aired whichever daytime TV talking head group was slotted for the time Seth went to break. Currently, it was *Good Morning America*.

"We're here with actor and director Benjamin Rodriquez," Robin Roberts said. "Now you've been a busy guy lately. Two movies coming out around the holidays. Do you get any time to relax?"

"Well, I am taking a break now. I've been filming three movies back-to-back, and it will be great to just take some time off and spend with family," Benjamin said.

"Yes, your lovely partner, Jade. And your daughter, Olivia. She's how old now?"

"Three! Yeah, she's great. I'm looking forward to that."

"And what do you guys like to do?"

"Oh, you know, we keep it really low key. Just hang out. Jade will pull out her guitar and we'll have little jam sessions in the family room. The three of us"

"Love it! So cute! And do you cook when you get to be home?"

"Oh, no! Not me," Benjamin said, laughing "Nobody wants that. I do make a mean PB&J, which is probably the most underrated comfort food. Simply the best."

"Perfect! Crust or no crust?"

"Oh, gotta have crust!"

"Gotcha. Okay, well, *Murder Shifter* is the film starring Benjamin Rodriquez. It comes out November 15. And *A Christmas Miracle* comes out December 1. Ben, thanks for stopping by and chatting with us this morning."

"Oh, thanks for having me."

"Absolutely. Up next, which country singer's cat is blowing up right now on Twitter? We'll dive into that story after this break," Robin wrapped up.

A smattering of people already sat in the break room, and Seth made his way to an empty corner of one of the tables after buying a Mountain Dew. From his phone, he opened Facebook. Not sharing much or commenting on anything. Just scrolling. Infinite scrolling.

All of it the same. Failed gender reveals, people pranking each other, tabloid fodder, and other click-bait. "You'll never believe what this star from this twenty-five-year-old movie looks like today!" He'd eventually find a video or link that grabbed his attention, but after watching for a bit, he'd get annoyed and turn it off. Only to open it again not two minutes later in an instinctive sense of amnesiac muscle memory. The cycle continued for fifteen minutes while he sucked down his soda and he'd head back.

Head back into the larger cycle of watching robots apply paint to door panels. Up and down. Up and down again. After work, he'd head back to the even larger cycle of sitting in silence in his dark apartment. Laying around until it was time to stare at the ceiling and contemplate how he got to this point. What poor choices did he make in this extreme choose your own adventure book had guided him to this spot right here? Was it too late to change?

"Seth! You were supposed to be back seven minutes ago," Mr Ballick, the shift manager said. "Stop staring at the wall and go break out Paul."

"Shit. Yeah. Sorry. I'm on my way. I lost track of time."

"This is the third time this week you've taken a late break, son. Next time it's a write-up."

"Yeah, I understand."

Seth slid his phone back into his jeans pocket, threw out the empty bottle, and headed back to the floor.

After work, Seth stopped in the apartment complex lobby to grab his mail. A voice hollered out to him, and Seth froze. He pinched his eyes closed as he let out a low groan.

Approaching him was a shorter, chubby man with rosy cheeks poking out from behind a thick dark beard. Like the deep red sun emerging from behind the forest at dawn. Bald head, starting from genetics until he took control of the situation and finished the job himself. He was Buddha fused with Paul Bunyan, squeezed into an Alice in Chains t-shirt and ripped Levi's.

"Seth? Seth Roberts? Hey, man, how are you? It's Craig Boskins."

"Oh, hey! What's up? I haven't seen you in a while."

That was a lie. Seth knew he moved in down the hall from him weeks ago. If Craig had been there while Lauryn was still in the picture, he would have surely been over for dinner, or games, or something. Seth, however, tried to avoid a meet up like this. He hated it. The awkwardness of the scene. More than once, for reasons even he didn't quite understand, Seth went out of his way to take the back stairs while Craig waited for the elevator in order to create some space and avoid him.

The part that didn't make sense to Seth himself, was he actually liked Craig. While never close friends in school, they did get along well enough. Craig always cracked jokes and Seth often marveled at how easily he simply walked up to people to strike a conversation. Like a fucking superhero. On the opposite end of the spectrum, Seth recently stopped going to Starbucks at the corner because he knew the new barista they hired. He had wondered if Craig noticed Seth avoiding him, but his demeanor showed that was unlikely.

"How you been? What's going on?" Seth asked.

"Nothing really. I'm bar tending down at Kasady's. Trying to find a way to put this Business Management associate degree to good use other than giving my mom something to brag about to my aunt, ya know? What about you? How's Lauryn?"

"Fuckin' horrible, I hope," Seth said. It just came out. He ran his hand through his hair and massaged the back of his head. "No, I'm not sure, actually. We broke up a while back."

"Oh, shit. Really? My bad. You guys were together a long ass time. I'm sorry."

"Yeah, me too. I know. It was about eleven years. But, whatever. It's probably for the best, you know?"

The silence lingered as Seth looked for an exit strategy. He shuffled through the mail in his hands.

"Oh, God. What the fuck is wrong with me?" Craig said. "Like, C'mon, Craig. Pull your head out of your ass!"

"Nah, dude, it's OK. I've got a habit of bringing everyone down lately. It's a shitty power I obtained. I gotta go, though." He looked up from the three pieces of mail he had been shuffling around and forced a smile. "It was good seeing you."

"Yeah, stop by sometime. We should catch up. I'm in 308. I work nights, and sleep until about 3PM most days. But hit me up. Or even stop by the bar sometime. I work Tuesdays, Fridays, and Saturdays. Tuesday is $2 bomb night if you're feeling frisky," he said and laughed.

"Sounds good, dude. I'll see you."

Seth locked the mailbox and walked up the back staircase to his apartment floor. As he stuck the key into apartment 303, he looked to his right and saw Craig staring back with a wide smile. His eyes disappeared behind cheeks that puffed up and over. Seth thought he took enough time on the stairwell that he'd be in the clear. But no luck. When Craig saw Seth noticed him, he nodded his head back in a "What's Up?" gesture.

Seth replied the same, and chuckled as he entered his sanctuary prison.

The quaint, dimly lit apartment remained decorated to look like mature adults lived there. Generic paintings of wildlife bought at boutique shops scattered along the wall. Ceramic figures and his/hers mugs rested on a small floating shelf to the left of the entertainment center. A glass jar filled a quarter way with smooth stones sat on a side table between the couch and reclining armchair. Evenly mixed in, however, their personalities truly shined through. A framed poster of Memento hung on the wall beside the window. A Lego bust of Batman rested on the bookshelf, along with poetry books and novels, both graphic and not.

He wondered at what point was it sad to still have everything decorated exactly the same. Hell, the furniture hadn't even been rearranged. As if the rooms looking different would be the final nail in the coffin.

It forced Seth to think about himself before everything went bad. And how, when two people spent a certain amount of time together, their personalities easily melded into one cohesive being. They fused skin to skin, and swirled together to the point where it grew difficult to differentiate one from the other. This is why when ripped apart, be it amicable or not, an adjustment period occurs. Both people feel incomplete. Some filled the wound with drugs or alcohol or temporary meaningless human contact. Some attempted to fill it with food or exercise. Some, like himself, failed to clasp onto anything at all. They remained exposed, unfulfilled, and sore.

He had convinced himself they perfectly matched. Every movie, every anecdote, every meal reminded him of Lauryn and how she would feel about the topic at hand. Who was Seth, anymore? He didn't know. He easily faded into the background. Falling off the map for a while he would say. But at some point, he had cemented himself there. Off the map and into a chasm of self-loathing and half smiles.

CHAPTER TWO

Seth knew he'd be cutting it close. He half-expected to cancel the appointment all together, and didn't bother changing the time. He only stopped home to change out of his work clothes.

He shuffled around the dresser drawers, searching for a specific shirt to wear. He slammed the second drawer, before pulling the third, but it wasn't there either. He finally found it folded and in a pile on a chair in the corner of the room. His old work t-shirt from the Torwood Multiplex. Though he hadn't worked there in over ten years, he still sought it out often. He didn't know why. Be it superstition, or comfort, or security. The black short-sleeve shirt still held up fine, save for a couple small holes in the arm pit and small snag in the collar. Even before being employed, Seth spent much of his time at the theater.

As an only child with a father who worked a lot, Seth turned to video games and movies to escape. Many Saturdays, Seth rode his bike to the mall and caught a matinee by himself. Simon gave him $15. It was enough for an early-day ticket, a small popcorn, and a pack of sour patch kids. Seth smuggled in his own can of Dr. Pepper. One afternoon, he filled out an application for employment, which quickly turned into a job offer.

From day one, Seth absolutely loved it. He watched movies

for free. It wasn't strenuous. And best of all, nobody wanted to talk to him. It was a customer service job, without the need for striking up conversations. People came to the counter, hurriedly got their ticket or snacks, and scurried into the dark before the movie started without them. Movie sucked? Not his fault. Pissed your impressionable child saw a boob in the R-rated flick? Not his fault. His freedom and independence also blossomed a newfound confidence not present before. In a short time, he plugged into any position with ease.

On the best days, Seth manned the ticket desk with Travis. Travis Jones also went to Torwood High School, though they never crossed paths much before working alongside each other. Their shifts together flew as they spent much of the time debating hot topics such as 'If the Star Wars prequels got a bad rap' or 'Which Rocky movie was the best'. Not the deep conversations to organically grow roots and form a bond to withstand the ages. But it passed the time.

One afternoon, as they argued whether the Chucky movies worked better as camp than they did as a straight horror franchise, the boys were interrupted by the manager, Tim Schaffer, as he approached the desk between the two.

"Hi, guys. I'm sorry. Hey, Seth, we have some new people starting today. Can you show them around?"

"Yeah, I guess," Seth said.

"Thanks. They're a couple of high school kids. Make sure they know how important it is that they take this seriously."

Seth looked at Tim puzzled.

"You know I'm a high school kid, right?"

"Yeah. You know what I mean, though," Tim said.

"Working a movie theater is barely a step below defusing bombs in terms of stress, right? They need to understand," Seth said.

"And if they don't, we'll kill 'em," Travis said as he slashed across his throat.

"C'mon. You know what I mean," Tim pleaded.

"Yeah, I got you," Seth said.

"Great!" Tim said excitedly, like he successfully won a heated debate.

Training. The one part of the job Seth despised. He had to strike up conversations and get to know people, engage in small talk, and try not to overthink what was going through the other person's head.

Am I too enthusiastic? Too apathetic? Go too slow, and it seems like I'm calling them dumb. Go too fast and it's my fault they don't know what the hell they're doing.

About an hour later, Tim walked up with the new hires to pawn off.

"Alright, and this is Seth. One of our best employees. I'm going to leave you guys with him and he's gonna show you everything he knows. You're in good hands. Seth, what time are you here until?"

"Uh... three o'clock."

"Perfect. These guys are out at two today, so they'll be with you until they leave."

Tim stood silent for a little too long, leading to a weird silence.

"Well alright, I'll leave you to it," Tim finally said and walked off.

"Cool. Um... like Tim said, I'm Seth."

He shook each of their hands, an action he questioned the rest of the day.

The new hires consisted of Brandon and Lauryn. Brandon only lasted about six weeks and didn't contribute much during that time. His slightly hunched back gave the impression he was always apologizing for something. But as Seth shook Lauryn's hand, he was drawn to her eyes immediately. Large and almond shaped. One glowing sapphire and the other a warm cinnamon; a few shades darker than her skin tone.

"H-Hi. I'm Seth."

"Lauryn," she said.

"Right. You knew that already. I'm kinda stalling, I guess," Seth admitted.

The group chuckled, and Seth sighed in relief.

"Honestly, nothing here is all that tough. Anyone can do it. The hardest part is just staying awake through the orientation video you guys just watched. So, you're actually in the clear now. Oh, and being familiar with what movies are coming out. You will undoubtedly be asked questions about 'that one movie with the guy who was in that cop movie last year' or some other vague questions like you're some kind of mind reader. Lauryn, hand me that bag, please. I'll show you how to make the popcorn. Make sure to keep this stuff flowing and no one will really complain here. If we run out of this, that's when customers start getting all pissy and start to revolt. Just keep 'em stuffing their faces and they won't cause you any problems for the most part."

"Good to know," Brandon said.

Seth's heart bounced off his rib cage. He had forgotten Brandon was even there with them. Seth spent the next few days showing the group around, and they were working on their own before the end of the week.

One slow, rainy Sunday afternoon a group gathered around Seth and Travis while they engaged in another deliberation.

"Superman would kick his ass with ease," Travis said disgustedly.

Seth massaged his eyes with his thumb and middle finger.

"No, dude, I'm not saying Batman is the greatest superhero. He's just a guy in a suit. Even with all his gadgets he'd get destroyed. But Superman is lame anyway. Self-righteous prick. Him and Captain America can just fuck each other and get out of the way."

"That would actually be pretty hot," Lauryn interjected.

"Listen, what I'm saying is, Batman's style is the best. The guys that drop in, don't really say anything, kick your ass quickly, and boom- they're fuckin' out. No fuss. Not wasting any time. They got shit to do, so intimidation is key. Him, Wolverine, Punisher, even Daredevil. Just getting shit done."

"Not a chance, dude," Travis said. "I require a little more flair. Give me Spider-Man any day over those guys. They're boring. Spider-Man, Deadpool, Michelangelo. Anybody that will talk shit to you while they're fighting you? At the same time? It's no contest. It's a special talent that can cut you down emotionally, like, on a personal level. Make you rethink who you are as a man, as they simultaneously put you in the hospital. That shit stays with you, man. Bones heal. But Mikey humbling you in a nunchuck battle before you take a big green foot to the jaw? You remember that shit forever."

"He's right," Lauryn said. "That's why Catwoman is a better character than Batman."

"What?" Seth said "You're kidding, right? You're messing with me."

"Hear me out. She's got a great back story. She's thought of as a villain, but she's not killing innocents or trying to take over Gotham. She's just trying to live her best life and steal some diamonds from rich assholes. Batman's stubborn ass gets in the way. Why does he get to decide what's right and wrong? Gotham is brutal, so you know that whenever he takes the time to get all up in her business, some poor bastard is getting bludgeoned and robbed within two blocks. She's not evil, sometimes even more of an antihero. It all makes her more mysterious. And she straight up fucks with Batman's head. Like, all the time. She's way more interesting than Bruce Wayne and his daddy issues. With his 'Ahh, my one rule!' bullshit. Is she a foe, an ally, love interest? She's all of them. Plus, she uses a whip, which everyone knows is the most underrated weapon."

Seth's jaw dropped to the floor. He had a crush on her before. He was infatuated now. The way her dark wavy hair bounced as she emphatically made her points. The way she hit him in the shoulder, not once, but twice as she argued. He became lost in her words. In her eyes. In her sly smile, which grew wider as Seth realized he was staring at her for way too long.

"What about Iron Man?" Brandon said.

"Oh, fuck Iron Man," Seth said, snapping back to reality. "He's just Batman without the combat training, detective abilities, or any worthwhile villain. Just a bitch made dude in a suit fighting other dudes in iron suits. Sometimes he's even got a sidekick who also has, yup you guessed it, a fucking iron suit. He's the worst."

"Brandon, did you empty the trashcans down the left hallway screens like you were supposed to?" Travis asked.

"No, I forgot. Should I go get those now?"

"They're probably overflowing right now."

"So, yeah?"

"Yeah, I would think so."

"OK," Brandon said as he sighed heavily and shuffled away. "I like Iron Man."

"Listen, Lauryn," Travis said "We're all going to Frank's to get some food after work. You should come with us."

"Yeah, that sounds cool," she said looking at Seth.

Travis threw the rag he was holding at Seth. "And tell this guy he needs to come this time, too. He always seems to skip out on us."

"Wait, why don't you go?" Lauryn asked.

Seth balled up the rag and threw it back at Travis. "I go sometimes."

"You've gone twice!" Travis said.

"I don't know. I just feel like going home after work sometimes."

Travis and Lauryn leered at Seth as if imposing their will on him.

"OK, OK I'll go!" he conceded.

"Great!" Lauryn said. "I gotta go clean screen three. I'll see you guys later!"

Seth continued staring at her as she walked away.

"You're welcome," Travis said.

He pushed Seth's shoulder, rocking him to one foot and then swaying back.

"What for?"

"Really? Don't worry. She likes you too. It's pretty obvious."

"I don't know what you're talking about man," Seth said.

Travis cocked his eyebrow and looked at Seth.

"OK, dude. Sure," he said as he walked away shaking his head.

Frank's was a small 24-hour diner about two blocks away from the theater. The younger employees regularly hung out and got food after work. Usually just burgers and fries, but it hit the spot. Seth arrived and sat in his car for ten minutes or so before heading in.

"There he is! I was starting to think you flaked!" Travis said.

"Nah, man. I'm here," Seth said and sat across from Travis.

Lauryn walked in shortly after and sat next to Seth. Travis smiled at him, and he smiled, knowingly.

"So hey, Seth, I've been meaning to tell you. You lied to me, you know?" Lauryn said.

His palms grew sweaty as he swirled his Dr Pepper around with his straw.

"Really? About what?"

"On my first day. You told me that 'anyone can do this job'," she said as she waved her hands around and deepened her voice.

Seth let out a relieved, yet hearty laugh "Oh, was that... was that me?"

"I mean, obviously. I thought it was spot on." She grabbed a french fry from a community basket in the middle of the table. "But anyway, Brandon proved you wrong."

"Yeah, you're right. I guess the bar can be lower than I thought. Sorry about that."

"You're forgiven. This time. Don't let it happen again."

"Deal. But really, though, we're even. Because you gave me homework that day."

"Oh yeah? And what was that?" she asked, amused.

Neither Lauryn nor Seth realized it, but Travis sat across from them, watching as if he witnessed his son walk for the first time.

"You made me look up the word for two different colored eyes," Seth said.

"Heterochromia," she said.

"Well, I know now. I already looked it up."

"You could have just asked me. Everyone else does," Lauryn said.

"Didn't want to come off as creepy on your first day."

"Yeah. Makes sense. So, enough time has passed now, I guess?"

"Exactly!" Seth laughed.

"Well then, I'm sorry I made you take fifteen seconds to Google something. That must have really cut into your personal time."

"Oh, I'll forgive you this time. Just don't let it happen again," Seth said, mocking her prior cadence.

Though they were with friends, Seth and Lauryn would come to acknowledge that as their first date. Seth often thought back on that night. If one's entire life were spread out on a timeline and graphed in a series of highs and lows, that time would be among the highest. He did all his firsts with Lauryn. They took pride in it. When others would jab about how they were inexperienced and only knew each other, they bragged about how two people could click as well as them at such a young age.

But those were merely memories. And as he sat, alone in the lobby of the therapist's office, it seemed a lifetime ago.

CHAPTER THREE

In the waiting room of Dr Fredrick Englund, Seth nervously shifted his weight in the brown leather chair. He hated the idea of this whole thing. Hated the idea of talking to a professional shoulder to cry on. Hated the idea of someone prying into his business. Hated the idea this implied something was wrong with him. Lauryn really wanted this for him.

She basically forced him to talk to somebody. One of the last things she talked about before leaving. Why? Just because of a rough patch in life? Like he couldn't figure things out on his own? After all, she had been going to therapy for a while, and he never noticed any difference with her. What could she tell some stranger that she couldn't tell Seth, anyway?

But no. He decided he would make this attempt. For her. For them. Maybe she would come back. Maybe if he had done this sooner, she wouldn't have left at all.

The carefully designed office bloomed in warm, earthy colors. The reception desk with the dark cherry finish. The paper-thin carpet in a pewter gray. Even the framed pictures were of autumn forests and old country houses, hanging from a wall painted in flat beige with just a hint of red. It was an obvious Jedi mind trick to help put the patient at ease and open up. But it wasn't working on Seth.

He absorbed the crisp October evening from the single window beside him. The sun melted into the sky casting an amber sheen to everything it encompassed. The reds and oranges of the maple leaves outside perfectly blended into the doctor's waiting room. They weaved themselves into the fibers of the carpet, and splashed across the walls, reminding him he couldn't hide from the reality of the outside world.

He browsed the collection of magazines to pass the time. Old issues of *Sports Illustrated* and *People*. Thanks for the insight on whether the Lions could finally get a playoff win. The big game was eight months ago. They didn't make it. Another wild card loss. *People Magazine* offered *10 Summer Exercise Tips and the Stars that Swear by Them*. If Seth rolled his eyes back any harder his optic nerves would snap.

When the doctor finally came out to grab Seth, he startled him.

Dr Englund was much younger than Seth expected. Late thirties, maybe. In shape, but not overly athletic. His flowing blond hair parted to the left. It connected to a patchy beard that, Seth guessed, was supposed to make him appear older and more distinguished. But it didn't quite match the rest of the look.

"Seth, good evening. I'm Dr Englund. Nice to meet you."

"Hi. Nice to meet you, too."

"How has your day been?"

"Good. Thanks."

It really had been, but the answer was more of a reflex. He could have woken up today with his foot chewed off by stray cats who climbed into his apartment after some passerby shattered his window, and he would have said the same. Seth learned early on most people did not care how your day was going. Not really. But they do possess an inherent urge to break the silence and be polite, which overcomes and forces the question. God forbid two people just walked by each other without a word. That, coupled with the fact even the best of friends don't want to be tied down and burdened by the issues of another person. So, the answer was always, "good," if he answered at all.

He also found he didn't even have to answer the question asked. If he just stated the day of the week, people would agree with it and move on. As long as he knew how many days away from Friday, he had a quick draw reply to any question that came his way.

"Have you ever talked to someone in this environment before?" the doctor asked.

"No. Never."

"OK," Dr Englund laughed. "I get that often. Well, personally, I like to start off with a little explanation of how I do things. Go ahead and have a seat."

He gestured to a set of chairs on either side of a small coffee table, with the same soothing color scheme bleeding in from the waiting room. It reminded Seth of a relaxing setup at a coffee house more than a place for crazies to complain about their neglectful parents.

"Is this where you diagnose me?" Seth asked.

"No, no. No diagnosing. We are just talking. I believe the most important thing that we can do is have a dialog. A way to get our thoughts and feelings out in the air, and not keep them in. Be it good or bad. So, I'm going to ask you some questions to start out. And I do have this pen and pad here. I may jot some notes down, and I may not. It depends. But either way, I will let you see everything I've written down, if you like. I like to be transparent. I hold no secrets. So, tell me a little about yourself."

"What exactly would you like to know?"

"Let's start simple. What do you do for a living?"

"I work at a car factory. Torcon is the name of it."

"I've heard of the place. How do you like it out there?"

"It's OK, I guess. It pays the bills. Ya know?"

"Many would love to have that. I feel like there was almost a 'but' at the end though."

"Well, I feel like… I don't know. Like I should be doing something more, I guess."

"What would you like to do?"

"I don't even know. Something more substantial."

"What's stopping you?"

"Oh, God. Time? Location? Commitments? There's quite a bit."

"Like what?" Dr Englund asked.

Seth silently searched for a response, but couldn't think of anything offhand.

"Have you tried volunteer work?" Dr. Englund said. "You could help out at the Torwood Mission if you're looking to make a difference. Or they're always looking for assistance down at St Margaret's."

"Yeah, but I'm already working, like, over sixty hours a week. Doesn't leave time for much else."

"Well then, what about just for yourself? The big three for self-care really are sleeping well, eating well, and exercising. How are you in that department?"

"Oh, God. Not at all, not really, and not lately."

"OK. Is there a reason?"

"Oh, well. I lay in bed and try to sleep, but can't. So then after work I guess I'm too tired to cook or exercise."

"What do you do instead of sleeping?"

"Just lay there, usually. Trying to sleep. Rolling around for the most part."

Seth watched as the doctor jotted down something on his notepad.

"Seth, I'm going to shift gears here now a little bit and hit you with the big question. The hard one."

They both laughed. Though Seth did get a little nervous, he appreciated the levity.

"Please branch out on my previous question and tell me, in general, not necessarily in your occupation, what it is you want to get out of therapy?"

Seth thought for a minute. He focused on the hole in the thigh of his jeans and began picking at the loose frayed strands of denim.

"Nothing really, I guess. Is spiritual nirvana too cliche an answer?"

"Nothing? Ok, I guess we are done! That was quick. Make sure you stop at Evelyn's desk to take care of the co-pay."

Seth sat caught by surprise. This wasn't what he expected. But at the same time, he wasn't upset. More than any office decor, Dr. Englund himself was finding a way of making Seth feel like he had known him forever.

"Seth, whose idea was it for you to come in today? Did you make the decision on your own?"

"I scheduled for myself. My girlfriend wanted me to come in. Well, ex-girlfriend, I guess. It's complicated." Seth paused before adding, "She thought I needed to talk to somebody."

"Why would she think that?"

"I don't know. But that's why she left. After eleven years. Up and left barely saying goodbye. Like I'm toxic now or something. But I've always been able to figure things out on my own. The whole time we were together, too. Nothing changed. But I guess now she thinks I needed help for some reason."

"But you don't?"

"No. No offense. I tried, and you seem cool, but this isn't for me. I'm wasting your time and mine. Is every first session just looking to convince the patient they need therapy? Job number one? You probably have a whole waiting list of whack jobs that I'm taking time from. Who's gonna save them?"

Dr. Englund ignored the question, instead letting the uncomfortable silence linger. When Seth began shifting around in his chair again, Dr Englund changed the topic.

"Seth, early impressions are you appear to use sarcasm and deflect when you're nervous. Is that fair?"

"I suppose."

"Would you say you get your sense of humor from your mother or your father?"

"Never really knew my mom. So probably my dad, I guess. We've got pretty similar personalities."

Dr. Englund scribbled on his pad some more. He waited for Seth to elaborate. But he didn't.

"So would you say you have a pretty good relationship, then?"

"Yeah, we do. Or did. He… he passed."

"I'm sorry to hear that."

"I mean. It's been a couple years. And you didn't even know him. Or me half an hour ago. I'm fine. Really. People die of heart attacks all the time. Life goes on, right?"

Again, Seth snuffed out his answer.

"Seth, do me a favor and exhale. Drop and relax your shoulders. Please know, this is not an interrogation. It's a conversation. Incredibly open and, of course, confidential. Know though, it is extremely normal to be apprehensive about talking to someone about how you are feeling. Especially if you're the type of person who tries to internalize and sort out issues on your own. It can be difficult to materialize those thoughts into something tangible. Something that you feel is coherent. But, again, the importance of it is about getting what you want. That's what all of this is about. What is it that you want to get out of this, Seth?"

"I want... ugh. I don't know. This was a mistake. Sorry for wasting your time."

"Seth, do you keep a journal?"

"What? No," Seth scoffed.

"I didn't think so. But I would like you to start. Just for a trial. I think it would help. People who generally keep their thoughts and feelings inside do so because they need to make sense of them before letting others know what is going on. The problem is the root of that feeling can get lost along the way to make sense of it. I'm a huge proponent of what is called stream of consciousness writing. It's where you just write down whatever you are thinking off the top of your head. It often doesn't make sense, and that is perfectly fine. And I know many people who no longer use a pencil and paper for it. It is becoming quite common to use the audio or video recorder on cell phones, since the accessibility is there. I would like for you to do this exercise each night to express how you feel about your day."

"I don't know."

"You keep saying that. 'I Don't Know.' What exactly don't you know?"

Seth thought about it, but didn't answer the question. Treating it as rhetorical.

"Tell me, Seth, are you a religious person?"

"What? I was raised Lutheran, I guess. But I haven't gone for years. More agnostic now. Why is that relevant?"

"What do you want for Christmas?" Dr Englund said.

"I uh… what? I don't know," Seth said.

"Because you feel put on the spot. You're thinking too hard about it. Even though it is a basic question for this time of year. And trying to break down what you want in life is the same way. Have you ever blanked when giving an order at a restaurant even though you looked at the menu a good five minutes prior? It's natural. When you get put on the spot, which is sometimes how people feel when starting therapy, it can be hard to clearly sort through problems. Getting down your thoughts and feelings in a journal is incredibly important. It helps to sift through all the crap. That's all therapy is. A helping hand to peel back the garbage and get to the core of what makes us happy. Here, I keep a lot of these, and I want you to have this one."

He handed Seth a blank composition notebook with a black and white spotted cover.

"That way you can have some good practice before our next session. Same time next Tuesday work for you?"

"Um, yeah," Seth said.

"Great. And just so you know, this was a productive first session. I'd like for you to use the journal. Whether you have a good day or bad. Take some time and get this done. Happy, sad, angry, hungry, tired, beaten down, whatever. It may seem insignificant, but that's the purpose of the activity. To turn your thoughts and feelings into something corporeal."

CHAPTER FOUR

Up and down. Up and down. First, clementine metallic. Then it would change to bright arctic white or tsunami blue. Up and down. And up and down again. Another day limped on as Seth watched the robots spray the color onto the door panels.

"You ever think about who names this shit?" Seth said.

"Huh?" Paul asked.

"The colors. Who's the lucky bastard in charge of deciding if a yellow is more of a dandelion or a mustard? Whether it's paint, or crayons, or… or paper. I mean, I don't even think it's bright in the Arctic. Is it? Isn't that what makes it the Arctic?"

"More all of the snow, I'm guessing," Paul said.

"All I can think of is a tsunami coming and some poor family in the Philippines is scrambling to gather what belongings they can fit into a couple hastily packed bags before they evacuate their home. And Mom's done a head count and all the kids are accounted for. Dad's gotta carry the little one because she's terrified and not that great of a walker yet anyway. So, they roll out. But as they're running away to safety, before they can be sure that they don't get swept away in the disaster, they have to stop and do an about face to admire how pretty blue that wave of murdering chaos is. And how they'd love that shade on a practical mid-sized sedan."

Paul quietly let Seth's words register, until he laughed so heartily his whole body shook. He grabbed Seth by the shoulders with his giant paws.

"Seth, man, you need to relax a little. So intense all the time. Anyway, you wanna go on your break first or you want me to?"

"Nah, man. You go ahead. I'm gonna try and hold off awhile longer. There's usually a huge line at the coffee machine right now. I'll let that clear out."

"OK, buddy. Sounds good to me. I'm starving anyway. I don't keep this figure by skipping snack time," he said, laughing to himself as he rubbed his stomach. "Gregory is going in to do midday cleanup on the robots. He'll probably need a hand."

As he walked away, Paul called out.

"Hey, Seth!"

"Yeah?"

"If it makes ya feel any better, them color namers probably get paid a lot more than you, too!"

Seth laughed. "Yeah, you're probably right! Thanks, man! I hope you choke on your Skittles."

Paul sarcastically saluted in Seth's direction and continued walking to break, leaving Seth to stare at the door panels some more.

The robots made a mechanical whirring sound as they moved. Like a zipper rhythmically being opened and closed. The air valves popped in synchronization with the robot movements as the color triggered on and off. It was a tightly choreographed dance between all involved. On this day, it didn't take long for Seth to join in.

His breathing mirrored the actions of the robots. Inhaling on the upper strokes. Exhaling on the downward strokes. In and out. Up and down. In and out. Up and down. The breaths grew heavier and heavier with each rotation. Soon his eyelids joined, tethered to the breathing They opened and closed in time with the rest of the routine. Until they broke free, going off on their own slower than the rest. Slower and slower. Closed and open. Closed and open again. At one point, they grew too heavy to open back up.

CHAPTER FIVE

Seth snapped back to himself to the sound of a crash and someone screaming. Screaming in pain? Hard to tell, as it was muffled. But panicked nonetheless.

"Seth, stop the line! What are you doing?!"

He gathered where he was and what was going on. A piercing buzz alarmed close by.

"Seth, stop the fucking line. Now!" a voice yelled.

He sprinted over and pressed the red safety stop button. All at once, the sounds went quiet, except for one last dull buzzing which let everyone in the area know the line had stopped. Paul and Mr Ballick pulled a screaming Gregory Karsin out from the spray booth and laid him on the plant floor.

Finally able to assess the situation, Seth noticed one of the door panels had fallen off the track. White paint mixed with blotches of blood and streaked across the floor from Gregory being pulled to safety. Anyone within earshot rushed in to aid him as he still screamed in pain.

Stunned, but wanting to further assist, Paul grabbed a mop and bucket to clean up the spill. Mr Ballick must have called for help, as the Torcon on-site medical responders quickly rushed in and took him away. However, the evidence of the event remained.

One of the door panels dislodged from the line and snagged Gregory as he wiped down the booth. Caught in the line, he was dragged over thirty feet before being noticed. By then, the damage had already been done. His leg snapped from being pinched in place while the line pulled at the rest of him. His shoulder lacerated by the fine inner edge of the metal door panel itself.

Seth ran to the broom closet to grab another mop, but he was stopped in route. Standing in his way was Mr Ballick. Vincent Ballick was tall and rail thin. He was in his late fifties and would have had a thick head of silver hair had he not used cheap comb in darkening dye on it regularly.

"Seth, they'll clean that up. I need to talk to you in my office," Mr. Ballick said.

He was both soft-spoken and direct in his way of speaking. Never yelled, but the angrier he was, the more his voice lacked any real emotion or emphasis. As he called Seth to the office, he was nearly monotone.

Seth had always respected Mr Ballick. He was one of few people who checked in on Seth when his father died. Vincent and Simon started at Torcon together. He and his wife, Judith, had known Seth since he was a child, with him and Simon often coming over to attend cookouts or Superbowl parties. While Vincent climbed the corporate ladder, Simon focused on being a single father to an only child.

Inside the office, Vincent sat down at his desk and motioned for Seth to sit across from him. He pulled open the top drawer and removed an individually wrapped peppermint lifesaver. He released it from the plastic and popped it in his mouth, a habit he adopted after giving up cigarettes twelve years ago. He ate them so often the scent emanated from him. The department often joked you could smell the mint fog coming before ever seeing Ol' Ballick himself pop up.

Vincent removed his glasses and rubbed his eyes with his thumb and index finger.

"Seth, please explain to me what happened."

"I don't know," Seth said. "I was watching production, and I must have dozed off for a minute."

There was no point in lying, and that wasn't Seth's way anyway.

"There's multiple, very preventable, things that failed here. Not only were you sleeping on the job, but you didn't catch the dislodged product. You weren't being the extra eyes during midday cleanup. I'm sure there's more but I still need to review the entire incident and check in on Greg."

"I'm sorry, Vince. I screwed up. I know that. I can stay over and clean up. Whatever you need."

"That's not gonna be an option, Seth. Are you under the influence of any drugs or alcohol right now?"

"What?! Of course not. You know me."

"Good." Vincent let out an audible exhale at the answer. "I'm gonna need you to take a drug test immediately. And we are going to have to do an evaluation of your situation. I'm worried about you, son. And I'm not just talking about today. This has been an ongoing thing for you. Even before today's incident, there have been continuous issues with your work performance. Your attendance has been suffering. You were late four times just in the last month. If I can be brutally honest, which I feel I can, you have just been going through the motions ever since he passed. Your father I mean."

"Wait, Vin-"

"Now, I told you that if you needed anything at all, to come and talk to me. In or outside of work. Come over for supper. Or just to see some friendly faces. We can try to reach out all day, but if it's all radio silent, well there's really nothing we can do. Judith and I really care about you."

"I know. I'm... I'm just going through some things right now," Seth said.

"Seth, when you come in to work, I expect that you come in ready to work. Any outside bullshit needs to stay just that. I have gone to bat for you many times for some of the small shit, but I can't ignore this."

"I get it," Seth said solemnly.

"Do you? Gregory was rushed to the hospital because you weren't doing your job."

"I know. I don't know what to say."

"Nothing. Not a thing. Now, know that what I say next really kills me. And is strictly business. But we are going to have to put you on suspension while we review everything. The accident. Your recent job performance. Your attendance. We will review with you when we have our decision."

"What?! Vince, I need this. You can't do this to me. I've been here for ten years. Doesn't that help me at all? C'mon, man."

"It would if this was the only infraction. But like I said, it's been a growing issue. Your performance here. I'll need you to stop by the nurse's station so she can administer the drug test and clock out immediately after. Normally I would have to have you walked out, but I'm not going to do that to you. Please do not make me regret my decision."

"I understand," Seth sighed. "Sorry, Vince. I really am."

He stood up, and left Mr Ballick's office, for what he assumed would be the last time.

Seth was sincere when he said he needed this. But not because of the money. Never the type to live lavishly, he saved up enough to get by for a while, as well as being set up well by Simon. But he did not want to be alone. As much as he hated the monotony of the job, as much as the heavy hours had taken their toll on him, he hated being alone at home so much more. The dark. The quiet. That's where all the truths hid. All the insecurities and skeletons that he easily ignored while distracted. They got in his face and screamed so loud and so pointed, he smelled the stale decay of his happiness rotting.

Seth clocked out silently with his head down. Everyone looked at him as he walked by, statuesque from the waist up floating to the time clock and out the door. Across the factory, word of mouth had already spread. While the stares ate Seth alive, he appreciated Vincent not having him escorted out. That would have been exponentially worse. Especially since he hadn't even been fired. At least not fired yet, he assumed. While he was no fortune teller, he knew he couldn't come back from this.

He didn't stop for anything until he got to his car, but he didn't drive home. He didn't listen to the radio. He didn't even turn the engine. He sat there and stared off into the middle distance with his eyes fixed straight ahead, not focused on anything specific.

What. The. Fuck. He thought to himself. And like that, the dam broke inside his head. The self-judgment and questions popped in and out of his mind overlapping until he could barely decipher one thought from the other.

What happened? When did I become such a piece of shit? Everyone here hates me now. Who the hell falls asleep at work? I can never come back. They probably hated me before. Good riddance, I guess. But now, if for some inexcusable reason I am not fired, I'll always be that guy. I can hear it now. Oh, I'm going to break, Seth. Try not to kill anyone while I'm gone. Christ, this is my future.

He screamed and clenched his hands to the steering wheel so tightly his arms quivered all the way up to the shoulder. The primal outburst rang until he had expelled any and all air from his lungs. Seth swallowed hard, took a deep breath, closed his eyes, and put his head back against the headrest.

Leaving the parking lot of Torcon, he hoped no one noticed the little scene that just took place. But at the same time, what better way to one up the story of the guy getting sent home than adding that you also saw him losing his shit in the car immediately after? Perfect.

CHAPTER SIX

Seth dejectedly walked into his apartment and tossed his keys on the small square kitchen table. He grabbed a bottle of Yuengling from the fridge, unscrewed the top, and took a hefty gulp. He slumped down on the couch and turned on the TV to distract himself from the real world, if only for a while. Normally he'd put on a movie, or catch up on the latest hot TV show, but he had no interest in paying attention to anything right now. He just needed an escape.

His TV set had, at some point in the last year, defaulted to channel three when turned on each time. He had been holding out until the television finally bit it to get a new one, but the wretched thing wouldn't die. It had mutated to an 80's slasher villain. But instead of gutting Seth neck to navel, it forced him to watch a local affiliate for CBS.

On the television, Dr Phil talked to some teenage girl with long blond hair about her Instagram. The girl's mother, in tears, which Seth imagined were mostly for show, pleaded to convince her daughter to return to high school.

"Dr Phil, she just don't understand me!" The girl exclaimed. "I'm up to almost seven thousand followers now! Things are really taking off for me!"

The girl, whose name finally popped up on a footer as Rebeca Stinten, had a slight southern drawl, which matched up well with Phil's himself.

"Seven thousand, huh?" he said skeptically. "And I'm sorry,

you'll have to explain this to me. Are any of these people you actually know?"

"I know them from the Internet. Don't you get how Insta works? I thought you were supposed to be smart."

"Rebeca, you're putting your entire life out there into the public. Don't you see the problem with that? Everything you do becomes public record. And you're even putting your family through this too. Recording their actions unbeknownst to them. They sound like they want no part of it. That's actually against the law."

The audience exploded in thunderous applause and cheers.

"They'll sure 'preciate me when I'm rich and can buy 'em a house."

"What happens if this doesn't work out? You have no education or anything to fall back on. Have you ever even held a real job?"

"Oh, it's gonna work. I know it. Why should I go work at McDonald's when I can do this? Once I get more followers, Im'a get sponsors and I'll make about a hundred dollars per pic. That means picture, if you didn't know."

Seth swallowed his beer hard and sat up straight.

"Fuck this," he proclaimed, and changed the channel as the foam from the beer burned through his nose. He hoped the good doctor had a nice rebuttal, but Seth wasn't going to listen to that anymore. He couldn't. Especially not today.

He flipped the channel up, not even being able to remember the last time he watched TV on a Thursday afternoon.

"Last week, Amber surprised everyone by getting the last rose of the ceremony, sending Kimberly back home to Minneapolis. Find out how the chips fall and see Beth's reaction to having to face Amber after stabbing her in the ba-"

Click

"-edia backlash over the joke. Hundreds of people were outraged over the insensitivity. Rodriguez later went on Twitter and apologized, stating that he regrets his words, and did not mean to offend anybody that suffers from a peanut allergy. The damage may be done though, with both *cancelbenrod* and *nonutnovember* hashtags already trending.

His endorsements have yet to make a statement, but his followers on Twitter have dropped by around seventeen percent in the last twenty fo-"

Click

"Tonight at six on your Channel 24 evening news, which Hollywood starlet's new hair style has the internet going crazy?!"

On reflex, Seth hurled his bottle into the air. It flipped end over end until colliding with the wall, bursting into golden green shards all over the floor.

His chest pounded. Blood pulsed through the bass drum of his heart, beating over and over, louder and louder, reverberating against the hallways of his chest. A slow, throbbing ache climbed up his neck, to the base of his skull, and right between the backs of his eyes. And as if his body were merely creating a diversion for him to follow while it snuck up to attack, he suddenly couldn't breathe.

With rapid, stifled breaths, he grasped for air like a child frantically trying to catch a balloon being taken away by a gust of wind. Tears crept from the corners of his eyes. The failure to inhale caused him to choke and exhale faster. With nothing left to expel, he was only able to double over.

He thought back to what Dr. Englund told him and the breathing exercises they went over in case something like this popped up. Despite the doctor's well-intentioned advice, he never really did find a happy place. He always thought that sounded laughable anyway. It instantly made him feel the sharp crack of Tyler Durden smacking him across the face and telling him to stay in the moment with his chemical burn. He did, however, fix his focus on the broken glass on the carpet. He consciously relaxed his jaw. Seth held his breath, like he had a choice in the matter, and closed his eyes until he re-centered on breathing evenly. He slowly, yet triumphantly, took a single healthy inhalation. He let it out and followed it with another. Then another. After successfully breathing full intervals for half a minute, Seth unscrewed the cap of a half-full water bottle sitting beside him on the table and took a sip. God knows how long it had been there.

He crumbled to the floor, back against the couch, and his head in his hands. The apartment felt a little darker, slightly colder, oddly quieter. The feeling seethed from the walls. He didn't want to be here. Not now. He couldn't.

He used his last reserve of energy to slide back up and roll onto the couch. Seth pulled a fleece throw blanket down from the headrest and slept hard; the apartment still soaked in the aroma of beer.

***

Seth awoke to darkness outside. November in Ohio meant it could be anytime between 6PM and 6AM. He felt realistically either could be the case. His phone told him it was 9:34PM.

His head pounded, though not from a hangover. He'd only had the one beer, and a quarter of it had soaked into the carpet. He let out a hearty stretch and cleaned up the mess from his earlier tirade. After a long, much-needed shower he looked for something to eat.

The fridge options were scarce. Lots of condiments. Not much real food. Some black forest ham from the deli, but no bread. Opening the freezer didn't add much to the equation. Frozen waffles, corn dogs, and a half-eaten container of moose tracks ice cream. He planned on grocery shopping after work, but today derailed. He knew he should spend money wisely. But he needed to eat, and eating out tonight would not be the difference between a warm bed and an eviction notice. He grabbed his jacket and headed out.

Seth lived walking distance to Kasady's Tavern. Kasady's had a decent food menu for a bar. The burgers were standard issue, but the onion rings were good, and it all paired well with the seasonal brews on tap. Craig Boskins, who was tending bar, greeted him as soon as he walked in. It was a Thursday. Craig didn't normally work Thursdays. Seth knew this and had avoided the days Craig worked to prevent this. He must have traded shifts with someone. Too late to avoid it, Seth sat down at the bar and Craig walked right up to him.

"What's up, Seth? How you been?"

How have I been?! Oh, let's see. I've barely been able to sleep at night in months, but I did manage to fall asleep at work, which fate would have it almost killed a guy. Then freaked out at the apartment. And now I'm here.

"Oh, you know. It's Thursday." Is what really came out of Seth's mouth.

"Shitty day, huh? Don't worry. Tomorrow's Friday!" Craig laughed. "But I work this weekend, so it really makes no difference to me."

Famished, Seth ordered a philly cheese steak and a Blue Moon. He quickly finished the sandwich and onion rings, and polished off his second beer quietly as he watched the small television behind the bar. It was just reruns of Seinfeld, but he had seen them so many times it didn't matter the sound was turned down low. He followed along fine as the gang attempted to locate their car in the parking garage. He motioned for another beer, before taking a big swallow to finish off his current drink and proceeded to stare at the bottom of the glass while swirling around the remaining suds.

From the other end of the bar, Craig acknowledged with a thumbs up while assisting a couple of guys wearing matching work shirts with *Moe's Transmission Repair* on the front. As he slid Seth's beer to him, he said, "Hope you're ready for a rough workday tomorrow."

"I'm good. Cheers to unemployment," Seth said raising the glass.

"Oh, shit. Really?"

"Maybe. I don't know. They'll let me know, I guess. Until then, here I go."

"I'm sorry, man."

"From Torcon, even. The town staple. Everyone either works there, used to work there, or knows someone who works there. They fire me? You know we had a forklift driver once who came to work drunk? Dude was nodding off in between driving skids around. They let him keep working! Said, 'Oh he's not that drunk. Let him sweat it out. We need drivers.' Are you kidding me? And they get rid of me?"

Seth's face twitched with realization.

"Hey, I guess I'm the missing puzzle piece now," he added.

"I don't get it," Craig said.

"Oh, never mind," Seth said deflating again. "Hey man, I don't got shit to do tomorrow, can I get a Captain and Coke next?"

"You got it. How you getting home later? You want me to call somebody?" Craig asked.

"Oh, I'm good. No one to call."

He continued conversing with Craig who easily pulled double duty manning the bar and catching up with Seth. It didn't take long before all inhibitions fled, and Seth's internal monologue melded seamlessly with his external monologue. Craig bounced between offering advice and standing as a sounding board.

"My dad would never show me if he was upset. He was a single father who sacrificed everything. If he was tired, or beaten down, he would never show me. I didn't even realize how hard he was working until I got older. Then, at that point, I always thought about how fucking selfish it would come off if I complained about anything. Ya know, though, the best memories I have with him are Friday nights when I was growing up. Every Friday he'd pick up pizza and a two-liter on the way home from work, and we'd play video games together. We'd play all night. He started doing that as young as I can remember, and I loved it. It was our thing. And it wasn't even a huge thing. But when I think back at some of the best times I had, it always comes back to that. And I don't, I don't even mean that in a negative way. I genuinely miss it. Sounds kind of lame, right? Playing Mario and eating Pizza Hut."

"No. It doesn't. It sounds nice, Seth," Craig said.

"And that's where I'm still at. Ya know? Man, you ever just feel... stuck? Like no matter how much you run or kick or scream life finds a way to pull harder into the same stationary position?" Seth perked up again, "Oh, shit! It's like those fucking goombas. You ever play Mario 3?"

"Well, OK," Craig said. "That's it. When you start trying to mash up Nintendo with psychological introspection, it's time to cut you off."

"No, man. Hear me out. Mario 3 had this flying goomba, right, and it would drop little baby goombas on Mario. They swarmed you, making you almost immobile until you flipped out on the jump button to escape. That's me, dude. Fuckin' Mario being attacked by mini goombas and running from an angry sun. This town is a black hole. You can't get out. I thought I was doing all right. But here I am. Single. Unemployed. Drunk."

Seth let out a half chuckle hearing how pathetic he sounded. He continued, more reflective and less hostile.

"You either end up at 7-11 watching stoned teenagers try and steal Doritos at 2AM, working at that god damned Ford plant making piece of shit door panels, or laid off from that very factory with a bad back popping Percocet like they're Altoids."

"Oh, come on," Craig said. "It's not that bad here. And no greater power other than yourself has you tethered to Torwood, Ohio. I can promise you that."

"Oh yeah? Even Nicole Bradburn- our God damned valedictorian, 4.1 GPA, went to college twenty minutes from here for some reason."

"Cheaper to attend locally?" Craig said as he collected the empty glasses from the bar.

Seth slapped the bar for emphasis.

"Came back to teach Geography and Sociology at THE Torwood High School. And you even! Shit, Craig, why do you stay here, man? You could go anywhere you like. But here you are serving drinks to sorry fucks like me. Don't you want more?"

Craig disengaged and let the energy simmer down, taking time to give the bar top a quick wipe down, and collect the tips that had accumulated along it. As Seth finished the drink in his hand, Craig came back and leaned in close to him.

"You remember Gracie Sedrup from high school?" Craig asked. "She was a sophomore when we graduated. She considers herself a social media celebrity, now. Does that count? An *influencer*, I guess."

Seth again let out that same half chuckle. "No shit?"

"No shit. She's even marrying some dude she met online. They're vlogging the whole wedding planning. Of course, they're also broke as shit. Her celeb status isn't quite Kardashian levels, yet. They have a GoFundMe going to throw a Cinderella themed wedding. Horse-drawn carriage arrival and all. Give 'em $50 and you get a t-shirt with their picture and wedding date on it. You even get to pick white or ash grey. They're claiming that donating would 'really help my brand'. Whatever the fuck that means."

"Oh, Jesus. Really?!" Seth practically vomited out. "Fuck them! Seriously. Fucking parasites. All of them."

Taken aback, but pleased with himself, Craig asked, "All of who?"

"Every Instagram socialite trying to make me feel like I should be even remotely interested in their life. What is wrong with people? Acting like they're owed something just for letting us share their oxygen. Have you noticed how many pieces of shit have that entitled view of the world? It's a disease."

"Fuckin' aye," one of the other bar patrons hollered.

Unbeknownst to him, all attention from the handful of people left in the bar slowly directed itself toward Seth. As he talked, he grew louder, and more pointed. He no longer seemed to be talking to anyone in particular. It was less a conversation and more a campaign speech.

Craig grabbed the almost-empty glass from Seth with one hand, and mockingly peeled back Seth's fingers with the other.

"Whoa, whoa, whoa," Craig said. "Let me just grab this from you before you toss it out of excitement."

"I'm serious!" Seth went on. "I have busted my ass in the same soul sucking building for ten fucking years. And what do I have to show? Nothing but an ongoing review of my entire meaningless career because I slipped up one time. I've been there so long they can get rid of me and hire someone else for half of what I'm making. And you know why it happened? Why I fucked up and am on 'indefinite suspension'? I can't sleep, because I sit up at night thinking about how my life is shit. Then, I overcompensate with caffeine to drag myself out the front door in the morning. And I do that six days a fucking week, trudging into that place to have what little energy I can muster steadily drained out of my debilitated skull. So, in my spare time I try to escape reality for a minute and look online, only to see these opportunistic ticks trying way too hard to trick me into watching them prank their fucking friends, or watch them just react to other people pranking their friends. It's nothing more than a lucrative form of voyeurism."

"Man, you are so right!" Someone yelled.

Seth looked around to locate the origin of the words, only to notice everyone around him looking his way and cheering him on. He heard the same voice speak up again.

"Watcha drinkin' friend?" the man asked. The words low and deep like they slowly spilled out of his mouth.

Ron, one of the men in the Moe's Transition Repair shirts, had slid down next to him. "Craig, can I get two Makers?" He looked again at Seth. "Man, I worked at the same auto shop in Detroit for eighteen years. I liked the work itself. Love working on cars, man. But my hours were all over the place. Drove my kids nuts when we tried to plan anything. Most times my weekends were shot. But I always felt like I was working toward somethin', yeah? Then, all at once, the owner sold it to some franchise. They got rid of just 'bout everyone on the team. Brought in their own people an' left us with nothin'. Took me three months to find work after that. You think my landlord cared about that at all? Hell naw."

They raised their shots.

"To the little guy," Seth said tapping his glass to the other.

"To the little guy," Ron agreed.

CHAPTER SEVEN

Seth woke up groggy with his head pounding. Initially forgetting the incident yesterday at work, he jumped up panicking he was late for his shift. As the room spun due to his misguided burst of energy, the whole shit-show slowly seeped back into memory. Followed by disbelief, and then shame.

He sat on the edge of the bed. Partly to recenter himself and not vomit, partly to figure out if he was more hungover or still drunk. He didn't remember walking home, but here he was in his bed. In some gym shorts, no less. As he grabbed a plain white t-shirt from the top drawer of his dresser, a clanging sounded from the kitchen.

Oh, God. He thought to himself. First thinking he came home with some bar girl. A one-night stand would be extremely unlike him, but since he didn't remember leaving, he couldn't be positive about anything. He looked back at the bed. The side he didn't sleep on remained untouched, so that seemed unlikely. A break in, then? Did he, in his drunken stumble inside, forget to shut the door behind him? Leaving his apartment wide open for the taking? It would be fitting. Maybe they'll kill him. He might just encourage the thought. For a brief, fleeting moment he accepted his fate. Ready to check out and be at peace. Who would mourn him, he thought. If he died today, who'd even remember him tomorrow? Things could have been so different.

Seth grabbed an aluminum baseball bat from between his dresser and the wall, took a deep breath, and slowly opened the bedroom door. He crept out with the bat cocked back. He expected to see all his belongings upended and broken all over the apartment. Instead, his assailant was making coffee and warmly greeted him.

"You're up!" Craig said. "Tell me. Who the fuck has frozen waffles, but no syrup? Like, what's the point? You got me eating some dry ass Eggo-ho-holy shit! Were you gonna hit me with a bat?!"

"God damn, Craig, you scared the shit out of me. And please don't scream. For the love of God."

The daylight of the particularly sunny Friday morning spilled over into the living room in abundance, forcing Seth's attention to the carpet as he conversed.

"And what are you doing here anyway?"

"Saving your life, bro. The breakfast is just payment," Craig said.

"What happened?" Seth asked, trying to piece last night back together.

"So, you don't remember? I was wondering. Well, you closed the bar not even realizing that you hung out while I cleaned up after close. Too busy singing Tom Petty songs. By the way, do me a favor and fucking learn more than just the chorus to *Runnin' Down a Dream*, please."

Seth collapsed onto the couch and pulled the throw blanket over his eyes to block the sun.

"Why Tom Petty?" he asked.

"Yeah, I don't know. One of the other guys at the bar was named Ron Pettry, and you kinda filled in the gaps yourself. Anyway, I was just going to drop you off after I got you in safe. But as I was leaving, I heard a crash from the bathroom. You didn't answer when I asked if you were OK, so I checked in and found you passed out on the floor with your pants at your ankles. I got you in some shorts and in bed on your side. Not gonna choke to death on puke on my watch," Craig said. He poured a cup of coffee and blew on it before taking a sip. "I watched a little Netflix while I made sure you didn't die and ended up falling asleep on the couch. By the way, your TV is dumb. Keeps resetting to channel three. Like I'm in a hotel or something. Took me a minute to find the input button for the XBox."

"Yeah, you get used to it," Seth said. "Thank you. You didn't have to do all that."

Seth slowly peeled back the blanket from his face and looked up at Craig.

"So, wait. Oh God! So, you saw my, um, well."

"What? Your dick? Yeah, man. It was there with us too," Craig said. After seeing the shameful terror on Seth's face, he added, "No biggie. I never understood why people get so weirded out about 'em. You know, I have seen and held at least one dick every single day for the better part of thirty years. Now, if you were Ken doll smooth, then I might have a couple questions."

Mortified, but unable to change the past, Seth moved on.

"OK, man, I'm gonna go take a piss. Probably sit down while I do it and put my head in my hands. You know, real pathetic like. I'd say make yourself at home, but you're already eating my food."

Seth went into the bathroom, grabbed ibuprofen out of the medicine cabinet, and dry swallowed two of them.

"Uh, Seth? Check this out. Did you see Kasady's Twitter feed this morning?" Craig said.

"Kasady's has a Twitter?"

"Dude. Everything has a Twitter."

Seth finished in the bathroom and walked up to Craig, who was on his phone. To his horror, they both watched Seth from last night at Kasady's Tavern yelling about his life, entitled social media celebrities, the Torwood black hole, the internet, and everything in between.

"Who posted this? Can you take it down?"

"I don't know who posted it. Just someone from last night, obviously. But are you crazy? This is awesome!"

"Awesome?! I sound like a drunken lunatic!"

"Well…"

"Oh, shut the fuck up. This is serious."

"OK. OK. It's not that serious," Craig said. "And anyways, hear me out. One, it's already been re-tweeted enough that it's gone, bro. There's nothing you could do if you tried. And two, people fucking love it! Look at these comments. 'Preach! Finally, someone who gets it!' Another one says, 'This dude has it all figured out. Hell yeah!' This one just says, 'My hero. I raise my glass to you, sir.' And sure, there's plenty of your obligatory racist and homophobic chatter. But this is great! It's not like you got caught picking your nose at a stop light or going all Darth Maul with a mop handle. This is not a bad thing. The internet has chosen you to be their leader for the day. And besides, it's not like many people outside of Torwood will see it anyway. Or care for that matter. Kasady's is a shit bar from a small town in a state that people only think about during big election years. So just relax and ride this wave. Before you know it, it'll be eclipsed by something, else and no one will remember." Craig grabbed two more waffles out of the toaster and added them to the stack on the plate. "But I'm gonna go back to my place and get some things done. Try to take a nap at some point before I go back into the bar at four. See ya, man. Hopefully that hangover doesn't completely derail your day. Eat those waffles. Oh, and get some Pedialyte. People swear by Gatorade, but there's so much sugar in that shit. I'm no doctor, but that can't help anything I wouldn't think. It was good catching up with you. Congrats on the dick. And sorry about your job." His eyes narrowed and his face straightened. "Really, I am. If you want to chill later and have a conversation you'll actually remember, I'm here."

"Cool. See ya. And thanks. You know, for helping me out." Seth shot his attention from the floor up at Craig. "Hey, you're real right? I couldn't handle hallucinations on top of everything else."

"Bro, you're wound too tight."

Craig grabbed one more waffle and held it between his teeth as he carried his coat and opened the door to walk out.

Seth sat down, still reeling from seeing his inebriated self at the bar. It was like a weird out-of-body sleep paralysis. He wanted to shake himself and say, "Shut up. Shut up! Stop! Everyone is staring at you, you idiot!" But there was nothing to be done. The more he watched, the more it drained him.

How could Craig think it was great? Easy for him to say. He wasn't the one people were sharing. Or maybe it would be different if the roles reversed. Some people crave the spotlight. Go out of their way for it, doing dumb shit in front of a camera in exchange for a myopic taste of internet infamy.

Seth had little interest in being the center of attention, and wasn't ashamed of it either. Even though others sure acted like he should be. They told Seth he needed to talk more. Be open. Meet people. That wasn't how it worked. The worst thing said to someone closed off was they just needed to open up and put themselves out there. Always said the same way; demanded with blissfully ignorant condescension. Like something was broken inside, and could be corrected if the right extrovert came along to save the day.

Or maybe it wasn't so bad, Seth thought. *Maybe, once again, I'm just stuck in my head, spiraling. Over-thinking something insignificant into a world changing ordeal that will derail life as I know it.*

Either way, he couldn't put off going to the store any longer. The sooner he could get back home, the better.

CHAPTER EIGHT

The alarm ripped Ethan out of his sleep at 6AM sharp, as it did every Saturday. It went off again at 6:10, because he hit the snooze button just as routinely.

"You're gonna be late, babe," Audrey said as she rolled over and threw her arm over Ethan's body, contradicting the words which rolled softly off her tongue.

"Yeah, I'm getting up," Ethan said.

As he leaned in to kiss her, she turned her head leaving him to land on her cheek. He raised his eyebrow confused.

"Sorry. My breath smells."

"Yeah, so does mine. And I won't see you until tonight, so give me a kiss."

He kissed her lips gently and rested his forehead on hers.

"Your breath is gross," he whispered with a smile.

"Oh, shut up," she said, and threw a pillow at him, which he narrowly dodged.

"Shh, you're gonna wake the baby."

Ethan walked over to the crib near the foot of their bed. Their six-week-old son, Hayden, still lay asleep. He ran a single finger from Hayden's shoulder to the baby's hand.

"Morning, little guy," he whispered. Ethan stood at the crib and quietly admired his son. "I know it's still early to tell, but he's definitely got your chipmunk cheeks."

"Yeah, let's just hope he doesn't have your giant nose to go with it," she snapped back.

Ethan made a sarcastic face, which Audrey mimicked, and he went in to go take a shower and get ready for work. He worked weekends at Thompson's Hardware Store. Monday through Friday he worked at UPS unloading trucks. Neither job gave him an abundance of hours, or a semblance of a future, but he made enough money that Audrey could stay home with Hayden while he worked as long as they lived modestly.

He took a moment while the shower warmed up and stared at himself in the mirror. He even thought he looked beat up. Stubbly beard. Bags hanging under his eyes, hooked to each corner like hammocks. His eyes were red and dry from falling asleep with his contacts in last night. He worked an extra shift at UPS yesterday, which got him home with enough time to eat some food Audrey saved for him and crash on the couch. He placed three drops of Visene in each eye.

As he entered the kitchen dressed and ready for the day, Audrey greeted him by wrapping her arms around him. She wore a pair of his boxer shorts and a tank top which showed off the tattoos across her chest and down her left arm. She pushed her short coal black hair out of her face before pouring herself a cup of coffee.

"You want some?" she asked.

"You or the coffee?"

"Ha-ha. Funny guy. Don't start something you can't finish."

"Yeah, you're right. Nah, no coffee for me. I gotta get going. What do you got going on today?"

"Jen is coming by at noon. I'm going to finish up her shoulder today."

Audrey gave tattoos from the spare bedroom. She had been employed at a local shop for a run, but booth rental and scheduling forced her to stop. She figured she could order supplies for herself cheaper than the booth rental anyway. She gave them mostly to friends and family, as well as any inquiries from word of mouth. She missed out on the walk-ins that a shop provided but made decent side cash under the table. During the week, she took online schooling for graphic design at the University of Florida. All of which allowed her to stay home with Hayden while also working on something toward the future.

"Cool," Ethan said. "Need me to grab anything on my way home later? I think Jordan might come over later, too. If that's cool."

"Fine with me. Yeah, we need wipes. Your kid won't stop shitting."

"Mmmhm. Just my kid, huh? I see you using them for yourself. You guys have the same problem it seems."

"Oh OK, whatever. Just make sure to get the lavender scented ones." After a small pause, she added, "Hayden and I both prefer those."

"Deal."

Ethan grabbed a Red Bull out of the fridge and after second thought grabbed an extra one. He gave Audrey a long kiss goodbye and started for the door. Before he walked out, Audrey called to him.

"Hey, babe!"

"Yeah, what's up? Everything OK?"

"Yeah, just wanted to say that I love you, and I know how hard you work for our little family."

Ethan smiled. "I love you, too. Thank you."

"Our little family," he said to himself as he walked to the car. Those three words alone would be enough to get him through the day.

***

Ethan Warner worked in the flooring department of Thompson Hardware in Gainesville, Florida. He started working there to pick up a second job when he and Audrey found out they were having a baby. Ethan worked every day between the two jobs, as well as any extra shifts he could pick up between them. When he started at the store, he worked full eight-hour days on both Saturdays and Sundays. But as they scaled back hours, he hardly worked enough to make it worthwhile anymore.

"Just curious, how many hours you guys been getting?"

Ethan asked Lori and Jordan.

"Man, this week I only got twenty-eight hours," Lori said. "And I had to work five days to get it, too."

Jordan added, "Yeah, you got seniority. I only got eighteen. And my availability is wide open."

Lori worked for Thompson Hardware since she was a junior in high school. Now, a thirty-nine-year-old divorced mother of three, Lori served as the unofficial mother to all the new hires that came in. She watched over the new kids and showed them the ropes. Which managers to avoid and which ones to trust, the rules that were enforced to the letter and which ones were more laxed. She made sure they knew that break and lunch times were audited daily, however the dress code was more or less ignored as long as you wore your green Thompson Hardware vest.

Ethan and Jordan were those new guys, even after working at Thompson's for months. They came from the same hiring class and bonded quickly. Both had similar lean builds with dirty blonde hair, Ethan's short and swept to the side, while Jordan's shaggy hair often hung over his eyes. Ethan stood roughly five inches taller than Jordan, and Jordan's baby face made him appear much younger than nineteen. Ethan often had prickly stubble across his cheeks and neck.

"Yeah, they won't get rid of nobody, even when they don't need your ass anymore," Lori said. "They'll scale your hours back, tryin' to make you quit on your own. That way they don't have to pay you unemployment."

Ethan said, "Well I'm not gonna quit. But I'm killing myself for an extra seventy-five bucks a week. Last Saturday, I picked up Cindy's five o'clock shift. I worked four hours in the morning, and then came back that night to work another four hours. Whole day was shot."

"That's just how it goes," Lori said. "It goes up and down depending on the season. It'll jump up again soon after Thanksgiving. And you're one of the final ones in the running for that assistant manager position, right? That will bump you up and guarantee forty."

"That's gonna be huge," Ethan said. "I could finally leave

UPS and stop breaking my back. I'll finally be able to think about the future instead of just wondering how I'm getting to next week."

"When you're manager, can you change the uniform color to red? This green isn't suiting me," Jordan asked.

"Yeah, man. That'll be my first order of business."

"I knew I voted for the right guy."

"I don't think it comes down to a vote, dude," Ethan said.

"Not for manager. Jeez, you conceited ass. I meant for biggest ass kisser. There's a tally in the men's rest room. Handicap stall. Grant's winning though, by a lot. Sorry."

"Great, can't wait to hear him whine about being picked on. Again."

An older man with short, stumpy legs walked up to them. His angry demeanor came off more comical as he hastily limped up and scrunched his dry wrinkly forehead. "Excuse me, can you call someone to mix paint? I've been waiting over there for fifteen minutes and haven't seen anybody!"

"Yeah, we will get someone right away," Lori replied.

"Thank you," the man said, and continued to mutter something as he huffed away, but the trio couldn't understand what it was.

"Lori, aren't you working paint today?" Jordan asked.

"Yup! I'll just get over there and apologize for his wait. Complain about my lazy co-workers or something and he'll end up bein' sympathetic towards me. Works every time," Lori said with confidence.

She chomped her gum at Jordan's direction and headed over to mix the paint.

"I don't know, man," Ethan said "I'm fucking burnt out. I gotta think of something. I thought I'd be fine, but it hasn't even been six months with two jobs and the baby, and I'm struggling bad. I just want to do good for Hayden. Give him what I never had. And yesterday Audrey said we should start a savings account for him. I don't even have a savings for myself. Did you know that as soon as kids are born now, you're advised to start an account for them to have money for college? That's some shit. If you don't start right away at birth, you're already behind the 8-ball."

Ethan looked over at Jordan whose eyebrows furled as he pulled at the loose white thread, undoing the embroidery of the "T" on his Thompson Hardware vest.

"I never really understood the appeal of vests," Jordan said. "What's the purpose? In case your arms are warm, but your nipples are cold? Just a weird garment"

Ethan laughed in disbelief. "Never mind, man. Good talk."

"No, listen. I'm just fucking with you. You're doing great. Trust me. It still cool if I come over tonight and hang out? I got into it with my dad again this morning. Don't really feel like going home right away. He was giving me shit for just wasting time here instead of finding 'an actual career' whatever the fuck that is." Jordan continued talking while still intently picking at his vest logo. "Hey man, you're older and wiser than me. What do you see me doing with my life? I'm startin' to think my parents aren't just trying to humble me before they announce we've actually been rich the whole time and let us dip into the trust fund. And I'm behind in following the great career paths for straight C students from Gainesville Vocational."

"Shit, dude. I'm, like, three years older than you. And I'm barely skating by as it is. Maybe I'm not the best person to follow."

"Are you serious?" Jordan said. "You have it all. Someone who loves you, a child, a house you're renting. You're living the dream." He stopped plucking at the threads long enough to look at Ethan. "For real, though."

"Yeah, you're right. I am lucky. Anyway, yeah, stop by later. We will be grilling out."

"See? Out grilling meats and living the American dream."

"Yup. Meatless hot dogs and frozen burger patties. Just like the rest of the elite."

CHAPTER NINE

Seth did not leave the apartment for the next four days. He ignored calls from a handful of people asking about his Kasady's video. He ignored texts. Nobody was actually checking in on him. Not like they really cared. They all wanted to know about the video. Almost non-stop, he read the comments and watched the views and retweets rack up. He wasn't sure what constituted a viral sensation, but 60,000 views in four days sure seemed like a lot to him. Definitely more exposure than he signed up for. So he decided to cut himself off from it.

For four days, Seth spent quite a lot of time in bed. Each day, somewhere between noon and two in the afternoon, he'd peel himself away to relocate to the worn-out living room couch, where he remained until eventually falling asleep with a movie or show rolling in the background. At some point, he would wake and go back to his bed.

He didn't even realize it at first, but for four days, Seth barely spoke a word. However, that inner monologue freight train rolled on. Reminding him what a failure he was. How his dad would be so ashamed of him. How he should be more ashamed of himself. How he hasn't even registered in people's minds other than that fucking video. Life pushed forward like normal for the rest of the populous, leaving him behind as dead weight. Soon, he would become a shadow of a memory. A fleeting thought that randomly flickered in the subconscious. Unable to be grabbed or examined. Hardly tangible enough to materialize. He'd become that song you can't quite remember the melody to. That movie you vaguely remember watching one rainy Sunday afternoon but can't describe any actual plot points.

He naturally thought of the last time he saw Lauryn. They had just gotten back from a party thrown by one of her work friends, which left him emotionally drained. He never wanted to go in the first place, but they hadn't gone out in a while, so he felt he owed it to her. After about an hour, he hinted at being ready to leave. He offered to Uber home by himself and let her stay. Even though she wasn't quite ready, she left with him. As Seth sat silently on the way home, he felt Lauryn staring at him. At the time, it felt like disgust. Looking back, he realized it was loss. Or possibly guilt.

"You OK, babe?" she asked.

"Yeah. Just tired," he replied.

"You know you can talk to me, right? About anything?"

Seth attempted to force a smile, but only managed a smirk from the right side of his mouth.

"I'm good, Lauryn. Really."

"OK," she said, and gently pulled his hand to her lips. She kissed the back of it and squeezed it hard.

Back home, as he slunk into the couch and turned on the TV, he could hear her in the bedroom. He assumed she was talking to friends and getting an update on the party. But as she came out, she grabbed her keys. For a moment, she stopped and looked at Seth. Though their eyes never met for a last time, he felt her pause. He sensed it, not knowing what it meant at the time. Her hair, styled for the night out not long ago, was now pulled up. Her eyes, red and weary. It all seemed so obvious looking back. She had wanted him to stop her. All he had to do was go and intercept her from walking out that door. But he couldn't do it. Couldn't, or didn't?

He watched it play out regularly in his mind. Many times, he saved the day. Got over himself and stopped her. Grabbed her by the face and made sure she knew he needed her. That he wanted nothing more than to be able to tell her everything that bothered him. Every fear. Every feeling. Every thought. Sometimes he even yelled at the piece of shit on the couch.

"She's leaving, you worthless fuck! And you're just going to sit there and let it happen. You'll tell everyone that it didn't work out. But you'll know the truth. You were never good enough for her anyway. You don't even deserve a good-bye. Look at you. You're pathetic."

As he laid there drifting through the past, his phone chimed.

What now, he thought. *Who wants to comment on my life this time? Tell me how hilarious I am, like I'm not suffocating.*

It was a calendar reminder. *Dr Englund Appt- 5:00 PM*, flashed across the phone screen. Everything in his being told him to cancel. He did not need this right now. He did not need to be judged. To be lectured. But something, deep down shined through. An airy whisper from within bubbled to the surface and told him he needed this session more than any of the others. He mustered enough energy to get ready for the day and head out.

***

"Seth, good evening. It's good to see you," Dr Englund said, and gestured to the open seat next to him. "How have you been feeling?"

Seth laughed. "Fucking terrible, actually."

"Oh? And why is that?"

"What? You don't have the internet?" Seth said.

"I'm sorry?"

"There's a video of me going around online being drunk."

"Oh," the doctor said. He sat up straight and crossed his legs. "I'm assuming you didn't know this was happening?"

"Right," Seth said, as he picked at the drawstring of his sweatshirt.

"And how has this impacted your life since you first saw it?"

"Well," Seth thought for a minute. "I feel like I can't go outside, because I might be recognized."

"And being recognized would be bad? You're aware people

do know you exist?"

"Well, yeah. Would you want to be known for being the drunk guy? On top of that, I'm complaining about what happened at work. So any hope I had of going back there is probably gone?"

"What happened at work, Seth?"

"Oh shit, yeah, you don't even know about that, do you? God, it has been a week," Seth said as he rubbed his eyes with the palms of his hands. "There was an accident at work. A guy I work with was rushed to the hospital, and it's kinda my fault. That and the damage to the product that was being painted at the time. Probably costs way more than I even make in a year. I can't imagine I'll be back. And of course, if I lose my job, I lose my insurance. So, actually, this may be our last session."

"Oh, we have options, Seth. Your well-being is most important. Don't worry about our sessions right now. However, I thought you were looking for a reason to leave that job anyway. You talk about it every week."

"Well, yeah, but not to just free-fall instead. That's not what I meant."

"No free-fall. I'll be your parachute. I'll help guide you, so you land on your feet. So now for this video, other than the fact that people recognize you, does it reflect badly on you personally?"

"Well, yeah. I'm just running off at the mouth about everything, telling everyone how crappy my life is. Feeling sorry for myself. It's embarrassing."

"What can you do about it?"

"Huh?"

"Well, it's out there, right? You can't change that. Remember, affect what you can control. So now what are your options? How do you move forward?"

"So far locking myself in my apartment has been the plan. But I don't think I can sustain that. This is basically the first place I've gone since it happened."

"And that's fantastic that you came today. It shows great progress believe it or not. There's a time where, if this happened, I might have never seen you again." Dr Englund said to both their amusement.

"Yeah, I did do that, actually. Kind of fell off the face of the Earth. Which is easy for me to achieve these days, with no one even watching anyway."

"Seth, I believe it would surprise you how wrong you are. You have to give people an opportunity to see you. Otherwise, what are they supposed to do? But, Seth, the fact that you chose to be here today is a great sign. Not long ago, you were telling me that I was wasting my time talking to you. It shows you want to be more open. To let people in."

"Yeah. I guess." Seth laughed.

"So now the way I see it, you can own it, or you can hide from it. But only one of those paths leads to feeling better in the end. Seth, you have a knee-jerk reaction to shut down if something unexpected comes your way. Almost a reflex. But instead of imploding under the weight, let's focus that energy outward. Have you been writing in your journal?"

"Some. I actually prefer the audio recordings. It feels more natural."

"Good! Good. And how does it feel afterward?"

"I don't know. Good, I guess."

"Seth, I don't do this often. But I'm going to give you homework this week. I want you to find a way to step out of your comfort zone and put yourself out into the world. Don't worry, I'm not asking you to suddenly be the center of attention in a room full of strangers. Start small. Reach out to someone you haven't talked to in a while, or strike up a conversation with a stranger, or I don't know. Sign up for a cooking or art class or something. You know, something small."

"Really!? Small? None of that seems small."

"I know. It is a big step. I can assure you; you will breathe a little easier afterward, and you will see that you have plenty to offer."

"Look, I get it," Seth said. "And when I'm sitting here, and removed from things, it's easy to say, 'I need to hang out more.' or 'I need to enjoy myself more.' But other times I'm sitting there minding my own business and I can hear my own voice. 'Nobody really likes you. Your friends talk shit about you when you aren't there. And why wouldn't they?' And that voice is so loud. The more I try to shake it off and drown it out, the louder and more guttural it grows until the words are being screamed right in between my ears and I can't focus on anything else. I've gone to parties before and after an hour or so, I can hear it. 'They're just being polite. They don't really want to be talking to you. No one wants you here. They didn't even mean to invite you. They invited Lauryn, and you just got to tag along. You're not smart enough. Not funny enough. Not good enough.'. And the room zooms out until I become so self-aware of every move I make that I just have to leave." Seth shrugged his shoulders. "Which is fine, I guess. Maybe I'm better off this way. Some people are just meant to be loners, right?"

"Is that a question? Are you trying to seek agreement, or convince yourself? Seth, I get what you're saying. I really do. But you need to listen to yourself. You went from agreement with me, to expressing your fears, which is great. That's healthy. But the last part, where you justify your fears to validate decisions you don't even want to make, that is where we have to focus. You even know what you're saying isn't true."

Seth said quietly, almost to himself, "I was always by myself growing up. Only child, and my dad worked a lot. So, I'm good at that. But I think it was easier then. You know, for years it was just me and my dad. And he... he knew it. He worked a lot, but I didn't mind. I didn't truly appreciate it when I was little. But I never thought anything of it either. He spent all his time taking care of me. Making sure I was provided for. He didn't remarry. I don't ever remember him with an actual girlfriend. I feel guilty now, looking back on it. He deserved to be happy, too. Right? I was scared to let him know how hard it was for me to fit in. Scared he'd be disappointed in me. But he may have been the best person to talk to about it. He was probably so lonely, and I didn't even think about it. How could I? As a kid you think your parents got it all figured out. We actually never talked about how we really felt about anything substantial. It was always movies, or sports, or TV, or music.

I was always amazed at our relationship versus Lauryn's with her parents. Her parents were divorced, and they hated each other. But she had both of them. So, while me and my dad got along great, we never really hugged. Or told each other 'I love you'. It was always like, an unspoken agreement or something. But Lauryn, she would have knock down drag out screaming matches with her parents, and her brothers. They'd call each other names and wouldn't talk for weeks. Vile things that I would think could absolutely shatter a bond between family members. They'd say what they said, and then not talk, and somehow everything was OK soon after. But when they got along, they were so close. They'd never leave or hang up the phone without saying that they loved each other. And they'd call each other every day. It was the damnedest thing and so different from what I had.

I'd always wonder which is better, ya know. Because we always went the more passive aggressive route. Don't talk about your feelings, just throw out a smart-ass comment and go about your day. Maybe deflect with a little humor for extra seasoning." Seth tapped the arm of the chair repeatedly with his finger and paused for a beat. "He died so suddenly; all I can think is all the things I should have said. But at the same time, it wasn't how we were. If I went up and gave him a hug and told him how much he meant to me, it would probably freak him out." Seth rolled his eyes upward, shook his head and smiled. "God, I can hear him now. 'What are you dying? Or on drugs?' So, I don't know. Which is better do you think?"

"Do you think your father knew how you felt?"

"I guess so. I don't know. He had to have, I think." Seth sat forward again in the chair, and took a hard swallow before continuing, "I didn't even cry, when he died. I didn't do anything. And I don't mean that in some hard ass, 'I never cry' kind of thing. I just didn't. Is that weird?" Seth asked.

"Do you think it's weird?"

"I wouldn't think it's the fucking norm."

"Well, Seth, everyone grieves differently."

"Yeah, but it's my father. A good one, too. Can you imagine how that looks? Sitting up front and showing no emotion? Like a fucking sociopath? I was worried about it, actually. I still am. I Googled it even, soon after, seeing if there was some disorder or something I should be worried about," Seth said.

"That's the worst thing to do. You know that, I'm sure," Dr. Englund said.

"Yeah, but I had to know. It told me I either had Schizoid Personality Disorder or Dry Eyes Syndrome," Seth laughed as he said. "So, there's some levels to choose from, I suppose. Do I seem like I have a disorder to you? Where does reserved loner end and emotionally depraved hermit start?"

"Well, Seth, let me ask you. Do you get upset or angry?" Dr. Englund asked.

"These days more than ever, I think," Seth chuckled.

"Do you get sad, even if you don't show it outwardly?"

"Yeah."

"Do you want to find someone you love, get married, and have a family at all?"

"Well, yeah. Some day."

"OK. Well, this isn't an official diagnosis or an elimination of one either, but my first impression is that you do not have SPD."

"So then...what the fuck is wrong with me? I'm just broken?"

"No, Seth, not at all. It sounds to me that you're a healthy, yet hurting person that needs a little help finding ways to get an outlet for emotions."

CHAPTER TEN

"You can see the numbers here behind me. Over ten thousand people have come from all over to our own Fort Wayne for a chance to be the next United Superstar of America! Will one of these hopefuls have what it takes? Tune in this coming Tuesday at 8PM and find out." Chelsea turned back to the crowd behind her. "What do you think?! Are you the next US of A?!"

The crowd answered with an uproar of screams and cheers.

"For Fox 55, this is Chelsea Winters. Good night."

"And we're clear!" Ted, her camera operator, said. "That was great!"

Chelsea gave an unenthusiastic smirk and nodded her head. Another bullshit assignment. It ate her up.

"We got more to do, or should I start packing up?" Ted asked.

"Yeah, we're about done. Probably just go and get more panning shots of the crowd screaming. The editors love running that at double speed during the voice over."

"Heh. Yeah. Cool, I'll be back."

She held a bachelor's degree in journalism from Georgetown. But if the circus came into town. Or a pet adoption. Or a celebrity caravan made an appearance. She was on the scene reporting for Fox55 News. Somewhere between her outgoing personality and face for television, she had been pigeon-holed as the face of Fort Wayne fluff piece bits.

She headed back to the van and grabbed her phone from her jacket pocket.

"Call Charles Baker," she said slowly, emphasizing each syllable.

"Calling Charles Baker," the phone repeated back in a monotone voice.

"Hello. You have reached Charles Baker. I can't answer right now, but please leave your name and message and I will call you back as soon as possible. Thank you."

Thank you? She thought to herself. *Thank you for what? Leaving a voicemail?* only to be startled by the beep that soon followed.

Chelsea groaned and ended the call, leaving nothing but her disgust behind for Charles to listen to later. That was if he even listened to the message.

She wasn't even supposed to be there right now. Covering this crap. She was supposed to be following up on a child murder in the upper east side. But it turned out they already cleaned up the scene and no one wanted to talk. She wasn't surprised. Good stories never had anyone that wanted to talk. On top of that, they sent Crispin Sanders over to that area. What a waste. The guy had the personality of a doorknob. He needed something juicy like a butchered juvenile backdrop to come across as a likable human being.

Yet another story pulled from her grasp due to its graphic nature. The murders, assaults, muggings, all handed off to others for her protection. Just last week, a robbery led to a shooting on the corner of 4th and Main. They sent Allen to cover it. It wasn't in the greatest neighborhood, and the suspect was still at large. Are you kidding me? Allen, the guy who grew up in fucking Oak Brook? The guy who has only been here for a couple of months and was already getting more screen time than her? When does it stop? When does recognition come? How long did Barbara Walters and Dianne Sawyer deal with this shit?

"All right, boss lady. I got everything packed up. Let's roll," Ted said.

"Great. Let's go. I don't know if you feel it. But if I have to do another day of screaming prima donnas, I'm going to fucking lose it."

Ted chuckled. "I understand, Ms Winters."

They'd already been there for hours. Collected interviews with contestants who seemed interesting enough to talk to. All of them guaranteed they'd be the winner when all's said and done. She had to respect the confidence. The singing took a backseat to the life stories of the contestants. Sad back stories and underdogs overcoming the odds filled the time between the show's singing spots. Nobody even cared if they could sing. What's the story? A talented boring person was such a waste. But a sultry lounge singer voice attached to a young girl who needed the prize money to pay for her addict mother's rehab? That's riveting. The secret Chelsea knew, though, was everyone could have a story. A little editing here, some sad piano there. Suddenly, the guy who packed up his belongings to chase his dream was now a poverty-stricken vagabond in need of a stroke of luck.

Ted drove the news van, while Chelsea rode shotgun and uploaded some publicity shots from the day to the Fox55 social media accounts. She hit send on a selfie of her bright, excited face with as many energetic contestants that could fit in frame. She captioned the picture, "Are one of these the next USofA? #FtWayne #USofA"

She sighed and tossed the phone onto the dashboard.

Ted smiled and looked over at Chelsea. "It doesn't even make sense. You ever think of that?"

"What's that?"

"United Superstar of America. There's only one winner. So who's being united? I don't get it. I get they wanted to try and make a USA thing, but I don't know. Just seems they could've tried harder."

"I never even thought about it, but you're right. That is stupid. We gotta stick together, Ted. We're similar, you and me. If we work together, we'll go places. We have to."

"I'll keep the camera ready, Ms Winters."

CHAPTER ELEVEN

Seth spent yet another night in his apartment. Not held behind lock and key. No steel bars blocked him from venturing out. He lived as a prisoner all the same. He bounced with pong-like precision between movies, video games, his phone, back to movies, and to television.

"On behalf of our channel, I would like to address something we reported on the other night," the TV anchor said. "We unfortunately found after airing, the hashtag 'no nut November' is not at all associated with peanut allergies, and our sincerest apologies to anyone offended after using the link."

He shook his head as he turned off the TV, and ricocheted his attention back to his phone. On a video of a girl dropping by to fill the world in on her day, he decided to read the comment section instead. Those usually provided a yang to the yin of the actual video, keeping the balance of the universe intact.

He stopped at a reply from someone named MagnetoWasRight1999. A gif of Seth from the bar making fun of social media influencers captioned, *The Hero We Need*.

Another replied to that comment. "Where is he when we need him?"

Seth continued through comment after comment about his bar video. Not a thing negative. He wasn't sure whether it was the recent stream of consciousness exercises, which he referred to as "Journal Vomit", or the third glass of Red Stagg he powered through. But an idea struck him. If the world called on him, who was he to remain absent? After all, he still needed to do his journaling for the day.

Step out of your comfort zone, Seth thought in the doctor's voice. *Well, this is going to be uncomfortable as fuck.*

He still wanted to crawl into a hole whenever he thought about people laughing at his expense from the last time. He silently screamed through his teeth each time a screen grab was uploaded to the Internet with some topical bold-faced font to give it relevance again. He didn't want to be one of those, "Listen up, cuz I'ma hit ya with some straight talk" vlogger douche bags which always seemed to be recording from the driver's seat of an old pickup. He didn't want to be seen. Not like this. No, he needed something else.

He rummaged through his bedroom closet, looking for anything to spark an idea. There was an aluminum baseball bat, and a couple of beat-up pairs of tennis shoes loose on the floor. He grabbed an Adidas box, which probably used to be the home of one of those pairs of shoes but now contained a dead Fitbit and three iPods. Two classics and a shuffle, only one of which he bought for himself. A chest at the foot of his bed contained old Halloween costumes.

Seth and Lauryn both loved going to costume parties and they tried to outdo the previous year every Halloween. He rifled through the blankets and old hooded sweatshirts. Nothing much left, really. There were a couple masks that he could find. He tried on his full latex Nosferatu mask from Halloween four years ago and immediately started to sweat profusely. He forgot how hard it was to see and breathe out of the thing, let alone talk and be understood. He grabbed a Batman cowl from the year before that. He was Christopher Nolan's Batman, while Lauryn was Catwoman. He wanted her to be the Michelle Pfifer version, but she opted for the more classic Julie Newmar. Either way she pulled it off, of course. Something about wearing that seemed a bit too heavy handed. But on the other hand, his parents were gone, too.

His father passed two years ago. His mother split when he

was a toddler after deciding the pressures of having a family were apparently too much. Just another item on the pile of shit that Dr Englund wanted him to pour his soul out about. Then he saw it, sticking out slightly from the cape of the Batman costume.

"This could work," he said aloud to no one in particular.

He pulled out a plastic skull mask bought from Dollar Barn three years ago. He had bought it to wear while handing out candy for their apartment building's Trick or Treat night. Classically off-white with black shadowed eye sockets and jawline, only now it was scuffed and worn from being stored away in the bottom of a wooden trunk. The elastic band had snapped, and the bottom of the jaw was cracked away, but that was fine. He re-tied the band, and using a utility knife, he cut away the teeth and chin. Though the plan was to give him better room to talk while wearing it, what remained was a sort of post-apocalyptic marauder look, which was not the motif he wanted.

From the closet, Seth grabbed some old acrylic paints left over from his brief time trying out painting canvases. Seth was suggested to try new hobbies and see what clicked to help find his identity again. The paint, all dried up now, would have been thrown away if not buried and left to die. He added some water to the colors to make them usable, and even then, the choices were limited.

He painted the mask a light gray. Having to dilute the paint enough to make it usable, the finished product was washed out and transparent enough, the scuff marks and shadowing were still visible. However, it did clean up the look rather nicely. He then added deep red around the eyes, filling in the sockets. As the mask dried on the table, he took a step back, impressed with what he constructed with scraps in his apartment. Funnily enough, he never liked his actual paintings and they also ended up in the bedroom closet.

Seth hung a king-sized black flat sheet on the biggest wall in his bedroom. He propped his phone and fixed it into position with electrical tape and a cereal box. He took and reviewed enough pictures to get the positioning right, giving the ability to keep his text paper just off camera.

He sat down at a folding table and finished off his glass of Red Stagg as a courage power-up. After putting on his recently spruced-up mask, Seth stared at his phone. He took a deep breath, reached his index finger out slowly, and hit record.

"So, I've been going to see somebody about how I'm feeling, and it was suggested that I continue on and do this. I don't know what this is yet or what it could be. But I'm supposed to just talk about what's on my mind and how I feel. And lately I've been tired. Just sluggish and not... not myself. I look around and it seems like everybody else is doing great. I know it's not true. I know it's all fake, but it's just how it feels. The same for everyone, I guess. You try to escape for a minute, but all you see is everybody else just living their best life. Making you feel even shittier than you did before. It's like the internet isn't even escapism anymore. It's just your life. And if you're not there, you're missing out. If you're not being reacted to, then you're just finding another way to throw yourself into a downward spiral. Living in a bunker while the world moves on without you. But if you are there, then it consumes you. That's it. There's no middle. You can log in every day and stay tapped in and know what's going on and just let it swallow you whole. Or you can break away and detach from the world and be clueless. Floating through life.

"And I know I'm rambling and I'm sure there's better analogies. But whatever. I don't know what the fix is but I know life isn't supposed to be like this. It can't be. There's got to be something else. But we're just driven into this corner where you can either conform and roll over and play their game. Or you can disappear and it's like you don't even exist. Which is how I feel about seventy-five percent of the time. That I'm just... there.

"You know, I remember when I was young, and I wouldn't speak up much because I feared what people would think of me. Like if I said something stupid or, you know, just had all the attention on me. And I found out that if you don't speak up then no one thinks anything of you. At all. You don't have a voice. You're not there. You fade into the background. An afterthought. But now everybody's got their fucking vlog and checking in to each and every place they go to and keeping tabs of what they do on a daily basis. Every meal. Every store. Every vacation. And don't forget to like and subscribe! Subscribe to what? You're fucking life? I'm just trying to get through my own life. Why would I want to follow yours? I don't even know you.

"What happened? Wealth is measured by internet followers above all else. We're so infatuated by celebrity that we'll do anything to gain notoriety. Just put a camera in front of us and a chance at relevance and we'll dance and sing, or eat spoonfuls of seasoning or laundry soap. Until that gets too dull, I guess. Then what to up the ante? Shoot our best friend or lover for a laugh? That's been done, too. It's all been done.

"In June of 2017, a Minnesota couple attempted to make a YouTube video where the girlfriend shot the boyfriend with a .50 caliber desert eagle. Pedro Ruiz held a book up to his chest that was supposed to stop the bullet, but instead, the shot penetrated through the entire book, and Pedro died from a single gunshot wound to the chest. He left behind a daughter and pregnant girlfriend. That girlfriend ended up getting charged with second-degree manslaughter. Are you not entertained?

"You think that's an isolated incident? I'll give you another, the year after that, Adrian Walters thought his followers needed to be with him as his car hit a milestone. So, on the Kansas back roads, he went live as he hit one hundred thousand miles on his Civic. Except, of course, to up the thrill factor, he was pushing a hundred miles per hour. As the odometer rolled over, he lost control and also rolled over the god damned car. He died instantly. Boom! Instant Karma! Don't forget to smash that like button.

"The list is endless. Someone needs to let people know that their lives are not that interesting. There used to be warnings about the dangers of what to post and not on the Internet. Be mindful, they'd say. What's online lasts forever. But now it's been normalized to a state where shells of humans are convinced it's standard practice to live stream every waking hour of their existence. I can't wait until the first presidential election that digs up old ill-advised tweets and selfies from the candidate's teen and twenty-something years. Or God forbid there's ever a child abduction and the poor kid can't be found since there's no picture of them without cartoon dog ears and a snout.

"And then the parents. God, those terrible parents who somehow both exploit and feed off their children. Dolling them up and sitting them down to talk to a camera and wait for validation at the expense of actual human interaction. It's the natural perverted evolution of the pageant and dance moms. The number of disillusioned kids sitting in front of a camera and opening toys is sickening. Contributing nothing to society other than single frame shot commercials for children too naive to realize they're being used for an advertisement. All backed by the adults who have convinced their young that the masses really need to see them unbox an action figure. Child labor is abhorrent unless the kid's got dimples. Then it's lucrative.

"These companies have grown to have so much power and leverage that they're determining what's popular. More than that, they're burying what isn't profitable for them. They started out as a vessel for the people, now people are the vessel for companies to spew their message and advertising. Nothing is genuine anymore. It needs to stop, but won't as long as sentient mannequins can feel important for two minutes watching the likes rack up."

As he pressed the button to stop recording, sweat droplets collected on his forehead. His intestines wrung and flopped in his gut. But somehow, and for reasons that he could not begin to explain, he felt amazing. He felt free. It was similar to the feeling he had after stream of thought writing or doing the audio recordings, only amplified. Reviewing the playback, he was simultaneously proud of and horrified at the product. It was raw, and honest, and vulnerable in all the ways that Seth usually wasn't. He also deviated from his notes, and some spots trailed off. It wasn't well lit, and he stammered in places. He expected that, though. He took issue with the majority of videos online; many of them overly edited monologues that poorly spliced together sentences and soundbites attempting to make a single coherent point. Slap a colorful ridiculous thumbnail to click on, and off you go. The main page of YouTube was an endless sea of vibrant boxes and obnoxious faces. It always seemed disingenuous to him.

   He knew if he didn't upload the video tonight, he would lose his nerve. It was now or never. He used a video editor to correct some of the brightness and sound level. And that was it. He watched his video another three times. Each time he admired it more. It indeed felt gimmicky concealing his face underneath the mask, but this was the only way it was going to happen. From behind the mask, he could openly say things to the internet that he couldn't dream of saying to anyone face to face. And if the world hated it, nothing would come back on him. It gave Seth the freedom to be honest, for the first time in a long time.

CHAPTER TWELVE

For days following Seth making the video, it was all he thought about. He had moved on from being suspended, and lonely, and even the Kasady's video. He had even made a few more and uploaded them. Nothing routinely, but he enjoyed it enough to continue. Maybe there was something to be said about the vlogger life, after all.

The knock on his front door sounded in a short, rapid burst. Since no one else came by, he knew it had to be Craig, who randomly popped in here and there for what reason Seth couldn't put a finger on. Craig seemed to him like the type to get a foot in the door, then knock the damned thing down and kick his feet up on the coffee table of your life.

"What's up?" Craig said.

"Oh, it's Monday."

"Yeah, another week."

Craig held out his hands containing a small blue bag overflowing with tissue paper.

"What's this?" Seth asked.

"So, I may have been wrong about the bar video. That thing's got legs, man! I underestimated your viral ability. Or overestimated the internet moving onto a skateboarding bulldog or something. Either way, I was wrong. Rather than let you say I told you so, I bought you something. Oh, shit you got pizza?! You mind if I grab a slice?"

There it was, Seth thought. Craig walked past him and

tucked the bag into Seth's chest like a football handoff. He pulled back the tissue paper and looked inside. The bag contained a black coffee mug with a yellow smiley face on it. Not the new age emoji style, but the classic "Have A Nice Day" yellow smiley face.

"Uh, thanks, man."

"Yeah, I noticed last time I was here you only had a couple mugs, and maybe this happy little guy will remind you to look on the bright side of life."

"You know, I think maybe that's all I needed."

"I'm going out and doing trivia night tonight. You should come with me." Craig said as he folded the cheesy triangle in half and took a bite.

"I don't think so, man. I don't want to just intrude on your group."

"Group?" Craig said confused. "Oh, no, no. I'm not even on one yet. I usually join some random group I meet that needs an extra person. It's a great ice breaker, actually."

"How is that even possible?"

"It's easy. C'mon."

"Nah, I'm just gonna hang out here."

"Dude, it can't be healthy to be here all the time."

Craig hung his jacket on the back of a kitchen chair.

"I'm not here all the time." Seth snapped back.

"OK, hey you got anything to drink?"

"No, hold on. You came here. Why? Just to make me feel like shit? I'm fine. Not everybody needs to be surrounded by people all the fucking time."

"Whoa, OK. My bad. I'm sorry. We can stay in."

"What do you mean 'we' can stay in? I thought you had Trivia Night."

Craig shrugged his shoulders.

"There'll be others."

Before he could reply, Seth's phone rang. *Torcon* stared him in the face as he peered down at the screen. He answered as quickly as he'd ever answered the phone before.

"Hello?" he said.

"Hi. Is this Seth Roberts?"

"Yes, it is."

"Good afternoon. This is Cheryl Andrews from Torcon."

"Yeah. Hi, Cheryl. How's it going?"

"Good. Thanks." Her tone remained unwaveringly cold and businesslike. "I called to let you know that our internal review is complete. We have concluded that a three-week suspension is an appropriate corrective action. You will be able to return to work next Monday."

"Wait, really?"

Craig, who only heard Seth's half of the conversation began miming questions to pry for information. Seth waved them off.

"Yes. You'll be placed under a probationary period of ninety days. But other than that, it's business as usual."

"That's amazing! Thank you."

"To be honest, much of it had to do with Vincent Ballick having glowing things to say about you."

"Really? Wow. And... how's Gregory?"

"Still healing. Still in the hospital. We don't know specifics. But even if we did, we couldn't disclose, obviously."

"Right. But thank you. I'll see you soon."

"Yep. Have a good day."

"You too."

Seth put the phone down, and turned to Craig, who stood ready to burst with curiosity.

"Dude, they're letting me come back."

"I thought you said you were fired."

"I thought I would be," Seth said.

"So, we're going out to celebrate!"

"Nope!"

"Dammit. OK then what are we doing."

"Again, with the 'we'. I'm about to stay in and watch something."

"OK, that works for me."

Seth watched in awe as Craig grabbed a beer from the fridge and sat down on his couch. He couldn't stop the smile from crawling across his face. He conceded and sat down next to him.

"I was about to start *Gothic Runaway*. You watch that yet?" Seth asked.

"Never heard of it," Craig said.

"I heard it's good. It's got Andrew Garfield in it. His kid ran away, or maybe was kidnapped, or something."

"Who's that?"

"Wha... He was Spider-Man," Seth said.

"Oh, I never saw them."

"His Spider-Man movies? Yeah, they're actually better than they get credi-"

"Any of them. Never really cared."

"Any Spider-Man movie? Even the Sam Raimi ones?"

"Comic book movies at all. Not really my thing."

Seth paused the movie still on the title screen to focus on more pressing matters.

"How? Not even accidentally? On TV or anything? They're always on somewhere."

"They're all the same. Some normal ass has something extraordinary happen shattering his mundane life. They run from their destiny until they don't, and they save the world. Kinda boring."

"I'm honestly shook," Seth said and resumed the movie.

They watched in suspense as Andrew Garfield looked for his son all over the rainy Seattle setting. After forty minutes, as the first red herring showed his face, something dawned on Seth.

"Wait, that's the third time they mentioned Nirvana for no reason. Is this another movie set in the fuckin' 90's? What is the obsession?"

Craig shot up and placed his beer on the coffee table.

"Oh hey! I know this one. Technology, bro."

"Technology?"

"Yeah, I read an article about this. People who make horrors and thrillers both love the eighties and nineties because it eliminates the 'why don't they just use their cell phone' thing. You can't even get lost nowadays. Let alone locked in your creepy neighbor's cellar. The always online lifestyle hadn't happened yet. The nineties are super popular right now because they don't even have to change much beyond getting rid of the phones and iPads. That and the sweet, sweet nostalgia of course. For the eighties, they need to put up wood paneling and find that brownish orange floral couch."

"Pretty sure people still go missing all the time," Seth said.

"For real, dude. Pull out your phone."

Seth did as asked, slipping his phone from his pocket and handing it to Craig.

"You don't even lock it?" Craig asked, appalled.

"The hell would I have to lock it for?"

"I don't get you. Anyway, look. It shows your big ass head right here at the apartment building. Give it six months they'll probably sync with Netflix and be able to tell what the hell you're watching."

"That's depressing."

"It's the price we pay for everything being just within reach," Craig said. "People say they want privacy. But really, they wanna sit in a recliner and say 'I'm kinda cold,' and have the thermostat automatically kick up the temp a few degrees."

"Yeah, I guess," Seth said. "You really never watched a comic book movie?"

Craig took the leftover discarded pizza crust from Seth's plate and started eating it.

"I saw the Batman movie with Mr. Freeze when I was little. Does that count? I thought that was cool. Arnold's the man."

CHAPTER THIRTEEN

The night air chilled the sand on the beach next to the lake. Music blared, melding with the howls of wildlife hidden in the trees.

Nights like these found a way to manifest themselves. Word of mouth spread far and wide without being able to pinpoint the epicenter. If one were to ask around, there would be no concrete answers. A friend told a friend who texted ten people who in turn mentioned it in the break room at work, and those people added the location to their Snapchat story.

Someone found a way to bring a keg, which three clueless high schoolers stood next to as they watched a YouTube tutorial about how to tap it. While there were no trees fallen in the area, a massive pile of branches and debris flickered ablaze as a homing beacon for more people to congregate. Joints were passed around among the dancing bodies. While the night was early, numerous spots littered throughout were occupied by conjoined bodies lost in embrace. Most of which discrete. Some unashamedly in the open.

Jordan's skin glistened in orange flashes by the roaring bonfire. He scanned the area from the perimeter, looking for familiar faces and planning his way forward. He walked up to a group consisting of a few people from Thompson's. Grant, Becca, and Heather.

"Oh, shit. Trailerman made it!" Grant said already slurring his words.

"What's up, Grant? I see you started early."

"You all alone tonight?"

"Yeah. Just me."

"Good for you, Trailerman," Grant said as he pushed against Jordan's shoulder. "I didn't even know you could detach from Ethan's dick long enough to venture out."

Jordan smiled and shook his head.

"Don't mind him, Jordan. He was already like this when he got here," Heather said.

"Why does he keep calling you Trailerman?" Becca asked.

"Oh that? Grant thinks he's clever and wants to remind me that I live in a trailer park. It's all he's got to keep him happy."

"You see, Jordan here is gonna work for me one day. I'm on the fast track to manager," Grant said to the girls. "Mr Thompson said it himself."

"He says that to just about anyone, bro. Don't get too excited. He uses it for motivation."

"He ever said it to you?"

Jordan quietly kicked the sand around with his foot.

"OK. I'm gonna go…anywhere else but here." Jordan said. "Becca, Heather, I'll see you at work tomorrow, yeah?"

"Yeah," they said in tandem.

"Cool. Grant, keep knocking them back. I hope you pass out face down in the sand."

"I'm so fucking sick of you," Grant said.

Jordan turned to respond, but Grant punched the side of his face, knocking him to the ground. Grant erupted in laughter.

"Oh, man. Who's down in the sand now?!"

Grant looked around, and to his dismay no one else was laughing along with him.

Jordan picked himself back up and wiped the sand from the side of his face. "OK, you fucking tool, let's get right to it and stop beating around the bush, shall we?" Jordan looked over to the two girls who had stopped talking to make sure that Jordan was OK. "Ladies, Grant here is acting like a fucking twat because he has no social skills and is actually shy. So I'll be his wingman. He feels like he needs to puff his chest and behave like this, because it will make you want to sleep with him. Is this true? Do one or both of you want to have sex with this man tonight?"

They both looked back at Grant, rolled their eyes, and walked away.

"Oh, I'm sorry man. I really thought that would work for you. Maybe next time if you follow up with spitting on the guy you knocked down, you'll drop some panties. Nice try though."

As Jordan finished his sentence, he launched off his back foot, fist in the air, uppercutting Grant in the jaw. He continued on running. While Grant regained composure, Jordan serpentined through the party crowd. When Grant finally shook off the sting of the punch, Jordan was nowhere to be found.

Jordan made his way through the crowd and grabbed a Busch Light from a cooler. Not his first choice, but as he looked back at the keg being worked on like a group of chimps trying to crack a safe, he knew his options were limited. At least until he found more people holding, since what he already spotted being passed around looked to be dwindling. Jordan cracked the beer and slipped into a group of people huddled around a phone. He assumed it was a rescue mission for the keg tappers, but instead they watched a man sitting behind a desk wearing a mask and talking.

"Nah, man my cousin sent me this." The guy looked to be in his early twenties, but short and stocky. Black frame glasses with the right earpiece held on by electrical tape. "She said this guy is all about taking back the power."

"Man, you talking about Felicia? That girl is on crack anyway. Who even is this dude?" asked another. He was roughly the same age, but around a foot taller with darker skin complexion.

"No one knows. The internet is just calling him "The Founder." You just don't get it because you're from Iraq or some shit. You guys have never had to rise up against oppression."

"Motherfucker, you know I'm from Tampa. My parents came here from Lebanon. And you sound fucking stupid. Did you fail history that badly?"

"Just listen. And then tell me how stupid I am. He's speaking the truth. He's taking on social media. He's talking about how companies don't care about their employees anymore. He made a whole video about how people don't give a shit about each other because they're too worried about not being able to provide for their own."

Another chimed in. She had a lighter complexion and spoke with a Hispanic accent while she attempted to be the voice of reason. "Yeah, I was reading about this a couple days ago. He's spitting hot takes on all sorts of shit. Dude actually said that we're all being pit against each other, so we take ourselves out rather than realizing we are all being screwed over all the same. He's got a handful of videos. He don't post often enough to blow up. He's smart like that. Flying under the radar. Trying to let word of mouth carry through to the people before mainstream media gets a chance to shut him down."

"Let me see that," Jordan said. He positioned himself and focused on the small screen.

"You're not saving the world. Sharing a post and adding a hashtag do nothing. Changing your profile picture does nothing. Stating that you're keeping a problem on your mind is not working toward making it better. And please, for the love of God, stop trying to inspire the masses with uplifting messages. It's pathetic and forced. The Internet is spilling over with self-righteousness. Get over yourselves. Here's some advice. Just don't be an asshole. Use your head. That's it. That's the only uplifting motivational advice you need.

"I know you. I see you. You're sitting there, hating your life, and wondering when it will get better. It never will unless you do something about it. It isn't out there behind a stock photo of the forest with block lettering stating some quote that may or may not actually be Emerson. I'm sick of acting like if I only had things fall in my favor that I'd be doing something else. The world is nothing but a sad carousel unless you finally get thrown off and-"

"I heard he's actually a congressman, that's why he can't

show his face," the girl added.

An eruption of cheers stole everyone's attention. Two people high-fived over the keg.

"Looks like they got it," one of them said. "Let's go while we still can."

"There you are you piece of shit!"

Jordan looked up and saw Grant heading his way. Two other guys marched alongside him. Jordan planted his foot to run, but it slipped. He fell and his elbows dug into the sand. He shot back up and ran away, looking back periodically to make sure he remained a good distance. He ran into the front bumper of his car, before tumbling inside and driving away, leaving his assailant and the party in the rear-view mirror.

What wasn't behind him, however, was the feeling of being cut down in front of every person at the beach. He also didn't realize how hard Grant punched him until his adrenaline waned and his left eye throbbed at the second red light. More importantly, he couldn't stop thinking about that video. And what they had said. Who was he? What else did he have to say?

When Jordan walked in the door at home, his mother and father sat on the couch watching TV. His sister had fallen asleep in the recliner, covered in a fleece throw blanket patterned with coral and colorful fish. The lights were off, but the glow of the television illuminated the room enough for his father to ask, "The fuck happened to your face?"

Apparently, Grant's solid connection already started to show.

"Nothing. I'm fine."

"Hopefully the other guy has two black eyes."

Ignoring that, Jordan walked down the hall to his room and rolled into his bed. In the safety of his bedroom, he slipped away into a rabbit hole of videos. There were only a handful of them. But he watched every one right after another. Jordan clung to each word as a life preserver. He was rescued by the message. This man. This anonymous face fixed behind an icy white skull. The eyes, enlarged and cherry red, attracted Jordan's focus while the words tag teamed him into a hypnotic state.

He finally found his calling. He found someone who understood him.

CHAPTER FOURTEEN

Stanley McGrady sat in the back of Reformation Church's basement and sipped on his black coffee. The steam spiraled up from the Styrofoam cup, dissipating in the air above him. He listened from the back row to the others in attendance. Always listened. Never really talked.

He didn't have to. He didn't have anything to add that wasn't said better and more interesting by the others here. He never drove his car through a playground or left his children home so he could go and get plastered. Those were the stories that really drove the point home. The rock bottom stories people needed to get off their chest and hope for forgiveness and warm embrace.

One bar fight that got out of control. That's all it took. One douche bag that got his ass beaten for running his mouth. But maybe Stanley shouldn't have gone so far. The pictures presented to the court seemed to think so. Police photos showing eyes bruised and swollen shut along with a crooked jaw that had since been wired shut.

His wife seemed to think so as well. He had been committed to repairing that, though. It's the main reason why he's here. No more missing meetings. No more making excuses. They'd be a family again, soon.

Stanley never really talked about his journey, but he would today.

"We've got a big day for someone here today," John said.

"Our brother Stanley, here, has his ninety days in today. Come on up here Stanley."

The applause in the church basement echoed, making it sound like hundreds were in attendance rather than the dozen or so people waiting for his inspiring words. John handed over the chip and leaned toward Stanley and whispered into his ear.

"Congrats, man. You earned this. Take your moment. It's a big deal."

John Murphy was Stanley's sponsor. Early on, Stanley swore he didn't need one. It wasn't until his wife, Donna, thought they needed a break that Stanley really started to struggle. Ironic.

Stanley attended the meetings as he needed to, but it was just a means to an end. His real sense of support and community came from the group he met online. Instant Karma. He found solace and a brotherhood in the words of The Founder. The movement started simple. Online discussions about how inspired people were by the pointedly honest videos they all stumbled upon. Perhaps "stumbled upon" was a poor word choice. The videos called out to them. The group shared theories and research about who made them, and what would come next. It all very recently spilled over into the real world. They began meeting at diners and soon would be coordinating full-blown protests. They planned to take their mission to the streets in an effort to bring attention to the atrocities of the elite.

Stanley had pulled himself up by his bootstraps and started a towing company with his brother, Ray. It did well enough, but the trucks need more upkeep than they're worth. Keeping a crew of reliable people was damn near impossible, and Stanley's mug shot making the rounds in the gas station local pamphlet *Indiana Incarcerated* wasn't good for business.

Later that night, when calling in to say good night to the kids, he attempted to once again explain the situation to his wife. He hadn't seen her in months, except for weekly couples therapy and when handing the children back and forth every other weekend. They talked on the phone multiple times per week so he could talk to their children.

"Donna, I'm going to the meetings. You're not listening to me. I'm just saying I found an additional group that really speaks to me," Stanley said.

"Okay. Because I swear to God, Stanley. If you decide to just up and quit again. I couldn't even. You found this on your own?" Donna asked.

"Right. Not ordered by the court. I'm doing all the right things," Stanley said. "I got my ninety-day chip today. I was actually hoping you'd be there."

"I know. I'm proud of you. I really am. And I'm glad you're serious this time and trying. I just... I don't know. It's going to take time. Baby steps. Just like Dr Richmond said."

"I miss you," Stanley said.

It was a desperate attempt to receive some kind of affection back. Even if only verbal; something he took for granted for years. But all he received was a long silent pause. Stanley pulled the phone from his ear and slid it down his cheek where it propped up his deflating head.

"Do you want to talk to the kids?"

"Please," he sighed.

"Kids!" Donna yelled away from the phone. "Daddy's on the phone!"

"Daddy!" one of his girls hollered excitedly.

Stanley and Donna had three children together. Emma was six, Chloe was eight, and August was ten, about to turn eleven next month.

"I want to talk to Daddy," Emma said.

"Hold on let me put it on speaker phone."

"Daddy, guess what."

"What baby?"

"Um, this is Emma. Ms. Samuels let us take Harry out of his cage at play time, and and and... and then he peed on the desk."

"Oh yeah?" Stanley chuckled.

"Yeah. Okay, love you, bye!"

Stanley listened to the pattering of feet running away.

"Ugh, you always hog the phone!" Chloe yelled at Emma.

"Love you, Dad. Good night."

"Good night. I love you, too. Is your brother there?"

"Yeah. August you wanna talk to Dad?!"

"Hey, Dad," August said.

"Hey, man, how was school?"

Stanley's conversations with August tended to be more back and forth. Not the onslaught of information hurled at him from his younger daughters.

"It was good. I had a math test today. It wasn't even that hard."

"Awesome. I'm sure you did great. Hey, I'm gonna try to be at your soccer practice tomorrow. I'm trying to have Uncle Ray work late and cover for me."

"Okay."

"Hey, I mean it, man. I should be there."

"Are you and mom getting divorced?"

"No, of course not. Who said that?"

"Bobby Gretter did. He said his dad moved out too and then his parents got divorced and then his dad grew a beard and eats a lot of spaghetti and jar sauce."

"No, buddy. Me and your mom love each other very much. We just need to work some things out and I'll be home. Besides, I already have a beard. And I'm a phenomenal cook. You know that. Am I right?"

"Yeah," August laughed in agreement.

"Okay. I love you. Go ahead and put your mom back on please."

"Love you too. Good night. Mom, here's Dad again."

"Thanks," Donna said. "Hey. So, you got the hamster pee update, I heard."

"I did. Listen, you don't use the 'D' word around them, do you?"

"Dick?"

"No! Divorce."

"Of course not. But he's old enough to know something is going on, Stanley. And kids talk to their friends like anyone else when they don't understand something."

"Okay. Because we will get through this. Baby steps, right?

Just like you said. You forgive me, you said?"

"It's not that easy. But yes, we're trying to get through this."

"I'm gonna try to be at soccer tomorrow. Going to see if Ray can stay late and cover for me."

"Please be there. I swear to God, Stanley, if you got his hopes up again to just not show up."

"I should be there."

"Well, if not, I'll see you Thursday at Dr Richmond's. Six o'clock, Stanley. Not 6:07. Not 6:15. Six PM."

"I get it. Okay. Good night. I love you."

Extended silence again. It was worth a try.

"Good-night Stanley," Donna said as endearing as she could muster, and ended the call.

CHAPTER FIFTEEN

The Thompson's Hardware break area consisted of two rooms. The main break room contained a 27" flat-screen TV, a lounge area with two couches, and three vending machines. One for coffee, one for soft drinks, and one for snacks. All badly outdated and overpriced by about fifty cents.

Lori tipped Ethan and Jordan early on that if you filled out a "machine malfunction" form attached to the wall, the vending machine company reimbursed you no questions asked. They didn't abuse it, but it came in handy more than once when Ethan didn't have anything to eat, but was graced with that little tan envelope with $1.25 in quarters with his name on it.

Inside that bigger break room was a smaller room with a door connecting them. Back when smoking indoors was legal in Florida, this had been the smoker's break room. While no one smoked inside of it since 2003, the walls remained stained yellow, and a slight tinge of nicotine still secreted from the walls and six-foot plastic table. It wasn't the best way to spend your fifteen-minute break, but it did give Ethan privacy to call and check in on Audrey and Hayden.

As Ethan was about to call, Jordan popped in and interrupted him.

"Dude, check this out!"

Jordan plopped down and put his phone in Ethan's face. Jordan's in your face attitude weighed on Ethan's patience at times. But the way Jordan's voice went up in pitch whenever he was excited made Ethan laugh every time. He pushed Jordan's phone away.

"Man, does it have to be right now? I was just about to call Audrey."

"God damn right it does! Look!"

He moved his phone back into Ethan's face. A YouTube video started of a guy in a beaten-up skull mask merely sitting and talking.

"Jordan, what the fuck is this? Who is this dude? Some *V for Vendetta* knock off? What's with the mask?"

"I know! Awesome, right?"

"If you really wanna know, kind of forced at best. Unnecessarily theatrical at worst."

"Whatever, just listen. Dude's legit."

The masked man spoke of fair working conditions and employees being taken advantage of in the workplace. And how wages were used against the populous to create competition only benefiting corporations. Ethan watched on as it almost felt like he was being talked to directly.

"It's blowing up right now on Reddit. And you're wrong about that mask. That damn thing is fire. He should make merchandise, if he's smart."

"OK, man. I can't wait until you get your overpriced t-shirt," Ethan said. The more he watched, however, the more the video made sense. "Instant Karma? That's his name?"

"Looks like it, he's got a handful of videos up. Talking about his life. Talking about struggling. And shit, get this! Now, it's even here in real life. People are gathering and fighting against corporations and lawmakers about stacking the deck against us. I heard he might even be somebody important. Like a celebrity undercover feeling guilty about his lifestyle. You think it could be Tom Cruise?"

Ethan laughed.

"No, I don't think it's Tom Cruise. I'll check the rest out later. Now get the fuck out of here so I can call Audrey."

"You need privacy for that, huh? At least wait for me to leave before you unzip your pants."

"Oh. Fuck you!"

***

Jordan Tillman and his family had grown older and apart somewhat as families do. But at the behest of his mother, Janet, every Sunday at 6:30PM, the family unplugged from their lives and ate a home-cooked meal together. Janet, Jordan, his father Doug, and his sister Beth all put their phones away, turned the TV off, and had a nice meal without distractions.

Jordan swiped his hair from his eyes, as he looked up from his plate.

"You guys seen that Instant Karma group on the news? They're kind of blowing up."

He knew they'd seen it. They had to have. He also had to feel the water before knowing if he could come out and talk about how interested he was. Sunday dinners had an unspoken rule not to discuss politics. Just keep it light and breezy and reconnect. Instant Karma was a weird gray area under that umbrella.

"I was watching something on them earlier," Janet said. "It's all over Facebook about how dangerous they are. Do you think it's true? Is it the guy, or a group?"

"It's not dangerous. That's all lies. And they still don't know," Beth said.

Jordan smiled. He figured he could count on Beth.

"They're just making noise," Doug said.

"I don't think that's the case, Dad," Jordan said. "What he's saying makes sense. There's a whole thing now because of him."

"Just a bunch of entitled kids that don't want to do hard work. Not everything is so easy. I've worked my whole life to provide for this family. Hard, honest, respectable work. It wasn't easy. But I didn't cry about it either."

"Exactly! You're a perfect example. What do you have to show for it other than a broken-down truck and a rented double wide?"

"'Scuse me?!" Doug said.

"No. Not like that. I just meant, like, their movement is trying to help people like us. And trying to, I don't know, get people to think for themselves."

Doug dropped his knife and fork in the middle of cutting his Salisbury Steak.

"How's that? By dressing the same and being told what to think by this lunatic?"

"So, you have looked into it?" Jordan said smiling.

"I know enough."

That was all Jordan pushed the issue. He had an out and could move on knowing what he needed to know. He may talk to Beth more about it later when their father wasn't around. While he drifted off elsewhere, he moved around his mashed potatoes, molding them into a clean oval. He then dotted two gravy eyes while he thought about how they should set up a protest here in Gainesville.

After dinner, Janet cleaned up the dishes. Doug already moved outside to work on his Dodge Ram. Jordan and Beth still sat at the table, staring at their cell phones downloading the messages they couldn't immediately see while the phone sat on the kitchen counter.

"Jordan, come here for a second," Janet said, and pulled him aside. She slid the window curtain, donned in a blue and white checkerboard pattern, out of the way with her pinkie finger and looked out at Doug in the side yard beside the trailer. The engine of the truck swallowed his head while the soft yellow glow of the flood light beamed from the top of the shed behind him.

"Jordan, in case you couldn't tell, your father is more stressed out than normal. I wouldn't take what he said to heart. He's just under a lot of pressure right now."

"Oh, I get it. It's my fault for not following the no politics rule, right? I thought he was fine. Why, did he say he was actually upset about it?"

"No, no. He didn't say anything. You know him. He won't." Janet hesitated and took a deep breath. "Look, I hate asking this of you. It's not fair, and I know it. But would you be able to help out around the house a little? For just a little while."

"Yeah, what do you need? Dad changing out the oil soon or something?"

"No. Not like that," Janet sighed. "Look, the shop is giving him a hard time about his short-term disability claim. It's holding up him getting paid, and he's too damn proud to admit it. I always said we would never have our children pay rent to live under my roof, but we would really appreciate it if you could help. Just for a little bit."

Jordan pulled her in close as she held back tears.

"Mom, mom, mom, of course! Don't even sweat it."

"You shouldn't even have to worry about things like this. But they're threatening to turn the water off." She said wiping her nose and eyes.

"Oh, stop. It's fine. Why didn't you say something sooner? If I wasn't here bumming off of you guys, I'd be paying rent anyway, right? I need to get used to it." Jordan hugged her again before adding, "I was gonna head out soon though. You gonna be OK? I can stay home if you want."

Janet sniffled and wiped her eyes with her palm. "No. Go. Get out of here. Go have fun."

***

The natural spotlight of the open night sky shone on the dirt patch of a back yard Ethan and Audrey transitioned to a makeshift patio. A small round table functioned as the point which plastic chairs orbited around. The firepit on the side gave off warmth and an amber-red glow. The cookout came and went, but a few stragglers remained still drinking and conversing.

Along with Ethan, Audrey, and Jordan, Audrey's younger sister, Gwen, was there. As well as Marcus and Phillip Benson, brothers who worked with Ethan at UPS.

The rental home barely exceeded a thousand square feet. It contained one great room, kitchen, bathroom, and two small bedrooms. A perfect starter home for a small family just getting on their feet. Many their age floated in the gray area between living with parents, a dorm, or in a cramped apartment. Their oasis was often used as a hangout for cookouts, game nights, movie nights, or any other general partying. While Ethan looked at it as a stepping stone for something much greater for his family, Jordan viewed it as a goal for a vision board.

"Anyone need anything while I run inside? Jordan? Another beer?" Ethan asked. "I was gonna check on Hayden."

"He's fine." Audrey slurred as she waved her drink around, splashing some onto the dirt. "You got the baby monitor, right?"

Tonight, Ethan had baby duty, and oversaw the monitor in case Hayden decided to wake up. Ethan and Audrey took turns kicking back without worry, so they could keep him home. The group stayed outside to not worry as much about keeping voices down, but the neighbors were quick to call the police for a noise complaint if anything got a little rowdy after 9:30PM. It pushed quarter after eleven, and they grew louder as they lost inhibitions.

Like the best of late party conversation, no one remembered how they arrived on the topic. But the group showed off tattoos, and what, if any, the meanings were behind them. Jordan popped up as something Audrey said sparked inside his brain.

"Wait, you have a tattoo studio at your place? That's awesome!" Jordan said.

"No, no," Audrey said. "That, sir, would be illegal. I do, however, give tattoos here for free. And if people want to make a donation to the 'Diaper Fund' box I have next to the tattoo chair, then they're more than welcome. Most people are gracious enough to donate between fifty and two hundred dollars. Diapers are expensive."

Jordan's face turned from intrigue, to impressed, to determined all in a single seamless shape-shift. He pulled out his phone and began typing away. After a moment, he pushed the spider-cracked phone screen into Audrey's amused face.

"Audrey, will you tattoo me?" Jordan asked. "I want this on

my forearm."

"The Instant Karma mask? Yeah. I could. It would be $40 for just the basic design. Or I could texture and shade it and shit for a little bit more."

"No. Basic is perfect."

"Wait, you've heard about this?" Ethan asked. "It's not just something that Jordan came across in a break from PornHub?"

"Yeah, it's popping up all over," Marcus said. "Marches, protests, walks. In Jacksonville, they were protesting outside the water treatment plant earlier this week. After they had something go wrong and put the city under a water boil advisory. They got the action news attention, and it sounds like it was fixed quickly just to try and keep it from blowing up nationwide."

"See? I fucking told you!" Jordan said, pointing at Ethan. "It's changing the world. Now where's that beer you were getting me?"

"I'll get the damn beer, hold on. Am I the only one who hasn't heard of this? Where the fuck have I been?"

"Probably working," Gwen said. "Or maybe your head's just buried in the sand."

"I'll bury his head somewhere," Audrey said cackling.

"Hey-oo," Gwen said high-fiving her sister.

Ethan laughed. "You guys are out of control. I'll be right back."

As he pushed himself up out of the plastic chair, he groaned and his shoulder popped.

"Oh my God, Old Man River. You gonna make it?" Marcus asked.

"Yup. Just slowly falling apart. Don't you worry about me."

***

Hayden awoke later that night, a little after 1:30AM. Ethan, still lying in bed awake and restless, took the baby into the living room to feed him without waking Audrey- who he helped into bed recently and instantly began snoring.

He didn't know why exactly, but he could not stop thinking about that video Jordan showed him at work today. He sat in the recliner, Hayden tucked in his arm suckling away at a bottle and pulled up the video again on the laptop. Ethan clicked on the link to Instant Karma's YouTube page and watched a few more videos while Hayden feasted.

One video in particular reached out of the laptop and viciously grabbed him. It took a firm grip on each side of Ethan's face and cemented it in position while he absorbed every word. In this moment, this masked, unnamed person sat eighteen inches from Ethan. They sat together in the dark room, lit only by the vibrant glow of a computer screen, and talked about feelings of floating without direction. About being unable to make a plan to advance because the minute you stopped treading water and look ahead you immediately begin to drown. So he, like Ethan, would blindly kick his feet below the surface just to give the impression he was relaxed.

He resonated in a way Ethan wasn't accustomed to. Audrey gave him an extremely deep connection, and they shared almost everything, but he never talked to her about his exhaustion. About feelings of being meaningless. He loved the fact that she could still stay with Hayden, for now, while going to school. If they also paid for daycare, it wouldn't be worth her working anyway. He repeatedly told himself this situation was temporary, but something had to give eventually, right?

He perused the YouTube comments section and found a link to a Reddit page dedicated to Instant Karma. He fell in and stumbled into a small community of people who looked at this guy in the same way Ethan did. Oddly enough, no one claimed to actually be him. Just a bunch of people with similar beliefs, and fears, and frustrations. There were even talks of small meetups and protests. This was so much bigger than a handful of inebriated fools in his back yard. More than a group inside of his tiny world of Gainesville, Florida.

As he slid the cursor to get swallowed further, Hayden whined and snapped Ethan right out of his trance.

"Shh, shh, shhh. I got you." Ethan said, hushing his son. He maneuvered the baby's position over his shoulder. "You got a full belly now, my man? Ready to go back to bed?"

Ethan closed the laptop with his free arm and headed back down the hall. On the way back to the bedroom, Ethan patted Hayden on his back repeatedly, which the baby reciprocated with a hearty burp.

"Oh, jeez, dude. You sound like your mama."

He gently placed Hayden back into his crib and collapsed next to Audrey. Hayden let out a couple weak whimpers and didn't peep afterward.

"God, I love that you sleep good," he said to himself. "Now if I can just do the same."

But he could not. He laid there face up, wide-eyed, and anxious. Ethan wasn't sure how Instant Karma managed to weave itself into his psyche and not let go, but as he tossed and turned trying to find a comfortable position, his mind stayed on that group. He wanted- no, needed- to know more. He picked up his phone and checked the time. 3:18AM.

If I fall asleep in the next two minutes, I can still get two hours and forty minutes of sleep before my alarm goes off.

It must have worked, as that was the last thing he remembered until morning.

CHAPTER SIXTEEN

Up and down. Up and down. First pomegranate red, then the color would turn to dark roast, and then salsa sparkle. Up and down. Up and down again. The robots shifted and sprayed without missing a beat. Back into the same routine, same as Seth. He never thought he'd be back here. Back to this. But here he was. After the initial greetings he received at the start of the shift, everything was eerily normal.

He knew the machine would keep on moving along without him here, but nothing was mentioned. Even when welcomed back it felt as if he had returned from a vacation. Not from a three-week suspension after a man almost lost his leg due to reckless negligence. As Seth followed the product down the line, checking off on each color, he looked around at Torcon running as a unit. Albert stocked supplies for the day. Mr Ballick and Paul reviewed the incoming production line schedule, even himself with the damned clipboard. He couldn't help but notice how the entire thing just felt so trivial.

Did any of it matter? Did he matter? A man snapped his leg in half- shattered bone tearing through the skin like an arm of the living dead breaking free of its soil prison. A wet brew of hot blood and thick paint thoroughly cleaned not forty feet from where they stood. They pressed on like it never happened.

Some team. Where's the compassion? Where's the "Torcon

Family" mindset now? That was all well and good when trying to make people come together and produce car parts, he guessed. But when it meant it. When people really needed it. When it meant actually looking out for one another and reaching out and being a fucking human being- then it's too much. Apparently, that went out the window when it wasn't beneficial to the company's bottom line.

When Seth's father died, the initial support felt great. Torcon sent flowers to the funeral home, and a flood of co-workers showed up to the wake; less to the actual funeral. But in a complete 180, he received push back from HR for wanting to take more than the allotted three days of bereavement. Corporate decided three days was plenty for an immediate family member dying. Then they held his pay after he forgot to get a note from the funeral director stating he attended. Upon his return to work, it felt the same as today.

And that was it, he realized. The same eerie feeling of something not being right with the world. The feeling of a small-town hero upon the realization that the area had been overrun by aliens. It was like he never lived in their plane of existence in the first place. Simon Roberts had given thirty years of his life to this company, literally. His heart gave out on the plant floor, and rushed to the hospital, dying in route. After the metaphorical dust settled, he was never mentioned again.

While Seth wasn't sure what should have happened, he knew something didn't sit right. Maybe it would have been a bench in his name, or start a memorial wall, or even something as simple as a mass email from HR about how "Torcon lost one of their own." But nothing. Seth had come back to work, and it was just business as usual. Same as with Gregory- though he at least should be able to come back, of course.

Perhaps he weighed it differently due to a guilty conscience. While Seth wallowed in his apartment, Gregory had rehabbed in a hospital after surgery repaired his right leg. As judgmental as he was, Seth hadn't reached out to Greg himself either.

Aside from that, Seth started to find it laughable how people stressed out so much from anything that happened here. Was he like that before? He knew now, nothing he did here mattered much. Torcon barreled forward whether he existed or not. It made sense, but how was he the only one who realized it? They freaked out about component shortages, product defects, staff turnover, customer demands. It was fine inside the bubble they created within this facility. But actual people lived outside that bubble with actual problems. Homelessness, unemployment, disease, famine, diminishing self-worth, the crushing weight of unmet goals and expectations. All of which tipped the scale in terms of gravity, and none seemed to exist here. It wasn't a sense of complacency. He felt that here before. Go through the motions and do a good job so no one's the wiser. With fresh eyes and what should be his newfound look on life, it all seemed so inconsequential.

Like muscle memory, Seth took his break in the same spot he had for ten years. No one talked on break, which was fine with him. They imploded into their own little worlds. Actual signal was hard to come by, seeing as they were essentially in a giant box constructed of metal and concrete. He wondered how quickly the revolts would start and the Torcon family would crumble if they decided to do away with the free Wi-Fi in the break rooms. Would it be an instantaneous foaming at the mouth and sprinting attack like *28 Days Later*? Or more of a slow but overwhelming boil over like *Night of the Living Dead*?

The television talking heads went on about how Ben Rodriguez, in the middle of his public relations mandated apology tour, had been left by his girlfriend, Jade Armstrong. This was especially newsworthy in Torwood, as she happened to be a hometown celebrity.

Jade Armstrong grew up in the area and blossomed at a local art school. She charted a few songs as a country musician and escaped Torwood by working hard and having actual talent. She latched onto stardom and left town like the fastest sperm to an egg, while the rest withered and died. She also was vicariously lived through by every slack jawed fuck who didn't make it out of here and still worked a nine to five. So, of course, whenever anything remotely newsworthy happened regarding her, all the local news channels went on a days long Jade Watch with live updates. Breaking news like how she visited her parents over the weekend or stopped in a downtown deli. When she received her nomination for the Country Music Awards Best New Artist category, the local news played her music for two weeks when they signed off each night.

Seth collapsed his head back, letting it hang freely off the back of the chair.

"Oh, for fuck's sake," he accidentally thought aloud.

"I'm sorry. Are you 'Oh for fuck's saking' Jade Armstrong," a voice asked from two tables away.

"What?"

The deep gravelly voice paired with a face he hadn't seen before. With the regular turnover and how little he paid attention, this wasn't alarming. What did slightly alarm him, however, was the face connected to a body of a woman who had to be just under five feet tall and weighed maybe a hundred pounds. She looked to be in her early thirties, but that accusing tone carried at least fifty years' worth of smoking cigarettes made from rolling crushed asphalt in fiberglass insulation.

"I consider Jade a close personal friend of mine. We went to high school together and were on the same debate team. Or at least we would have been if we were in school in the same years. We were six years apart. I even DM'd her when she started dating that Ben Rodriguez fool and I told her that he is no good for her. She can do so much better than him and he'd end up breaking her heart. And look what happened. I don't want to brag but I'm basically the matchmaker of my group of friends. I have matched up every single one. Still looking for the special someone for myself, but that's beside the point."

"What is your point?" Seth asked.

"What I'm getting at is that if you are defending Ben

Rodriguez in this whole thing then you and me are going to have problems and I don't think you want that. So, I'm just wonderin', would you say you are Team Jade or Team Ben?"

Seth, still trying to figure out if this were really happening or if he'd fallen asleep on the job again, said, "I don't even care."

"About which one?"

"Any of it. Are you serious right now? It doesn't matter. And I don't mean that in some nihilistic care-free nothing matters sort of way. I mean it doesn't fucking matter. At all. You don't know her and she damn sure doesn't know you. You shouldn't even have an opinion. Break ups are fucking hard. Just leave them alone. You gotta have actual things in your life that are more complicated than that. Or maybe not. I don't know you. But I do find it comical that you're ready to battle in the middle of the work break room about this. Go ahead, dude, and fall on a sword for someone who doesn't even know you exist. Fine by me. But based on this conversation alone, I'm 'Team Ben'," Seth said air quoting for emphasis.

"Whatever. Don't call me dude. My name is Alicia. And, really, why are you even here anyway? They told me about you. I heard you killed a guy here or something."

So, people were talking about it, Seth thought.

"OK. Good talk. Tell Jade I'm a huge fan when you see her at the next 2000's Debate Team Reunion," Seth said as he left.

After only forty-five minutes of Seth being back on the floor after his break, Vince flagged him down.

"Seth, they need to see you in HR."

"You know what it's about?" Seth asked.

"Not a clue, son."

He handed his clip board to Vince and headed to the front offices. Walking through the main hall up to HR felt like traversing through a Torcon propaganda center. Slogans and posters hung proudly with smiling faces from company cookouts and summer family days. "Every person is an equal piece to the Torcon puzzle." Seth wondered how many people in that T-shaped puzzle were even still around. He didn't remember seeing any smiling faces today while on the floor. Or even in the break room. Everyone either with their head down taking a well-deserved nap, or mindlessly scrolling away on their phone.

"Seth, come have a seat," Cheryl Andrews, the HR Manager, said.

Cheryl's long, thick auburn hair hid away in a tight bun pulled back behind her head. Freckles spread across her cheeks and the bridge of her nose, connecting the crow's feet in the corners of her eyes.

"Seth we've had a complaint raised about you this morning."

"You did?" he said, surprised.

"What happened in the break room? Alicia Whitt was pretty upset about something that you said."

Seth laughed. Probably ill-advised, but involuntary.

"Is something funny?"

"No. It's nothing. Just a misunderstanding, I guess."

"She says that you verbally attacked her and were incredibly rude. Seth, while we normally wouldn't make such a big deal about something that is essentially a he said/she said situation, the fact that it's so soon after your suspension and employment review is a cause for alarm."

"Uh, a suspension that wasn't about behavioral conduct or insubordination. It was some one-off Final Destination type shit that I felt terrible about, which is why I took the suspension without a fight. Even though the whole thing really being no one's fault."

"Seth, I need you to reflect on just where you see yourself within this company. I'm hoping we can right this ship. But I need you to put forth the effort if you would like to remain here."

He knew he should have felt threatened by that. But she raised an interesting point. Did he wish to remain there? His going along with the current had led him to this point, and he wasn't in any way excited about it. Maybe he needed to hit the eject button now before he sleepwalked through another decade of this.

"Thanks, actually. You're right. You've given me a lot to think about. Um, are we done? I can promise you won't see me back in here again."

"Yes, we're all set," she said in a self-congratulatory manner. "I'm glad we could set this right."

"Yeah, me too," Seth said as he walked out.

When he returned to his work area, Seth pulled Vince aside and immediately told him he was quitting. He explained that he was moving on to something else, not knowing quite what that would be yet. But he needed to make some changes.

"You sure?" Vince asked. "Tell you what. Sleep on it, son, and talk to me in the morning."

"No need. I've never been surer of anything in my life. Look, Vince, I'll finish out this week and next, but I gotta get out of here. That time off might have been the most eye-opening thing for me. I'm seeing life through a new lens."

"I was going to say, you've got a new energy about you."

"I'm trying. I feel different."

"Well, even after you're done here. Don't be a stranger, yeah? Our door is always open for you to pop in."

"I know. Thanks," Seth said.

The next week flew by. Seth slept better at night. He woke up refreshed and ready for the day. He ate breakfast and arrived at work early rather than rushing to clock in on time. He had a better attitude at work, too. Somehow recently snapping his life and routine like a glowstick, illuminated something in him and he reverted to a model employee for a job he was days away from no longer being a part of.

Much of his last day was a merry-go-round of people saying goodbye. They made small talk about him getting out of there and getting a fresh start. When the inevitable question would come up about what the plan was, Seth gave out answers like "That's classified" or "Porn Star" or "Professional Sandwich Artist."

"Hey, Traitor," Paul said toward the end of the day.

Seth chuckled.

"Hey, Paul, what's up?"

"You're really doin' it huh?"

"Yeah. It was time. I started feeling like I was skating on thin ice anyway. Figured I'd pull the trigger before anyone else could."

"So, look. I know there's no way in hell you'd want an actual going away party. But you gotta let us take you out for a drink after work today. It's your last day."

"Man, I don't know."

"C'mon, it was Vince's idea, and it's all Albert's been talking about."

"Oh yeah? Well, I guess I'll go then. You know, for Albert," Seth said.

CHAPTER SEVENTEEN

The brainstorming session for the afternoon and evening news stories took place each morning in FOX55's briefing room. Charles Baker started every meeting by blowing smoke up everyone's ass, praising the best new team in Fort Wayne. He'd say how lucky he was, and he was blessed. Trevor Rogers, the head anchor, would lap it up and offer a reach around by means of reciprocation. He'd praise Charles for how easy his job was when guided by such an inspirational leader. Chelsea would see how far her eyes could roll back into her skull and wait for her turn. She usually came in with her own story ideas to bounce around, before being shot down and told what her pissy little assignment was.

"Charles," she said. "Three houses have all been burned down in a neighborhood on the west side in the last few days."

"Yeah, I saw that. A few kids burning down abandoned houses. There's nothing there."

"On the same block? I don't think so. They're all houses that people in the area have been fighting with the city to demolish for close to a year. Saying the unkempt yards and boarded windows are killing property values. I think there's more to it. Here, look. I'd like to check it out."

"Nah, forget it. I've got something better for you. There's a new cupcake shop opening today on 3rd. We need to be there to promote it, and you're the best for the job."

"Charles, you've got to be kidding me. That shit isn't even news."

"Chelsea, look. I get it. You'll get your big story soon enough. But everybody must pay their dues."

"I'm not even the newest field reporter here. Ever since you sent Allen to report out on the opening of the public pool, he's been getting the real meaty stuff."

"It's just the way the straws were drawn. That was only-"

"It's winter, Charles! The damned pool closed for the season two months ago. Give me something."

"You'll get the next one. I promise. Hey, grab me a cupcake while you're out at the opening, will you? And hey, make sure to ooze that Fox55 charm."

Chelsea silently shook her head and walked away.

***

After the shop opening, Chelsea sat quietly in the news van as Ted drove them back to the station. Pockets of run-down areas fluidly mixed in with up-and-coming ones as developers carefully picked where to give new life as others fell further and further apart.

"God. I never noticed how terrible things were getting," Chelsea said. "Kinda sad."

"Yeah. We always used to go there when I was growing up," Ted said, pointing off to Dos Conquistadors on the right.

The old restaurant used to be an inviting orangish beige while in operation, but Dos Conquistadors was just one of a growing of shut down businesses in the Fort Wayne area. As they passed, Chelsea couldn't help but notice the white skull painted on the chipped brick of the building face. It wasn't the skull that grabbed her attention so much as the eyes. Vibrant red. Almost piercing her. The orbs followed her as the van rolled down the street.

"Let me ask you something, Ted. Is this what you thought you'd be doing at your age?"

"I mean, I never thought I'd be a company president or anything. Just happy to have found a place. My dad was a school custodian. My mom was the lunch lady at the same school."

"That must have been fun growing up."

"Yeah, it was interesting, all right." Ted paused and laughed to himself. "I learned how to fight at a young age, I can tell you that. Not sure if you know, but kids are assholes."

"Oh yeah. I can imagine. Ted, we're a lot alike you and me. We're fighters. I see it in you. We have to fight to get ahead. Don't lose that."

Chelsea's mind began to drift off when she spotted another skull tagged on a towing company fence. Same color scheme. This one had the eyes larger, and the skull more in the shape of a muffin than a human head. But there was an attempt.

"You know what the hell that is?" she asked Ted, pointing to the graffiti.

"I think it's a mushroom."

"No. No, it's a skull. I saw another a few miles back."

"Huh. No idea. Think it's a drug thing? Like a 'Get Your Heroin Here' sign?"

"I don't know. But we're gonna find out."

***

That night, like the loose thread of a sweater, Chelsea pulled and pulled unraveling the mystery that was Instant Karma. How it started rising in pockets across the country. Rallies and protests had already taken place in Columbus, Pittsburgh, Lexington, and reportedly as far south as Nashville. Originally written off as viral marketing for a new video game, it looked to be gaining ground and recognition.

At each pop-up event, people wore the same cheap mask. Trivial details differed, but the broad strokes were the same. A generic skull found at any dollar store or discount section of a year-round party store. Some were painted white or gray. Some left alone. But all having the eyes painted in a deep blood red.

She found a handful of self-made videos online of the events, which gave off a particularly haunting vibe. The tense atmosphere accented with the bizarre visual of dozens of identically-faced beings chanting and marching. The same image Chelsea saw tagged on buildings while driving around the city. Not drugs, probably. Each answer she found unearthed further questions she jotted down. How has no one else poked around at this?

She didn't wait until the morning meeting the following day. She stormed into Charles Baker's office as soon as she arrived at work; hellbent on taking this on.

"Charles, we need to look into Instant Karma."

"What?" he said.

"Instant Karma. Ted and I were driving back from Cupcake and Chill-"

"Who's Ted?"

"My camera man."

"Oh. Didn't realize you were on a first name basis. Anyway, go on."

"So, Ted and I, we drove by this graffiti of these faces. I was looking more into it and these faces are actually a group of people across the country that are fighting for... well I don't know what they're fighting for. But that's the point. We need to dive into this. Find out about them. Are they dangerous? Where'd they come from? You know?"

"No."

"No?"

"No. Not happening. Not worth our time. The story's got no legs. It'll get no traffic online. No shares. We've got nothing to go on. And the more you explain it, the more I'm convinced it's just a huge publicity stunt. In a few days you'll probably find out it was teasing a new Terminator movie or something."

"Mr Baker, please. If there's nothing there, we'll stop talking about it."

"I'll do us one better," Charles said. "We aren't going to cover it at all. Let ABC do it. They can be the ones to issue an apology with their pants down."

"You're making a mistake. I'm telling you. This is big."

He rubbed his bald head and sighed. His desk phone started

ringing, and with an index finger, he motioned for Chelsea to hold on.

"Yeah, this is Charles," he said into the receiver. "OK, can you hold for one sec? Thanks." Charles directed his attention back at Chelsea. "I'll tell you what, give me a day to look more into it. I'll see if it's deeper than it looks. But I'm telling you, at first glance, it looks like more of that 'chain yourself to a tree to occupy Wall Street' nonsense that's wasted our time too often already."

"Great! Thanks, Mr Baker. I'll see you in the meeting."

"It's Charles!" He tried to call out to her as she walked away, but she had already disappeared.

CHAPTER EIGHTEEN

"Yeah, I don't know, man. But something clicked in me, and I knew I had to get out of there." Seth victoriously paced around the living room as he talked on the phone with Craig. "I looked around and just felt like I didn't belong." He popped a couple BBQ chips in his mouth as Craig said something on the other end. "Yes. I know I say that about pretty much everywhere. This was different though. I think maybe the universe was trying to shove me in the right direction with that suspension. I just had to make the final leap." He paused again. "No, dude, I don't think God broke a man's leg because I'm depressed."

Seth froze and cut Craig off from whatever he trailed on about. His attention hijacked by the news anchor on the television screen.

"I gotta let you go. Yeah, yeah everything's good."

On the TV, Seth's own face looked back at him. Not his face, exactly. But his face hiding behind a mask, with a black backdrop.

"Who, or what is Instant Karma?" The newsman asked Seth. "What do they want? It appears the movement was started by this man, who, as of the airing of this piece, is still unknown."

Seth stood mouth agape in shocked disbelief. His surprised curiosity ever so slowly morphed into a wide grin. He watched with the same abstract out of body feeling as the

Kasady's video, which thankfully had mostly sunk into the quicksand-like trappings of the internet. This time, the surreal feeling built him up, however. Without breaking his fixed gaze on the TV, he sat down on the couch and turned up the volume even more.

"His videos are garnering popularity and attention as he uses them to speak about himself and society as a whole," the anchor said. "Videos covering topics ranging from public issues he claims others are blind to, as well as personal issues that come off more as a video diary than any traditional kind of news topic discussion forum. While he still has not come forward, his messages have resonated with a growing number of people. Protesters gathered outside of capitol buildings in four states at 10:30AM yesterday.

"The questions about what Instant Karma's message might be, stem from the group not appearing to have a singular goal. While other groups call out specificities such as animal cruelty, treatment of minorities, or global warming, the lack of a focused message is causing many to wonder if there is something more sinister at play here.

"Was yesterday's public demonstration just a warning? What happens if this goes from merely four states in the Midwest to places such as New York and Los Angeles? Our sources say future synchronized protests are already being planned for the coming weeks. We will continue to follow this story and dive deeper into the questions brought forward by what we already know."

Seth sat in a stunned silence. He knew the videos had a fair amount of views and was skeptical but proud of it. A small number of viewers had subscribed to him. A handful of messages trickled in and thanked him for his words, which he, in turn, thanked back. But this? This was far bigger than he could have ever imagined.

He Googled "Instant Karma". After the John Lennon song, and YouTube links to his own videos, was a link to a Reddit page. On the other end, Seth dove headfirst into an entire world he never knew he created. People discussed their favorite videos and planned meetups. Some dissected the videos, trying to decipher hidden meanings.

Instant Karma grew in popularity despite itself. The low-quality videos were not uploaded regularly. They didn't have advertising or sponsors or featured promotions. They were all merely a single-camera monologue of a man in a mask. And people hung on every word. It spread organically. Rising in popularity authentically in a short amount of time through word of mouth and the fact those who found the group felt they had stumbled across something of a secret club.

What started as a public video journal for Seth spread to comment sections and internet chats before spilling over into the real world. Call them meetings, or protests, or rallies, it didn't matter. They began getting noticed. Some marched the streets for higher minimum wage. Some protested health care and pharmaceutical companies right outside their headquarters. They took on news stations, city municipal buildings, state capital buildings; all in the name of toppling the leverage in favor of everyday people. They demanded transparency. They demanded fairness. They demanded to have a voice in the conversations about their well-being and everyday life.

Seth threw his head against the back of the couch and ran a hand through his hair. He spent the next hour in awe reading every post on that page. More meetups were planned in Fort Wayne, Nashville, Philadelphia, Buffalo, Cleveland, and Ann Arbor. Tuesday at 10:30AM. He had to go. He needed to witness this. He could be in Fort Wayne in about two hours, and nothing was more important.

One thing that didn't sit well with Seth from the report, was questioning the motives of those individuals. Or maybe they weren't being considered individuals, after all. The motives of Instant Karma. Could he call them that? Is that what this is going to be? At this point, he didn't think he had a choice in the matter. Like the branding of most things the media got its vice-like grip on, the brains behind it don't really get a say in the nomenclature before it catches on.

Seth walked to the bedroom and used the unexpected inspiration to record again. He'd gotten better with practice.

He had an actual stand and ring light to hold the phone. He experimented enough to find the perfect distance. He prepped his tools, put the mask on, and hit record.

"I feel like I'm being lied to. Maybe lied isn't the right word. But for sure manipulated. Try and find a news station, local or national, that doesn't skew information one way or another. They're all owned by rich and powerful people who have rich and powerful friends and will not air something which doesn't help push their own political agenda.

"So maybe you decide to get your information from the internet instead, but that's even worse. It has the same problems I already mentioned, compiled with the need for ad revenue brought on by views. We are nothing more than hosts to be fed upon. If I see a news article that interests me, I'll click on it. That tells a computer somewhere I'm interested, which gives me more articles in that vein. Each time learning more and more about me, sharpening the pinpoint until the only stories I'm even shown are ones I already agree with before clicking to read more. And I will click it for sure, because I need to share it with internet friends. I need validation for my beliefs. Otherwise, I might have to find different beliefs.

"No matter what the event, it's always delivered with the same breaking news urgency to manifest reaction. Whether it's a plane vanishing with all passengers inside, a revolution in a country most of us couldn't find on a map, or the release of a new iPhone. They'll kick down your doors and force you to absorb it all. Strapped to a chair with our eyelids pinned back Clockwork Orange style if necessary. It is shoved down our throats through broken teeth, and given opinion pieces, and turned into memes.

"News stories aren't finite anymore. They live. They breathe. They evolve. Everything is breaking and more important than the last morsel of information you were fed. Everything is *be the first*. Not *be the truth*. Because the truth is subjective. Facts are debated. We decide what news stories to believe, and which to cast aside. If something doesn't fit in the narrative we've already established, just pretend it doesn't exist. And after all, why wouldn't we? Stories are reported on with different viewpoints depending on what channel or website you see them on. It's like if a movie released with different endings depending on whether you lived on the east coast or west coast. And while everyone argued online about which version was real, the studio just laughed and counted the money.

"What happens if there is no news? Then we will find anything to pummel into the consciousness of the general public. But an actress getting a haircut is not news. A musician tweeting about the news, is not itself news. But that's what we've come to accept, isn't it? I guess, it isn't new. People have obsessed and imitated celebrities as long as there have been movies and music. From James Dean and Audrey Hepburn to Johnny Depp and Madonna to Jennifer Aniston to Justin Bieber to Beyonce'. But it's all bullshit. It doesn't matter. Nothing they do should have an impact on how you live your life. They're barely even real people.

"And how did we get here? At 8:46AM on September 11, 2001, a national tragedy struck and staggered the country. It left people coast to coast reeling with equal parts anger, devastation, and curiosity. Every single person alive at the time remembers where they were and what they were doing when it happened. Our generation's JFK assassination. This moment in history led to the dawn of twenty-four-hour news. And the world stayed watching. Ready and waiting for updates and answers. But when we inevitably put our country back together again, that delivery method was too profitable to turn off.

"So, here we are. We have more coverage of the news than actual news. These channels are filled with opinion pieces and spin the story to feed into a rhetoric. Every fact questioned. Every event politicized. Every scrap of information tossed to us, and then picked apart, and stretched, and debated until it snaps under its own overworked brittleness. Then we're simply served the next item and it starts all over again.

"Think hard for a minute. Think of a recent issue that

flooded the media with 'round the clock exposure. How did it resolve? Where did it go? It naturally faded away. It went silent when the new hot topic came and replaced it.

"We deserve better than news stories cherry picked to service an already created belief system. We are being divided by it. Turn off the TV. Turn off the computer. Put down your phone. Talk to people. Make a stand. We deserve better. You would be surprised how much common ground we have as people.

"I didn't appreciate it at the time, but my previous job was in an automotive factory. You want to talk about a melting pot? That's the place to go. It's no wonder politicians make sure to hit multiple manufacturing facilities on the campaign trail. I worked with people from all walks of life. Right out of high school to bordering retirement. People that grew up a few miles from the place and others that moved from other countries and barely spoke English. Black, white, rich, poor, gay, straight, and the entire spectrum in between. And for the most part, everyone got along. You would have young kids with face and neck tattoos joking around with little old Vietnamese ladies. Degreed engineers working closely with rough looking biker dudes. Nobody thought anything of it.

"The people you see at work, or the grocery store, or in line at McDonalds are all on the same side as you. We all just want to take care of our family and live a decent life. Everything else is just bullshit to keep you grinding and hungry."

CHAPTER NINETEEN

Chelsea sat at her desk, defeatedly scrolling Twitter. Post after post on Instant Karma covered by colleagues all down her feed. She slept on it without fighting hard enough and might be too late now. She knew in her gut she needed to tackle this, but didn't.

One post stated a rally for Instant Karma happening in Downtown Fort Wayne on Tuesday. This was it. She would be there, covering for Fox55, and she wasn't taking no for an answer this time. She hurriedly walked the hallways looking in through the offices for Mr Baker. She popped her head into the command center and saw him talking to Trevor.

"Ah, Mr Baker!"

Charles and Trevor both turned to her.

"Please. Chelsea, it's Charles. I don't know how many times I need to tell you."

"Sorry. Charles. This. We need to cover this," she said to him as she showed him the message from the phone.

"I don't know, Chelsea. You think it's really going to be a story? I wouldn't be surprised if it's just a few kids wandering and screaming about safe spaces."

"It's already a story, Charles. A big one. And you slept on it. Trust me. Please. I'll make sure of it. I won't let it fizzle. This is just starting, and you'll want to be at the head of it. We need to cover this. *I* need to cover this. I deserve it, Charles. Look, we think the same, you and me. I know it. I know you want us to be there for the next big story just as much as me. Let me do this. I'm not taking no for an answer."

Amused, Charles looked at Chelsea, then back at the phone. His small round glasses slid down past the bridge of his nose-making him almost Dickensian in his peering concentrated face.

"OK, Chelsea. This one is yours. Make sure it tracks. And make damn sure it's actually worth covering. Last thing we need is for this to be a dead end and scramble to find a restaurant that has roaches or something. Or maybe we'll get lucky and there will be a pileup on I69 to keep in our back pocket."

"Thank you so much! You won't regret this. I swear!" she said and floated back to her office.

CHAPTER TWENTY

Tuesday morning came quickly for Seth. He looked forward to something for the first time in recent memory and arrived early. He sat in the car watching the setup and organization before heading in. Seeing his own words boldly painted onto posters caused his stomach to percolate in excited nervousness. Signs ready to be hoisted into the air stating *You Can't Divide Us, Instant Karma is the Truth,* and *We Deserve Better.* Another randomly read *Honk for Justice!*, which made Seth chuckle at its absurdity.

A masked Seth weaved his way through the crowd. He was mindful not to speak much as he feared people recognizing his voice. He knew, however, he could quietly blend into the crowd, not too dissimilar from how he approached any other day.

A roaring sea of masks adorned the faces of like-minded people; all different ethnicities, religions, backgrounds, and ages. It doubled down on what Seth vented about just the other day. Crack the shell and people are all the same. Have the same fears. The same goals, and dreams.

The news report was not lying about the police presence either. Officers posted outside the rally on both sides of Washington Dr, stood attentive, but didn't engage with the members. They didn't converse with the rally or attempt to mix in. With not much to do other than hang out, they simply stood in observation.

A local news field team arrived and captured the event. Creating a great contrast against the matching group, was the camera man in his navy blue Fox55 jacket and the nicely dressed field reporter conducting the talks. She walked traversed the crowd and asked for interviews, and it didn't take long before a handful agreed. One such person was close enough to Seth that he could listen in.

"Hi, I'm Chelsea Winters from Fox55 News. Do you mind if I ask you a few questions for a moment?"

"No, go right ahead. You want me to take my mask off for it?" the man said. He wore a plain gray T-shirt with a screen-printed decal of Seth's mask. His posture along with his salt and pepper hair gave the tell he was middle aged, though his face was hidden.

"Totally up to you. What's your name?" Chelsea asked.

"Stanley. Stanley McGrady. I'll take it off. That way my kids can see me on TV later," he chuckled. Stanley removed his mask, revealing a thick beard which also was graying and matched his hair.

Seth laughed to himself. *We are still fighting for fifteen minutes of fame, I guess. Can't change everything immediately.*

"Good morning, Fort Wayne! We have Stanley here at the rally of Instant Karma. How are you? This is quite the event. Did you expect it to get such a reaction?"

"I'm great! Yeah, this is something isn't it? I wasn't sure what to expect today, to be honest. You never know with something like this. It could go either way. Maybe it's a large group and organized. I've been to protests before that was just a few folks standing around. But I came prepared with extra materials for making signs for everyone."

"Nice. And what is it about Instant Karma that connects with you?"

"He's just real. No polish, ya know? It's refreshing. He speaks his truth, but he's also not afraid to show that he's human and trying to figure it all out like the rest of us. He's not out there just saying things for attention or fame. And what he says makes sense. Makes you sit back and think about your perspective on shit. Sorry. Stuff."

Chelsea laughed. "No problem. This isn't live. We will edit it out. So, what is it exactly that you folks are here protesting?"

"Oh, this isn't just a protest, Chelsea. This is about sending a message. We need to let the people in charge know they must do better. To stop trying to drive a wedge between the citizens politically and understand that the only way we can move forward is if we work together.

He's making better sense than I felt I ever did, Seth thought. *It's like they picked my brain and pieced my words into coherence.*

"Stanley, are you from the Fort Wayne area? How far did you travel for this today?"

"I live just outside the city. About half an hour north of here. But I woulda gone as far as I needed for this. I feel it's that important."

"And please, help the Fox55 viewers understand. Why the masks? What do they represent?"

"The masks unify us. They make us one voice instead of a collection of random people," Stanley said.

"Thank you so much for your time," she said.

"Thank you, Chelsea."

Chelsea motioned Ted to cut the camera. They collected their belongings, packed up the van, and left.

Seth enjoyed his time, but soon after the news coverage left, and the crowd began to dissipate, he decided to head back home as well. The entire way back to Torwood, he ran through the protest in his head. It was amazing to see. Seth didn't expect much attention at all, and mostly showed up out of curiosity. But news? And police? This was crazy. Surely it couldn't get much bigger and had to peak soon. If not already. He enjoyed the validation, but these poor people had to figure out he didn't have the answers. He's just another guy bitching and whining about his problems on the internet. Finding an outlet. Trying to find happiness one day at a time. Soon they'll move on to someone else, like any other internet fad. But, as Craig once said, it couldn't hurt to ride the wave from the shadows until then.

***

That night, he eagerly turned in to watch the news report covering the rally. Unable to be everywhere this afternoon, he needed to see it in a larger scope. Being the age of instant gratification, the piece already had posted to the Fox55 website.

"Good evening. I am Trevor Rodgers. The growing political activist group 'Instant Karma' took to downtown today to spread their word. In this Fox55 exclusive, we went to find out a little more about the group, and their message. Chelsea Winters, who was on the scene, has more."

Chelsea Winter's pleasant, upbeat voice spoke over panning clips of the rally.

"Police were on hand today as the activist group "Instant Karma" took over downtown Fort Wayne. Over fifty people gathered with signs and megaphones to protest and spread their message. Authorities kept the situation under control, but tensions were high as concerned citizens looked on and wondered what exactly their motives were. We stepped up and asked the members in attendance what attracted them to the movement, to get a better idea of what they're all about."

The video cut to different attendees being interviewed by Chelsea.

"Instant Karma is all about wanting to be better. Better education, better representation, just being better people. The little guys who feel marginalized and want to take a stand."

"Chelsea, this is about sending a message. We need to let the people in charge know that they must do better."

"We have to do something. We have to get our point across and get attention."

Chelsea's voice-over took control again.

"I also made a point to ask about the leader of the group. The unnamed man behind the videos, and the masks themselves."

"It's like, when I watch the videos, he's speaking to just me.

He knows what I need to hear to feel better about myself."

"He's just simply relatable. He has it all figured out."

"What he says makes sense. Makes you sit back and think about your perspective."

"If I see someone walking down the street, or on Facebook, in the mask. Or driving down the street with a window sticker, it's like, yeah. That's my brother. That's my family."

"The masks unify us. They make us one voice instead of a collection of random people. We have one voice. One goal."

"And just how far they are willing to go to meet that goal?" Chelsea asked.

"As far as I needed for this. I feel it's that important."

"When you get this many of us together. People are gonna notice."

"With unease about the group steadily rising, the public deserves to know. Would Instant Karma use violence to get noticed?"

"I don't see anyone who would want to stand in our way. Let's say that."

"I wasn't sure what to expect, to be honest. You never know with something like this. It could go either way. But I came prepared."

"So, as Instant Karma continues to grow, and we find out more of their message, we also remain committed to keeping our viewers up to date and safe. For Fox55 News, I'm Chelsea Winters."

The feed cut back to the studio and the head anchor seated behind the desk.

"Wow. Eye opening stuff, Chelsea. Can't wait to hear more. Up next, is owning Chihuahuas racist against Mexicans? One group from Utah thinks so, claiming it gives the owner the satisfaction of owning a foreigner. We dive deeper after the break."

Seth's hands trembled as he slowly shut the laptop. The viscous silence clashed against the piercing rampage in his head. He only listened in on one of those interviews, but he knew what happened in all of them. Bullshit sound bite treatment. This was never about learning more. Why should we expect anything less? He understood now he needed to take a stand. He held a responsibility for this.

Up to now, the videos were self-contained. A moment in time that discussed the world, but not directed at the world. This was different. He knew he had to do something to get ahead of any negativity. Clear the air. Actually address the information and address the group itself. These people already looked up to him. And now they needed a leader to take a stand for them.

"They've already done it again. Eyes and ears are everywhere, but they think they can spread lies about us. We are growing larger and more focused every single day. We get beaten over the head to support the military, but then the people fighting the wars right here get villainized. The class war, the war on poverty, on religious freedom, the war for equality, for basic human rights. How is it different?

"Every one of you is a chain link in this wrecking ball. Crashing the status quo is what will get us noticed. We demanded better. And in response, those who should get the message, instead doubled down and cast us as the enemy. I was at the protest in Fort Wayne this morning, and it was incredible.

"It wasn't disruptive, but it was big enough to be noticed and make noise. They are missing the point, aren't they? We don't need them. We have transcended their control. They need us! They rely on us to tune in, to follow their word, to blindly share their skewed half-truths and flat-out lies with friends. Hell, they rely on us to give them something to talk about in the first place. So let them know. Dig your heels into the dirt and scream until your throat is bloody and raw. 'We don't need you!'

"And yes, there are things that we as people could have differences about. But look past that and instead look at what the average person can all agree on. Despite age, race, or religion. Fairer wages. Cheaper medical care. Keeping our families safe. A congress that actually cares, and is present, and fights for who it is they represent. Say you don't trust the government and everyone high-fives. But then, while everyday people bicker about what needs to change and how the ones in power are fucking us, they're producing sneakier ways to separate themselves from the bottom-dwellers. It's comical to me. It's like no one cares. You struggle, 'til you die. Then you're free. Then they care what you have to say. Hasn't anyone taken in the numerous examples of putting differences aside to defeat the common enemy? When we work together, we are so much stronger than they could imagine.

"And trust me, I know how this sounds. I'm not far off from the conspiracy screaming talking heads vomiting out to 'Wake up, Sheeple', force-feeding buzzwords like 'puppeteer' and 'indoctrinated' like we're playing 'Tinfoil Hat Bingo.' But that's not what this is. This is about looking at where you are in your life and wanting better. Wanting more. More than working your ass off just to be replaced at the snap of a finger when you begin to break down. More than having to choose between buying groceries or paying the electric bill. More than relying on a support group to help find a place in the world after the government was done with you. More than hiding away who you truly are because you think the repercussions may not be worth it. More than… sacrificing spending time with your children in exchange with providing for them."

Seth choked realizing mid-sentence this hit closer to home than originally intended. He let out an audible sigh and continued on more subdued.

"Complacency and apathy are what keep the balance of power from shifting. It won't come easy. It won't be given to you, even though Instagram makes it seem like you're the only one not sipping margaritas on the beach somewhere. You aren't alone. And… and that's something I am still struggling with myself. So, I get it. Trust me. But remember, we are one voice. We do not need them. They work for us, and soon they will fucking understand that."

Seth stopped the recording. No signing off this time. No subtle awkward joke because he didn't know how to end a conversation, let alone a YouTube video. He cut it out after driving his point home and left it to linger. He thought it came off as a stamp on his words. All it caused were more problems for him later than he imagined.

CHAPTER TWENTY-ONE

Jack Thompson himself made the rare appearance at the Thompson's Hardware Store today, which meant he finally was going to announce the new Shift Manager position. He gathered the team members all in the back room before the store opened and raised one hand to quiet people down and gather their attention.

"So, I've given this a lot of thought. But at the end of the day, the choice for the Shift Manager opening really made itself. Since they've been here, they've made quite an impression with their work ethic, teamwork, and dedication to the success of the store."

Jordan grabbed Ethan by the shoulder and shook him vigorously. Ethan looked back at him and smiled.

"And that's why I'm happy to announce that Grant Seiter will be filling the Shift Manager position starting immediately. He's going to be training with me and will fill in as we see fit. Please offer him your congratulations and support."

A smattering of applause drifted by from the dozen employees in attendance. Jack Thompson firmly shook Grant's hand followed by others that stuck around. Jordan turned to check on Ethan, who was already gone.

Back on the floor, Ethan stared off, focused on nothing in particular. He thought about Hayden. And Audrey. And money. And time. Does Hayden even know who he is? This is the most crucial time in his baby's life for who he'll feel comfortable with. And he's never there. Hell, Hayden probably even knows Gwen more than him. How long will things be like this? He was supposed to get the promotion at Thompson's, quit UPS, and start to have an actual life.

Ethan finally focused on a hand waving back and forth in front of his face.

"Ethan. Earth to Ethan. You with us?" Lori asked.

"Yeah, sorry, Lori. What were you saying?"

"I'm going to Arby's for lunch. You want anything? They got two for four Beef 'N' Cheddars."

"Nah, I'm good. Thanks, though," he said and went back to work.

Lori gazed at him, her head cocked accusingly.

"Ok. What's going on? You hate Arby's, and I got zero reaction out of you. Something's not right. Tell me. What is it? Woman problems? You know I got about seventy-five pounds on Audrey if I need to kick her ass for you. Let me know."

"Nah. No, nothing like that," he laughed, vaguely adding, "It's just… I'm just thinking things through."

"That's the main difference between you and Jordan."

Ethan sighed and ruptured open spilling his thoughts all over the desk of the Thompson's Hardware flooring department.

"God. Lori, what the fuck am I doing here? Ya know? I am so tired. And for what? I shouldn't even care that much about not getting that stupid position, but I can't keep doing this." He began to pace back and forth behind the desk. "It's like, I know something's gotta change, but can't afford to actually do it. They got me. You see all these stories of people quitting their dead-end jobs and liberating themselves. Giving their middle finger to the man and following their dreams. How is that even remotely realistic? What you don't see is that kind of thing always comes with a giant step backward before any payoff. I don't get that luxury. I'm barely ahead as it is. You don't get handed what you want in life just by quitting what you don't. How could I tell Audrey and Hayden that I up and quit my job, but don't worry I have a plan that may never actually come to fruition? It just seems selfish when I even say it out loud."

"What plans? Have you talked to her about it?" Lori asked.

"No. I don't want her to worry. And that's the thing! I don't even have any fucking plans. I have never been able to catch my breath long enough to make any. I just know I can't work every single day slinging boxes and peddling flooring," Ethan said.

"So, what, stupid? You think she's not worried now? You ain't foolin' her. I can tell you that, for sure. Listen, Ethan, you're no good to your family if you're a zombie all the time."

"If I tell Audrey how drained I am, she will run out and get a job."

"Because she loves you," Lori said.

"No, look," he said. "You realize everything she does? She's going to school full time online right now for graphic design, and the tattoos, and taking care of Hayden. I mean, if she was also going to work on top of that? One of those would have to give, and you know it wouldn't be our son. If she drops out of school because of me, we'll just both be unhappy. I'd never forgive myself."

"But listen, you don't get to make that decision for her. She's an adult. If the tables were turned, what would you want her to do? Would you want her to quietly be miserable, or tell you how she felt?"

"Yeah. You're right."

"Of course I am!" Lori said as she stood up straight and pretended to fix her nonexistent collar. She looked back down the aisle, saw it was empty, and turned back to Ethan. "You're better off without that job anyway, you know. Don't get trapped here, Ethan. Trust me."

"Huh?"

"Don't get trapped here." Her tone was dry and uncharacteristically sincere. "You know I wanted to be a teacher?" she asked, already knowing the answer.

"Really?" He asked.

"Yup. I wanted to teach kindergarten. That's the best age if you have the patience for it. My plan was to graduate high school, move out of this dumpster of a city for college, and be a teacher. When I started here, me and some of the other guys would always make fun of all the lifers working at the store. How could they be so complacent, right? Fucking losers. Then halfway through senior year, I got pregnant. Of course, I still kicked ass and graduated with honors. I walked to get my diploma with Evan in my belly and had him in July like a god dammed superhero. And I know I could have kept on pushing and attended college locally, even with the baby. Plans change. You adapt. It's what you do. But Evan's dad, my ex-husband, said I should hold off a year until things settled down. So, I did. I worked here part time and spent the rest with Evan while John went to school for Civil Engineering. The next fall, the time wasn't right still, and I waited some more. Then we got married. And then I had Emily. And then Brian. It was years, but I look back and it feels like it all happened in a blink."

Ethan could see the corners of Lori's eyes redden and well up.

"And then the same man that wanted me to hold off until the time was right, suddenly didn't want to be married to a woman with no goals and just worked at a hardware store anymore. And before I knew it, I had turned into one of those fucking lifer losers that I used to make fun of so badly."

Lori wiped her eyes and shook her head back and forth to fling away the feeling of regret. Even though her ex-husband couldn't see her right now, she would not give him the satisfaction of getting under her skin.

She continued. "Look, I love my children more than life itself. And I would never trade my family for anything. But every day that I come to this place, I sit in my car before walking in and stare at the building wondering what could have been."

"I'm sorry, Lori. I had no idea."

"Yeah, I don't make a habit to be a bleeding heart in front of everyone." She forced a half smile. "Ahhh... so, you're welcome."

"You know it's not too late, right? You're not stuck here."

"Aww. You're sweet, babe. But I'm afraid you're wrong. Go home and talk to Audrey. She will have your back, I guarantee it. The longer you wait, the further you get stuck in a place like this. It's quicksand."

"Thanks. And you're not a loser. You practically run this place, despite what Grant probably thinks."

"I'm not worried about him. Ethan, just remember, there is a big difference between compromise and sacrifice. Compromise is necessary. Sacrifice is dangerous. Never sacrifice yourself to try and make someone else happy."

"Yeah. Thanks," Ethan said.

CHAPTER TWENTY-TWO

"Seth, do you know what object permanence is?" Dr Englund asked.

"Like that thing babies have?" Seth said.

"Well, kind of. You're thinking of the right thing. Babies lack it, though. But essentially, it's the knowledge that objects exist even though you cannot see them. It goes for people too. Some adults can have that same issue with people. Like an out of sight, out of mind line of thinking. The ones you see all the time are there, and if you don't see them, it's like they don't exist. Think of some people, and you don't have to name who they are, but think about them and tell me how or why you fell out of touch."

"Nothing really happened. We just did."

"Exactly."

This resonated deeply. Not just human beings, but anything. Activities, people, shows, responsibilities. What Seth worked on at any given moment was all that existed in the world. During his suspension from Torcon, it easily wasn't a part of his life anymore. He didn't even think about it. His life always had been nothing except for what sat right in front of him, and he never noticed.

Dr. Englund tasked him with reaching out to people he hadn't talked to in a while. Anyone he may have been scared to reconnect with. Maybe someone with unresolved issues, or an old friend that drifted away. He didn't know which part of this assignment caused his throat to swell up; casting out the line to reconnect or knowing after twenty-eight years of paper-thin friendships, he had no short supply of people to choose from.

"And what if they don't reply?" Seth said.

"Then nothing changes, right? But what if they do?"

Seth thought that may be even more terrifying.

The doctor added, "Look, if nothing else, maybe they'll just be happy you aren't reaching out to sell them on a new business opportunity."

This pulled out a genuine laugh from Seth.

"It's time. You've been doing well. I feel like I can push you a little bit now. Nothing is going to be scarier than the scenarios playing out in your mind. And I can guarantee that whatever you already have running through your head won't happen. Just shoot a message out there. I'm not even asking for you to speak directly to anyone. Just choose five people and extend out a hand."

Seth sat at his kitchen table after the appointment, making a list of people he thought he should reach out to.

"Good lord. It's not that fucking hard," he said aloud to no one. "You're not an alcoholic making amends for fucking people over."

He had two. Travis, whom he fell out of touch with after graduating and leaving the movie theater job, and Vincent Ballick. Those were easy. He strained to think of more. Well, he knew the last spot already. Whether he wanted it to be or not. The answer rang out as a siren to not be ignored. A pulsating beacon screaming out to Seth even though he tried to look away. As if everything so far merely got him to this point right here and work up the courage to reach out to her for practically the first time since she coldly and silently shut him out. He sat alone with a task and a means to connect and a twist in his gut so severe his stomach acid wrung out from inside the belly.

His heart thumped. He set his phone on the table and wiped sweaty palms back and forth on the thigh of his jeans. He'd get to that later. Suddenly the rest of the plan appeared so much easier. He had Vince's number still. It hadn't been that long, and in hindsight, he did owe him an apology. Seth didn't have Albert's number, and he wasn't on social media. But he sent a Facebook message to Paul Musgraves and James Moore, another floor worker from Torcon. He kept those short and sweet. They were more or less filling the quota as he shot out a simple message saying, *"Hey. Hope you're doing well."*

Seth originally planned to tell Travis it's been too long, and they should catch up. That old chestnut. But upon some slight Facebook stalking, he learned Travis moved to Boston with his husband Amir and their daughter Nevaeh. So, he shifted gears.

"Hey, how you been? Looks like you're doing well. What have you been up to?" After pausing for a moment, he added, *"Oh me? I'm spiraling, thanks. Dad's dead. No friends. No girlfriend. No job. And just the constant reminder every time I venture out or even look online that I have nothing going for me."* He sat back and looked at what we wrote, deleting it back to, *"What have you been up to?"* Then, *"I'd love to meet the family sometime."*

Vincent was easy. *"Vince, I know you probably hate me. And I'm sorry. Don't think I take lightly you bringing me back. But I just couldn't do it anymore. Sorry if I put you in a bad spot. Even though I didn't realize it early enough, you always had my back and looked out for me. I appreciate you."*

The heavy feeling in his chest lifted with each message. A simple task, much more about getting out of his own head than reaching out to people.

That crafty Dr. Englund, Seth thought.

Lastly, he needed to fire off the hardest one.

"Don't think, don't think, don't think," he repeated to himself to work up his nerve.

No wonder something like this normally happened at 3 AM, tag-teamed by an individual and their drink of choice as a wingman. It's not that weird, right? It's not like he's been blowing her up since she left and begged to take him back. Much in the same way Seth unwittingly just let her walk out the door and out of his life, he also never even reached out after that first day following. It had been radio silence on both ends. Even after being together as long as they had, Seth reacted much in the same way as he did with anyone else. She was gone, and he was alone, and balance was regained in the universe. It was only a matter of time. Everyone leaves. That was the Roberts Family Crest that should be sewn into throw pillows and crochet coasters and littered around him. It didn't matter if it happened today, a decade, or a quarter century. Everyone will leave, and you will be alone. Death and taxes and solitude. But that was the old Seth, not quite different from the new Seth, but he was trying. Life brought him here. Some kind of chakra crystal astrology bullshit believing spacey star gazer would explain this as the universe testing him. The devout would say that God works in mysterious ways. Seth Roberts would just say that the world is full of weird shit.

"Okay," he said to himself, "It needs to be one message, so I'm not blowing her up with back-to-back texts. But not too long because then she may not even read it."

He typed, *"Lauryn, how have you been? I still think about you. I would love to get lunch together sometime. Not in a begging you to take me back kind of way. More in an old friends catching up kind of way. I get it if you've moved on. You should. I've got some things to tell you about. I'm pregnant..."*

Don't make dumb jokes you fucking idiot.

Delete delete delete

"I feel like I'm finally in a better place, and I just want to talk to you again. There's actually no one else I'd rather talk to about it."

He hit send. Unplugged from what he just completed; he was back in the kitchen area of his apartment. Seth had little choice after but to stew in the atmosphere. The TV remained off, an odd occurrence for him. The lights all cut except for the room he stood in. Seth pictured the scenario of each person in his head simultaneously. Them reading the message, shaking their head dismissively, putting the phone down and returning to whatever thing they were doing before that.

Never giving it a second thought. He grabbed a beer from the refrigerator, only to put it back and pull a bottle of Red Stagg out of the freezer. This called for something a little stronger. He began to pour some into a small glass when his phone vibrated on the table.

She actually messaged me back. Why didn't I do this months ago? he thought as he glided from the counter back over to his phone. It was Travis.

"Yeah, man. My mom still lives in Torwood, so we are back in the area quite often. Next time we're in town we'll have to catch up. It was good to hear from you. Tell Lauryn I said hi."

Seth sighed into deflation. "Sounds good, man. Looking forward to it."

It vibrated again almost instantly. He really wasn't looking to get into a conversation with Travis. This time, though, it truly was Lauryn.

"I would like that. Do you have time on Saturday? We can meet at Aha Bistro at noon."

He stared at the message for far too long before replying. "That would be great."

CHAPTER TWENTY-THREE

Ethan ignored the vibration from his watch shaking him back to the living. He stayed over an extra two hours at UPS last night, not getting home until 12:30AM. Audrey and Hayden already had passed out in the bedroom. He let out a soft grumble as he peeled himself out of bed.

"Give me a second," Audrey said. Her voice cracked as she was not fully awake. "I can make you some coffee if you want."

She slid out of bed right behind him. Quietly as to try and get a few minutes with Hayden still sleeping.

"Cool, thanks," Ethan whispered.

He splashed water on his face and brushed his teeth. When he shambled into the kitchen, Audrey sat at the table with coffee for him.

"You look like shit," She greeted.

"Thanks," Ethan said, still trying to wake up. "It's the look of success, apparently."

"That so?"

"I don't know. Sounds good, I guess. I'm gonna be honest, I don't know how much longer I can do this."

"So don't."

"I know we need the money, but I'm fuckin'- huh?"

"So don't, babe. I never see you. You never see the baby. I never asked you to kill yourself. That's been you this whole time. It's not worth it. It's obviously wearing you down."

"We need the money."

"We'll always need more money. But what is it? A little more than an extra hundred dollars a week after taxes and everything? Don't kill yourself for that, babe. Besides, we could use you here even more."

"I just want to be there for you guys. You already do so much. I don't want Hayden to ever think... I want him to have what I... I don't know. It's stupid."

"I get it. Really. But you're not him. You're here. You're present. Hayden is lucky to have you. There's more to being here than working and making a bunch of money."

"I know. But I feel like, you're already going to school and doing the tattoos. And being a mom, and I just... look. I don't know what I want to do. Just know I promise I will give you more than what we have now."

"Dammit, Ethan. I love what we have now. Stop beating yourself up so much. When's the last time you just stopped and breathed for a minute? Look at me, we're a team. You understand?"

Ethan grabbed Audrey, held her close, and let out a massive sigh.

"Oh, wait a second," Audrey said. "Did you... did you think you were the strong one? Oh man, that's cute. Come here, baby. Let momma hold you." As she spoke, she ran her nails back and forth between his shoulder blades. "No honey, you're the looks in this operation. I'm only with you for that ass."

"Ok, Ok. You're hilarious. I get it," he said. "I'm doing it today, then. I'll have my weekends free with you guys. Unless you want me to wait until after his birthday or something."

"Nah, I'll have to work out a new schedule with my other suitors, but we'll make it work."

"Oh, yeah. I'll make sure to give you my schedule. Make sure you can fit everyone in. Really though. You guys are the best thing that's ever happened to me."

"You too babe," she said, still holding him.

"OK I'm out of here. Love you. Tell the other dudes I'm way bigger. That's all I ask."

As he walked out the door, Audrey threw a kitchen towel at him, hitting him in the back before it floated down to the floor.

***

Grant, or Mr. Seiter as he demanded to be called since the promotion, took no time to start looking and talking down on people working the same job he held not long ago. What this place saw in his management ability, other than the dowel rod shoved deep into his ass, Jordan didn't understand.

As Jordan cashed people out at the front of the store, Grant talked to a man who recently came through his line. The customer gestured angrily and seemed to motion his way. Soon after, Jordan was approached by Lori.

"Mr. Shitstick told me to take over for a bit so he can talk to you. Not sure what it's about, but it sounded urgent," she said.

Jordan handed the scanner over, grabbed his bottle of water, and headed to Grant.

"Hey," she said as he walked away, "Play it cool, yeah?"

"Oh. Always," he said with a smile.

As he approached, Grant struggled to hold back a grin, while the fellow beside him held a receipt and a scowl.

"Jordan, come here, please," Grant said.

"Yes?"

"We received a complaint about you. Do you know what that would have been about?"

"No, not really."

"Can I?" Grant said to the customer while taking the receipt and coupon, before turning back to Jordan. "This gentleman came and raised an issue about you not taking his coupon. Does that ring a bell?"

"Oh, yeah. Really? They-"

"So, you do remember after all."

"Well yeah. But-"

"Jordan, we don't have the name recognition of the bigger stores. We pride ourselves on great customer service and-"

"It was expired. And not even for the same caulk he was

trying to buy."

"He said you were being rude about it. Is that true?"

"I didn't think so."

"Jordan, we can't have you belittling customers."

"What? I didn't-"

"Please apologize to Mr. Westing for your attitude," Grant said.

"You gotta be kidding, right? The guy tried to basically rip off the store."

"You think $5 is worth losing a happy customer over? Is that right, Jordan?"

"Oh please," Jordan said.

Grant scribbled a note on his clip board and shook his head.

"And now insubordination? This isn't looking good."

"I'm sorry," Jordan said softly, looking at the floor.

"Sorry. What was that? You'll have to speak up," Grant said with a smirk pressed on his lips.

Jordan cleared his throat and looked up at Mr. Westing.

"I'm sorry I didn't take your coupon," he said. This time more clearly. "It was my mistake."

"Thank you," Grant said.

Glenn Westing looked more agitated than before.

"Now that's all well and good. But I still am owed money back."

"Yes, of course," Grant said. "Follow me up to the service desk and Nancy will take care of you right away." His attention turned to Jordan. "Jordan, since Lori already has your register, why don't you just go grab a mop and clean up the bathrooms?"

Jordan ran his tongue across his teeth in a single sweeping motion.

"That's not even in my job description, Grant. I'm a cashier. A decent supervisor would have that memorized by now."

"No? I'd hate to suggest to Mr. Thompson that you're being problematic," Grant said. He seemed to have forgotten all about Glenn Westing and his problematic coupon. "I've seen where you live. That cute little trailer. You know as much as I do how much you need this job."

Jordan's eyes narrowed. Several responses of varying acidity swarmed his head, but all that came out was, "I'll go grab the mop. Help you out this one time."

"That's a great idea," Grant said.

"Am I going to get my money or not?" Mr Westing prodded again.

"Yes, sir. Right this way," Grant said, and led the old man to the service desk.

Jordan watched the duo walk away for a moment, before he strolled to the supply closet, grabbed the cleaning supplies, and cleaned the bathrooms as was asked of him.

Soon after, while he sprayed down the urinal with a cleaning agent, Ethan entered the bathroom.

"Hey, dude. You OK?"

"Yeah, I'm fine. I don't let him bother me too much. It's just, God he such a fuckin prick, you know? Part of me knows I shouldn't fuck with him so much, but also—"

"He just asks for it. Oh, I get it. Just be careful, man. As much as it sucks, that prick has authority now."

"Hey," Jordan said "I just saw there's going to be an Instant Karma rally on the sixteenth here in Gainesville. We should go, man. You, Me, and Audrey. This shit feels like it's really gaining traction. We should be a part of it. Bring Gwen and the other guys if you want."

"Absolutely! I'm going to be having weekends off soon anyway."

"Oh, shit! You did it? When?"

"Today. Told your BFF I'm putting my two weeks in. I'm guessing they just don't put me on the schedule anymore now. We'll see. But it's gonna be a huge relief. Not to mention I'll get to actually enjoy some family time."

"You big softy," Jordan said as he shoved his friend. "You guys make me sick. Really though. I'm happy for you kids. It's the American Dream."

"Living the American Dream all right," Ethan said. "Exhausted and barely scraping by while raising a son out of wedlock. Just like Norman Rockwell painted. Hey, what time you get off? You need a ride?"

"Nah man, I'm good. Thanks though. Car is fixed!"

Jordan finished his cleaning tasks, even going heavy on the lemon freshener. It didn't quite kill the public bathroom smell, but did mask the majority of it. Afterward, he returned to the register to finish his day. As he stood, staring at time pass on the clock, someone stormed in the door. The slam against the wall perfectly synchronized with the entrance chime in a jarring commotion. Grant looked around Thompson's Hardware with suspicion. His hair, usually meticulous and neatly parted was awry, falling across his reddened perspiring face.

"All four of my tires?! Really?! You think I won't find out who it was? AAA is on their way, and I've got nothing to do but look up the parking lot video. Mr Thompson will hear about this and there *will* be levels skipped in the corrective action escalation! I can promise that!"

Jordan smirked and Grant's eyes darted at him.

"Is something funny, Tillman? You wouldn't know anything about this would you?"

"No sir, Mr. Seiter," Jordan said. "If there's anything I can do just let me know."

Grant ignored the offer and scuttled off into the back office where the surveillance playback access was located.

Jordan pulled out his phone and shot Ethan a text.

"Your boy just ran to his office damn near crying. You know anything about that?" Jordan asked.

"Awesome. I mean... What? That's crazy," Ethan replied.

"You really slash his tires?"

"Nah. Just let most the air out. Fuck's he gonna do? Fire me?"

CHAPTER TWENTY-FOUR

Seth arrived at Aha Bistro twenty minutes early. He tried to look calm, but his leg bounced up and down as a sort of release valve to keep from bursting. It felt like a first date all over again. The restaurant air had a chill to it, but he was sweating nonetheless. He looked over the menu, though he had it memorized, then changed to staring at his phone and then back to the menu again.

He pretended not to notice her enter. She wore no coat, but an oversized white sweater with flowing arms. Her black leggings ran into black and red boots.

"Hey," she said as she walked up to him.

She slid her hands under the table, and Seth could tell she was picking at her nails.

"Um, thanks for meeting me today. God, that sounds so formal. I don't know. This is harder than I thought."

"No, you're fine. It's good to see you. How have you been?"

"Good," Seth said, trying his best to sound sincere. "How about yourself?"

"I've been good, too. Doing a lot of soul searching. Trying different things. I've been painting a lot, actually. I go to the park and take pictures, then use them as reference for painting. I'm not ready to paint in front of everyone yet. Feels weird."

God, is this what we're doing? Seth thought, *Small talk?*

He wanted answers. He wanted reasons. It disarmed him, how easily he fell into a rhythm with her. Like the last few months never happened, and he was just sitting there, across from his girlfriend eating lunch, talking about their mundane day. Her eyes penetrated his callous skin, making him feel right at home again. It surprised him how any negative feeling he manifested toward her floated away like the ashes of a snuffed-out fire.

"I started therapy," he blurted out. As if those were the magic words she waited for all this time. "Dr Englund. I go on Tuesdays."

"That's great, Seth. I'm happy for you. How do you like it?"

"I... I like it, actually," Seth said realizing it for the first time himself. "It's grown on me. You know I'm not the greatest at talking about things, but it made me realize that I do have some issues that I've been working through."

"Oh really?" she said sarcastically.

"Yeah, I guess you would know more than anyone. So, are you seeing anyone? Have you been with anyone?"

Lauryn's eyes shot up from her coffee and through Seth's soul.

"No, not like that! Oh, God. Sorry. That's not my place. Never mind."

"No, no. You're fine," she said smiling. "It's fair. Um, no. I haven't been with anyone since."

He didn't know if that made him feel better or worse. While it gutted him to think about her leaving him for someone else, that would have at least made more sense.

"Then, why did you just leave? Without saying anything? And not only that, you never even talked to me afterward. You became a ghost."

"Honestly, I didn't know how to. I figured you hated me. I was scared to. After I left, I wanted to reach out, but never felt like I could."

"I could never hate you." He reached across the table for her hand. "I lied. I haven't been well at all."

"Seth I-"

"No, listen. I need to say this. I don't know what I want to do, but I quit Torcon. I couldn't do it anymore. So, I have nothing. Nothing to keep me here except unanswered questions. No friends. No family. No job. No relationships. But I still feel like I can't leave. I can't move forward. I can't just keep doing the same fucking thing day in and day out anymore. And I wanted to say that if you don't want to be together that's fine, but I would love to still be in each other's lives. And now I find out that you would rather not be with anyone at all than be with me. I am literally worse than nothing at all."

"Seth it's not like that."

"Isn't it? Everything was great, I thought. Weren't we good together?"

"We were," she said.

"Then what? I don't get it. Because it seems like we were perfect, and when life got hard, and I was at my lowest you just walked away."

"I didn't just walk away, Seth," Lauryn said much calmer than his tone.

"I needed you! I lost my father, and you left me when I needed you!"

"Fuck you! That's not fair!" she yelled back, and then repeated softer. "That's not fair. I loved your dad. And I loved you. And we grieved, together, for the father that we lost. Because when my own dad wasn't there, he was. But Seth, when it was time to lean on each other and pick each other back up, you shut me out. You shut everyone out. How much do you even remember looking back before our breakup? The time between your father dying and me leaving? There was a lot of time in there, Seth, that you were not present for. You stopped communicating with me. You're the one who became emotionally detached. And I tried. I said, 'Oh he's still having a rough time. I understand. I need to give him space. That's how he operates. I need to give him more time. I just need to support him.' But that went on and on. I tried to get you help. I figured maybe I was too close to it, but if you could at least talk to someone..., anyone. But it starts with you. I was exhausted, and I needed to move on. And you can hate me, and think I'm selfish, and tell people that you're all alone now because I walked away. But you walked away from me first. I just did it physically. When the writing was on the wall. And maybe you're right. Maybe I should have tried harder. But you can't help someone who doesn't want to be helped. How I did it was wrong. I know that, and I have to live with that every day and feel shitty about it. For as long as we were together, you deserved better, deserved some kind of closure. But if I didn't just leave, I knew I wouldn't have the strength to actually do it. I couldn't face telling you I was done. But, Seth, I was more alone and isolated living in that apartment with you than I have been since actually living by myself. It was suffocating."

Seth sat silent. Equal parts broken, furious, apologetic, reflective.

"Goodbye, Seth. I'm sorry. Maybe this was a mistake," she said. Lauryn stood from the diner table, softly kissed Seth on the right cheek, and walked out.

The rest of the patrons at the restaurant stared on with rubber necks. Some poorly acted like they hadn't noticed. Seth threw cash onto the table and walked out.

While driving back home, he texted Craig letting him know how he screwed it all up. This wasn't how the afternoon was supposed to go. This was supposed to be the next chapter in Seth and Lauryn's relationship. Not the ending chapter. The natural evolution was never supposed to become estrangement. And now, there was no question. He had conjured up hundreds of scenarios of why she left. None of them being he had driven her away. That realization ballooned in his chest.

***

Back at the apartment, all Seth wanted to do was release. If he gained anything from therapy, it was the weightless feeling after getting his thoughts and negative energy expelled from his body. He finally knew, even though it killed him. He knew it was over and it was his fault. Of course it was. He was jobless. And it was his own fault. He had nobody to care about him. And it was his own fault.

He walked to his bedroom and slipped on his Instant Karma mask. Somehow, behind the mask, he no longer felt alone. As stupid as it sounded, he had started to believe it himself. An entire group of people looked to him for guidance and had his back all the same.

He pressed record, and sat in front of the camera, silent. The lump in his throat stole his ability to speak, as he slid the note papers in front of him back and forth.

"I am alone," he said. "Not in a Lydia Deetz suicide note kind of way. I don't think. No, this is something else. Almost epiphanic. Is that even a word? I don't know. It feels right. Everything is finally clear to me, unfortunately."

He slid the papers again, this time they fluttered onto the floor, as he swallowed hard and continued.

"This was supposed to fucking help me. Get your feelings out they said. Find an outlet. Well, I tried the fucking painting. I tried the journaling. And the jogging. When am I supposed to feel better? Because it's not doing anything. I still sit there afterward, head spinning, thinking of a thousand different reasons why I'm a piece of shit.

"I don't even know what I'm doing anymore. They all say the same things. Reach out, talk to someone, reconnect with friends and family, keep busy, find a hobby. Fuck off. Every single person will tell you what to do to pick yourself up. They'll kiss your forehead, boot your ass, and send you on your way to collapse in solitude. But at least they helped, right? They'll tell others later about how they helped someone that day. What a good fucking Samaritan they are.

"Reach out? To who? Because maybe people don't like me as much as I like them. What if I'm just a burden they feel obligated to be around at this point? What do you do when you're convinced the people you consider yourself close to don't feel the same?

"I'm at a loss. I am just tired of feeling like this. And I'm starting to think that there is something wrong with how I think, or operate, or something. I don't know. I've never been the type of guy who can articulate how I feel. Because I think that either people won't understand me, or they'll judge me, or I'll just be seen as a nuisance. I've thought a lot lately about the people in my life. And I... I can't think of a single one who I could call. Not one person who would be excited it was me on the other end. We all drift apart over time. Messages get fewer and farther between. The riptide of life sweeps people away, other than a yearly Facebook 'Happy Birthday'. Or running into each other in the store and saying, 'We should definitely get together soon', and then not.

"I don't blame anyone else, though. It was my doing. I found that out today. Now that I think about it, I can't remember the last time I had a deep meaningful conversation with anyone. 'Emotionally detached' are the words that stick out to me the most. Blinding me like a flickering neon sign in a dark empty room.

"I don't know. This fucking derailed. Or maybe it didn't. Maybe it's exactly the window into my thinking that I subconsciously wanted. Don't forget to subscribe to this fucking train wreck!" he said sarcastically with two thumbs up. "Gather round kids, maybe next week he'll fucking hang himself on camera. Ugh...whatever."

He pressed the button on his phone to stop the recording. He sat at the desk, and disgustedly stared at himself in the phone screen. A sorry hermit looked back at him. One in a cracked, corny skull mask. A black flat sheet behind him.

This is the guy people look up to?

"Fuck it!" He said aloud to himself and uploaded the video.

CHAPTER TWENTY-FIVE

Seth awoke with a ton of bricks falling on his chest. With the realization of what he uploaded last night, he vaulted out of bed and logged in to delete what he considered to be a timed grenade floating out there ready to detonate and make his life a living hell again.

To his surprise, not only had the video been viewed thousands of times, but his inbox flooded with people supporting him. They asked if he was okay. They told him they often felt just as alone, even when hanging out with friends. Some messages told him simply that he mattered. Once again, he felt pride in the community he had started. He sat stunned and overwhelmed reading the stories shared by warm strangers. They didn't need to do this. But they cared. This must have been what crowd surfing felt like. The sensation of being carried by a wave of supportive strangers. He decided to leave the video up. It seemed disingenuous to take it down now.

He would follow up soon to say thank you. For now, he wanted to lay low and needed a break.

Seth sat in his apartment; the curtains drawn closed. All lights off. He melted into the couch for hours, and that may turn into days. He hadn't decided yet. The only thing to strip himself from the couch was the alcohol in the fridge, of which there was plenty.

Right now, the outside world did not exist. No Torcon. No

Instant Karma. No therapy. No expectations. No judgments. The only things real and tangible were Seth, and the ambient tractor beam coming from the corner of the room.

He didn't hear the knocking at the door initially. It melded perfectly with the gunfire between Neo and Agent Smith. But it eventually lured his attention away from the TV. Even after he heard the knocking, he didn't budge. Maybe he was hearing things or maybe they would just vaporize so he didn't have to get up. To his dismay, the knocking continued.

Seth finally shambled over to the door. Craig's face looked comical through the eye hole. His already round bald head ballooned into a realistic render of an amusement park caricature, which Seth couldn't help but laugh at. He unlocked and opened the door begrudgingly, greeting Craig.

"What's up, man? I was just hanging out," Seth said.

"Nothing, I was just about to go out and grab a drink. Wanna go?"

"Nah, I can't tonight."

Craig scanned the apartment. No lights. Beer bottles and dishware littered about. A basket of unfolded clothes sat on the recliner. Whether dirty or clean he had no idea.

"No, no, no. You're not doing this. This place oozes of self-pity, dude. The brooding energy is so thick I can taste the shit. Nope. Not today. C'mon, bud."

Craig walked in and grabbed the curtains, stopping to turn to Seth before throwing them open.

"You're not going to start hissing if I open these, are you?" Craig asked.

"Funny," Seth said.

Craig flew open the curtains illuminating the apartment.

"See, still daylight outside. Didn't even know that did you?"

"Okay, man. You made your point. Look, I fucked it all up. I thought I was course correcting my life. Turns out all my grand decisions only drove me right off a cliff."

"Oh my God. Are you actually talking in metaphors? You didn't fuck anything up. Just apologize. You know that's a thing that people do, right?"

"It's not that easy."

"It is. Way easier than you're probably going to make it. Now get dressed. We're gonna do something."

"I said I don't feel up for it, man. I just want to lay low right now."

"Well, you can't stay here and sulk," Craig said.

"Sure, I can. I'm getting surprisingly good at it." Seth said as he plopped back onto the couch.

"Everyone has their talents, I guess. Okay, so you're not in the mood to hit the clubs."

"I don't think I ever have, or ever will be in the mood to hit the clubs," Seth said.

"Come grab food with me then, at least. You gotta eat. I know you don't have shit here to fix. You probably haven't even bought syrup yet for them waffles. If after you get the stank of this place off of you and some food in your belly, and you're still not feeling it, then we can come back here and brood together."

"I don't know, man. That's really more of a solo thing. You may cramp my style."

"I'm not good at it anyway, so I'll just be taking notes."

Seth shook his head in the understanding that Craig wasn't taking no for an answer.

"OK. Fine."

While Seth got ready, Craig spent the time picking up the loose bowls and mugs, as well as throwing out the beer bottles sitting on the coffee table and floor and kitchen counter. Seth emerged from the bedroom to Craig finishing up washing the small amount of dishes in the sink.

"You didn't have to do that," Seth said.

"Bro, that would have bugged me the rest of the night. I did it for my sanity. Not for you."

They sat in the dining area of Brock's, a nearby bar and grill. Seth ordered a double cheeseburger and chips, along with a Bud Light. Craig ordered a buffalo chicken sandwich, sweet potato fries, fried pickles, and a local IPA to wash it all down.

The television behind the bar played the evening news and

focused on an Instant Karma protest in Milwaukee. A mattress factory which employed much of the city halted plans to relocate after the activist group pressured the parent company to dedicate funds and upgrade the facility to stay in that area.

"Seth's attention focused right past Craig, toward the news.

"Oh, yeah. You see that?" Craig said. "That's fucking awesome, right? I don't know man, just something about that whole group seems cool. I don't get the hate."

"Yeah, dude. It's crazy how it's blowing up. You don't think they're dangerous then? I guess they're saying the dude that started it is a menace," Seth said.

"They're just trying to flush him out, I think. They don't like the mystery surrounding it. But nobody important is saying it."

"How so?"

"It's just like, if he was really a concern to anyone in power, they'd find him in a heartbeat, right?" Craig paused to take a swallow of his beer. "But that's also part of the appeal, I suppose. There's no set conclusion. It can be whatever it needs to be."

"So, you're all for it? You think he's helping?" Seth asked, still looking at the TV.

"Yeah, I think so. I haven't been too close to it. Do you think it's just one guy? I kinda figured there was a few making the videos. Just the vibe I get," Craig said, before sliding the fried pickles over to Seth. "Want any?"

"Nah I'm good. But yeah, it's for sure one guy. I think it's obvious. What do you mean 'Whatever it needs to be?' What should it be?"

"Oh, God, I don't know, man. It's just, there's no set, like, mission, I guess. Other than tackle the patriarchy or some shit."

"It just looks to me like they're fighting for the little guy. Whatever fills that hole."

"Yeah, I suppose," Craig said as he wiped buffalo sauce from his mouth. He popped up with a smile. "It definitely created a hole where the cheap Halloween masks used to be, though. Know what I mean?" Craig laughed and raised his hand for a high five, but Seth didn't finish it. "Now that's just rude. Why you got so many questions about this thing anyway?"

"I don't. Just making conversation. You're the one who dragged me out. Now you're upset that I'm engaging?"

"Whoa, buddy. I'm not upset," Craig said while looking back over his shoulder. The TV moved on to the regular Instant Karma wrap-up and talked about questions and caution around the group. It showed a YouTube clip of one of the earlier, poorer quality videos.

"I just, uhh…no. Hold on," Craig said.

His face changed expressions on a dime. His eyes narrowed as he looked at Seth, then back at the TV again. Any unassuming person would think Craig had lost his train of thought, or possibly suffered a mild brain aneurysm. Seth, however, was steps ahead of what was happening as Craig looked at him and cocked his head. Panicked sweat beaded on Seth's forehead before Craig even said the words.

"It's you."

"What? You're insane, dude. Have another drink, why don't you. Two more, please!" Seth yelled to the waitress just a few tables over.

Craig folded his hands together thumbs down in an upside-down "U". He moved them between his own eye line, and Seth's head, like a director surveying their upcoming shot. He covered all of Seth's face except for his mouth and closed one eye to focus.

"It is you! Fuckin' aye!"

"Shhh, man," Seth said. "I don't know what you're talking about. But if I was, would that be- "

"Fucking awesome!" Craig said finishing the sentence. "This is huge. I need answers. Like, how? And why, and… shit! You're him!"

"Yeah, OK. You're right," Seth said rapidly quieting his tone in an attempt for Craig to do the same. "Dude, I don't even know how it happened. I was doing my therapy exercises and decided to put it online one night. And it felt great, man. Even before I knew people actually watched them. It felt amazing and, like, I got a rush just from venting to a camera for a while."

"Who else knows?"

"Dude, nobody. I don't fucking talk to anyone but you."

"True. You are my favorite hermit."

"Thanks."

"My pleasure. So, what now? Have you seen the impact this is making? You're huge! Just that for instance." Craig said, pointing to the TV. "You're the reason those people are keeping their jobs. Do you realize that?"

"Honestly, I thought about quitting soon. I can't be this guy."

"The shit you can't!" Craig blurted. "You don't see it, but I do." He took off his ballcap and ran his hands across his bald head. "Oh my God this makes so much sense. OK, you hate attention. I get it."

Seth shot him a suspecting look.

"Well, OK, so I don't really," Craig continued. "But I can respect it. Look, pull your head out of your ass for a minute. That shit at the bar that you dissolved into a sad puddle about. That shit was empowering. You had the whole place on your every word. Those weird debates you used to have at the movie theater would draw crowds."

"You knew about those?"

"Dude, I worked there for like a month."

"What? When?"

"Are you serious right now? That hurts. We'll have to circle back to that one eventually. But, dude, people have looked at you like this for as long as I have known you. So, puff your fucking chest out for once and realize it. It's like they say. Some people are born with great power, and some people have great power thrust upon them. And then have great responsibility… about it."

"Wow, that was surprisingly motivating before dying off at the end."

"Was I close? It felt right."

"I think my brain popped. You managed to piss off both English Lit nerds and comic book nerds."

"I'm equal opportunity," Craig said.

"So, what happened to just a few minutes ago where you said 'It's whatever' and 'you're not that close to it'?"

"That was when I thought it was just some tool with a Messiah complex. But you're that tool. So, it's different. We gotta celebrate. Excuse me, two more please," Craig called out.

"I just ordered us two more."

"Yeah, but those were dinner drinks. I just ordered celebration drinks. Totally different. They can't be the same drink."

"Right. What happened to us heading back after we eat?"

"Fuck, you're right. OK, we can finish up and head back. I need you to spill the beans on everything anyway. 'Cause people are for sure running with rumors since they have no real information about you."

When they left, a cold evening mist hung in the air. The cloudy sky offered little assistance in guiding the way back, but they hardly noticed. For the entire walk home, Craig prodded Seth for information. Seth offered answers hesitantly at first, but whether it was the alcohol sloshed down with dinner, or Craig's natural charm, after the sixth or so question, Seth answered without reservation. They tackled everything from the following, to the mask, to the backlash, to Seth's retaliation to the backlash.

"Why'd you name it Instant Karma?" Craig asked.

Seth spun around to face Craig as he talked and began walking backward.

"I didn't name it! I said it, like once, in a video and that's what clicked, I guess."

"Kind of a dumb name."

"Well, use your powers to get something else going," Seth said as he waved his fingers.

"Has anyone reached out to you? I mean, about the videos."

"Like news people?"

"Just anybody I guess."

"I can't bring myself to read any of the comments. Fuck that. But I do read any messages sent my way. Mostly positive. Some hateful. Occasionally sexual." Seth turned back around and walked with Craig in stride. "It's kinda fucked up how many nude pics get sent to me wearing just a skull mask. Both chicks and dudes. But it's cool reading about people that say they're going through the same shit that I am. Feeling the same things. Kinda legitimizes it all. Makes me feel a little less Wizard of Oz like."

"Dude, they're already behind you. I think if you let people know who you are, it would change things."

"Yeah, change for me. The best thing about this is I can go on with my life. I can continue on forever if I want. Or I can drop this at any time. But either way, it's in my court."

"It's not James Bond, man. You can't just pass the torch on to someone else when you're done with it. You don't realize exactly what you've done. People believe in this to their core. Some are taking it ridiculously seriously. Almost scarily. And you're downplaying it like it's a community service side gig."

"No, I do get it. Why do you think I was contemplating quitting? And I think if people knew who I was, it all would fizzle out. The mask is perfect because it's bigger than just me. That changes the minute it's just Seth fucking Roberts and his sad vlog."

They remained mostly quiet as they walked inside the building and up the stairs. They stopped at Seth's door.

"Think about it, man, is all I'm saying," Craig said. "I think it'd be a nice burden off you. But that's just me. I'm an attention whore. But imagine that rush you talked about earlier amplified with people knowing it's you. You could drop the disguise and start to merchandise. Hey, that's got a ring to it! Anyway, I'm headin' home. Think about what I said."

As Seth walked past Craig and into the apartment, Craig stopped him.

"Oh hey, guess what," Craig said.

"What?"

"You're an influencer now."

"Man, get the fuck out of here," Seth said, shoving Craig toward his own place.

"You and that Cinderella wedding are gonna put Torwood on the map, yo! Oh hey, Mr Alverez!" Craig yelled out to the apartment super rolling his cart at the end of the hall. "How's it hanging? You ever gonna fix the light by my door? It's still out. Just hook me up with the bulb and I'll put it in myself."

"Well good luck with that, man. I'll see you later." Seth said as he walked back inside.

CHAPTER TWENTY-SIX

Jordan walked into the kitchen, grabbed his keys off the counter and a Red Bull from the refrigerator. His father sat at the kitchen table with the pieces of a disassembled coffee maker in front of him. Doug had complained about it being on the fritz for about a week. Today must have been his tipping point. Jordan had assumed he would be buying a new one, especially since he could have used Jordan's employee discount from the hardware store. He should have known better. Doug normally mumbled under his breath with something torn down to pieces in front of him. If not some small kitchen appliance or a radio, he was elbow deep into the front end of his truck.

"Fixable?" Jordan said.

"Absolutely. We'll get it," Doug said. Then after looking up, he added, "Where are you headed?"

"Just out. I'll be gone most of the day."

Doug looked at the mask hanging from Jordan's fingertips.

"You're not wasting your time down at that rally, are you?"

"Yeah. I'm going. Sounds like there is going to be a lot of people gathering there. Wanna come?" Jordan asked looking for levity.

"Jordan, those people are a fucking joke. Just a bunch of crybabies making noise about this until something else comes along. Then they'll jump ship and follow that instead. I've seen it so many times in my life."

"No, Dad. This is different. We aren't a bunch of bleeding hearts tying ourselves to trees. We are reclaiming our voice. Letting big brother know that they do not control us. Letting the world know that we are together. Demanding better lives. We are-"

"Jesus Christ! Enough! You already sound brainwashed. You want to better yourself? Learn a trade. Go to school. Do something that fucking matters. If you're looking for shit to do, I have a ton of work around here. At least then you'd have something to show for it. Stop floating through life like a God damned joke."

Jordan's body sank.

"Is that what you think?" he asked.

"That came out wrong. But I'm worried about you, son. You need a plan."

"I am doing something that matters. Just because you wasted your life away in a thankless back-breaking shit hole doesn't mean I need to."

"Jordan, I forbid you to go down there."

Jordan scoffed and slammed the door behind him on the way out.

The Florida sun was unapologetic, despite barely pushing springtime. The pulsing beams of the unusually high temperature reverberated off the blacktop. The rain, which came and went last night, had all but dried but could still be smelled throughout the air, and the humidity sat heavily on the chest. Those in attendance marched to fight for raising the rate of minimum wage for the state of Florida. Corresponding protests were synchronized in Tampa, Ft Lauderdale, and Tallahassee. It was already being spun how the greedy working class didn't understand how an economy works, as Florida had a higher rate than the national average. Instant Karma argued the high cost of living made that fact inconsequential.

Ethan, Audrey, and Jordan all absorbed the energy permeating from the crowd. As expected, the gathering showed smaller than other recent demonstrations from the likes of Pittsburgh and Lansing. Midwest college cities were hot spots for activities such as this. The crowd appeared around thirty to fifty people, though over seventy-five talked big on the message boards. Unsurprising. So many people expressed outrage online, but never followed through when time to physically do something. The entire world would scream "Revolt!" in solidarity, but many remained nonexistent when they realized it would take turning off the television and leaving the confines of their living room.

"Look over there. There's more than I thought," Jordan said.

A solid row of police officers donning riot gear stood statuesque along the outskirts of the sea of crimson eyes and angry chants. Their presence had been the norm as more and more protests popped up. The chat rooms also discussed them. Having described their company as an unwarranted means of intimidation, but largely harmless if ignored; or at the very least unprovoked.

"Yeah, officially they say the police are here for the safety of the rally attendees," Audrey said.

"Oh, OK. Sure. They're here for my benefit," Jordan said.

The day before, Audrey had made shirts for the three to wear. Using plain white t-shirts as a canvas, she designed and drew with fabric markers and her own artistic abilities. Audrey and Ethan's both had realistic skulls with the eye sockets colored in a bold blood red, which spilled over and oozed down the face into a puddle in which the skull sat. Under the bloody pool were the words "We still see right through you" Jordan's was more minimalist, per his request. A simple drawn-on version of the growingly iconic skull logo, with a stylized lettering I and K beneath it. Jordan had also bought a mask the day before and painted it for today's event.

"Jordan, you painted the eyes orange," Audrey said.

"I know, I know. I couldn't find any red. It was the best I could do. I was hoping no one would notice, but, ugh. I had to go to three stores just to find the damn mask itself."

"Nah, it looks good," Ethan said.

As the trio snaked their way through the crowd, they

overheard other attendees conversing.

"It's not even one guy," one said. "There's a whole team of them. That's why they wear masks. They want to make it appear like just one person. Because we are all one voice."

"No. It's just one guy. The mask is because he's really a congressman," another said. "Can't remember where I read it, but he's a senator in New Jersey or something. He can't let people know who he is, or he won't have information for us anymore."

"Ethan, you hear that?" Jordan asked. "You think this stuff is true? It kinda makes sense."

Audrey said, "I don't know man. It would explain why he always wears it."

"Nah," Ethan said. "He's just a normal dude who found a way to speak his mind and help unite people. And look around. He's doing it. He built this."

"OK! Here we go!" a woman screamed into her megaphone. The amplification squealed from her unfamiliarity with how to operate the device. The group began the march down Oakwood; a slow, steady crawl.

As they marched through the street, continuing to chant about fairer wages to coincide with record profits, Audrey looked at Ethan and smirked. She hadn't seen this passion from him in some time. She missed it. Ethan looked at her, and through a sort of mind reading few people share, they silently agreed everything would work out. They were part of something bigger than themselves and would use this to help make a better world for their son. Lost in each other, the protest around them blurred into the background.

Jordan found himself chatting with more of the protesters. Curious to learn what he could about the man behind it all. He talked to a middle-aged man with a tight buzz cut. His arms and chest swollen and toned, with a midsection even bigger due to a steady intake of cheap alcohol.

"The red eyes are a symbol for recording," he said. "Record everything to memory. Record and expose any misgivings or undermining of the people. Expose the lies and corruption.

Put it all out there."

"It's not just one guy," Jordan told him. "There's a bunch of them. That's why they wear masks. They want to make it appear like just one person. So, they keep it simple with a black background and one camera."

"Nah, man. He's one guy. But he's ex-military. Two tours in Iraq, I heard. His face got fucked up by an IED, hence the mask. But he flipped it on them and is using it to his advantage."

"Oh my god, that makes so much sense," Jordan said in awe.

"You guys are so simple," a woman said squeezing between them. "It's obviously a resourceful woman with a voice changer. You can tell by the posture and how she always wears baggy t-shirts to hide her figure. She knew misogynists wouldn't follow if they knew the truth."

Another man, this one with a darker complexion and his hair pulled back into a knotted bun, chimed in. "Naw you guys gotta look deeper, see. If you add up how many seconds of each time he pauses in his speech. The time of each pause correlates to that letter of the alphabet. It's mind blowing. I'm still deciphering it, but it's gonna be huge."

As the other protesters chanted, Jordan screamed. He screamed every syllable, in an attempt to be heard by everyone who needed to listen. Every declaration others stated through megaphones, he served as the exclamation point stamped at the end. As he yelled, he pumped a sign, high and proud, displaying a wrecking ball crashing into a wall made from letters spelling Status Quo. It allowed Ethan to track him down. But also attracted the attention of the Gainesville Police Department.

"C'mon, Jordan. Chill out. The cops are starting to watch you."

"Let em, dude! This is awesome. Scream with me."

Jordan turned his gaze to the officers standing by. They still hadn't moved but talked amongst each other. He looked them in the eyes, in an attempt to steal their attention.

"We Are One Voice!" he yelled their way. While speaking

directly into them, Jordan moved to the outside edge of the crowd.

"Settle down, sir," one of them yelled back.

"You work for us! And you need to fucking understand that!" he screamed.

The crowd jumped at a sudden boom and Jordan collapsed to his knee with a crippling pain in his side. The rubber slug bounced around the feet of protesters before rolling to a stop, along with the majority of the march.

"Hey, what the fuck was that?!" Ethan roared at the officers.

"That was bullshit! We're allowed to protest, you fucks!" Audrey added on.

The crowd around them checked on Jordan, pulling him to his feet. Others piled on disgruntlement toward the GPD who began approaching. Some protesters pushed their way closer to the police.

Into the tight crowd, a can launched with smoke billowing out. All around instantly dispersed while covering their mouths and eyes. The people slow to react coughed uncontrollably while blinded by a dense smoke that caused their eyes to water and burn. Jordan dropped to the ground once again; coughing, eyes and nose running. He pleaded for help, but everyone around him had scattered. He brought himself up slowly and staggered out of the smoke. He looked around for Ethan and Audrey, but all he could make out was blurry movement. He felt someone grab and pull on his arm.

"Jordan! Thank God. We gotta go," Audrey said.

He ripped his arm out of her grasp.

"Fuck that! I'm done, man. Done. Done being told I'm worthless. Done being called a joke," Jordan said.

"Jordan, breathe," Ethan said. "How's your chest? No one thinks you're worthle-"

"They absolutely do! All the time. I get shit on at work. I get shit on at home. Even my friends don't think I'll amount to anything. I am sick and fucking tired of being treated like less than a person. Of people making jokes behind my back. You think I don't get it, dude. But I do. More than you, probably. Everyone looking at me all the time like some fuckin' piece of trash. I work my ass off. Same as you. So why do I get shit on so much?"

"OK. I'm sorry. We can talk about this more later. But this is getting out of control."

"Out of control for who? We are winning! This is what it's all about. Breaking the chain. Starting something better. And we need to create the narrative. Otherwise, it all falls apart. Don't you watch the videos?" Jordan asked grabbing Ethan by the shoulders. "Don't you see what's happening here? What the fuck did you even come here for? Because when this gets talked about later, it'll be twisted like we're the fucking problem. They'll cherry pick a few people to make an example out of. Drag them through the dirt to keep the rest of the group quiet. But there are too many of us to ignore and silence. We need to speak up. People worried about getting loud and demanding what's owed to them? That is what is keeping us down."

"Jordan, c'mon. We got to get you checked out, dude," Ethan pleaded.

"I'm good! I'm finally good," Jordan said. "Better than I've been in a long time actually. You should be coming with me."

"Jordan, please," Audrey said. "We need to get you to a hospital. Your ribs-"

"For what?" Jordan scoffed. "I'm still tickin'! Ethan, let's go raise hell and fight for something."

"Dude, not like this," Ethan said.

Violence swarmed around them, moving closer as they talked. If they didn't leave now, they'd be trapped in the tumult. Ethan knew he'd have to leave with or without Jordan.

Jordan said, "Of course like this! Ethan, man, you're scared to do anything because you have too much to lose. But that's exactly why you should be front and center in this."

Jordan paused for a moment, hoping Ethan would wake up and follow him. Instead, Ethan withdrew. Jordan did the same in the opposite direction, quickly disappearing into the crowd like taillights in the misty night air.

Ethan called out once more, but the only response he saw

was another explosion of tear gas as they covered their mouths and retreated.

Jordan headed further and further into the abyss. He only hesitated when it suddenly dawned on him his chest no longer hurt. He knew it would be unbearable later but would ride the adrenaline high for now.

As he weaved his way through the discord, he spotted a police officer restraining a young woman writhing on the ground in attempt to roll her over and zip tie her wrists. The slippery heat added a protective aspect as she repeatedly pulled her sweaty arms out of his grip. Jordan spotted no other officers in the immediate area not occupied by other protesters. He darted forward and dropped his shoulder. In one fluid movement, Jordan tackled him off the woman, rolled, and continued quickly through the crowd.

The cop, Victor Burne, yelled out after him, but Jordan already vanished. He turned back around to the woman, but she was gone as well. He climbed to his feet, fuming, and began ripping people to the ground, searching for his assailant.

About fifty feet ahead of him, another GPD officer held two rioters at bay with a shield and baton. One of the two, a stringy white male, looked close to the guy who attacked him. Close enough, at least. The officers locked eyes and Officer Byrne fired a rubber bullet directly between the shoulder blades of one of the two, propelling her forward. As she stumbled, the other officer shoved her backward to the ground using the end of his baton.

On instinct, the Instant Karma member still standing whipped around to see what happened. As he turned, a sudden sting shocked him on the right side of his neck as another rubber slug came in. He folded to the ground, convulsing. Clutching his throat, he tried to simultaneously gasp for air and scream for help. Neither came to him. Just a stuttered whimper as he inched closer to his fellow protester, now unconscious.

He didn't even know her name. Didn't know who she came with, if anyone. While they hadn't met officially, they were family. He draped his arm and back over her to protect her on the ground as best he could while using the other to wave for help.

Nearby, Jordan assisted a group attempting to push past the barricade while two officers struggled to hold the steel barriers in place. When the structure started to give, they swiftly let go and grabbed the batons and pepper spray from their belts. They swung freely on the rioters as a jungle explorer would hack away vines.

One by one, Instant Karma dropped. The protesters who continued to put up a fight were gifted pepper spray to help take them down. With one unified shove, Jordan and the others still standing successfully knocked the two officers backward and off balance. Jordan picked up a discarded protest sign from the ground and ripped the poster board from the 1x2 wooden stake it was duct-taped to. As an officer raised his baton to come down onto Jordan's shoulder, Jordan reeled with the stick. He faded back just enough to slip the force of the baton swing. With pendulum-like momentum, he came forward again and struck a blow to the side of the off-balance cop's knee, catching it just behind the kneepad. The officer screamed out and buckled to the blacktop. Within seconds, he was pounced on by other protesters who ripped away at his gear. Defenselessly lying on the ground, the officer had no choice but to protect his face and head with nothing but his prayers and hands for cover.

Jordan darted his eyes around for the other officer, who moments ago blocked him at the barricade. They were nowhere to be seen. What he did see, however, was a Gainesville Police Department SUV unattended not far away from him. He crouched down and crept over to the vehicle, reached in, and grabbed a megaphone sitting on the passenger seat. Jordan climbed on top of the car and addressed the crowd.

"Look around you! This is the response we get for trying to improve our lives! Make no mistake, we will get what we are owed one way or another. The people who are wearing masks are your brothers and your sisters. We stand together. Anyone who isn't wearing it? Well, they can either get out of the way or get dealt with! We will take what is ours. We will silence those that try to stifle or manipulate!"

Jordan stopped suddenly with his legs swept out from under him by the handle of a nightstick. His back slammed against the hood of the police cruiser in a metallic thud. Three GPD officers held him down and attacked with batons and riot shields. He coughed and wheezed, struggling to regain his breath. Jordan braced himself as best he could, covering his face and already bruised chest with a shield he wrestled away from an officer. It helped, but a few good hits to his abdomen were a shocking reminder of the rubber bullet hit he had taken not fifteen minutes ago. Jordan's left arm wrenched as his protective shield disappeared.

Pinned on the hood of the SUV, he writhed to break free from the onslaught. They weren't arresting him. They were making an example out of him. One of the officers ripped away the mask Jordan had still been wearing. As he fought for control, and with every bit of survival instinct left inside of him, all he could manage to do was scream. Rather than a plea for help, or even a surrender for mercy, all he managed to expel was a single sentence. Every bit of it subconscious. Jordan barely realized the words emanated from his own mouth. He would have sworn someone else said it if it didn't hurt so much in his chest and throat to say aloud.

"I am Instant Karma!"

One attacker pulled him off the car hood by the legs of his jeans, and Jordan fell again onto his already throbbing back. Coughing rather than breathing and watering from the nose and eyes, it took everything within him to continue fighting.

A piercing crash coupled with a flash of intense light and heat distracted the officers. Jordan grabbed his mask and crawled under the SUV. Beside the cruiser, a city trash container laid next to debris strewn about and aflame, along with shards of glass from the window which broke on impact. In front of him, away from the riot, he spotted a clearing to escape. He didn't want to, but knew he wasn't going to help any further here right now.

As Jordan scrounged up any remaining upper body strength, he dragged his lower half out from under the vehicle. Every part of him ached. He climbed to his feet and made his way toward the alley. He leaned against one of the barricades which stood where the march never quite made it to. He composed himself, looking back at the free-for-all still taking place. Police fought with civilians like the result of a bar argument. Cars parked by the curbs along the route growled in flames. Shop windows shattered. Clouds from tear gas canisters still dissipated slowly in spots. As Jordan limped to safety a voice boomed from behind him.

"Oh, there I found you, mother fucker!"

Jordan turned around to the cop he tackled earlier marching toward him. It felt like an eternity ago at this point. A pinching sensation hit his collarbone and the middle of his chest. Before he registered what happened, he dropped to his knees with a paralyzing pulsing sensation all over his body. He cried out in agony, fully falling to the ground.

"Not so fuckin' brave now, are you!? Roll over and put your hands behind your back."

As Jordan attempted to do just that, he was immobilized yet again by the electric charge and let out an involuntary scream. Somewhere between a yelp and a whimper.

"That one was just so you learn some respect. Now roll over."

On his stomach, with his hands behind his back, Jordan realized the ride was over. He was going to jail. His father, who will see this on TV and know his son was arrested, will give a vindicated speech about what a crippling waste of time this was. How Jordan came looking for a reason to be unruly, without listening to any counter argument.

He closed his eyes and laid waiting for the pinching click of steel handcuffs. Waiting. Waiting. After what seemed like forever, Jordan rolled over and saw three protesters restraining the officer. One of them, a giant of a man, had his forearm around Officer Burns's neck stabilizing the grip with the other arm. Another one zip-tied the officer's wrists together. Whether they were lifted off this cop in a twist of sweet irony, or they came from somewhere else, Jordan didn't know and forgot to ask later. The third companion stood beside Jordan, offering their hand.

"Come with us," the voice said.

Initially surprised to hear a woman's voice come from behind the mask, he took her hand and stood up. He looked again at the officer being lifted by the bigger guy, only to fall back down to his side.

"Guess I got a little carried away with the choke hold," he said. He was calmer and better enunciated than Jordan had expected for a hulking man in a skull mask and tank top.

"You OK?" the girl asked Jordan.

"Yeah, thanks," he said.

He pulled the taser clamps off his chest in a single winced tug. Jordan looked again at the cop on the ground. He cocked his right leg and launched it forward into the ribcage of the fallen GPD Officer.

The cop let out a distressed heavy cough.

"See? Still alive," said the third person in the group of saviors. His dark arms and neck contrasted with the bright white shirt and mask he wore.

"Great. Let's go," the girl said.

In the safety of the alleyway, Jordan took comfort in the stability of a dumpster behind Connie's Coffee and Cookie Stop. The shade of the alley kept the dumpster cool and refreshing against his bruised and aching body. He leaned against it and slid down back against the wall.

"You were fucking amazing out there. What's your name?"

"Uh, Jordan," he said, puzzled.

"Well Jordan, good to meet you. I'm Tyler. Juggernaut over there is Shane. And this is Caitlin."

"Sick tattoo," Shane said looking at Jordan's forearm.

"Why didn't we think of doing that?" Tyler said.

"I'll have to show you to my tattoo lady. Really, she's a friend, so she could hook you up. You guys saved me out there," Jordan said.

"Us?" Caitlin said. "You were a badass out there. You really took control."

"Thanks."

"You sure you're OK?" Shane asked.

"Yeah. Yeah. I'll be good."

"Here, let me see your phone," Caitlin said.

She added her information into it and tossed it back to him.

"You killed it today. We're definitely going to have to work on something together soon. This whole thing is only getting more serious. We need people like you."

"That sounds great."

Jordan peeked around the dumpster to see Officer Byrne in the distance slowly climbing to his feet, and he instantly saw red again.

"He deserved so much worse," Jordan said, coiling into the sharp pain of his ribs.

CHAPTER TWENTY-SEVEN

Jordan showed up to work at Thompson's Hardware the following day with a grin on his face. He held his side as he limped up to the time clock.

"Dude, are you OK?" Ethan asked as they clocked in and took the floor.

"Yeah, why? I'm sore as shit. But I wasn't gonna miss your last day."

"Where were you? What happened? I tried getting hold of you."

"I just laid low."

"Laid low? Bro, your face is all over the internet!"

The way Jordan lit up was equally harrowing and refreshing to Ethan.

"I know! Isn't it fucking awesome?"

"I am Instant Karma? What was that shit about? What does that even mean?"

"I don't know, man. It just kind of came out."

"Look, I feel terrible. I shouldn't have left you like that. But it was too much. God I should have taken you back with us."

"Ethan, I'm a big boy. I decided to stay. You didn't leave me. Look, it's all good. I'm sorry too. It got way worse than I even thought it would have."

"Yeah, the cops were here yesterday, I guess. They're fucking looking for you."

"Really?"

"I heard on the news they're trying to get a bunch of people for all sorts of stuff. Resisting arrest, assaulting multiple officers, and stealing police equipment."

"They fucking started it!"

Several looks from the straggling Sunday morning customers shot their way. Ethan and Jordan ducked down and continued the conversation just above a whisper. Jordan proceeded to explain what happened to him at and after the rally.

Ethan listened to every detail, as growing concern for his friend festered. Relieved he was OK, but also taken aback by how Jordan's energy percolated as he spoke. As Ethan focused on Jordan's eyes lighting up, and his eyebrows rising, and his mannerisms livening, the words Jordan spoke faded away into the shadows of the hardware store. What stood out to him, was the cut in Jordan's bottom lip not even healed enough to scab over. And the rolled toilet paper still shoved in his nostril to prevent any nosebleeds.

"Look, man. I don't think it's smart for you to be here today. You look like shit, and you know Grant will throw you right under the bus. Probably have them drag you out in front of everyone."

"Shit, I didn't even think about him. Ok, I'm gonna complain about food poisoning or something and take off."

"Go hang out in the stall. I'll tell everyone you can't leave the bathroom. They should let you go home. You need to lay low."

"Thanks. Sounds like a plan. Hey, we're good, right?"

"Yeah, man. We're good."

***

Doug sat at the kitchen table to eat his lunch when a soft knock came from the front door. He looked down the hall expecting Beth to come running with her purse screaming, "I got it I got it I got it!" as was the norm when her friends stopped by to pick her up. After another knock came with no response, he put the newspaper down and stood up to answer it.

"Hello?" he said, as he pulled the door open.

Two men stood at his door. The one in front was a grizzled gentleman in what looked to be his late forties. His bottom lip hung below a full, bristly mustache, and his head donned thick tight fade. He pulled out a badge from around his neck and presented it to Doug.

"Sir, my name is Detective Jeffery Larson from the Gainesville Police Department. I'm looking for Jordan Tillman. Is he home?"

"What's this pertaining to?"

"He's wanted for questioning regarding the riots downtown yesterday. Is he home?"

"No, he hasn't been home since this morning. Riots you say? Where?"

"You hadn't heard about them? Even from your son?"

"I don't really watch the news. Too depressing."

"Do you know when he will be back?"

"Not sure, he may have had to work this afternoon out at Thompson's. You have teenagers? It's a full-time job trying to stay on top of them coming and going."

Detective Larson looked at Doug, who remained reserved yet curious. He scanned past him into the living room and visible parts of the kitchen.

"Is there something I should be concerned about officer?" Doug asked.

"Detective," he said. "When Jordan gets home, please have him give me a call."

Larson clicked his tongue against his teeth and pulled out a small metal case from the left pocket of his slacks. The cold, hardened police officer wasn't his normal demeanor, but his mind raced. Many of his team sustained injuries yesterday, and the investigation opened into the event had him on edge.

"Will do," Doug said, matching the subtle intensity of the officer and took the card. It was crisp and sharp on the edges. With bold dark lettering, and a debossed golden shield with

"GPD" in the middle. He studied it for a moment and put it in the breast pocket of his olive-green Dickie's T-shirt.

"Thank you. Have a good day, Detective."

"You as well."

Doug stood in the doorway and watched interestedly as they returned to the cruiser. He closed the door, reflecting on the trouble his son had undoubtedly gotten himself into. He told him not to go. He told him not to get wrapped up in that nonsense. He knew Jordan well enough that he would surely do something to get himself into trouble.

Jordan meekly crept into the living room behind his father. Walking down the hallway from his bedroom.

"Dad, thanks! That was awe-"

"Don't!" Doug sharply interrupted. "Don't you dare thank me. For fifty-two years, I have never even been questioned by the police. Let alone had to lie to them. What the fuck did you get yourself into? You are supposed to be a fucking adult. Start acting responsibly. You're nineteen years old. There are actual, real consequences for the shit that you do. And it's not fair to your mother and I when you bring this shit to my door."

"Dad, I-"

"You need to go."

"Fine, I'll hide out for a while. Wait for this, and you, to cool off. I'll be back for dinner later."

"No. You need to go. You can't stay here. You need to get out."

Jordan stood in the shadow of his father; silent and shattered.

"Where am I supposed to go?"

"Don't. You're a smart guy. You brought this on yourself. Your mother and I can't go through this anymore, Jordan. This isn't like you getting busted for weed in high school. Or that time when you were thirteen and got picked up for squatting in that vacant trailer down the road. This is real. This has real world consequences. You need to pull your head out of your ass and grow up. I told you not to get involved with it. And instead, you get a fucking tattoo!" he said pointing at Jordan's forearm.

He had forgotten about that.

Jordan tried his best to match his father's intensity. He always yearned for the stoic reservedness Doug permeated. However tall he stood to his father in this moment, head high and chin up, he buried how fractured he was. His throat constricted and the back of his tongue slid deep into his windpipe. Jordan's eyes burned and grew heavier as he held back all emotion in a way to save face. This didn't bother him, he told himself. And Doug would soon appreciate everything Jordan has done when he sees the work Instant Karma is doing. He'd have to.

Jordan spun around and walked back to his room. He threw all the belongings he could fit into a blue Nike duffel bag stored under his bed and filled a lawn bag with clothes. He decided to go out the back door so as not to walk past his father on the way out.

CHAPTER TWENTY-EIGHT

"All right, guys. Here you go," Stanley McGrady said as the slid the cups across the table.

At the end of his weekends with the kids, Stanley always took them out to a late lunch and ice cream. Partly because he knew it may ruin their dinner. Just because he worked to repair his marriage didn't mean he couldn't have some harmless fun with it in the meantime. All three of the children ordered root beer floats, while Stanley got a plain twist in a waffle cone. As they enjoyed their ice cream and listened to the Top 40 hits playing over the speakers, Emma talked about what she wanted to accomplish the next time they came over.

"Daddy, have you ever seen the Lion King?" she asked.

"Oh yeah. Many times, sweetie. Great movie."

"I want to watch it next time I come over. And can we color? I like to color. I want to bring my iPad since you don't have one yet. But Mommy wouldn't let me."

"Of course. And I'll try to get us another iPad for Daddy's place."

"Would it have Angry Birds?!"

"You still play that game?"

"It's the best!"

"Then, I'll make sure it does."

"Hey, Dad, those guys are recording us," August said.

Stanley looked up to see a group of high school aged children with their phones pointed at him and the children from a couple of tables over. Three of them wore thick, black-framed glasses, but all of them looked like they bet each other to wear the oddest combination of clothing they could find at Goodwill.

"What are you doing?" Stanley asked them.

"We know you. You were on the news talking about that wacko group," said one boy in a black choker and a cardigan.

"Yeah, they actually let you be around kids? Didn't you say you'd kill a dude if they got in your way?" said a girl with ear gauges and blue hair. Her oversized t-shirt had been cut off just under the armpits. Leaving the sleeves hanging down to her elbows while the bottom of the shirt ended just below her breasts.

"I never said that," Stanley said.

"What's she talking about, Daddy?" Chloe asked.

"Nothing. It's fine. Let's just go. You can finish that in the car," Stanley said.

"Kids, do you know this man?" choker boy asked.

"Of course," August said.

"Has he hurt you?" said one of them wearing a plain black t-shirt over a long-sleeved fishnet shirt. He had his head shaved, but a blonde mustache that twirled at each end.

"Listen, get the hell out of here, will you?" Stanley said.

"Just hold on a second. Can you prove that these are your kids?" blue hair girl asked.

"Excuse Me? Who the fuck do you think you are?" Stanley said.

One of the girls looked past Stanley and focused on the children. Two others continued recording.

"Listen, honey, if you need to come with us, you can. He can't hurt you. Do you need to use my phone to call your mom?"

"Stop it! You're scaring my family! Come on, guys. Let's go."

Stanley and his family left the shop. Two of the teenagers followed.

"Hey, where are you going? Why can't you just prove it to us? Is that so hard? If they're really yours this shouldn't be a big deal!"

"Listen. You can shut up and get fucked or I swear to God-"

"Hey, this man might be dangerous! Someone help!" twisty mustache yelled.

Sporadic bystanders within earshot began looking their way.

As August climbed into the car, Stanley buckled up the girls and they pulled out. His tires squealed as they exited the shop parking lot.

Somehow, he had to explain the entire situation to Donna. He had to get ahead of it before the kids poorly detailed the afternoon and created an even bigger hole to dig out of.

Soon after, Indiana Highway Patrol followed Stanley for a half mile before turning on their siren and lights. He spotted them as soon as they pulled up behind him, and knew it was only a matter of time. He sighed and pulled over right away.

Two officers walked up to the car. One stayed on the driver's side and motioned for Stanley to roll down the window. The other approached from the passenger side and focused more on the back seat.

"License and registration please," the officer said.

"Was I speeding, officer?" Stanley asked.

"Sir, we had a call about some minors that may be in danger. Can you step out of the car please?"

"Look. It's just some asshole kids at the ice cream shop. Of course, these are my children."

"Step out of the car, please."

Stanley sighed, unbuckled himself, and exited the vehicle. As he stood in front of the truck. Car after car slowed down as they drove by in order to get a look. Trying to piece it together in their mind. That didn't matter to him. His mind fixed on what his kids thought right now.

They already questioned him after the news interview. Everyone did. He bragged ahead of time about being on the news and made sure to let them watch. That backfired. Instead of glowing about their father being on TV, he had to assure them he was still the same lovable dad they'd known. Hard to do when he only saw them every other weekend. He thought the fires were put out. He didn't expect a rogue group of self-righteous crime stoppers making a scene.

After the police spent fifteen minutes questioning Stanley, they turned their attention to the children.

"Kids, can you please tell me your names?" one officer asked.

"August. That's Chloe and Emma."

"And you all know each other?"

"They're my sisters," August said in an insulting manner.

"Where you all coming from? Looks like you got some ice cream."

"Yeah, we always go," August said.

"And do you know who this man is?"

"Of course. That's our dad."

"Where's your mom?"

"Listen! That's enough!" Stanley said. "I have a right to be with my kids. Would you ever ask a single mother where the fucking father is?"

"Sir. Please calm down! We are talking to the children," one said.

"Now, little man. Do you know where your mom is?"

"Yeah, we're going there now."

The two officers huddled together momentarily and walked back over to Stanley handing him back his driver's license.

"Sir, you're free to go. Sorry for the confusion. Please understand this is all about keeping our children safe. We wouldn't be doing our jobs if we didn't follow up on the call. Have a nice evening."

Frustrated as he was, he understood. His jaw hit the floor itself when he watched the news story. Stanley tried contacting the station to clear things up but was given the runaround. Multiple attempts to call out Chelsea Winters and Fox 55 news directly only got him blocked by both parties. He decided to put his head down and move on as best he could. But the station's daily segment on Instant Karma mostly entailed false narratives and stoked the flames on the hot button topic. They often went back to that day and replayed soundbites carefully crafted for the occasion.

He found solace, however, in The Founder speaking to Stanley through a channel the two of them shared. The video of the aftermath felt like a direct line straight to Stanley. To know The Founder himself attended the very same rally as him was exciting. No, he was not violent. Pushback was to be expected. With this guidance and the support of his brothers and sisters, he'd make a better future for his family. He had to.

CHAPTER TWENTY-NINE

Jordan clocked out from work and walked to his car. His 2002 Oldsmobile Alero wasn't known for being extra roomy, but luckily for him, there weren't many belongings to take around with him. He surprised himself how quickly he transitioned into a nomadic lifestyle. He mostly used fast food as nourishment in the first place. The real blow was psychological. Though at nineteen, homelessness passed as commendable and glamorizing. He'd brag about the ultimate freedom. Bouncing from place to place with nothing to tie him down.

But when parked outside of Walmart and sleeping in his car, there was no one to spin it for. Nobody to convince he lived the dream as a young free spirit with the wind in his sails.

Washing his clothes one garbage bag at a time at the laundromat grew tiresome. Showering at his 24-hour gym wasn't prestigious. Jordan came up with a routine that worked and secured a brave face. But that meant nothing when reclined in the driver's seat to sleep each night. His nightly decision whether to fight the seatbelt buckle jabbing him in the abdomen or tuck his feet in and lie down in the back. The neon glow of the store front, combined with the overhead parking lot flood lights left much to be desired when it came to sleeping conditions.

He searched YouTube for "I am Instant Karma". Video after video of him being restrained by police. Different angles of live camera footage. Reaction videos. News segments. Both local and national. Messages from fellow members showing their support and signing off with the phrase. He'd exploded. He'd never admit it to anyone, especially not Ethan, but he watched them often. He'd sort by the upload date and see the new ones.

His phone flashed and the video disappeared.

"I love you. This will all blow over soon," his mother texted him.

She messaged him every night, and he'd message back assuring her he was just fine. He owed her that much. Better than fine, he said. Doing great actually. Leaving was the best thing for him. She also invited him to shower, eat, and do laundry, but he was too stubborn to concede. Jordan wondered if his father remained adamant about him being banished, or if regret had settled in. Didn't matter either way. Jordan would make sure Doug Tillman lived with knowing he pushed his son out. Jordan drew a line in the sand and swore to himself to not cross it. Looking back wasn't an option. Especially now.

Last Sunday, during the weekly family dinner, Jordan drove up to the old home. He sat in the car and, through the window, observed the family dynamic without him. Not much different it turned out. They managed to laugh and eat and work together as a unit without all the pieces. Maybe, Doug was right. Maybe, Jordan did bring the stress and anxiety into the home. He pulled back out and just drove. Drove for hours.

All he surmised was he had to be on the right track. Setbacks aside, he felt needed. He had a community. They were building something. Something everyone benefited from, whether they saw what was right in front of them or not.

Jordan knew, down to his core, he joined a crusade for the people. He would do the dirty work and help kick the shit up to make the world a better place. Even if the Doug Tillmans of the world had their heads buried in the sand too deep to realize it. Throughout history, progress never came without blood and sacrifice. In order to make an omelet, you needed to break some eggs.

But none of that mattered tonight. It was hard to feel like a warrior with your head lying on a garbage bag full of clothes in the rear seat of a two-door coupe. Bigger pictures and vision boards didn't translate well from that position. Jordan removed the Tampa Bay Buccaneers cap from his head and placed it over his eyes in attempt to block the light. Tomorrow, he would make moves and change the world. For now, he could do nothing but tap out on another deflating day.

CHAPTER THIRTY

Raymond Chambers leapt out of bed at 8AM.
Today's the day, he thought.
Today had purpose. He took the first half of the day off from work to prep everything he needed. Today, he'd finally make a name for himself. He ignored the pounding on the bathroom door as he enjoyed his shower.

"Raymond! You better not use up all the fucking hot water. That takes some balls when you haven't even paid your part of the bills in two months," screamed his roommate, Landon.

Landon's disgruntlement rolled off him same as the warm water raining down from the shower head.

Fuck him.

Here on the west coast, everyone either already broke into show business, or were days away from closing the deal on their big break. Landon thought he was hot shit ever since he'd gotten the part in that Dorito's commercial last Summer. Funny thing was the guy would never even touch something like a Dorito normally. Unless they started making them out of quinoa. Pretentious prick. What the hell kind of a name was Landon anyway? It sounded like he was built simply to be a sniveling colossal douche bag in someone else's story. But Landon would have to work for it today. Because Raymond wasn't biting.

He stepped out of the shower and finished prepping for the day. The overall planning was a no brainer. Where to step.

Where to turn. He'd rehearsed it so many times he performed it in his sleep. He worried about his dialog. Raymond looked over his lines again, memorizing every minute detail. He knew which words to emphasize, where to leave a dramatic pause, which inflection to leave on certain words to make it his own. Some people suggested he just wing it. That the authenticity and emotion was more important than the actual words themselves. That seemed like nonsense to him.

The California sun was especially brazen today as Raymond walked the five blocks to work. In tow, he had his backpack with him as he did every day. It usually contained his lunch if he packed one, laptop, and clothes to work out in at the small gym next door to the office. Today, he also carried an additional gym bag. The extra baggage wasn't too heavy at first, but after deciding not to Uber this morning, he second guessed himself as the sun, along with his own nerves, forced him to sweat profusely.

Raymond worked as an intern at the social media start-up, Banter. Banter focused on small interactions between friends- being able to share short video clips, pictures, and instant messages- all capped at bite-sized lengths for ease of use and quick distribution. Created to be a refuge away from other hyper-political and overly celebrity-influenced social media platforms, he assisted with the built-in editing features of the app.

An intern for a little over six months, he was promised a full-time job after Banter officially launched and could sustain a bigger payroll. Initially excited to get into the next big name in tech on the ground floor, the excitement faded over the last month or so. He stood now at a crossroads. Raymond was confident, though, after today he would no longer be at Banter at all.

He walked through the glass double doors into the foyer of the shared office building Banter called home. Inside, a metal detector led to a set of turnstiles that unlocked electronically by key cards distributed to all employees. To the immediate left of the employee entrance, stood a larger gate used for deliveries and functioned as direct entry into the facility. The complex allowed for the daily operations of four businesses, but currently, two of the suites were vacant. Without much foot traffic in and out of the building, one person worked as doorman and security for the building.

From behind a cozy booth just inside the entry doors, Jim Varnes greeted Raymond. Jim luckily stumbled into a cake security job for a bunch of nerdy tech kids. Isolated all day inside of a booth registered a few notches above solitary confinement for a social person like himself. But in the downtime, he ironed out his screenplay, which he claimed would be the next Hunger Games. Jim savored the temporary company as people walked in, and could not help excitedly striking a conversation, as he discovered he wasn't the last human alive, after all.

"Morning, Raymond! You just getting here?"

"Yeah, I worked it out with Gavin and took a half day today," Raymond said as he caught his breath.

The cool breeze of the air-conditioning vent hit him as swiftly as the greeting. Raymond stopped for a moment to recharge.

"Ah, good call. It was a beautiful morning! Do anything good? I heard the waves were perfect early on."

"Nah, didn't get a chance to. Maybe later. My buddy just got a new board. We'll see if he will let me borrow it."

"Yeah, definitely. Any news on the merger?" Jim asked.

"No, not really," Raymond said, picking the bags back up. "Hey, Jim, can you buzz me in? I walked three blocks before I realized I forgot my wallet this morning."

"Sure thing! You sure got your hands full there!"

"Yeah, I didn't want to have to run back home after work today. I'm heading straight out after."

"You just missed the rest of 'em. They all went for lunch. I think it's Baja Taco day they said."

"Thanks! Have a good one."

The delivery door buzzed and clicked as Jim pressed a green button. Raymond squeezed himself and his bags through, twisting his torso enough to slide by.

Raymond stopped before he hit the stairs. He shook his

head and turned around.

"Oh, hey, Jim," he said. "That guy is out front panhandling again. He's being really aggressive this time. Can you go and take care of it?"

"Again? Jeez. Yeah, that guy doesn't take a hint. I'm on it."

"Thanks."

Raymond moved from Nashville to San Francisco when he turned twenty-two years old to pursue his dream. His father wanted him to join the military. Get an education and life experience that way. Raymond's father, uncle, and grandfather all were Marines, but he wanted to carve his own path. He knew in order to make connections and gain experience, he needed to move out where the action was.

Both of his roommates, Landon and Kevin, aspired to be movie stars. They routinely told Raymond to follow them to auditions. Get his name out there. Kevin even told him to fill the opening in the acting workshop he attended, to get his feet wet. But that didn't interest him. With Banter coming to an end, though, who knew what the future held.

He knew they'd all be at lunch. The office cleared out at the same time every day, and he banked on being alone. Raymond walked into the office common area and stood at the entrance, looking over the floor. Completely empty. He walked to his desk and sat down, unloading the baggage onto the floor.

Set to go live weeks ago, Banter was abruptly put on an indefinite hold. The initial news shocked everyone inside the office. They'd all used the full app between each other and ironed out most of the bugs. They were as ready as they would ever be. Finger pointing began over who might be the sudden hold up. Who didn't have their end of the interface adequate, after all? The reality was much more exciting.

Pathfinder, the rising star of internet search engines, gained their wealth and popularity by selling advertising to anyone who would pay. What they lacked in political bias, they made up for in influence. Pathfinder's size could both absorb anyone they saw as potential competition, as well as pay handsomely whenever murmurs boiled over whether they rapidly grew to a monopoly. Lately, their attention fixed on rolling out their own social media platform, Speakeasy. They recently put into motion acquiring Banter for the nice round number of one hundred million dollars. With no intention of launching Banter as is, they grew infatuated with the app's video editing and aimed to use that code for their own program. In turn, everyone employed at Banter would be paid, whether retained or not.

Raymond bent over and unzipped the backpack. Inside sat two smaller drawstring bags and a mask. He took a small pause and let out a hefty exhale.

During development, Gavin Shemple, the creator of Banter, saved money by offering developers shares in the company over much of a salary. He theorized employees would feel more invested since they owned a bigger piece. As a result, he also lowered initial capital required during a tough and unpredictable start-up.

The video editing Raymond worked closely with, was what Pathfinder wanted. Not being a full-time employee, he held zero shares of the company and was informed recently the acquisition left no room for him. However, the experience he obtained should look good on a resume.

Inside each drawstring bag contained a mixture of ammonium nitrate and aluminum powder. Small amounts of the mixture were routinely used in target shooting to report on a successful hit. Generous amounts of the mixture would cause an explosion large enough to ruin a company that left you soon to be unemployed and penniless.

He slid the mask over his face and pulled his jacket hood over his head. He worked at Banter long enough to know where the security cameras faced, and where the blind spots remained where contractors still needed to install. Raymond carefully walked the office floor with his back to the cameras and his hood up. Grabbing the drawstring bags, he slid one into the cooling room which housed a bank of servers. He dropped the other bag by the glass window looking out to the Pacific landscape. From his hoodie, he pulled two cans of spray paint. He tagged a skull and dotted two ruby-colored eyes over the Banter banner hanging on the main wall. From the duffel bag, ironically branded with the Banter logo, he pulled out his rifle and a spare phone. The live feed would first be seen by Instant Karma groups and then branch out to wherever needed.

"Gavin Shemple," he said into the phone. "You have been found guilty of taking advantage of your employees. You step on the heads and throats of individuals who have poured countless time and energy into building something great. Draining life from them and leaving them discarded while you accumulate power and wealth. You thought you could steal ideas, work, and wages without consequence. Well, we do not sit idly by while you destroy the lives of so many hard-working people. Our message will be given. Our voice will be heard. I am Instant Karma!"

Raymond attached the phone to a stand on his desk and continued recording as he finished the job. He fired first at the bag by the servers. The eruption blew a hole in the wall, causing it to cave in and force the surrounding desks to take flight. Even at close to a hundred feet away, he staggered backward, falling over from the force of the blast. The successful report loud enough to be heard for miles.

He had no time to admire his work yet. He didn't have much time before the area swarmed with police and fire trucks. Raymond shook off the feeling of being leveled by an F150 and fired at the remaining mixture bag by the windows. Shattered glass jetted out from the second story of the office complex and rained down on passersby below.

He stood accomplished and satisfied as he basked in the disarray. He took the fire escape at the back, tossing his mask and unnecessary sweatshirt in the stairway trash. For a bit, he joined the crowd below, blending into the panicked mob. What better way to hide? As first responders gave medical attention to the civilians unfortunate enough to be below the explosion, fire fighters rushed the building searching for injured inside. Raymond waited long enough to not attract attention, and wandered off toward the beach.

CHAPTER THIRTY-ONE

"Seth, open up the door!" Craig said as he pounded repeatedly. "Open up, dude. I know you're home. You don't fucking go anywhere. Put your god damned pants on and open up. Good morning Mrs. Reynolds," he said softly, quickly shifting tones when a mother and her young daughter walked by. Meredith Reynolds silently glared daggers and hurried her pace as she scooped up the child. "Oh, please. It's nothing she doesn't hear on YouTube!"

Craig turned his attention back to the door as it unlocked and opened slowly. Not all the way, though. Just enough for Seth to peer out from behind the chain lock. His eyes appeared to have not seen the back of the eyelid in quite some time.

"Dude, you made me embarrass myself in front of Mrs. Reynolds," Craig said.

"Sorry. Well, I just was able to get to sleep and you woke me up. We're even, I guess. Besides, I'm sure she thinks you're creepy anyway."

"It's 3PM. How do I work nights and get up before you? And no way. If she wasn't forty-three and happily married, we could totally be together."

"Man, do you even hear yourself? What do you want anyway?"

"Oh yeah. Let me in! You need to see this."

Seth sighed and rested his head against the door before

unlocking it and letting Craig inside.

"God dammit, I'm serious. This is huge. Look."

The phone screen blinded Seth, not yet ready for the day, until the words slowly faded into focus. *Instant Karma Synchronizes Bombings Across Country.* He rubbed his eyes in disbelief and checked again to ensure the words changed. They did not.

"What the fuck? When is this from? Where?"

"I've been trying to get hold of you. They all happened a few hours ago. The same time in different cities."

"What got blown up? Did anyone get hurt?"

"Mostly news stations and buildings on the campuses of tech companies. They weren't professionals doing this or anything, so the buildings weren't totally destroyed, but still. They're still assessing the damage, and the buildings were mostly empty. No confirmed deaths so far. Quite a few injured, though."

"Oh, God. How did this happen? This is all my fault. Wait… tech companies? Like Silicon Valley tech companies? You mean we're all the way to California now?"

Craig's eyes narrowed at Seth who was obviously more pleased than troubled by the news.

"Seth, that's incredibly fucked up. But yeah."

"No, I know. Absolutely. Of course," Seth said, laying the empathy on thick. "But still…"

He had to see for himself the talk online. He clicked a bookmark which took him straight to the Instant Karma page. He looked at it every day. He kept tabs on his people but didn't remember seeing anything about that. Not even in code. Unless he overlooked it. Craig and Seth huddled around his laptop and searched over the page. Nothing. Nothing even responding to the attacks, which felt more eerie. Seth was trapped in the lull of a horror movie where the sound dissolved into an extended silence, right before something exploded out with the volume cranked back up. But nothing. No needle drop. Other than people planning another meet-up, it was like nothing happened worth mentioning.

"What are you going to do?" Craig asked.

"What can I do?"

"You can get ahead of it. You have to. At some point, it will come out that you are The Founder."

"Ugh. Don't say that."

"What?"

"Founder. It's cringy."

Craig shook his head in disbelief.

"Look. Call yourself whatever you want, man. But like it or not, you started this thing. And when, not if, when you're discovered you're going to want to distance yourself from this violence."

Seth slammed the laptop closed.

"Wait a minute, I was going to quit! You're the one who convinced me not to."

"I also said you should come forward a while ago. I didn't say you should quit and hope it goes away. I said get ahead of it and stop the attacks. Now. Make it known that you don't condone it."

Seth waved him off.

"You don't, right?"

"Of course."

"Look I gotta go. I'll text you later. Let me know if you need anything. Just do what you need to do and try not to over think it."

"Have you met me?" Seth said.

A guilty, yet nervous, grin arose on his face.

"Couldn't just start a fuckin' podcast like everyone else, could ya?" Craig said to himself as he walked to the door.

Alone again, Seth sat on the couch and thought about how far Instant Karma had grown. Not the bombings. Not the vandalism. After all, no one was hurt too badly it seemed. No real harm done. These people were sending a message. Not the message Seth intended for them to send, admittedly. But they'd surely be noticed now. No way they'd still be cast as some tiny, meaningless collection of misfits. They couldn't be skewed as insignificant. And if they were already misrepresented as about to boil over, might as well make it true.

He agreed with Craig, though. This needed diffused. They made their point loud and clear, but this was as far as it would go.

CHAPTER THIRTY-TWO

Chelsea Winter's Instant Karma report quickly became a hit. The protest coverage posted online by Fox55 received a record number of comments and reactions. People argued on the news station's Facebook Page, including name calling and even threats of violence. It was glorious. She tingled thinking about the possibilities this would open for her. Finally, she had leverage. She had a backing. Chelsea had been the darling of the news station for a couple of years now, but here was her chance to become respected.

Her nightly Instant Karma update offered her face time, in studio even, and highlighted the latest activities and rumors of Instant Karma. This came loaded with its own intro graphic and set backdrop. No more car washes or Fat Tuesday bakery visits. Crispen Sanders could get fucked. That was his territory now.

She even tried to bring Ted in studio to operate the camera, but he preferred being out in the field. To each their own. Probably for the best, really. She wondered how long she could act friendly towards him anyway. She was often put off by his thick scraggly eyebrows. Not to mention the faint sprinkling of Frito crumbs always stuck to the chest of the shirt.

As she sat just off camera and waited for her lead in, her stomach fluttered. It happened every time. The first few nights, she thought it was nerves getting to her. But she'd been on camera plenty of times. Mostly pre-recorded, but sometimes live. She soon came to realize it was the feeling of recognition. She had fans. She worked for a local news channel, but the reach of the internet gave her a national following. Charles never failed to mention how she blossomed into the station's viral sensation. As long as the engagement and shares kept flowing, she had free reign to report out on whatever she wanted as long as she kept it Instant Karma related.

"And now, with our Instant Karma update, here's Chelsea Winters."

"Thanks, Trevor. As Instant Karma continues to dig their claws into the fabric of our everyday life, more and more we are seeing their true colors shining through. For every time they help a senior citizen cross the street, they're holding a toddler underwater until they can no longer breathe. Metaphorically, of course. For now, at least. They'll save a local business, then go and destroy public property. They seem to be the very definition of a bait and switch. Gain your trust. Pay your dues. Then you must give the leader your firstborn.

"They very adamantly say they're fighting for the little guys, but why is it the good innocent American people who keep getting caught in the crossfire? Innocent people were hospitalized, some even in intensive care, after the latest attacks. Do I have to worry next time I go to the bank that it might explode because someone was mad they were charged an overdraft fee? Where are the authorities? Why is no one stepping in to put a stop to this?

"Fox 55 has been close to the action during the protests. Thankfully, due to our being on the scene, as well as local authorities, the cultists have been kept at bay here locally. Not everywhere can say the same. Take a look at this footage we obtained from one of our Florida affiliates. Utter calamity as society collapses right before our eyes. Fires. Vandalism. Fighting public servants. If the police were merely doing their job when the group began to attack, this is an act of domestic terrorism."

"Now, Chelsea, let me interrupt you for a sec," Trevor said. "Investigation is ongoing, but many reports are coming out that the GPD actually initiated the violence unprovoked during the march."

"Well, Trevor," Chelsea scoffed. "What I said was if the police were merely doing their job, it is terrorism. But some people seem to think this is OK. Even a step in the right direction somehow. But Fox55 will continue to keep you safe and up to date on the antics of Instant Karma. If you have any details or videos of the group that you would like to send in, please upload them to the Instant Karma section of our website. Or call 260-555-3289 to speak to the hotline. I'm Chelsea Winters. You can follow me on Twitter and Instagram @ChelstersFox55. Thanks, Trevor."

"Thanks, Chelsea. For Fox55 News, I'm Trevor Rogers. Good night."

"And we're clear!" sounded the voice of the stage manager on the studio floor.

As the lights above them dimmed and the outro music kicked on, Chelsea leaned in toward Trevor.

"Don't you ever fucking interrupt me again when I'm on a roll."

CHAPTER THIRTY-THREE

It all felt eerily similar as Jordan, Ethan, and Audrey participated in another protest together. They wore the same shirts Audrey made. The air was slightly colder, but even more humid. A tense aura hung over the event like an odd sense of deja vu.

Immediately after the last demonstration soured and left a black eye on GPD and the city in general, a bill quickly surfaced making it up to a two-year jail sentence to resist arrest. Six months for disturbing the peace. But this rally would not get violent like the last. Peaceful. Coordinated. This one would not get out of hand, even though there still stood a police presence. Justified most would agree. Smaller scale. Only the seriously invested individuals showed up today.

Jordan walked around most bothered. Different setting and without the intensity. Without the bite. Without any attitude or edge. But he still saw ghosts all over. He scoffed at the chanting and the signs. How was this going to be effective? Audrey was handing out bottles of water to fellow protesters.

Say what you want about how the last one boiled over. At least it got people talking. People took notice. What the fuck was this going to do? Did the assholes inside this building even know they were out here? Jordan imagined they were so preoccupied with circle jerking inside they didn't even know there was a protest happening. The continuous chanting and yelling and name calling, simply white noise to the powers behind the doors.

He imagined he could get inside. Scratch that. He knew he could get inside. At least if he were stopped, he'd have their attention again. Just weeks ago, he was on top of the world. He was the talk of all the news outlets. All the morning talk shows. "I am Instant Karma," rang from his tongue and reverberated throughout the internet. It became a rally cry for the marginalized. A slogan for the over medicated and underpaid. It was branding.

"Ethan, what are we doing man? We're losing steam," Jordan said. "We can't change the world with a sign and a sad whimper."

"Trust the process," Audrey said. "Think of it more of a slow burn."

"Yeah, man. It's like, a line in the sand," Ethan said. "Stand your ground and strategically move forward. You can't just storm the castle. What's that gonna get you?"

"Noticed, bro. It gets you noticed."

"You gotta be more tactful, dude. Look around right now. This is a beautiful thing. You're a part of something here. We are going to stop these assholes from passing a bullshit law that is set to punish things like this. That is really cool. This moment right here."

"How can it be cool if no one fucking cares? The news vans left half an hour ago. They haven't even looked out the windows. It's barely on Twitter. Set a fucking fire on their front steps. I'll bet they start paying attention then."

"Yeah? What did you gain from rioting with police? What, other than making a scene, did you actually fucking accomplish from that?"

He opened his mouth to respond, but nothing came out. Ethan was right. His ribs were still bruised and sore- probably broken. He drove a wedge between himself and his family. He's living out of his car. Meanwhile, there'd been no talk of higher minimum wage. No talks of anything except for finding yet another way to silence the people that are already only screaming because they're in need of assistance.

Jordan slid his mask from atop his head down over his face. He pulled one of the extra signs which had been stuck stake first into the grass and walked to the front line of the protest. Nothing between him and the enemy except for a metal barricade and a smattering of police.

He scanned back and forth attempting to recognize any of the officers, and more importantly, see if any of the officers appeared to recognize him. They didn't. He didn't. He figured he was as anonymous to them as they were interchangeable cyborgs to him. If they had lives, or a back story, or hopes and dreams, he didn't care. He didn't even look at them as people with conscious thought. Just a hive mind of oppression and unnecessary violence.

Jordan joined the chanting, but punctuated the lines with ferocity. He stared into the faces of the police as he spoke. He then stared past them. Through them. He began to scream right to the bodies behind the concrete walls. If he concentrated enough, he could speak right into their souls. Everything else, on both sides of the metal barrier, faded away. The clanging of midday construction and growls and horns of downtown traffic dissipated into the atmosphere. Jordan could only hear his own voice. His own words carried from his mouth into the psyche of those he felt wronged him.

"Protect our freedoms! This bill is unconstitutional!" Jordan yelled. "You will never silence us!"

He took half a step forward with his sign in the air.

"Get back!" he heard yelled back in his direction.

Jordan's concentration broken; he noticed the officers now in front of him. One with his hand at his belt unsnapping the clasp from the pepper spray and sliding a right foot backward in readiness if they felt the need to deescalate.

Jordan smirked. Maybe he had the upper hand after all. They were shaken. He stopped yelling and took a step backward.

"Okay, Okay. No problem," Jordan said in a tone matching the dry smile on his face. "You're doing a wonderful job today, boys. Really keeping the peace. Commendable." He then said, in a lower tone, "Tell me, how did you let those protesters beat the shit out of you all last time? One of you even got choked out. I heard, I mean. Is he here?"

"Excuse me?!" the officer asked.

"Oh nothing, just trying to make conversation," Jordan said.

"Come here. We need to ask you some questions. What's your name?"

"Instant Karma," Jordan said almost as a reflex as he backed away from the barricade and walked back to the group.

"Hey someone grab him. Bring him here!"

But no one did. No one even batted an eye.

Audrey looked off at the officer yelling and then back at Jordan.

"You do that? What's he yelling about?"

"Oh, I don't know. You guys were right, though. I gotta think about being more tactful about all of this. Less reactionary."

"Wildcard, bitches!" Audrey said in her best Charlie Day voice, but got zero reaction from Ethan or Jordan. "Really? Nothing? Fuck, you guys are the worst."

"Sorry, babe," Ethan said.

"Look I gotta get going though. I gotta work at four. Should probably shower and stuff," Jordan said.

"Yeah, gotta get all fresh and clean for them hot Thompson's groupies," Ethan said.

"Hell yeah. You know."

"Hey, if you need someone to come in and use the spray paint on the aisle floor to test the color, just let me know."

Jordan laughed. "I'm guessing some asshole's already got you covered. But I'll hit you up if you're needed."

"Sounds good. Stop by later if you want, man. We're just gonna be hanging out at home. Stay the night if you want," Ethan said.

"Yeah, yeah. I'll let you know."

***

The night was slow at Thompson's, and Jordan's shift came

and went without incident. He clocked out at eight, but afterward, stayed in the break room and watched TV while he charged his phone and relaxed. He had done so many times since being kicked out. He had nowhere to go.

Ethan offered regularly. But his place, which used to be a haven for Jordan, began to accentuate everything Jordan didn't have for himself. He figured he could hang out here until the store closed, at which time he'd drive off and sleep somewhere in his car.

Jordan slouched in the hard plastic chair with his feet propped up on the seat next to him. As he mindlessly popped Doritos into his mouth one after the other, he stared off while he half-way paid attention to the TV. He only sat up when Instant Karma was once again on the news regarding the day. To his surprise, their protest had made the news after all.

"Bill 1402," the news anchor said, "which has been dubbed Florida's Keep The Peace Bill is facing extensive backlash while being fast tracked following the violent riots earlier this month. The bill would stiffen as well as give clarity to certain punishments based on public safety. Supporters of the bill say that it would give peace of mind to those who have businesses downtown where, at least in our city, they are still reeling and cleaning up the aftermath of Instant Karma. Protesters gathered in multiple cities throughout Florida, including right here in Gainesville, to battle the bill they deem unconstitutional. We reached out to our district congresswoman but have not received a reply. We will of course stay close to this and update when able to."

Soon after, Jordan's phone chimed.

"Made the news today! Trust the process, man," Ethan messaged him.

"I saw that! Hell yeah!" Jordan replied feeling uplifted, but not as enthusiastic as his text back appeared. More cautiously optimistic.

"What you up to tonight? Wanna celebrate? Audrey is making margaritas."

Without replying, he slipped the phone back into his pocket. On his way out to the car, the phone chimed once again. He expected to see Ethan poking him for an answer, but it turned out to be Caitlin calling him. He wondered if it was intentional. He hadn't talked to her since the riot.

"Hello?" Jordan said.

"Hey. What you up to?" She asked.

"Chilling. Just got out of work. You see the news? We're trying to kill that bill."

"I saw. You were there today? That protest was cute."

"Yeah, I know. More than what you're doing though."

"You think?"

"I don't know. I guess? I haven't even seen anything else happening lately. But I just feel like we could be doing something more, ya know?"

"You saying Kumbaya and arts and crafts ain't cutting it?" she asked.

Jordan laughed.

"Yeah. Somethin' like that. Just hoping we didn't flame out early."

"You want to do something more direct."

"Yeah. Something like that."

For a brief moment, the phone went silent.

"You there?" Jordan asked.

"Hey, if you're free now, you should meet us at the corner of 13th and Berry."

"What are you guys doing there?"

"Just stop by. I'll explain when you get here," Caitlin said.

"OK. Cool. On my way," he said.

Jordan arrived shortly after and walked up to Tyler and Shane huddled over a set of lights.

"Hey, what's up?" Jordan asked.

"Oh, check this out, I had a great idea," Shane said. "You know those floodlight holiday decorations that circle the Christmas lights or ghosts and shit? Well, Tyler the genius here was able to replace the image. Tyler, let's see how it looks."

"All I did was change the template in front of the bulb. Nothing, really. Check it out."

Tyler plugged the lights into the portable power bank. Three flying skulls shone onto the ground between their feet.

"Holy shit!" Jordan exclaimed. "You actually got plans for this or just playing around?"

"Oh, we got plans," Caitlin said.

"Wow, are you trying to sound like a Bond villain? Or it just come out that way," Jordan asked.

Caitlin smiled.

"Just grab that book bag and follow us," she said and walked away.

Shane threw the lights and the bank into a bag by his feet and the three of them followed Caitlin to her car

CHAPTER THIRTY-FOUR

Ethan's phone vibrated to Jordan's call as he sat by the fire.

"Hey dude, you guys still got people over? Was seeing if it's still cool if I come by," Jordan asked.

"Yeah, we're still up and chilling. Come on over."

"Cool. I'm bringing a few others with me too if that's cool. We got some stuff to run by you and Audrey."

"Uh, yeah no biggie, I guess."

Shortly after, Jordan and the others showed up and joined the rest of the group in Ethan's backyard.

"Hey, there he is!" Ethan slurred.

"What's up, man?" Jordan said. He practically skipped up to Ethan and hugged him.

"Guys, this is Caitlin, Tyler, and Shane. They also are followers of the group. I met 'em at the protest downtown. They actually saved me."

"Nice to meet you!" Audrey said.

The others waved and gestured their heads in welcoming movement. Gwen raised her drink in a cheers-type motion.

"Oh shit. Were you still there when things got crazy?" Ethan asked.

"Yeah, we were," Shane said. "That's actually how we met him. He's already a legend."

"Can I get you all something to drink? I made margaritas. I'll be right back. They're in the kitchen."

"Oh no, I'm fine," Shane said.

"I'll take a beer. Thanks," said Jordan. "Actually, give me two. I gotta catch up."

"Margarita sounds good," Tyler said.

"It does. I'll take one, too," Caitlin said.

Jordan sat down in an empty chair by the fire.

"So," Ethan said. "Why are you so elated? Grant get his apron caught in the paint mixer again?"

"Bro, I thought you'd never ask. Check this out."

Jordan pulled out his phone and showed Ethan their masterpiece of the night. A video played of the four of them in their masks vandalizing a local news van. The windows left shattered. Spray painted all over the side of the van were sayings such as "Stop Dividing Us" and "We Don't Need You" and naturally, "I Am Instant Karma" was in full display taking up the back doors. The tires were not just punctured, but shredded. Swirling all around were those same skulls as they illuminated the van, then rolled over to the brick wall beside the sidewalk where the van was parked. They fluttered around like bats in the night sky.

"The lights were my handiwork," Tyler said.

"Beautiful, isn't it?" Jordan said. "It's like street art. We're fucking Banksy, dude!"

"When the hell did you guys do this?" Ethan asked.

"Eh, about forty-five minutes ago."

"Jesus Christ, dude. And then you decided to just come here. We've got people here. My son is sleeping inside. Did anyone follow you?"

"There was nobody there. We're fine," Shane said.

"And besides. Have you watched that news station?" Tyler said. "WKCP. Gainesville Florida's leading news station. Bringing you hard-hitting stories like 'Are Unemployment Rates Directly Tied to Depression and Drug Use?' and 'Model's Diet of Appetizers and Cocaine is Effective. But is it healthy?'

"I'm not talking to you," Ethan said. "I don't even fucking know you. Jordan, you just agreed earlier we need to be tactful. It's not a fucking game."

"We were tactful. They'd been planning this out for days.

This video already has fifteen hundred views and it's only been up an hour. That rally earlier barely got noticed outside of the area."

"You fucking uploaded it?! With what account? Your own? That's insane. They'll know it's you."

"Good," Jordan said. "I'm not scared. This shit is bigger than me, Ethan. It's bigger than you. Bigger than Gainesville, that's for sure. These guys get it. I really wish you would too."

"Look, I think this was a mistake. We should go," Caitlin said. "We've got a lot to go over."

"Yeah, I think that's the only decent idea you had tonight," Ethan said.

As Jordan and company walked back to the car, Audrey came out the back door.

"What the hell happened? Is everything OK?" she asked.

Ethan remained silent as the group left, confused terror splashed across his face.

"Ethan," Audrey called again.

"I… I don't know."

"Actually, it's getting late. I should get going too," Gwen said.

"Yeah, we're out of here too," Marcus agreed. "Audrey, it was good seeing you. Ethan, we'll see you Monday."

"Yeah. Have a good night," Ethan and Audrey both said almost in harmony.

Ethan sat back down by the fire again and quietly stared into the dancing flames. Audrey slid in right next to him, and then shifted over a little more like she wasn't already resting right against him.

"Need this?" she offered and passed off one of the three drinks she currently held.

Ethan smirked and grabbed the glass from her.

"Thanks," he said. "What am I supposed to do? The dude is going to get himself arrested or killed or something. Not to mention he's undermining everything people are actually doing to help. It's careless. I don't know, babe. Am I wrong?"

"No, Ethan. You're not wrong. But I don't think it's all him either. You just have to shine brighter for him and stay consistent."

"I can't keep him out of trouble. I'm not his keeper."

"Oh, stop. You don't have to keep him out of trouble. Just be there for him. Be the reminder that there's more than one way out of the hole he seems to think he's in."

"Yeah, OK. No. You're right."

"Naturally."

"How'd you get to be so smart huh?" Ethan said as he buried his mouth into the side of her neck. Audrey recoiled in a tickled reflex.

"Just a gift," she said as she downed her last drink. "Now enough of that. Put that fire out and come up to bed. I'm feeling just drunk enough to let things get especially interesting tonight."

Ethan finished the drink in his hand. He dumped the ice in his glass as well as the bucket of water next to the pit over the fire and followed Audrey inside the house.

CHAPTER THIRTY-FIVE

Jordan pulled up to Caitlin's house to drop off her, Tyler, and Shane. The whole group talked about the night's activities the length of the car ride and were still excited as they pulled up to the house.

"Jordan, come in and celebrate with us?" Caitlin said.

It was posed as a question, but Jordan heard it more as a command.

"Yeah?" he said.

"Yeah, man. You gotta come in with us," Shane said.

Inside, Jordan couldn't help but notice the entire house was extremely well furnished. He wasn't sure what he expected it to look like, but the whole thing looked surprisingly suburban. Complete with a Live, Laugh, Love plaque hanging above the back of the couch. Polished lamps topped with decorative linen shades sat on side tables bought at a legitimate furniture store rather than the furniture section of a department store. Pictures on the wall of Shane and Caitlin next to an older couple he assumed were their mother and father. A couple pictures of Shane and Tyler were mixed in. Giant gaps in the wall decor from photos which used to hang stuck out to Jordan the most.

They congregated around the distressed white country chic dining room table. What began as congratulating each other on their news van masterpiece, turned to planning for the next demonstration, turned to Jordan himself.

"Jordan, I've been looking for the right way to say this, but it all sounds awkward," Caitlin said. "I'm just going to blurt it out. I couldn't help but notice you had to move a bunch of stuff into the trunk to drive us around tonight. Where are you sleeping?"

"Oh, that? No, it's good," Jordan said.

"Listen, if you want, we have plenty of room. More than enough. I can't have you just out there alone. That's not good for anyone."

"You sure? That's not what I was trying to do here. And you don't know me that well. What if I'm a serial killer?"

"How do you know we aren't?" she said.

Jordan laughed. "That's fair."

"Stay as long as you need to. We don't have another spare bedroom, but the couch pulls out," Caitlin said. "Shane and Tyler are down the hall. I'm the room across from them."

"That's great. Thanks so much. Really."

"Of course. Look at me" Caitlin said. "Make yourself at home. Shane, help him bring his stuff in."

"Damn, bossy," Shane said.

"My bad. Go help him bring his stuff inside, please," she said, her voice drenched in sarcasm.

Outside with their heads in the trunk of the Alero, Jordan unloaded rapid-fire questions while beaming and smiling.

"You guys all live here?"

"Yeah. I had moved in to help my sister after the marriage ended. Tyler moved in shortly after since we wouldn't be getting a different place together anytime soon. We had joked around about basically starting a commune. This is the next step, I guess."

"This is amazing. You guys really all look out for each other."

"Jordan, you can put your stuff in the closet for now. We don't have any extra dressers or anything. We'll figure it out though."

"Maybe I'll just upgrade from duffel and trash bags to suitcases. Really, I'm not stressing about it. I owe you guys everything," he said as they walked back into the house.

"Remember that. I'm not asking for your firstborn just yet. But it's early," Caitlin said.

"Well, I do work. And I don't want charity. I'll absolutely carry my own weight." Jordan scratched at the back of his neck. "But is it cool if I go shower?"

"Of course," Caitlin said.

Jordan tossed his pillow on the couch and carried a balled-up wad of clothes into the bathroom with him. It was the first hot shower in weeks that didn't feel rushed. It was the best shower anyone had ever taken. He was convinced of this. Jordan didn't remember much after that. When he finished and changed, Shane had already pulled out the hide-away bed and left it fitted with a sheet and blanket. He melted into it, and while the others celebrated in the other room, their cheers slowly faded away as Jordan drifted off.

The bed sank in the middle. The metal support bar dug in right below his shoulder blades, but it didn't matter. He was not fighting a seat belt buckle in his hip. He didn't have to shield his eyes from parking lot spotlights. As far as he knew, he slept on the most luxurious bed in the world.

Jordan awoke the next morning and knew he was home. Looking around flooded him with pride. For the first time since he was a child, he belonged somewhere. More than at his parents' home. More than at Thompson's. With every fiber of his being, he knew this was where he was meant to be.

He walked around the house marinating in the aura. In the dining room, he greeted Tyler, who was already up and clicking away at his laptop.

"Whatcha playin'?"

Tyler looked up from the screen long enough to see who was talking to him and looked back down.

"Not playing. I'm working. I'm looking for something."

"Oh. Cool. Cool."

"Can't talk about it right now. I think I'm on to something."

"Great. Good luck, man."

"It ain't even about luck, but thanks."

Jordan continued through the hall and into the kitchen,

where Caitlin stood already plotting the next move with Shane. A large white paper donned with sharpie laid the plans for whatever happened next. Jordan felt like he was in one of those heist movies his father obsessed over.

"How'd you sleep?" Caitlin asked.

"Great, thanks. You guys are... I can't describe it."

"You're one of us, Jordan. I can feel it already. We're one big giant wrecking ball, remember? We do need to talk though."

"Did I do something wrong? I promise I'm going to pay for my fair share."

"No, no, no, it's nothing like that. I just don't have a good feeling about your friend Ethan."

"Oh, Ethan? He's in, I can assure you."

"I don't know. I think I see it already, Jordan. He won't do what we need to do. He's a liability."

"No. No, he's not. You gotta trust me."

Caitlin furrowed her brow and pressed her lips tightly together.

"Work on him. He needs to be all in. Him and Audrey both. They need to know that this is a commitment. The rebellion can't pick and choose when they participate. And the severity of the fight fluctuates with the object on the other side. Control is a funny thing. It's just a game of chicken. You need to sprint headfirst directly at whoever stands in your way. Do not flinch. They'll swerve. The reason they don't want to give up any power is because they are used to the opposition cowering. All it takes is a little hesitation to ruin everything that we've fought for. And if they plan on standing their ground, we'll blow up the fucking dirt beneath their feet."

"He's good people. We all want the same things."

"I hope so," Caitlin said. "For all our sake."

"Trust me. Look, you wanted the tattoos, right? I'll make that happen, and we can all talk. Maybe plan something together."

"Yeah. Yeah, OK. Make it happen," she said.

CHAPTER THIRTY-SIX

Despite how his attempted reconciliation with Lauryn went, Seth was not going to let that be the last they spoke. While not the outcome he hoped for, he did break new ground. They spoke for the first time in months. After the sting of clarity subsided, he still felt upbeat about it.

He decided he needed to reach out again. While he wouldn't outright admit it, Dr Englund's voice rang in his ear.

"What if they don't reply?"

"Then nothing changes. But what if they do?"

Seth exhaled and shook out his arms as if about to jump into the ring and fight. He wasn't necessarily more confident and able-bodied, but he started becoming more willing to fight his negative feelings with vigor. He picked up his sword and shield and began to type away.

"Lauryn, I apologize. I'm not happy at all about how our last conversation went. Can we try again? Please?"

After minutes that felt like hours, Seth's phone chimed.

"I'm sorry too," and then another *"I'm not either. Sure. Coffee tomorrow?"*

"Great. Thanks. 3:00? Normal spot?"

"See you then."

It was short and to the point, but the anchor that had been resting on Seth's chest lifted away, and he floated like a hot air balloon over to the couch.

Rain steadily drizzled down the next morning, cold and

crisp. Not enough, however, to snuff the utter glow bursting from Seth as he walked into the coffee shop. Lauryn already sat and waited for him. He asked her if she had already ordered, and when she said, "No," he nodded and offered to get both of theirs.

"Same thing?" Seth asked.

"Yeah. Same thing," she said softly.

Seth returned shortly with two piping hot mugs topped with a decorative steamed milk design and he slid one over.

"Thanks for coming. I honestly didn't even know if you'd message me back."

"I mean, I owed you that, I guess."

She was cordial, but understandably guarded. Her hair was tied back, showing the row of piercings lining both ears. Dangling from the lobes were two handmade dream-catcher earrings Seth remembered she bought from a flea market one afternoon years ago. She cupped her mug with two hands, breathing in the caramel aroma before taking a sip.

"OK, I don't know if you know this about me, but I'm absolute shit at small talk."

"Oh?" Lauryn played along.

"Yeah, and even worse at actually talking about myself. So just know I'm really throwing myself out there. Please, bear with me. This is hard for me. But I'm trying. Poorly. But I'm trying. I care about you. Like a lot. And it fucked me up when you left. I can't deny that."

Lauryn's naturally wide eyes grew larger, and Seth couldn't tell if she was offended or surprised. Before she could interject, he continued.

"But… I'm not good for anyone right now. So, I understand. It's not fair to you, how I was acting."

"That's…," she cocked her head, "very impressive of you."

"I said before that I started therapy. It really has helped. So, turns out you were right about that. And also turns out that I have issues with abandonment and vocalizing my feelings. So, to combat both of those, I'm asking that we keep some kind of communication open. You know, totally platonic. I still need to know that you care about me."

"That's a lot of pressure on me, no?" she asked.

"I'm not asking you to save me. I'm still doing a lot of soul-searching. I'm just asking you not to completely jump ship all-together. I just miss talking to you. I miss your energy. Need. I need your energy. I'm still trying to find my way without it? Think of yourself more like my mental health sponsor."

Lauryn took a moment to reflect the offer.

"I don't know. How do I know how you're doing on the day-to-day?"

"What do you mean?" he asked.

"I mean, I may need to check in on you from time to time. Over brunch or something. You know. To make sure that you're progressing nicely."

"If you think that's what the job will entail. It doesn't pay any extra."

"We didn't even talk about pay. How much you thinkin'?"

"Oh, the pay is horrible," Seth said. "I don't have a fucking job."

They locked eyes as they laughed, and Seth broke away. He tried to think of something to say to change the subject, but nothing came to mind. Lauryn, however, stayed fixed on Seth. She smirked as she set her coffee down, but didn't loosen her grip on the mug.

"So, what about the other thing? That doesn't fill the void?" she finally asked.

"What other thing?"

"You know," Lauryn said.

Seth thought she couldn't be talking about the first thing that popped into his mind. The only thing. Did Craig tell her? Do they talk to each other? Do they talk about him?

"I've got nothing," he bluffed.

"Really? You're going to make me be the one to bring it up?" Lauryn said.

Seth looked at her, squinting his eyes in an attempt to pick her thoughts. She couldn't have known, could she? Not only did that make him feel lame for thinking the mask was at all hiding his identity, but he also felt exposed. If she watched the videos and knew it was him, she still didn't reach out at all? As he talked about how alone and lost he was. Screaming into the abyss about how everything he ever loved has left him. How life just kept stomping us down.

But, she also came back. He, in a roundabout way, finally got across to her exactly how he felt, and she still showed up. He must have been silent a bit too long because Lauryn chuckled.

"You ain't getting in here, Professor."

"So, wait... you watch them?"

"I might have perused some of them from time to time." She bounced her head from shoulder to shoulder. "OK, I follow you. All right."

"And you knew it was me the whole time?!"

"Of course, I know it's you, Seth."

"Really? How could you tell?"

"Man, we were together for over ten years. You think a cheap ass mask is gonna make me not recognize you?"

"And you still never said anything? After everything I have talked about?"

"Honestly? I didn't feel like it was my place. I couldn't look away, but I also felt like it was a violation or something. Almost like, reading someone's diary. But at the same time, I finally saw the spark in you that had been missing for so long. You were enthusiastic and confident. And the more people behind you, the more you grew like you drew power from their energy. Just know I was so proud of you. Am proud of you?"

"Which is it?"

"Both? I mean, look I know it wasn't your intention. But this thing has grown a life of its own. Look around. Is it even your thing anymore?"

"Wait, is that why you really came here? Just to lecture me?"

"No, dude. But you can't just ignore it and shrug it off like everything else. It's not an old TV or a wonky car door. It's peoples' lives." Lauryn leaned in and said in a hushed tone. "People are dying. Because of something you created. Your fucking monster is killing the villagers, and it's up to you to put a stop to it. Look, Craig and I-"

"Craig? So, it was him that put you up to this. I'm such a fucking idiot. I thought you came here because of me. But no. You're only here because someone else asked you to talk to me."

"It's not like that. Everything I said was true. We're both worried about you."

"Worried about what? Maybe I have everything right where I want it. Maybe they're right for toppling the hierarchy and demanding the truth for once."

"Seth, just listen to yourself. Do what you need to do. Do you really have everything right where you want it?"

"God dammit. No," Seth said. "Fuck, what do I do?"

"They're already following your word, Mr Founder. Keep on with the brutal honesty sprinkled with the vulnerability. Seems to be working so far. Just, you know, reign it in."

CHAPTER THIRTY-SEVEN

Jordan excitedly knocked on the front door, eager to bridge the gap between his two groups.

"Ethan!" he said as the door opened.

"Hey, what's up guys?" Ethan said. "Come on in."

"Look, man. Umm, first off, I want to apologize for the last time. You know, the whole van thing. I shouldn't have sprung that on you like that."

"It's all good man. Don't even swea-"

"Oh, shit!" Jordan blurted out. "Van-dalized. Fuck, that's so good. Why am I just now thinking of that?"

"OK. Who's going first?" Audrey asked "The room isn't that big, so unfortunately, we can't all just hang out in there. Gonna have to take turns."

"I will," Caitlin said. She followed Audrey into the spare bedroom and sat down, awaiting the needle.

Caitlin, Tyler, and Shane would all be getting tattoos to match Jordan's. In an act that would keep them connected even when not donning the masks and fighting for the cause. Caitlin sat in the chair, her arm laid out with forearm to the sky, while Audrey prepped her canvas with alcohol after setting out the tools.

"You mind if I freehand the stencil? It's a pretty straightforward design, but I never freehand the real ink. It's not worth the attempt to show off."

"Yeah, whatever works for you," Caitlin said.

"Cool." Audrey sat down and began to sketch out the eyes, followed by the outline of the skull itself.

"Believe it or not, this is my first tattoo," Caitlin said.

"Really? That's wild to me. It's become such a part of my life, I don't even think of people not having them. Why now?"

"I've wanted one. I just overthink it, I guess. Whenever I come up with something I like, I never want it still after a few months, so it seems pointless. But I finally found something that speaks to me. I'm big on rebirth lately. But butterflies and lotuses are cliche as fuck."

"I do a lot of butterflies," Audrey chuckled.

"And something like a phoenix isn't really my style."

"You ever thought of a scarab?"

"No. Really?"

"Yeah. They've long been worshiped and seen as a symbol of rebirth and everlasting life. Plus, they look cool. So that helps."

"I like that. Like a scarab right behind my ear."

"That would look awesome. And I'm not just saying that, I swear." Audrey fired up the tattoo gun and started along the stencil lines. "It's funny. I'm all for the movement, but I still can't do the mask. I like the look. Intimidating. But I just can't get behind the whole dressing alike and becoming anonymous thing. I'd rather take the fight to them with them staring right into my eyes. See the person they're dealing with. I get it, but it's just not for me. I'd rather protest the old-fashioned way."

"If the old-fashioned way worked, we wouldn't still need to protest. The masks are what unify us," Caitlin said. "It's fitting, because that's how we're seen. Faceless, humanoid beings. No identity. No characteristics. Just shells. According to the powers that be, you're nothing but a social security number and a taxable paycheck. Nothing if not exploitable. And that... that's why he chose these masks for us. To take how the peasants are perceived and flip it on its head. Use the whole thing against them and fight for what we want. No, deserve. So, please. Wear it proudly, Audrey. You're part of the faceless army of Instant Karma."

"Yeah, I guess," Audrey said.

"Your son will thank us when he doesn't have to worry about the shit that we do when he gets older. Shouldn't he get to have a life where he can go to college without being price gouged and stuck in debt for twenty years? Maybe he'll be able to stay up to date with world events without having to do a background check on who owns the news station and what they're lobbying in Washington for?

"If I've learned anything in the last couple of years, it's that you gain nothing by sitting idly by. Things don't get better by patiently waiting. You need to take action. They're not planning to give up any of the power. Why would they do that? So, take it!"

In the kitchen, while Shane and Tyler waited for their turn in the chair, they planned out what to do next along with Jordan and Ethan. Ethan, while trying to not be a killjoy, helped formulate a plan they could all agree on.

"Look, we all want the same things, right?" Shane said. "The Founder says that we need to put our details and minor differences aside. Work together, and I want to do just that. He's right. Don't let the details get in the way of progress. So, tell me, Ethan. What are you willing to do to protect your family?"

Ethan said, "We just gotta do it smart. No hurting innocent people. No collateral damage. You can't simply 'ready, fire, aim' this shit or else you're in the news being called a terrorist or a Nazi. We're making progress."

Tyler groaned and shook his head.

"Whatever, man," he said. "You can fuck off with your progress. So much throughout history is still prevalent today. It's insane. John Lennon made Working Class Hero in the seventies. Hurricane Carter was also wrongfully arrested in the seventies. Rodney King was nineties. Animal Farm, 1984, Handmaid's Tale, Fight the Power, Fuck the Police, Killing in the Name. All made decades ago. Hell, To Kill a Mockingbird could be re-imagined to take place present day, and it would still fit right in. This shit isn't progress. It's a fucking merry-go-round.

"OK. OK. We get it," Shane said. "We'll come up with something. Ethan, Jordan says you're cool. Then you're cool. We trust him. He's a huge deal."

"He doesn't do anything half-assed. That's for sure," Ethan said.

They all laughed, and Ethan grabbed some drinks for the table. He twisted one open and set the rest down.

"You're really protective over him," Tyler said. "He doesn't have enough people like that."

"I'm sorry. Haven't you only known him for, like, a month?" Ethan said.

"I'm right here, you fucks. You do see me, right?" Jordan said.

"I'm just saying. It's important to have people in your corner. You know, if things get bad. We can rely on you right, Ethan?" Tyler asked.

"Absolutely," Jordan said. "I'd trust him with my life."

Ethan shook his head. Not in disagreement. But in disbelief at how this conversation was turning.

"So, what's up with Caitlin?" he said, steering focus away from himself. "She always so intense?"

"Yeah, that's just my sister," Shane said. "She's been through a lot."

"Yeah? So has everyone. That's why we're here," Ethan said.

"She can be very warm. But she doesn't like bullies. She just happens to see quite a few people as such. She wants to make them pay."

"So that's why you're here? To help protect her?"

"Me? Protect her? Please, dude. Back in school, I once saw her hold a metal nail file to a dude's neck because he threw another kid's lunch all over the floor just to be a dick. This is her mellowed out. Trust me. But yeah, zero mercy for people that punch down."

Shane looked over his shoulder back down the hall toward the buzzing of the tattoo needle.

"Ugh. Listen, it's not really my business to tell, so you

didn't hear shit from me." Shane took a swig from his beer bottle and continued at a lower tone. "She used to be married a while back. Her husband started off as a nice enough guy, but always kinda jealous. I don't even know exactly when it started getting bad, and she don't really get into it. Even with me. But they stopped coming around. Pretty much stopped talking to the family all together. And when she did come around it was like she was always walking on eggshells. Totally different person. She'd always have hoodies on, and her hair would be down. It was longer then. We live in Florida for Christ's sake. It's too hot for that shit. But one night my dad straight up pried it out of her. He knew something was up. Call it parent's intuition or something. He called me and we were going to go put the fear of God into him, but she stopped us. Said she'd take care of it. About a week later, she called me up crying. When I got there, there were police all over, and she's sitting on the front steps huddled over a glass of water like it's giving her life. She got home late from work, and he started accusing her of a bunch of shit. They started arguing and that girl shot his drunk ass when he tried putting his hands on her. They agreed it was in self-defense after they took her in and questioned her."

"Holy shit. That was her? I heard about that," Ethan said.

"And she says that I'm the hero?" Jordan said.

"That's terrible," Ethan said. "I never would have guessed."

"Yeah. I'm proud of her."

"That why you're here?" Ethan asked.

"I have my own reasons. But there's no one I'd rather have in my corner. We need better. And there's no one out there that is going to give it to us."

"So let me ask you again," Tyler said. "How far are you willing to go to keep your family safe?"

That question would eat away at Ethan all night. Picking at him just below the surface.

CHAPTER THIRTY-EIGHT

Stanley stood on the front porch, unable to believe what he just heard. Technically speaking, it was still his front porch. A place which once held so many great conversations and tender moments, now felt incredibly cold. The storm door stood between him and Donna, but so much more divided them. Her words lingered in his ears repeating over and over.

"They're scared, Stanley."

"What do you mean, they're scared? The whole thing wasn't even my fault. We got bombarded by those assholes. I explained what was going on."

"Well, apparently not well enough. I'm not going to force them to come over if they don't want to. They were already shaken up, and then with the bombings. What are they supposed to think?"

"Can I talk to them?"

She walked out to the porch, closing the door behind her so they could talk in confidence.

"I don't think that's a good idea. Frankly, I'm scared too. What I'm seeing on the news. I don't want my kids around it."

"Our kids, Donna. And you mean around me."

"Look, just give it some time."

"I don't need time. I need my kids!"

"And I need to protect them!" she snapped back. "Now I'm trying to be diplomatic about this, but you need to understand this is for their own good. Just... you gotta let this Instant Karma shit go. I know you're not a bad man Stanley. Not really. But with your history, and now this. It's not healthy. And it doesn't look good."

"I had Komets tickets for us tonight."

"I'm sorry," she said, and turned to head back inside.

"Wait. Here, take them. I'd still like the kids to be able to go if you want."

Donna took the hockey tickets and walked back inside.

"Stanley."

"Yeah?" he said, hopeful.

"You can't come over here anymore. Don't fight me on this. When things settle down. If they settle down. We'll work on supervised visitation."

The lonesome drive back home took far longer than normal. Stanley passed up his apartment and continued to drive. And think. An extra trip around the block extended through the neighborhood. Then further out around the city.

He wanted a drink. He wanted to scream. He wanted to go to the nearest bar, get blackout drunk, and beat the hell out of anyone who looked at him sideways. He needed to make a phone call.

He pulled over into a Speedway and called his sponsor, John. Stanley listened as the phone rang through to voice mail, and exhaled deeply as he tossed the phone over the steering wheel. His palms itched, and his mouth turned to sandpaper. He could get through this. He just needed to clear his head and breathe.

Stanley grabbed his phone again and pulled up the Instant Karma YouTube page. He could normally find solace here. The Founder had a way of speaking about just whatever his people needed to hear at that point in time. The best leaders always did. He forgot there was a new video he had yet to watch. Those more militant than him, the ones everyone seems to fear, went ahead and made a mess of everything.

"This isn't even really a video," The Founder began. "I mean, it's a video, but... ugh, whatever. I quickly need to respond to what was all over the news recently. This all is turning. Turning in a counterproductive way. After what happened, I don't think anyone is going to think of this as insignificant anymore. The claims about being something to ignore will surely stop. But at what cost? This will not accomplish anything. Vandalism and destroying property gain negative attention and won't actually change anything. It does nothing. Look elsewhere. We've grabbed their attention, now's the time to demand their ear. Do it the right way. Take the fight to the-"

The video cut out and the phone vibrated in his hands. The name John Miller flashed across the screen.

"John. Thanks for calling me back."

"Of course. What's going on?"

"I'm not doing good, man. I've lost my family. I'm feeling real low. I'm scared. I really want a drink."

"What do you mean you've lost your family, Stanley? Where are you right now? Meet me somewhere."

"I'm at a gas station just north of Fort Wayne. I'm just out. I don't know. I'm not in my right head space."

"OK, I'm on my way. Walk me through how you got here."

"My own children are scared of me. That bitch took them from me and turned them against me. How could she do this? She took everything away from me."

"OK now. Remember, Stanley, only obsess over what you can control. Donna is only doing what she thinks is best for the kids right now. You know that."

"No, not Donna. I don't blame her. I could never. Chelsea Winters. Chelsea Winters ruined my fucking life."

CHAPTER THIRTY-NINE

The bell above the Thompson's Hardware Store door gave off a familiar jingle as Ethan and Audrey walked inside with Hayden in tow. It had been a while since his old coworkers saw Hayden, or Audrey and Ethan for that matter. But it was the baby that garnered all the attention. That's just the natural order. They made the rounds and Hayden ate up all the affection he could handle.

Grant stood at his office door and peered out with a face that told Ethan the rod remained firmly in place up his ass. Ethan expected him to come out and tell him to move along and stop distracting the employees, but he all but disappeared after a few minutes.

They picked up an outdoor swing for their son, the main purpose of the trip. The Little Tikes swing was red and blue, and could be attached directly to the tree behind their house. After collecting all the tools needed for the job, they found Lori to catch up. They purposely sought her out last, knowing they'd talk with her far longer than anyone else at the store. They walked up behind her as she straightened up the shelves of the electrical aisle.

"Excuse me, miss. Do you sell lightbulbs here?"

Ethan was pleased with himself after seeing her deflate before turning around.

"Uh, yeah. They're actually right in front of y- Oh my God! Hey guys!" she said while hitting Ethan in the arm. "Asshole.

Oops. Sorry. Butthole. And look at you! Gimme that baby."

After holding Hayden and burying her face into his fat cheeks, Lori's demeanor straightened as she handed Hayden back over to Audrey.

"Have you guys talked to Jordan lately?" She asked.

"He came over a few days ago. I don't think I've talked to him since then," Ethan said.

"This is the second day in a row he's no call no showed. I tried callin' him and checking in, but couldn't get a hold of him. I'm only still here to fill in. I was supposed to leave already."

"That's not like him. Usually, I can't get him off the phone," Ethan said.

"I don't know. He's been acting different lately. Not his usual self. Have you noticed that? I'm pretty worried."

"Yeah, he's got some shit going on. I didn't think he was too bad though. Maybe I just haven't been paying attention."

"He's been missing a lot of work. When he's here he's…it's hard to explain. He's still Jordan, but there's something different I can't put my finger on. I'm worried about him."

"Yeah, ever since that riot thing he's been on edge a little. I'll see what's going on. Then I'll give him shit for worrying you."

"Thanks. That's the real issue here, you know."

Lori hugged them both, and blew raspberries into the cheek of Hayden, forcing him to expel a huge belly laugh. Afterward, they cashed out, but before leaving made a point to seek out Grant.

"Grant! How you been?"

"Ethan," he said. His jaw was tense and barely moved as he spoke. "Can I help you?"

"I'd like to fill out a formal compliment card for the exceptional service we had today."

"Oh yeah?"

"You have an employee. I think her name was Lori. Please help me take care of this."

Ethan pulled out a Great Thompson's Service card and began filling it out.

"*Today I received great service looking for a swing for my son. I was helped by Lori, and she went above and beyond to make sure my needs were taken care of.*"

"When you see Jordan, make sure he knows he's a strike away from losing his job," Grant said.

Ethan looked up at Grant, then back down to the card.

"*The stuffy manager in charge was very condescending and of no value for my visit here today. Didn't catch his name.*"

He slipped the card in the box and thanked Grant.

"Feel better, Warner?"

"Very much so, actually. See ya."

Audrey drove around for close to half an hour looking for Jordan while Ethan called him repeatedly from the passenger seat. They continued to get no answer. When Hayden started fussing in the back, Ethan dropped Audrey and the baby off at home. He continued the search by himself hitting all the spots he knew of Jordan hanging out. After about forty-five minutes of driving around solo, he drove by where the riot occurred.

The area still had not been completely cleaned and remained closed off. Some storefronts remained boarded up with plywood. Two streetlights needed replaced, giving the area an eerie unnerving quality. He spotted Jordan's Alero pulled over to the side of the street. Ethan pulled up right behind it and flashed his high beams. Nothing. He got out and walked up to the driver's side door. Looking through the windows, no one was inside. The doors were locked, though, which Ethan took as somewhat of a good sign. Scanning around the area, nothing stood out at first, but he finally saw a shadow standing on the roof of the coffee shop, facing the alleyway.

"Jordan! What the fuck?!"

No answer. He resembled a gargoyle peering down from its perch.

"Don't move! I'll be right there."

Ethan ran around to the fire escape and climbed to the roof. Jordan stood on the upper ledge, staring out into the night with his arms out.

"Jordan, what are you doing, man?"

Jordan stood flat-footed, knees bent on the concrete railing. His eyes fixated on the ground below him. The coffee shop roof sat high enough to feel the cool breeze blow gently against his back.

"This isn't really what you think, Ethan."

"Yeah? Then, what is it? Because from here, it looks genuinely concerning."

"More like, extreme meditation. I'm just thinking."

"What about?" Ethan said as he inched closer and closer.

"Everything, I guess. Choices. People. Life…death."

"Yeah, I don't like that last part. Why don't you get down from there, man. Come talk to me."

Jordan began slowly walking the ledge of the roof; one foot in front of another.

"We're talking now, aren't we? This is where it all happened, man. I can still feel the energy. It's electric out here. You ever wonder if you've already peaked? What would you do if you knew life would never give you another high point?"

"You know that's not true, man. Jordan, I'm not good with heights. Come here. Let's go grab a burger or something. We can talk about what's next for Instant Karma. Or anything else you got on your mind, really. I'm being totally honest. You're scaring me, dude."

Jordan didn't move. Didn't turn around. He instead spread his arms wider and closed his eyes. The night air breathed against his fingertips as he swayed following the direction of the current.

"Don't worry," Jordan said as a smile grew across his still face. He waved his fingers, letting them surf one by one on the wind fluttering beneath them. "People don't really want to jump most of the time. If you know what I mean. I don't think, at least. I haven't done studies or anything. Just personal experience. They just want to feel something. Enough to feel the adrenaline pump some life back into their heart and prove it still works. And then just before they cross over the point of no return," Jordan paused. He stood still and silent. He listened to the wind whisper into his ears just a moment longer. He felt the air caress his hands, starting at the palms and then diving off his fingertips. As Ethan was about to scream his name one more time, Jordan jumped backward, without breaking his gaze of the ground below. "They hope someone is there to pull them back."

Ethan clutched Jordan on each shoulder and stared at him. His eyes welled up as he searched for words that made sense. Instead, he pulled him in and held him tightly. He then pushed him back out, still clasping onto his shoulders at arm's length.

"Don't you ever fuckin' pull that shit again. OK?"

"I come here quite often, actually."

"Well call me instead of doing some shit like that, you hear? I'm here. Got it?" Ethan said.

"Yeah. I hear you. Really. I'm good though. So about that burger," Jordan said.

Ethan looked at his friend. The person who looked back, he hardly recognized. The bright-eyed and energetic demeanor Ethan gravitated toward and grew a quick bond with replaced with pain and reckless cries for help. Or maybe the pain was always there. Maybe he simply didn't see it before. Jokes to kill tension now seemed like ways to change the subject from hard conversations. Self-depreciation now seemed more pointed and less in jest.

"Yeah. Let's go," Ethan said.

They drove to a diner where they both ordered Bacon Cheeseburgers and Fries. Jordan ordered a Dr Pepper, while Ethan ordered a Pepsi.

"So, what's going on with you, man. I know you're bouncing around. Is that it?" Ethan said.

"Nah. I mean, it's not helping. It's just... everything."

"Want me to talk to your dad?"

"Absolutely fucking not."

"OK. Sorry. Fair enough. Grant playing nice?"

Jordan laughed.

"No. But I can take care of him no problem."

"He says you're about to get fired. Lori's worried about you too."

"Look. Nothing is going on with me. I'm just passionate about what we're doing. It's all I think about. How come me being serious about something is concerning to you?"

"It's not. It's just… look. You kinda blew up and even created a catchphrase with the 'I Am Instant Karma' thing. That's huge. I feel like maybe you're getting swept up in the moment of that and not looking big picture." Ethan paused, searching out his next words carefully. "And I think some people have latched onto you because of it and are using you as their mascot."

"Who? The other guys? We're a team. And I'm trying hard to bring us all together. I'm not being used. It's the next step of this shit. He's said himself that we need to take the fight to them. That they won't listen if you're not screaming bloody murder into their faces."

"Look, man. About Caitlin. Dude, they're using you."

"Is that what you think? You have no idea," Jordan said.

"And I know it's not just them. It's everywhere. But we don't need them."

"We don't need them? Who's fucking side are you on?"

"You know where I stand. Where do you? They're gonna fuck up and drag you down along with them. I'm not saying we gotta stay in the same lane. We can evolve. But they're not even thinking. It's all just a distraction and smothers the real fight happening each day. Destroying property and defacing walls downtown isn't gonna help fix the roads or help your mom get her pills cheaper. Last week someone tagged Instant Karma on the front window of the Hot Brew. It said online they used whole milk for someone's caramel latte when they requested almond milk. The assholes took it as trying to attack lactose-intolerant people. That's not helping anything."

"Yeah, and writing my congressmen and gathering petition signatures outside Costco doesn't do shit either. At least if we're making noise, they have to take us seriously. Whether it's making an example out of a news van, burning draft cards, or even dumping tea in the fucking harbor."

"Whoa, you a history buff now?" Ethan said, throwing a

french fry at Jordan.

Jordan caught it and ripped it in half with his teeth.

"Believe it or not, I'm not a complete idiot," he said. "Don't tell anyone though. I got a reputation."

"Man, I'm sorry. I know. I didn't mean it like that."

"Nah, it's cool. I get it," Jordan said. "Just extra sensitive right now or something. Look, I'm not gonna ask you to do anything you're not comfortable with. We'll try to meet somewhere in the middle. But I'm all in. Come with us for our next mission. It'll bring everyone closer together. One big happy family."

"I don't know."

"You said we'll take it bigger. No civilians harmed. No collateral damage."

"Sure, yeah OK. I'll go with you. We'll attack it from both angles. You come with me to the protest next weekend, I'll go with you guys," Ethan said.

"Deal," Jordan said.

"So, where you staying tonight?"

"I've actually been staying with the other guys."

"Dude. Really?"

"Yeah, man. They took me in. I owe them a lot."

"I offered you to stay with us," Ethan said.

"I know. But you got your own family and shit going on. Anything you do for me just feels like something I'm stealing away from Hayden and Audrey."

"That's not the case though."

They finished their food, and Jordan grabbed up the bill before Ethan had a chance to react.

"I said I was taking you out for a burger," Ethan said.

"Just shut the fuck up," Jordan said.

"Yes, sir."

CHAPTER FORTY

In an effort to keep the coverage fresh and exciting, Charles Baker decided to shake up the format for tonight's Instant Karma segment. For the past few days, views began to fall off. The shares and reposts even more so. Nothing alarming, but trending in the wrong direction. One would think that after the recent rise in violence, interest would be at an all-time high. But Tuesday's spot dropped six percent from last week. Wednesday's was another eight percent lower than that.

Trevor suggested they transition it into a weekly spot to prevent over-saturation. That didn't fit into Chelsea's plans. Tonight, Chelsea would moderate a debate based around the movement. Not just any debate. Two women, debating on the evening news, facilitated by a woman. If this didn't get the fucking internet backing, she didn't know what would. Unfortunately, on such short notice, they were all white women. Oh, well. It would have to do. The butterflies in her stomach felt more like wasps tonight the way they pulsed and buzzed. The hairs on the back of her neck tingled as she listened to her lead-in from Trevor.

"Thanks, Trevor. Good evening, Fort Wayne, and thank you for joining us. Our Instant Karma coverage will be extended tonight, as we bring in some guests to help discuss and debate the topic. I'm your debate moderator, Chelsea Winters. Sitting with us are Kentucky Congresswoman, Barbara Hope. Hello Mrs Hope."

"Hello."

"As well as Editor of the Pittsburgh Journal, Elizabeth Platt. Welcome."

"Good evening."

"Ok, we have a lot to unpack, so let's jump right into it, shall we? For those of you just joining us, we are talking about the activist group Instant Karma. Instant Karma, for anyone who may be unaware, started as a vlogger on a YouTube channel, and has grown into something much more. Mrs Hope, we will start with you. Before politics, you got your start as a lawyer in Lexington. How do you feel about Instant Karma? And not only the group, but also the man who owns the channel?"

"I feel sick, Chelsea," Barbra Hope said. "How does a country get to this point where everyone applauds this man? He's a cult leader for a growing terrorist group. Because of him, seven bombings have taken place. Seven. Synchronized at that. All by civilians dressed the same and mimicking his "costume". Whether you want to call it a gang, or a movement, or a cult. It is all the same."

"OK," Chelsea said. "But Ms Platt, you have said that you don't feel the same way. Is that correct?"

"Not at all, Chelsea. While, of course, many of the actions are abhorrent, there is also a lot of good coming from this. Those stories seem to get buried beneath the click-bait murder porn. Pardon the term. I hardly feel it is fair to hang him personally in this way. He did not condone the attacks and has spoken out against them. We need to stop the individuals that are committing the atrocities, yes. But separate the evil from the good. This is just another scapegoat that uninformed fearmongers use as an easy blame. First, it was music and movies, then video games, and now here we are. He hasn't committed any crimes."

Barbra Hope scoffed. "And with that logic, neither did Charles Manson. Should we have let him just run free as well? The point is, what accountability should we hold him, and others like him? People who use their platform for evil. I'm all for freedom of speech, but he is inciting violence."

"He never once suggested that someone do harm to another," Elizabeth said. "He is forcing us to take a step back and look at the world through a different lens. There are hundreds of people online that speak out in a similar way, that go unnoticed. He has something that caught fire. You call him a terrorist, others say revolutionist."

"Oh, that's absurd." Ms Hope said.

"OK. OK. OK." Chelsea said. "That was time there. Let's move on to the leader. 'The Founder' as he's been coined. What fault does he have in all of this? Mrs Hope, we'll start with you again."

"He's nothing but a hypocrite. He calls out social media celebrity, just to gain fame from it himself. He condemns the news stations, and they repay him by making him a daily talking point and spreading his word. No offense, Ms Winters."

"None taken," Chelsea said.

The congresswoman continued, "It is asinine that we allow this to continue. If he is so righteous, why does he wear the mask? Like some knockoff from that Anonymous group. I say he is nothing more than a cowardly criminal."

"Gaining fame?" Elizabeth Platt rebutted. "People still don't know who he is. This is no different than the countless other bloggers, vloggers, and public speakers who give the same kind of message. If he went on stage and did an hour-long TED Talk about not believing everything that you see and read online, there would be nothing negative to say. It is the same message, just packaged differently. Mrs Hope, didn't you, yourself, have an event where you spoke out on the dangers and addictions of social media? If someone had watched that and then blown up the headquarters of Twitter, should you be held responsible for that?"

"Of course not. That is completely different."

"How so?"

"Because of the instant feedback and the rapport with the viewers gained from running these channels. These people are called Influencers for a reason. They convey a message that *influences* people's actions and beliefs. Some use it to promote a beauty regimen. He uses it to destroy the world. If he has such great ideas, then why hide his face?"

"So that it's not about him. But about the message. Everything comes back to the mission."

"Why wouldn't he want the notoriety? If his ideas are so novel, wouldn't you think he wants credit? This whole thing is just a dangerous joke to them."

"Why would an author choose a pen name? Why would an artist hide their face? Since there have been people making content, there have been some who choose to stand by their work without recognition. Instead, living through the work itself and the reactions and speculations of others."

"All right! Thank you, ladies," Chelsea interjected. "We are out of time. I appreciate both of you being here with us tonight. And now, we will throw it out to you all at home. How do you feel about Instant Karma? Are they the percolating threat to our once rich and great society they appear to be? Or do you feel they're a positive group with well-intentioned people, but a few bad eggs? We will have the poll open on our Fox55 Facebook page. Feel free to follow that, and me on Twitter and Instagram @ChelstersFox55. Thank you all. Have a good night."

Trevor, who thought the cue was coming back to him to sign off, spoke into the dimming lights without a functional mic. He looked over to see Chelsea shaking hands with Barbra and Elizabeth, before being congratulated by the producers and Charles himself. He walked up to the group.

"Why didn't you throw to me?"

"What?"

"At the end. Why didn't you throw to me? I'm the anchor. I'm supposed to end the nightly news."

"I'm sorry, man. I was just feeling it," Chelsea said. "I thought we should end on that high note. Did you guys feel it?"

"I sure felt it," Charles said. "I've had this thought lingering for a little while now. But I think it's time. Starting tomorrow, Chelsea, you are co-anchoring the news with Trevor. I want you in bright and early tomorrow for promotional shots and we will need to move the camera angles around to accommodate the extra person."

"Really? Oh, this is great!" Chelsea said. "Charles, thank you so much. You won't regret this."

Trevor slipped over closer to Charles and grabbed his shoulder.

"Charles, are you sure about this? Don't you need to get feelers out or something? Make sure we can bounce off each other? We don't even have good banter."

"Well work on it. I'm very sure. I feel it in my gut. Chelsea, you'll have to hand the Instant Karma stuff over to someone else."

"Yeah, that's fine. Interest is waning anyway. Might be time to just cut it for all I care."

"Good. Like I said, bright and early tomorrow to iron out the details."

"Absolutely. Thanks, again," she said.

Chelsea appeared weightless as she sailed out of the studio, except for the *clack clack clack* of her heels echoing against the concrete floor of the parking garage. As she approached her car, she fixed onto something staring back at her from the shadows. Someone, at some point today, had painted the Instant Karma logo onto the wall in front of her car.

"Great," she said to herself. "These fucking people."

As she moved closer, the painting detached from the cement and floated toward her. To her surprise, the skull was attached to a black Carhart coat. No. Not graffiti. A real mask, with a real hood pulled up and over the wearer's head. Chelsea froze as the body approached her driver's side, standing right next to the wheel.

"Are you satisfied with yourself?" he asked. His voice came across gravely, but cracked with uncertainty.

"Excuse me?" she asked.

"You ruined my life, you know? Does that feel good? To know you personally destroyed a human being?"

"I'm sorry, do I know you?"

"Of course you wouldn't. I'm just a boost to your career. Something to throw to the dirt and dig your heel into as you climb higher. Twisting my words to seem like I'm about to do something terrible. Be violent. Why would you do that?"

"Are you violent?"

"I've just needed to talk to you. What do you think?"

"I think you have to know it was nothing personal. I'm just going to assume, judging by," she waved up and down at him, "you have issue with our Instant Karma coverage. We have millions of views on that coverage, though. It is currently the entire top ten in our trending topics. I assume you're recording this somehow. With your stupid fucking mask, or a phone, or something. People record every confrontation nowadays. So, listen carefully. Have you looked around lately? Big picture? Bombings and deaths around the country at your hands. Not mine. Looks like I was right about you all. Just ahead of the curve."

"Or wished it into existence."

"Look, this isn't even about you. Nobody cares about a peaceful protest. They want tension. Suspense. Even if nothing happens, viewers need to feel like disaster could erupt at any time. Or else what's the point? Why bring it up at all? It wastes their precious time that they could be watching crime documentaries with instead. It wasn't supposed to affect you personally," she consoled with the warmth of an arctic wind. "Besides, we might be totally moving on from it anyway. So, there's that too, I suppose."

"You ruined my life!" he said and took a step closer.

"Look, we aren't so different, really," Chelsea said. She took a half step back and put her left hand up between them. "I know quite a bit more about your cause than you suspect. I did my research. I'm thorough. And I get it. I want to be a journalist. Like, a real one. I have a degree and have busted my ass. But I've been at this station doing reports on bullshit going on three years. And now, just recently, have I been making a name for-"

She took the keys, strategically balled up in her hand, and drove them down like a handful of daggers against his temple, down through his cheek. He growled in pain as his mask twisted sideways. As he staggered backward and covered his face, Chelsea turned and ran. She stumbled slightly as she removed her high heels, leaving herself barefoot but more mobile. She sprinted to the stairwell and flung open the door. As she passed through the doorway, her head snapped back. The assailant grabbed her coat collar and whipped her to the ground smacking the back of her head on the concrete. She crept away until she no longer had the energy to move further. Her attacker followed as she scooted on her back across the parking garage. Her vision blurred. Her surroundings darkened. The world slowly shut down around her.

CHAPTER FORTY-ONE

When Chelsea became conscious again, she found herself secured to a chair with ratchet straps and her arms tightly trapped behind her. The single hanging light above her swayed back and forth causing the dim amber glow to dance with the shadows as she regained her awareness. She had no clue how much time had passed, but the back of her head throbbing reminded her how she got here. She was in some sort of office. Disheveled and unkempt. She'd assume it were abandoned if not for the up-to-date calendar hanging on the wall. Loose piles of papers stacked on the desk beside candy wrappers and open cans of Mountain Dew. A giant board full of key rings hung on the wall beside her. Looking out the office window, she saw her car on the back of a tow truck, with more trucks lined around outside. A chained gate with barb wire above it donned a sign for McGrady's Towing.

The fluorescent lights in the adjoining room buzzed and flickered, commanding her attention. Her gaze shifted downward to a man, seated in a chair in the next room with his head in his hands. He spoke to himself, barely above a murmur. No longer wearing his mask, she recognized him now.

"You don't have to do this, you know," Chelsea said. "I... I can see that you're second-guessing yourself. Please, just let me go. I won't tell anyone. Just get my car off the back of the truck and let me go. I said I wanted to be a real journalist. I wasn't lying. We'll just consider this an... an occupational hazard. A wake-up call for me. I won't say anything. I promise."

"I wasn't," he said.

"Wasn't what?" Chelsea whimpered.

"Trying to talk myself out of it. I wasn't. I know what I need to do now. I just need to figure out what to say. But this needs to happen. We can't move forward unless it does."

"Please," she sobbed. "I'm sorry. It was a mistake. I do remember you, now. Sam, right? No, Steve... or..."

"It's Stanley!" he screamed with enough ferocity his vitriol took flight from the back of his throat, misting the air. "It doesn't even matter. Because of you, my children think I'm dangerous. I tried talking to my ex-wife about it, get things straight, but she won't communicate with me anymore. Our lawyers have to talk instead now. I've been completely closed out. We were on decent terms, too. I've been going to meetings. I've been managing my anger well. I just wanted to be a part of something. Something important. You ruined that for me. I have nothing now." He chuckled to himself. "But our message is still important. I see that now more than ever. And try as you might, you will not silence us. He said destruction is not the answer, and I get it. I know what he's trying to tell us. Mindless vandalism just is not big enough to get our point across."

"I'm so sorry! I didn't know. You want a retraction? Stanley, is that what you want? We can do that. Right away. We can have it out by tomorrow morning. We'll get it all straightened out. Just let me go."

"It's too late now. The damage is done. There's no purpose in backpedaling. Because you're right, Ms Winters. No one cares about the peaceful option. Public opinion is far more damning than actual right and wrong anymore. So, let's give 'em what they want."

"Help!" Chelsea screamed as loud as she could, to no avail.

"You can keep screamin'. This lot is huge, and there's no one else working this late. I gave them all the night off."

"No. No, please. We'll do the retraction. We'll pay you for

damages. Please."

"You think this is about me? This isn't just for me. I'm making a statement for every person you and your kind have destroyed as a means to stand out. And if I let you go, the cycle will just continue. Ironic, isn't it? You wanted to create the news so badly. Now you won't even be around to see your biggest story."

Chelsea's demeanor flipped from apologetic to spiteful.

"You're just proving me right, then," she said, her eyes piercing through him. "And your children are better off with you gone. Why'd she leave you anyway, Stanley? Did you hit her, too? Hit the kids?"

"I would never!"

"You did something. No one goes to meetings just for the hell of it."

"Shut the fuck up!" he yelled, as he smacked her before grabbing the tape to close her mouth.

Stanley put his mask back on. Not to cover his face. That would matter little to him when he was finished tonight. He needed it, however, to draw in the strength of all his brothers and sisters to stand with him. Stanley McGrady doing this would simply be murder. But together, Instant Karma would send a necessary message. He took out his cell phone and began to record. Directing the video first at a restrained Chelsea Winters, and then reversing it to himself.

"Enough is enough. We will no longer stand idly by as lies are spread. All we want is to make the world a better place. Help out the little guys some. The backbone of this country is breaking, and when we raise our hands and make noise about needing help down here below, it's met with deception and manipulation. This is just one that steadily used her platform for shaping the truth in exchange for attention. So now, our voice has shifted. We are no longer asking. I am Instant Karma, and *we don't need you!*"

Stanley pulled his .38 Special from his coat pocket and pointed it at Chelsea Winter's forehead. Her mouth, still taped, gave a muffled scream. But her eyes said everything. From pleading, to acceptance, to disdain. Pure hatred which he felt down to his core. They shook Stanley for a moment. He stared back, though thankfully his eyes remained hidden. He felt she knew. Somehow. She could tell this was not what he planned.

Stanley took a deep breath and pulled the trigger. The screaming stopped instantly. He then turned the camera back at himself.

"It is too late for me," he said softly to the camera. "But our message is too important to be stifled. And as I go, more will stand up and take my place. This is not death. This is progress."

Stanley uploaded the video to YouTube and the Facebook pages of the local Fort Wayne news stations using a fake account he made recently. He sat back down and slid the gun between his tongue and the roof of his mouth. The barrel, still warm, soothed more than it should have. Like sipping on hot soup broth made from metal and nitroglycerin. Stanley McGrady sent his family a mental goodbye, as he squeezed his index finger, firing another round. The gun fell to the ground as Stanley's body went limp and fell to one side over the arm of the chair.

The boom from the gun echoed through the main office of McGrady's Towing and would carry across the country.

CHAPTER FORTY-TWO

Seth could hardly contain his excitement after seeing the news.

"Sun'N'Surf will revise their marketing strategy following intense pressure from groups such as Instant Karma. The swim-wear giant has come under fire recently for releasing advertisements for their newly released Active'N'Breezy lightweight swim-wear line for kids and teens. Advertisements many are calling out for being too sexual.

"The specific commercials in question mainly focus on children between the ages of eleven and fourteen donning the swimsuits while playing on the beach and in the ocean doing sporty activities such as playing football and volleyball, or wrestling in the water.

"A statement from Sun'N'Surf said 'We apologize to anyone offended by the campaign. The advertisements have been pulled while under review, but to clarify they only played out in slow motion to capture the fit and flexibility of the swim-wear line.'"

His smile grew ear to ear while he soaked in the glory. He and Instant Karma were doing good in the world, anomalies aside. The radical violence and skewed news pieces couldn't stop what was happening all over the country. *I am Instant Karma*, he thought. The pride felt in knowing his baby had grown to span all borders of the US. New areas popped up weekly, if not daily.

A map of the United States hung on the wall in his room and grew more and more congested. When Instant Karma began picking up steam, he used this to keep track, adding push pins to locations with confirmed action. Mostly green pins, but he added red ones for riots or violent attacks. He needed to make sure he still was doing the right thing. He kept track of everything, and since the red were few compared to their green counterparts, he remained at ease.

He'd done what he could to snuff out the violence. But who was he to tell people how to get their point across? He didn't know each and every situation. Did organized religion shut down based on the actions of the radically devout? No. The masses agreed on where the lines were and moved forward with their message. Time would show where the best of intentions lied. This morning's news only reassured Seth's logic.

Sporadic thoughts surfaced of whether he should finally come forward. He sat on the sidelines for better or worse, letting the cause live and die by the mask. A mask which grew larger than anyone could dream. But, did Peter Parker ever wish it were him and not Spider-Man that prevented a bank robbery or halted a runaway train?

While Seth basked in the glow of his accomplishments, his phone vibrated. He stared at it in confused surprise, as Lauryn's picture flashed across the screen. Somehow unsure what to do, he nervously answered.

"Hello?" he said.

"Seth?"

"Hey. What's up?"

"Umm... what are you up to?" she said.

"Just at home. Nothing really."

"Listen, I was supposed to go out with Lindsey and Angela later, but they bailed on me. I really don't want to sit at home right now."

"Is everything OK?"

"Yeah. It will be. So, I was wondering, would you want to hang out?"

Seth exploded silently.

"Sure. Tonight?" he asked.

"Yeah. Not a date! Just, you know, as friends."

"Of course. Of course. You have anything in mind?" Seth asked.

"Not particularly. We were going to get drunk and do karaoke. I know that's not really your thing. So, you can decide."

"OK. I'll figure it out. I'll text you later and we will meet up somewhere."

"Cool. I'll see you later, then."

"Yeah. Sounds good."

Seth picked Lauryn up that evening, and they headed to Crosswinds Lanes, a bowling alley close to Lauryn's apartment. They grabbed some drinks and shoes and headed to their lane.

"I didn't even think you liked bowling," Lauryn said.

Seth shrugged.

"I watched The Big Lebowski the other day. I guess it's been on my mind. This and buying an area rug."

"Oh god. You're not gonna be all cliche and quote the movie the whole time, are you?"

"I mean... not anymore."

"Good. Cuz this isn't 'Nam, Seth. This is bowling. There are rules."

"Wow. OK," Seth said.

Lauryn shrugged her shoulders as if to say, so sue me, as she walked away to grab a ball.

Seth picked up a spare off a two and seven pin, then rolled a strike his following frame. Lauryn chipped away four pins total before throwing three gutter balls in a row. After the third straight, she threw her hands up in the air.

"Oh my god. I fucking hate bowling!" she yelled.

A mother in the next lane, having a fun night with her three children, shot her an evil glare for the outburst. Lauryn winced and sunk as she walked back to her seat.

"Sorry," she mouthed to the woman and turned back to Seth. "I fucking do, though."

Seth smiled deviously. "Yeah. I know."

"I know you know, asshole," she said laughing. "So why are we here?"

"I mean, we need to make sure we don't enjoy it too much. Right? Otherwise, we might get mixed signals."

Her face lit up with delighted realization.

"OK. Well, what else did you have in mind after this, funny guy?"

"I don't know. I thought we could hit up Seafood Shack to grab something to eat."

"Ooh, greasy fast-food fish? You spoil me. Is the Seafood Shack even still open?"

"Should be. And then, you know, maybe we could just aimlessly wander around the mall but not buy anything."

"Fucking kill me," she said laughing. "I'm in. Can we just bounce around like pong and not have any structure to where we're going?"

"Absolutely!" Seth said.

She sat down on the hard plastic chair, while Seth approached his bowling ball to take his turn.

"So how many games you gonna make me struggle through?" she asked.

"Just this one. Don't worry. Tell you what, how about whoever can roll the most splits gets their greasy fast-food fish paid for?

"OK, deal. I'm gonna show you I'm the best bad bowler there is."

She did too, winning the bet three to one, which she made sure to gloat about.

Afterward, as they drove around, they reminisced about better times. Fun times. Game nights, and cookouts, and concerts. Nights in where they did nothing but lie in bed and enjoy each other. There was still baggage to unpack. Conversations to be had. But tonight felt light and relaxing.

They pulled into Seafood Shack and sat in the parking lot. Seth's muffler rattled as they looked on into the windows of the restaurant.

"I kinda forgot how run down this place is. Should we... do

you wanna do drive-thru or go inside?" Seth asked.

"Can you even still eat inside?"

"I think so? To be honest I don't think I've ever seen more than one car at Seafood Shack at a time."

"It's weird, right? It's not just me?" Lauryn asked.

"No, it's weird all right. They gotta be a front for something. Drugs?" Seth said.

"Something like that. Or maybe they've got a lair below with a hoard of vampires!" Lauryn said as she sat up with her arms folded like she was rising from a coffin.

"I doubt it's that cool. I don't even see commercials anymore. But they don't ever seem to close. They just sort of, exist."

"So. Drive-thru or go inside? How adventurous are you feeling?" she asked.

"Seeing as how I don't want the guilt of eating my food next to a tweaking homeless dude, I say we eat in the car," Seth said.

Lauryn smacked him in the shoulder.

"That's sexist as fuck. Why can't it be a tweaking homeless lady?"

"True. Sorry for being so close minded."

"Get with the times, man."

The two sat in the parking lot and ate their food in Seth's car. They both decided to play it safe and ordered the Fish Strips and Fries combo. Lauryn also ordered some hush puppies. She picked at her fries. After watching the traffic and listening to top fifty radio for a while, Lauryn broke the silence.

"So, I'm trading in the Buick finally," she said.

"Oh, yeah? Good for you. Whatcha getting?"

"Oh, just a newer but still used SUV. Yeah, it's time." She turned away from Seth and looked straight ahead. Without breaking her gaze straight ahead, she popped a few fries into her mouth. "So now, of course, to keep the universe balanced my dad isn't talking to me."

"Why would he care?"

"We got in a huge fight because I'm trading my car in."

"So?"

"So, he thinks I should just give it to him instead. His truck has been acting funny again."

"Jesus. So what? Didn't you even help him pay for that truck?"

"Oh, for sure. He actually said, 'Oh you won't get that much for it, anyway. After everything I've done for you, you should give it to me.' He was screaming at me over the phone. Called me a selfish stuck-up bitch for selling it out from under him."

"It's not his to claim. I still don't get why you bend over backward for him. I've told you this."

"Oh, I know. He's getting old, though. God forbid if something happened to him and I wasn't... ugh. I couldn't live with myself."

"That's not on you. You know that."

"Honestly it got worse after your dad, I think. The way that crushed me. How sudden it was. I started letting more and more slide because I was scared. And I'd just keep doing and doing for him. My mom too. You know the only thing they agree on is how horrible I am."

"You're a better person than me. That's all I know," Seth said.

Lauryn tucked her knees into her chest, letting them get swallowed by her oversized sweater. She wrapped her arms around them as she picked at her fingernails.

"I think I'm just scared that fighting is better than never talking to them again at all. And I know that's coming sooner rather than later." Lauryn wiped away the tears trying to form in her eyes. "But I'm a fucking adult, man. Why? Why do I even still care so much? Why does it still hurt? And then Angela said, 'Well, he's still your dad. You only get one.'"

"What a dumb bitch," Seth said in an exaggerated tone.

"Right?" Lauryn chuckled as she wiped her eyes again with her sweater sleeve. "Fuck that. You shouldn't get a pass just because you're family. You don't get to treat people like shit just because they can't go anywhere."

"I'm sorry. You don't deserve that."

"Full transparency? The other girls didn't bail on me. I bailed on them. After I got off the phone, you were the only person I wanted to talk to. You've seen it. I knew you'd understand."

Seth smiled at her and squeezed her hand.

"I'll always be here," he said.

"I know. Thanks."

They didn't spend much time at the mall. The ironic fun wore off quickly, and they decided to hang out at a place they enjoyed for real. Upon arriving at Kasady's, they were greeted excitedly by Craig from behind the bar. He handed them two Bud Lights. The dart board was open, and Lauryn challenged Seth to a game.

Seth finally achieved the happiness which felt so out of grasp not long ago. He was spending time with Lauryn at Kasady's. Craig tended bar but felt more like he was with them. The jukebox played the opening to No Diggity as Seth whipped another dart at the board. The pieces were finally falling into place. He never thought he'd have this feeling again. Unbothered with where this was going, or what the next step was, or even what was going through Lauryn's head at this very moment. Nothing else mattered. Right here, right now, felt like home. He had won.

"Hey hey, turn that up!" someone yelled to Craig pointing to the bar television.

"Breaking News out of Fort Wayne, Indiana. Newswoman Chelsea Winters is dead, having been tragically murdered tonight by a suspected member of Instant Karma. Chelsea, a news anchor for Fox55 out of Fort Wayne, had been covering the movement nightly for the station. We do have footage to share which was uploaded by the murderer himself, who was also found dead at the scene. He, as of this report, is still unnamed. Please be warned, the video we are about to share is quite graphic."

Seth dropped his last dart. He sunk into the barstool as he watched on with horror. Any prior feelings of peace and redemption curdled in the pit of his stomach as the familiar self-doubt seeped in. Any and all thought blurred together. He questioned why he hadn't put a stop to it. He thought he had. Why did he think he could mitigate the damage and separate the two? Had he just been in denial? He knew who she was. He recognized her right away. He spoke out against her. Was this his fault? Did he set this in motion? Or did she do it to herself?

"It truly is a terrible thing, Ronald," the other anchor said. "And she was such a pretty girl, too. Such a tragedy. We will continue to keep you updated as we find out more information. For Ronald Simpson, I'm Keegan Mathews."

Seth glanced over at Craig and Lauryn. He searched for reassurance. For comfort. But their faces said it all. It flashed across the both of them, flaring up like a grease fire. Only for a second, but Seth noticed all the same. Pure terror. They tried to hide it, and immediately after showed concern. Probably reacting to how Seth wore his panic across the forehead. But he knew the truth. They looked at Seth like a monster. Were they scared of him? Scared of the situation? Scared of what he had become? He didn't know.

"Oh my God. Seth, hey talk to me," Craig said.

"Yeah, you're looking pale. Stay with us. Wait, did they really comment on how hot she was?" Lauryn asked.

Seth tuned both out and sprinted to the bathroom. He sat down on the toilet of the first stall and tried to calm down, only for a second before jumping up and vomiting into the bowl. The stall walls closed in on him, growing higher as they tightly sealed him in. He flung the door open and marched out of the bathroom. He passed by everyone and went straight out the front door.

"I need to get some air," he said as he walked by.

"Hold on. Let me pay the tab," Lauryn said.

He didn't wait, or even acknowledge. He fled the bar.

What he saw on the TV burned itself inside the back of his eyelids. The way she glared right through the camera. The way her head snapped back and went limp before the sound of the shot even had a chance to dissipate. The way the killer used Seth's own words before pulling the trigger. He had to talk sense into this. Get ahead of it, if that's even possible. What could he say? What do you say to a group that has already gone way further than you could ever take them? Is it too late? Could he even stop it now? How can you stop a bomb that's already detonated? Can you hold back the radiation from a nuke that has exploded? Or are the only legitimate choices to hide away in the bunker or face it and hope to not become some sort of feral ghoul?

    He slammed the apartment door behind him and leaned against it. His chest thumped as the breaths came short and sharp. Seth stared fixed at the light switch in front of him as he swallowed hard and slowly inhaled. He walked straight to the bedroom and climbed into bed.

CHAPTER FORTY-THREE

Audrey placed Hayden into his crib. Swaddled tight in a blanket, his eyes slowly opened and closed as he lost the fight against sleep. He tried to glue his eyes to the mobile above him with colorful tropical fish swimming in circles above his head. But not long after, he was completely out.

Audrey stood bedside and watched him sleep for a while. She walked back into the living room and peeked around the corner as Ethan sat in the recliner strumming an acoustic guitar.

Long before Thompson's and Hayden and Instant Karma, they were just two kids in love. She'd often lie on the couch and listen as he'd pick away, sweeping them off to their own isolated plane of existence. She moved over and laid down on the floor, closing her eyes. Audrey transported to years earlier, floating in space on the memories.

After a break in the guitar, she said, "I haven't heard you play that in a while. I miss it."

"Me too," Ethan said. "I'm actually thinking of signing up for an open mic night again."

"I'd love that," she said as she rolled over and rested her head on her hands.

"Hey, remember this?" he said.

Ethan strummed away and began to quietly sing the chorus to Tennessee Whiskey. Audrey sat back up and joined in for the second half. When he stopped, the guitar rang out as they admired the moment. She rested her forehead against the bare knee poking through his jeans and then kissed it before standing back up.

"What if you didn't go tonight?" she asked. "They don't need you, do they? You could just stay home with me."

"Mm, I'd love that. But I already promised Jordan. He said he needs my help with the demonstration."

"They don't *really* need you, do they?"

"Hey, you're the one who said to grab him and go if the others want to do anything stupid again. Show him he has choices, remember? The poor guy has already been cast out by his own family. Hey, you should come with us."

"Gwen already said she couldn't stay over tonight. Or I would."

"OK. I won't be gone long. You gonna be up when I get home still?"

"I should be," Audrey said.

***

Ethan met the others shortly after. All of them dressed in black pants and long-sleeved shirts. Jordan walked up to him and handed him a mask.

"Jordan, I…"

"Just take it, man."

Ethan rolled his eyes and begrudgingly accepted.

"Hey, wait, the eyes are orange again."

"Yeah, that's the old one. I made a new one for myself. Eyes are red now."

"Is that the only reason you want me to take this? To hide your botch job?"

"Absolutely not," Jordan said, nodding his head yes.

"Man, you sweated all up in this thing. Better have Lysol sprayed it or something. If I get pink eye or some shit, I swear to God."

The plan was simple. A similar statement, only this time no destruction of property. A happy medium bridging the two ideals. No recording themselves this time either. The word would travel on its own. The work would speak for itself. Ethan still wondered how the others never got caught destroying the news van. They basically implicated themselves, but apparently the police were too occupied with other things to follow up on it. He figured the van was probably insured for so much they bought two more.

"Here, take this," Caitlin said to Ethan as she handed him the power bank.

"How many of these do you have?" he asked.

"Only a few."

Jordan and Shane grabbed the floodlights. Tyler carried the backpack. They climbed the seedy stairway of the parking garage dodging empty beer bottles and fast-food bags. They made their way up four of the six levels, stopping in front of a window which overlooked the downtown traffic. Shane took a finger and swiped across it, then looked at the grime left on his finger.

"No one ever washes these, I guess. Shoulda brought some cleaning supplies," he said.

"Nah, it's perfect," Caitlin said.

She hopped up on the ledge in front of the window to reach higher, and used the sleeve of her shirt to wipe away a circle about as tall as she was. She cupped her hands over her eyes and peered through. The street below was peppered with foot traffic as the businesses and local restaurants kept the area busy.

"OK, Tyler," Caitlin said. "It's all you."

Tyler reached into his bag and pulled out the red and white glass markers. Starting with the circular motion for the eyes, he moved his arm around in spiral-like patterns filling in the sockets with an even coverage. He finished with the white, drawing a massive circle around the eyes, before completing the Instant Karma logo filling in the white of the skull. He took a step back to admire his work.

However, this wasn't for the folks coming up the stairs. This was for anyone walking down the street. A symbol to peer down onto the passersby and offer hope. An allegory for the oppressed, belittled people of the city. It also stared directly at the medical billing office across the street.

"OK. Floodlights are standing," Ethan said.

Ethan and Shane positioned the tripods toward the window. A pair of them with two rectangle lights fixed on top.

"Let me plug 'em in!" Jordan said.

Caitlin looked at her watch, then back at Tyler. Jordan plugged the shop lights in, and the bulbs gleamed with piercing light, blinding everyone in the stairwell turnaround. Jordan jumped up onto the ledge and used his palm to wipe away at the dirty glass, making a small viewing window. His shoulders dropped as his arms flopped to his sides in disappointment.

"It didn't even work."

"Hold on," Ethan said.

Ethan and Shane moved the lights around, positioning them directly at the mural. The skull shined out into the night, projecting itself onto the buildings across the street.

"There we fucking go!" Jordan said.

Tyler looked at his watch. He walked up to Caitlin and whispered something into her ear.

"Let's go get a better view," she said.

They walked up the stairs to the fifth level. The outer wall had multiple openings overlooking the streets below. People down on the street who passed by on foot and bike and car stopped in their tracks and stood in amazement. They stared at the projection on the building. A few pulled out their phones and took pictures. One snapped a selfie with it, throwing up a peace sign and sticking his tongue out.

The group looked onward with pride. Even Ethan. The thrill of the night pumping through him, this was the kind of fighting back he could get behind. Jordan posted up for a high five, and Ethan smiled and connected. Shane put his arm around Tyler and kissed him on the side of the head while they looked out.

Ethan took a picture to send to Audrey, and noticed the rest weren't even admiring the street-level appreciation anymore. They kept looking at the medical office. Caitlin, once again, looked at her watch.

Suddenly, the Earth shook below them.

CHAPTER FORTY-FOUR

They felt the eruption first. Heard it immediately after. The flashing bright sky blinded the group with an orangish-ivory glow, as the medical billing office's exterior wall blew out and glass and dust and cement rained down in front of them. The streets below littered with shrapnel. The thunderous roar of the blast faded into screams as passersby below now laid in the streets pleading for help. Multiple people stopped and called emergency response while pulling rubble from the helpless. The Instant Karma projection shined on and around the fiery hole. Caitlin, Tyler, and Shane all looked on in admiration. Ethan shuddered at the chilling realization their mission tonight had nothing to do with the parking garage at all. Their current location merely served as an observation deck to the carnage across the street.

"What was that? What the fuck did you do?" he screamed out as he ripped the mask from his face. "There were people in there. People down there. Oh, God!"

"They don't matter," Caitlin said. "They're sacrifices for the greater good."

"Jordan, did you know about this?"

"No. But look at it, man. It... it's glorious."

Jordan looked on in awe. The explosion was beautiful in a way he had never witnessed before. Not in person. Not with his own eyes. Equal parts poetic and chaotic. He could feel the warmth brush up against his face. Vibrant and powerful and cleansing.

"You guys are fucking insane!" Ethan said.

"Jordan, he's going to draw attention to us," Shane said.

"I'm going to draw attention? Oh, fuck you."

"Ethan, I thought you were here to help with the cause," Jordan said.

"I told you he isn't one of us!" Caitlin said.

"Yes, he is!" Jordan replied. He held his hand up to get her to stand down. "Just a little shook, I think. Ethan, you need to calm down."

"Calm down? Jordan, they had to have killed someone. And it's like you don't even care."

"It was said to draw a line in the sand. So, we did. Which side are you on, Ethan?" Caitlin asked.

"We need to call the police. Or the fire department, or… fuck I don't know. Just call 911."

Caitlin positioned herself between Ethan and Jordan, as she looked Jordan in the eyes.

"Jordan, he's just going to get in our way."

"No, he's not! We are in this together, remember? One voice. We need him. Ethan, please don't be like this, man."

"Like what, dude? Act like a normal fucking human being? Man, what is happening to you?"

"Guys, we can't stay here," Tyler said, trying to refocus the group.

"We will not be silenced. Not by them, and most definitely not by you," Caitlin said, pointing at Ethan.

"Will you shut the fuck up?! I can't sit here while you drag my friend down," Ethan said.

"We aren't dragging him down. You're holding him back. Stifling his true potential while you continue to look down on him," Shane said.

"You don't even know us! Standing there talking about unity?" Ethan scoffed. "You fucks aren't trying to improve anything. Not worried about what the hell happens to those people. Hell, they might be part of the movement themselves. You got no clue what it is you're trying to gain in the end other than making the world hurt just because you do. That's not what I wanted. I know what the fuck I want."

"Jordan, we have to go," Tyler said. "Deal with your friend before we are forced to. He can't be acting like this. I knew he was soft."

"Go to hell!" Ethan said. "I think anyone around is a little distracted by the fucking building you blew up!"

"They don't matter," Caitlin said. "Do you realize how many children have to choke on a toy before it gets changed from a freak accident to a nationwide recall? Or how many people a prescription makes bleed from the asshole before it's taken from a known side effect to a class action lawsuit? Death is progress. No one cares until then."

"They're right, Ethan," Jordan said. He spoke softly and reflective. "I know you think I'm not as smart as you. Or as ambitious. I've been shit on by everyone. I'm not going to let you do it too. This is more important than any one of those people down there. Any of us, even."

"What?! You really think that? Don't be like this, dude. I'm sorry if that's how you feel. C'mon let's get out of here. Please."

"There you go trying to control him again," Caitlin said. "He's not your puppet. He doesn't need you. The test has been given and you've shown that you're not one of us."

"My puppet?" Ethan said, throwing the mask at her, but it quickly fluttered to the ground. "Who the fuck do you think you are? You're trying to speak for him. I'm trying to talk to him. To you, he's just the 'I am Instant Karma' guy. You treat him like a mascot. Doesn't need me? Look around! Jordan, you don't need this."

"Either get out of the way, or get dealt with. Remember, Jordan? Those were your words," Caitlin said.

"You don't get it, Ethan," Jordan said. "I warned you we can't half-ass this. The world doesn't change for people who don't want to get their hands dirty. I'm sorry you don't understand. I really am. But I've outgrown you."

Jordan turned around and watched out beyond the parking garage at the masterpiece across the street.

"I'm done. I came here to try and make sure you didn't do

anything impulsive. Or harmful. It's even worse than that! This was premeditated. I mean... whatever. I can't. I'm gonna go help them," Ethan said as he turned to walk away.

"We can't let him go," Caitlin said. "He can't be trusted." Shane grabbed Ethan by the arm.

"Get the fuck off of me!" Ethan said as he whipped around.

Shane reached out to grab him again, but Ethan swung his fist, connecting solidly to his cheek. Shane staggered back before lunging forward. With Shane bent and charging at him, Ethan grabbed him and twisted. Shane toppled, feet first in the air, as they both landed on the cement. From the ground, they traded blows back and forth until Jordan got between them.

"Guys stop!"

The two kicked off each other and climbed to their feet. They all stood still in silence while waiting for the other to come to their senses. Incoming sirens paired with the bellows of close by damage.

Ethan broke away, turning toward the exit to head back down the stairs.

"Whatever. Jordan, I tried, man. I'm fucking do-" he started to say, stopping as all the air expelled from his lungs mid-sentence.

He buckled to the left with a searing pain jetting from his abdomen. Tyler stood face to face with him holding the knife driven into Ethan's stomach right below the rib cage. He balanced his left hand on Ethan's shoulder and used it as leverage to pull the knife out and plunge it in again immediately beside the first entry wound. He wrenched the handle, twisting clockwise and pushing off against the shoulder again. Ethan stumbled back, collapsing to the ground. He wheezed and coughed up bloody pools lying on the cold concrete floor. Jordan ran over to him screaming his name.

"Ethan! Ethan! Oh God, what the fuck did you do?"

"We had to," Tyler said.

"Jordan, look around you. We can't stay here," Shane added.

"He's dying!" Jordan said. His voice quivering and

panicked.

"He was going to turn us in. He did not have your back like you think. Let's go!" Caitlin said.

"Why the fuck would I come with you?"

"Jordan," Caitlin said calmly. "Things are going to get much worse for us if we don't disappear now."

Jordan looked at the three people standing before him, then out to the flames which still waved across the street, and back down at Ethan. He had stopped coughing. Stopped moving altogether. Jordan took Ethan's hand and squeezed it. He pressed it up against his eyes.

He stood up and began to follow the other three to the stairwell, before he spun around and ran back to Ethan.

"Jordan, what are you doing?" Shane asked.

"Give me just a sec. I'm gonna... I gotta call an ambulance from his phone. I'm just gonna dial and leave it here."

"You can't do that. You hear the sirens? They're already on their way. We can't be here."

"We're wasting time," Tyler said, looking at his watch. "We should be blocks away already."

Jordan heard a struggling whisper coming from below.

"Jordan, don't... don't leave me. Please. I'm scared," Ethan said. He pleaded. He used what little strength in him to try and reach out.

"Hel... help is on the way," Jordan said. "I'll fix this. I'm sorry. You're gonna be OK."

"Jordan, let's go!" Caitlin said.

"I'm sorry," Jordan said again. He ran to the stairwell and out the exit door at the bottom. It wasn't until he got to their vehicle that Jordan realized he was still gripping Ethan's phone in his hand. He powered it off and slipped it into his jacket pocket.

The original plan was to go back to the house and watch the news for the response. But the group had to adapt and improvise. They drove around aimlessly for a while before stopping for gas and come up with a plan.

"We need to disappear for a little while," Caitlin said. "At least until we can assess the situation. But we made a statement tonight. That's for sure. God damn, my heart is still thumping! Look at my hands. Still shaky!"

"We should just go to the highway. Head north for now," Shane said.

"Anybody disagree?" Caitlin asked only to hear silence from the rest of the crew.

Jordan, who hadn't said anything up to this point after leaving the parking garage simply stated, "We need to make a stop first."

They arrived shortly after at Palm Villa Trailer Court. Jordan approached the steps, but stopped before heading up to the front door. He took a step back and slipped an envelope containing just under $1,200 cash into the mailbox beside the front steps. He looked up again at the door, turned around, and walked back to the car. From behind him, Caitlin squeezed his shoulders in warm reassurance.

From the side view mirror, he watched the silhouette of his father open the front door. His mother peeled back the curtains and stood in the window as they pulled away. They remained there until no longer in Jordan's line of sight. He stayed fixed on the mirror anyway. He imagined them running behind the car waving frantically to come back. But there was nothing. Just the dimly lit path through the court. No sound to be heard except the crunch of rubber tires rolling on the loose gravel street. The Palm Villa neon sign flickered as if to wave goodbye as they drove past it on their way out of the trailer park.

"Anybody need anything before hitting the highway?" Shane asked. "We got a full tank of gas, so speak up now. Otherwise, we're just cruising until we can't take it anymore."

CHAPTER FORTY-FIVE

Audrey knew what had happened even before officially being told.

"This just in," the television said. "Details are still incoming, but an explosion at a downtown medical billing center seems to be connected to the death of an Instant Karma member. The identity of the individual not disclosed at this time."

"That's right, Kevin. We do know the explosion happened late last night. Crews are on hand searching the building, as it's unknown if anyone was inside at the time of the explosion. In a nearby parking garage, the body of someone lying next to a discarded Instant Karma mask was found stabbed to death. Authorities are working to see if the two are connected, and if the body is truly a member of Instant Karma."

Audrey's knees buckled and she ceased nervously folding laundry. She had been calling Ethan for hours. It wasn't like him to not check in, let alone ignore her like this.

"And I'm sorry if this is in poor taste, but if he is part of that cult, then good riddance," the anchor said. "They're finally starting to just take each other out instead of innocent people."

"Oh, nope. Civilians were hurt, as well," the other one added. "That's the real tragedy. The probability of innocent people inside that building. Security? Maintenance workers? But here we are talking about a dead terrorist. What's the world coming to?"

"No," Audrey said to the TV.

"*Alleged* dead terrorist, Kevin," the anchors continued. "We are still waiting to see if there is security footage of the scene."

"Well, we can't speculate at this time, but we are actively looking into if the two events are connected."

"Stop," Audrey said again to the empty room, a little louder. But the news pundits continued.

"Not officially we can't. But they were right across the street from one another. It would be an unprecedented coincidence if they weren't."

"I'm sorry, but after the national media outlets have been unfairly targeted for months, is anyone surprised that it has come to this? Sometimes you can see a small leak in the dam and know the whole thing is about to blow. And while we don't know have confirmation yet, he was wearing the black jacket and the mask was right there, so…"

"Either way, the more of these goons taking each other out, the faster we will be past this whole thing. Since it's been shown that the authorities won't do anything about them. We just have to wait, I guess."

"*Shut up!*" Audrey screamed at the TV as she turned it off. Her thumb strained and pearl white from forcibly holding down the power button. Her arm outstretched and shaking as she pointed her scepter at the television. As if she had the ability to remove the duo from existence by holding down the circular red button.

Hayden had been sleeping in the corner, but he startled awake, and he began to wail. Audrey couldn't even hear him. Everything at the moment was muffled and distorted, like she was underwater. She collapsed to the carpet, laying there as the tears ran down. As she sobbed and attempted to catch her breath, she covered her face with the kitchen towel she still held, draping it over her eyes and mouth to block out the outside world, if only for a second.

In a sudden about-face of denial, Audrey snapped back up to her feet and scurried around to find her phone in the kitchen. Still nothing. No messages. No missed calls. She frantically called him again, this time without a worried tone to her, but more of determination. She had to be wrong. Of course, she was wrong. He's going to pick up and apologize profusely, and then she would kill him herself and they'd laugh about it later. It had to happen this way. Because he couldn't be gone. He couldn't be taken from her. Not like this. The universe wouldn't do that.

The knock at the door came as a distraction from the phone call she attempted to make. She dropped the phone on the kitchen counter and sprinted to the front door.

This was Ethan. He lost his keys, and his phone was dead. He fell asleep and had to bum a ride this morning from one of the other guys, who didn't have Audrey's phone number, so of course he didn't call. And holy fuck was she going to let him have it.

Audrey flung the door open to greet him with hugs and slaps and swears and love. When she saw who was standing on the other side of the white screen door, her stomach leapt into the back of her throat.

Two solemn-faced police officers stood before her. A middle-aged white man and a younger Hispanic woman. The male officer cleared his throat.

"Are you Audrey Helmse?" he asked.

"Yes."

"Ma'am, I'm Officer Bridges and this is Officer Vasquez from the Gainesville Police Department."

"Is this about Ethan? He didn't come home."

"May we come in?"

Audrey's hand trembled as she slowly opened the door and led the officers to the kitchen.

Officer Bridges walked with his hands on his belt buckle. He turned slightly to weave his wide shoulders through the kitchen doorway. Officer Vasquez completely disappeared behind his stature as they walked single file, reemerging as she sidestepped and stood in front of the stove. Her long hair pulled back in a tight ponytail, which she slipped through the back of her GPD cap.

"Ms. Helmse, you're going to want to sit down," Officer Bridges said.

"Is this about Ethan? Is he OK? Please, God," she said as she sat down at the kitchen table.

"Ms. Helmse, we're here today because unfortunately we have some bad news. Ethan Warner was killed last night from a stabbing into his abdomen and chest."

"What? No. No you've made a mistake," she cried. "You're wrong. It couldn't have been him. He was with people. What about them?"

"He had identification on him when he was found."

Officer Vasquez grabbed a box of tissues from a table in the living room and handed them over to Audrey.

"Do you have someone you can call that can come stay with you? You shouldn't be alone right now," she said.

Audrey grabbed three tissues from the box, holding them to her eyes and nose.

"Yeah. Yeah, my sister."

"Good. Call her we will stay until she gets here."

Hayden began to cry from the other room.

"Oh God, Hayden. What are we going to do?"

"Does the baby need fed? We can take care of that. Do you use formula?"

"He's breastfed," she said, and blew her nose. "I can't. I don't know what to do. Ethan can't be taken from me."

"Ms. Helmse, we're here for you right now. Is there any pumped?"

"There... there's milk in the fridge."

"Officer Vasquez, please assist Ms Helmse and warm up the baby's food. Ma'am, I'm going to grab the baby. If that's OK with you, of course. Hayden's her name? His name?"

"Yeah, um... his. Hayden is his name. Thank you."

Gwen arrived half an hour later. She embraced Audrey tightly and they cried against each other. She took Hayden, who had fallen asleep after breakfast, from Officer Bridges and placed him in his crib, shutting the door gently behind her. After giving Audrey and Gwen another moment together, Officer Vasquez approached Audrey and offered her a contact card.

"Ms. Helmse, I know this is a very difficult time for you, and there is no easy way to request this, but we need you to identify the body. As a formality. Also, we are actively investigating the circumstances of what happened to Ethan. We need to piece together the events of last night. So sometime in the next couple of days, when you are ready, we would like for you to come to the station and answer some questions for us. Or we can come back here if you would feel more comfortable doing that."

Audrey looked at Officer Vasquez, and rather than responding or grabbing the card, she fell deeper into the arms of Gwen. Gwen reached up herself for the contact information. She looked it over and slipped it into her jacket pocket.

"Thank you," Gwen said.

"Absolutely. We will leave you two alone now," Officer Bridges said.

CHAPTER FORTY-SIX

The gunshots which killed Chelsea Winters and Stanley McGrady reverberated from Fort Wayne, Indiana to the Atlantic and Pacific coasts. Daily news updates from both local and national outlets offered updates and gave opinion pieces on Instant Karma. Vloggers shared their condolences paired with sentimental background music. TMZ asked any celebrity they could wrangle to share their thoughts on the subject. Social media flooded with information and opinions and arguments on the state of the country. How did we get to this point? Who was at fault? What was the final straw?

But the real draw was the death and life of Chelsea Winters herself. Reports aired around the clock at length about her journey from small-town prom queen to national newswoman. Respected amongst her peers. A rising star in the name of journalism. And, of course, how her star trajectory tragically came to an abrupt end at the hands of this mob.

Interviews with friends and family of the deceased shared anecdotes and parting words. Reports leaked days after the incident Netflix quickly bought the rights to produce a ten-episode documentary series. The news machine quickly grew the ability to feed off itself to sustain life. Much in the same way some animal mothers eat their own young in order to survive.

Caitlin first heard about it in a diner booth a little north of Atlanta. After driving aimlessly for an hour or so, they hopped on I75 and traveled north as far as they could before pulling over to eat and refuel. They grabbed breakfast at the attached diner, keeping a low profile.

After the rush of the night before had waned and they traveled through the night with nothing but their thoughts and the clothes on their backs, it was mostly quiet. But while Caitlin, Shane, and Tyler blended in by displaying a nonchalant casual confidence, Jordan became a ghost. Silent. Unemotional. Disjointed.

He didn't sit in the booth so much as crumble. He ordered a ham and cheese omelet, but after eating just over half he began poking and sliding them around with a fork. While the rest of the table refueled and plotted out a plan, he remained detached, until he finally turned his head and looked at Tyler.

"You stabbed him."

"What?" Tyler said, initially unaware Jordan addressed him.

"You stabbed him, and now you're, what, debating on what fucking pancakes to order?"

"I had to."

Caitlin, sitting across from Jordan in the booth, tapped on the table between them and grabbed their attention.

"Shh, it had to be done. You know that." She spoke calmly and slightly above a whisper. "He was undermining the entire mission. He became unhinged. A liability. He attacked Shane. What choice did we have? Who are we to get in the way of progress? Any of us? Whether it's him, or you, or myself. He lost focus of the big picture. Of the message. That is what The Founder is letting us know. If you're not willing to do the work, then you need to just get out of the way. Otherwise, you're no better than the ones we're fighting against."

Jordan stopped looking at his food and stared out the window. Caitlin reached out and touched his hand.

"Look at me," she said. "This movement is growing by the day. And he will go down in history as one of the original members of Instant Karma. But unfortunately, we will lose some people along the way in this fight. You know that as well as I do."

"He might be OK. I haven't been able to check. We don't know for sure," Jordan said.

"We're strong," she continued. "But think of it like a plant. As it grows, you need to prune the dead pieces so that the strong ones can continue to grow."

"I get it. I'm sorry. It's... It's all my fault. I shoulda just had him stay home. None of this would've happened. I pushed him too hard. He would have come around. I know he would've, but I just don't know why he," Jordan sighed deeply and pushed his hair out of his face. "Why he couldn't fucking get it. You know? I'll... I'll be OK. I'm here. You know th-"

"Shut up! Check this out," Tyler said positioning his phone so everyone could see.

"More details from the horrible tragedy in Fort Wayne, Indiana. Reports now coming in that Chelsea's killer is Fort Wayne native, Stanley McGrady. Stanley kidnapped, tortured, and murdered the news anchor after she reported on his violent behavior and the malevolent intentions of the group itself. Instant Karma appear to have been using McGrady's tow truck company as a base of operations for the domestic terrorist acts carried out across the country. No word yet on whether there are more connections between McGrady Towing and Instant Karma. Fox55, the station home to Chelsea, will be holding a candlelight vigil, as they unveil a monument in her memory. For those not in the area, the event will be live streamed so all can watch and pay their respects. Well, I can assure you, I will be watching. And also hugging my family just a little bit tighter."

Caitlin slammed her palm onto the table.

"That's where we're headed. It's manifest fucking destiny. C'mon. We've got to keep moving."

"Can we at least keep moving toward a Walmart or something and get some clothes first?" Shane said. "We're all still wearing matching black. We look like we just finished a fucking heist. Not very low key."

"Yeah. We need some stuff anyway," Caitlin said. "We'll need new phones."

"What?" Jordan said.

"Well, they're definitely trying to track ours by now. They gotta go."

"I need mine," Tyler said. "I can't get hot spot from a damn burner phone."

"Here you kids go," the waitress said. She left to-go boxes and the checks. "Anything else I can do for you folks today?"

"Ah, is there any way I can get a travel cup for my coffee?" Caitlin said.

"Absolutely. I'll even bring you some extra creamers for the road as well."

"That would be so great. Thank you."

As the waitress turned and walked away, Caitlin addressed the group again in a hushed tone.

"OK. Tyler keeps his phone out of necessity. Shane, Jordan give 'em up."

"God dammit. I'm gonna have to put all my passwords in again. I don't even remember most of them. What a pain in the ass," Shane said as he tossed his phone onto the table.

Jordan quietly pulled his phone from his pocket and looked at it one last time. He had multiple missed calls from both his mother and father. A message notification from his mother stated, *"Honey, please give me a call back. We are worried."* He flipped it over screen down and stacked it on top of Shane's.

Caitlin collected the phones, along with hers, and put them all in a to-go container. Shane boxed up the rest of his french toast, as well as Jordan's discarded omelet. Tyler took a big gulp to finish his coffee, and they exited the booth to pay. On their way out, Caitlin threw the container of phones into the metal trash can by the front double doors.

Shane put his arm in front of Jordan and held him back.

"We're gonna need you to get your head on straight. We're moving on up and can't have you second guessing yourself. You hear me?"

"I'll be good, man. I'm good. Don't worry."

CHAPTER FORTY-SEVEN

"Gavin, what do you say about Instant Karma and the attack? Any comment about the allegations claiming you steal the work of your employees as your own? Does this change anything with the Pathfinder deal?"

"My client has no comment other than the contracts signed by each employee clearly state that any software created at our facility or by our employees is credited as 'Banter' software. Any report contrary to that is fal-."

Click

"He's nothing but a conservative Nazi warmonger. He's hellbent on chaos and destruction and would rather watch the whole country burn than promote change through the proper channels. The tried-and-true channels that have kept this country great for over two hundred years. And in this great nation, we use our words and character to set an example. Not spite and violence."

Click

"Managed to get Torwood's own Jade Armstrong to sing Amazing Grace at the memorial. Chelsea Winter's mother mentioned she was a big fan of the singer, and Jade and her team were incredibly touched."

"Who wouldn't be, Keegan? Let's hope she can bring some of those mourners back to Torwood. Give them a taste of a few local restaurants."

"Oh, I agree. Up next, what hot new craze can get you

beach ready by summertime? Here's a hint, it involves leeches, and Hollywood is swearing by it. Stay tuned."

Click

All Seth wanted was to escape it. Instant Karma haunted him. It was as if he remained anonymous to the people, but the universe still refused to let him have a moment rest. For once, Seth would kill to see something about a singing competition or a red-carpet fashion miscue. He clicked off the TV and tossed the remote beside him. He needed some air. His normal safety net of television only made matters worse.

He walked into the corner store and wandered aimlessly looking for something to strike his interest. The store had a faint earthy odor. The fluorescent lights above him hummed and stuttered. He disinterestedly walked past the Lay's and the Pringles and pork rinds. He finally found a bag of Honey BBQ Fritos screaming out to him. He grabbed those and then picked up a Mountain Dew from the cooler.

On his way up to pay, the sign for 2 for $4 all-beef hot dogs lured him in. He felt fairly brave today, and as they rolled over and over atop their metal log treadmill, he decided they might be just what he needed. He fixed up the hot dogs and waited in line to check out.

With nobody behind the counter at that moment, the line had grown five patrons deep. Mr. Petrov, the SwiftShop owner, argued with a man in black slacks and a royal blue fleece pullover while everyone waited.

"This is unacceptable!" Mr Petrov shouted. His bombastic voice, along with his Russian accent, snatched everyone's attention.

"Your rent is extremely past due. There's nothing else I can do."

"My rent is past due? Repairs are past due. I pay nothing."

"You're behind three months. Soon, I will have to get the lawyers involved if I don't receive it. We have been working together for many years, Mr Petrov."

"We don't work together nothing! I pay and pay and pay just to run my business. You do nothing."

"I've tried working with you. I can't make the repairs if the tenants don't pay on the lease."

"Fifteen years I pay! Six months now, roof leak. Drip drip drip. Over in corner. I had to move candy bins away to protect from water."

"Ms Goldsmith from Trash to Treasure next door has no issues."

"Ms Goldsmith has no customers! All day I am busy. People in and out. Always people. You fix roof. You get rent."

"If that's how this is going to go, you can expect notice here soon."

"Good. I call Action News. They serve *you* notice."

Mr Petrov walked back to the cash register, fuming, with a look of surprise smacking him when he saw everyone in line.

"Sorry everyone for wait. Hopefully, you enjoy show, though, yeah?"

As Mr Petrov scanned the Mountain Dew and hot dogs, he looked up at Seth.

"This not meal, is it? You're not teenager. You need nutrients."

"Oh, I'm good. Frito's are corn chips. It's right there in the name."

Mr Petrov laughed, and his face straightened immediately after. A move Seth recognized quite well.

"That guy sucks. Why don't you move somewhere else?"

"Bah. Rent is cheap. Location is good."

"You know," Seth said. "I don't think it's just the leak. I think there's mold in the ceiling too."

"Yes. I'm sure of it. It is sad. Every night I pray. Pray I come in next morning and see that group burn this place to ground.

"Really?"

"That would be something. I would just laugh loudly and warm my hands on the flames."

"Report him. Like you said."

"I bluff. I already called news station. They do nothing. Then I find out Greener Grass Realty is a sponsor for station. It's all backwards."

"That sucks. If there's anything I can do. I will. I've been coming here for a long time."

"Yes, you and girl would always come late night for snacks. I haven't seen her lately."

"Thanks for reminding me. Yeah, girl isn't around anymore."

"Ah, chin up. It will be OK. You see. You are young."

"Not young enough to eat hot dogs and pop, though, huh? Mr Petrov laughed as he bagged the snacks.

"Yes. Exactly!" he said.

"Have a good day," Seth said.

"You too."

Seth walked down to the small neighborhood park to eat his lunch. He also must have had a look on his face that invited questions about his opinions, because in between the hot dogs, someone called out to him.

"Hey, tell me something."

That's surely an intro into an awkward conversation, Seth thought. One he looked around and didn't see possible to escape from.

Two men at a close by table looked over at Seth intently. One older and bald, with a horseshoe of grey hair growth wrapping around the back of his head from ear to ear. The other, Seth guessed perhaps his son, had similar features but with darker hair and a tanner complexion. His hair had only started to recede, but the future looked none too promising for it.

"You think that woman deserved to die?" the older one said.

Straight to it, then, Seth thought before playing dumb.

"What woman?"

"You know. That newswoman. It's all over."

"Oh, I don't know," Seth said.

"Jesus Christ, Dad. Leave him alone," the other said.

"What? I'm just being friendly. You see. My son, the hippie, wants to go to the memorial tomorrow and pay his respects. I say good riddance."

"Of course, I want to pay my respects. She was murdered for telling the truth. Plus, it would be a great place to network and talk about my blog."

"Wrong. She paid the price for always scaring people. She knew what she was doing. She faced consequences. Tell my son she was a horrible lady."

"Dad, I'm not going to debate you on this."

"I don't... I'm not that close to it. Sorry," Seth said.

"OK, Dad. Leave the guy alone. It's time to get you back anyway."

A woman jogging stopped and jumped into the conversation.

"You guys talking about Chelsea Winters? God that was terrible. And then the guy killed himself to get away with it. Coward."

"Thank you!" The younger man said. "The whole movement should be snuffed out one by one and arrested."

"I mean, they're not all bad," Seth said. "They've done a lot of good. You can't hang them on a few people, right?"

"A few?" the woman said. "It's getting out of control. They ought to find and try the leader of theirs, is what they need to do. He shouldn't get away scot-free. He knows what he did."

Seth quietly balled up his garbage and collected it in the plastic SwiftShop bag.

"Bullshit!" the older man declared. "That man is a modern-day hero. They'll write history books about the changes he championed. Make no mistake."

Seth had heard enough. He ejected himself from the conversation and continued to walk around the park and soak in the sunny afternoon. The birds had started to show back up with the warmer weather, and the rain that had come in the last few days had the trees and grass looking exceptionally green and full.

His phone chimed and showed a text from Lauryn.

"Hey call me. I need to talk to you."

Ugh. He'd do that later. He appreciated she didn't immediately shun him after the ordeal, but he couldn't get her terrified face out of his mind. God, it would have been better to not have to think about what she thought of all this. Would be easier at least. As he walked, he replayed in his head over and over the news report. The shame spiral guided his fingers to Dr Englund's phone number. He hit send and asked if there was any room for an emergency session.

Dr. Englund, surprised Seth would request something like that, offered to meet him later that same day due to a cancellation in his schedule.

"Great. Thank you. I'll see you then."

CHAPTER FORTY-EIGHT

"Seth, what brings you here today? It sounded urgent," Dr Englund asked.

"Do you think there are people who don't deserve to be happy?"

"You already know my answer. Everyone deserves to find happiness."

"OK, well I mean, do you think some people are destined to not be happy? I mean, how do you even weigh happiness unless there's also perpetually miserable people to compare to? Like one of those you need sadness to appreciate the good times, but larger scale. Some of us are destined to get stomped repeatedly to let the others fly, correct?"

"I don't quite follow."

"I feel like the universe is pulling me in a million directions, and I don't know what to do."

"That's great, Seth. We can work with that."

Seth's face straightened, and his shoulders sank.

"What do you mean?" he asked.

"Well, it wasn't that long ago you said the universe had left you behind and you had no purpose. Now it's giving you multiple avenues. I'd say that's something," Dr Englund said. His matter-of-fact manner left Seth speechless. The doctor continued. "So, do any of these directions lead somewhere positive?"

"I don't know."

"Ah. There's that *I don't know* again."

"Sorry. OK. I feel like I take a little step forward, finally make some progress, and get my feet pulled right out from under me. Every time I get a little bit closer to the right track... you know." Seth mimed jerking a steering wheel and paired it with an explosion sound.

"So then where are you now, if not on the right track?"

"I told you," Seth said. "I don't know what to do with myself. Nothing I do is right. Every decision I make is the wrong one."

"You mentioned that you and Lauryn had a good conversation. Anything more on that front?"

"We actually, uhh, yeah we actually hung out last night."

"See. That's great!"

"Yeah, but I think I screwed up again. Now I don't know what to do. She messaged me this morning."

"That's good."

"But I don't know how to respond."

"Respond by telling her how you feel. You said the big component of repairing things was opening up and being honest with her. Don't stop now."

"It's not that easy right now."

"So, you'd rather push her away again? Your words. Not mine."

"No. This is different."

"How so?"

"Well, I don't know."

The doctor wrote something down on his pad and flipped back to a previous page.

"Seth, do you think your reaction of shutting people out stems at all from your mother leaving you at such a young age?"

"I... never thought of that." Seth leaned back in the chair, only to shoot forward again. "What the fuck. You just have that in your back pocket this whole time?"

"Seth, you mentioned before that your father dedicated his life to providing for you. That you grew up to feel selfish he didn't have a life of his own."

"Yeah. I remember that."

"Do you think subconsciously you sabotage yourself because deep down you think you don't deserve to be happy?"

Seth heard another explosion, this time in his own head.

"Why do you say that?"

"Let me hear you say it. Out loud. Say 'I deserve to be happy'."

Seth gripped the armrest tightly.

"This is stupid."

"Humor me."

"I deserve to be happy," Seth said in a low droll.

"That was almost convincing," Dr Englund said. "OK, let's do this. Never mind happiness. Maybe that's too much for you right now. Let me hear you say, 'I'm worth being around.'"

"I... huh?"

"You heard me."

Seth rapidly bounced his leg up and down, using the balls of his feet as a springboard.

"This isn't getting us anywhere," Seth said.

"So where is it you want to go?"

"To have some kind of purpose that doesn't hurt everyone!" Seth blurted out. "Whether I know them or not! I realized recently that everyone is worse off because I am around. It's a fact. Whether it's something I said. Or did. Or didn't do. Doesn't matter."

"Oh, Seth. You must know that is far too much pressure to put on yourself."

"It's true. I don't expect you to take me on some 'It's A Wonderful Life' type shit. But it is," Seth said.

Dr Englund set the notepad down on the arm of his chair and folded his hands on his knee.

"It's unfair to both yourself and to Lauryn to clasp on to her as your gauge of success and failure. There is so much more. You've come such a long way. Do you think that's the last hurdle? Because maybe that's an unattainable goal to base success on."

"It isn't just her. I feel like a bunch of stuff blew up in my face all at once. Like a chain reaction."

"Technically speaking, a chain reaction doesn't go off all at once. It's back-to-back, but, you know, semantics."

"For example, Instant Karma. You've heard of it, yes?"

"Of course." Dr Englund gave a quizzical expression. "Are you involved with them?"

"More or less. What is your take on the whole thing?"

"My personal beliefs aren't what we're here to talk about."

"Humor me."

Dr Englund sighed and hesitated before answering.

"I think, like anything else, it is a makeup of the sum of all of its parts. Some good. Some bad. The bad gets the attention because that is what's dangerous to ignore. Just like someone with a mental illness is more than just their illness, but to ignore it is irresponsible and dangerous to the whole person."

"You can never just answer a question, can you?"

"My entire job is to rebuttal any questions thrown my way with the patient looking inward for the answer."

"So just non-stop laying down the Uno Reverse card?"

"Is that what you think?" Dr Englund said smiling.

"Damn, you're good."

"Seth, in all seriousness, you should be careful with latching on to groups such as Instant Karma. They naturally attract stranded people searching for any kind of solace."

"That's funny. Well, it's a little more complicated than that."

"I've seen people look for answers in the wrong forms and it didn't end well for them. If you're searching for peace, some things have an ability to appear like everything is figured out. But they're toxic in the wrong situations. Be careful. Please do not hesitate to call me anytime you feel the same as you did today. That's what I'm here for. Remember, let me be your parachute."

"Thanks, Dr Englund. It's not that big a deal yet. I can jump ship at any time. Thank you for seeing me today. I actually feel much better."

Seth returned straight home after the appointment. His head was clear. He decided he'd make one more video, and then be done. He'd make everything right. He grabbed a bottle of water and took his position.

"I can't put my finger on exactly when we got here. But this can't go on. Not like this. The worst has happened and there's no turning back. We can do remarkable things. We *have* done remarkable things. Made *real* change. But also done real, irreversible damage.

"People have died, and that's on all of us. We own that. This isn't working anymore. We need to transcend. Don't be influenced by some garbage on the internet. I'm not the inspiration you want me to be. I can't. I'd love to, but you need to look inward. I'm no one. No one worth admiring anyway. I don't even know who I am. I've tried being the leader you need me to be. But I can't. Not like this. Not *for* this.

"This isn't even about me. Despite everything, look at what we've done. You've all shown that when we work together, anything is possible. It isn't about a single person. It never has been. A person is fallible. We've seen that. It's the ideas, and the message that we get across that are important. People aren't supposed to be worshiped. It doesn't hold. Times change. Ideals change. Society moves forward, and people once thought of as progressive are looked back on as close-minded and hypocritical. We need to stop doing this to ourselves. Elevate someone into a god-like status and at some point, they will let you down. It never fails. You build anyone up enough and, in time, they'll fly straight into the sun. It's inevitable. Wings melt. Gods fall.

"And they should. No one is better than the rest. That's been the heart of this movement all along. That's why carving monuments and dedicating days to mere mortals has always been problematic. We sin. We're biased. We're impulsive. The pendulum swings the other way bringing an inevitable backlash. Because the majority of us are down in the shit just fighting to survive. So, I say fuck em! Tear them all down. Whether you're building a statue of some supposed war hero or putting a celebrity on a pedestal they don't deserve. Nobody is worthy. Yet we allow it to happen over and over again. That's not new. Nothing I've said this entire time is breaking new ground. It's been going on forever.

"We can't allow ourselves to be taken down by the actions of the individual. Our message should be what lives on. Eventually all of your heroes will reach a status where they either sacrifice themselves, or become sacrificed by the devoted. Words should carry meaning, not the flesh and blood behind them.

"For that reason, I am done. This will be the last video for a while. Maybe forever. We must do better going forward."

CHAPTER FORTY-NINE

Jordan, Shane, Caitlin, and Tyler pulled into a Walmart off I75 North in the middle of Georgia for supplies, and a change of clothes. Keeping things cheap, they stuck to clearance and non-brand clothing.

"Nothing fancy. Pants and shirts," Shane said. "Maybe a jacket or sweatshirt if you can find it cheap."

"I've got blood on my shoes," Tyler said.

"Dammit. OK. Get shoes. Throw those away."

"Fuck. I loved these too. Fuck that dude."

Jordan's eyes shot Tyler daggers, which went unnoticed by him. But not by Caitlin.

"That dude," she emphasized, "will be remembered favorably. In the end, he will be celebrated. Do not be disrespectful. OK. You three meet me back in electronics in twenty minutes."

They picked through what was available, grabbing some seven-dollar graphic tees and store brand jeans.

"Hey, I'm getting these," Jordan said as he pulled a pair of sunglasses from the rack.

When the boys met Caitlin over by the cell phones, she already had some picked out and threw them in the cart. OK, we all set?"

"We need some snacks for this road trip," Tyler said.

"Beef jerky and Twizzlers are a must," Shane agreed.

"Hell yeah," Tyler said.

"Listen!" Caitlin said as she forcibly grabbed the handle of the cart. "This is not a joyride. We are on a mission. It's not a fucking vacation. Stop acting like clowns."

"So… we can't eat?" Jordan said.

Caitlin rolled her eyes and ran her fingers through her short hair.

"OK. We can get some food. But same thing, keep it cheap. So, no beef jerky. We need to use cash when we can. Never know when the cards will start being tracked."

They cashed out and as they walked toward the exit, Jordan stopped.

"Hey, I'll meet you guys in the car. I gotta take a shit."

"OK. Hurry up," Tyler said.

Jordan slipped into the single person bathroom and shut the door, locking the hook and eyehole behind him. He pulled a phone out of his inside coat pocket and turned it on. The colorful Google letters bounced on the screen as the phone loaded. He typed Hayden's birth date into the keypad and the phone finished waking up. He knew what he was about to do was in poor taste, but he needed to talk to her. Needed to know. As shitty as he felt, he had no choice. He scrolled down to Audrey's number and pressed send.

CHAPTER FIFTY

Audrey screamed as the fine hairs on her arms and the back of her neck stood at attention. Her body temperature plummeted to arctic levels. It couldn't be.

Ethan danced across her phone screen in some horrible prank or supernatural summon. Either way, she could not move to answer the call. She stared in paralyzed disbelief until the phone eventually went dark again.

"No. No, no, no," she said, wishing it back.

The phone lit up again displaying the same incoming call. She broke free and swiped her thumb to answer.

"H-hello?" her voice cracked.

"Audrey. It's me."

"Ethan?"

"No. Jordan. I have his phone."

"Jordan? Jordan! Jordan, what the fuck!?" she asked through tears and gasps.

"Audrey, listen to me. I'm sorry. We had to leave."

"Leave where? What the fuck happened? They won't tell me, yet. What happened to Ethan?"

"So, did they get to him? Did he make it?"

"The police came here this morning and said he got stabbed. They want to ask me a bunch of questions, and I just want to know what happened and why nobody will tell me and why I lost him. Why did I lose him?" she said. She bounced between talking and screaming and crying.

"So, is he? Did he..." Jordan said.

Audrey didn't respond, but her breaking on the other end of the line was all the confirmation Jordan needed.

"Audrey I... it wasn't supposed to go this way. I swear. But he will be remembered. We will celebrate him. This is bigger than him. Bigger than all of us. What we are doing is going to change things. It's gonna be huge. People will look back on him and celebrate him. I'll make sure of it."

"What are you eve...? Do you hear yourself? You're fucking delusional. Did you see it? Were you there with him? You were, weren't you? I swear to God, I will kill you. He loved you! And you failed him. How dare you call here? What happened to him, Jordan? To Hayden's father? You know what happened. I know you do. Jordan, where are you?"

"You know I can't tell you that. But I just need to make sure you know that I do love Ethan. When this is all over, his name will be synonymous with progress. I've gotta go."

"Jordan, no. Don't hang up. I need to know. Tell me what happened. Jordan, please. Please! You owe me that. How did it happen? Was it you? Was it one of your fucking group? Was it someone who saw what you were doing and you ran? What!?"

"Goodbye Audrey."

"No. No please talk to me. Jordan."

As the phone cut out, Audrey collapsed onto the floor of the house. She would have screamed again if she were able to breathe. She clung to the phone like she could wring her life back out from it.

Jordan sat down on the toilet behind him and let his head melt into his palms. Finally having the shock fall away and able to catch his breath, he sobbed silently for minutes. They were supposed to do this together. They were a team. It was never supposed to be like this. But he had no choice but to press on in Ethan's name. As hard as it would be. He didn't lie. Ethan's name would be synonymous with Instant Karma. With battling in the trenches. With progress. He'd make sure of it. He owed it to him. Jordan took another second to himself and walked back out.

He powered off the phone and threw it into the trash can of the Men's bathroom.

CHAPTER FIFTY-ONE

Jordan regrouped with the others as they huddled around the car. He wore newly acquired sunglasses and a baseball cap to hide his tired, swollen eyes.

"OK. We ready?" Shane asked.

"Yeah. I'm good. Let's head out," Jordan said.

"You think it's smart to be driving this the entire way up there? I'm sure by now someone has to be looking for it," Tyler asked.

"You know, that's good thinking," Caitlin said.

"Told you he's a genius," Shane said.

"I mean, it's kind of a no brainer, right?" Tyler said.

"Damn, just take the compliment, will you?" Shane said.

They split up and walked up and down the rows of parked cars trying to open doors without success. Finally, Shane pulled the handle of a utility van, and the door popped open with a hefty satisfying click. He called everyone else over to help him.

"Really? The white windowless van?" Jordan said.

"You got anything better?" Shane said.

"I guess not. Pedo van it is. Tyler, you know how to hot wire this?" Jordan asked.

"That's messed up. You asking because I'm the only black guy here?"

"Uh, no. I asked because you're the electrical guy here."

"I'm just fucking with you. Of course, I got this."

Shane unscrewed the license plates from the old car they readied to abandon. Caitlin and Jordan stood watch while Tyler worked his magic. Before long, the van turned over and fired up.

"Damn I'm good," Tyler said to himself as he played a triumphant drum solo on the steering wheel.

They threw the necessary belongings into the back of the van, piled in, and pulled off.

"We'll pull over somewhere soon where we can swap the plates," Caitlin said. "But we need to keep moving. That memorial is tomorrow."

They drove for another hour before finally feeling safe enough to pull over. They parked in an out-of-business Sunoco off the highway, and Shane hopped out and traded the old plates for the new ones.

"Is that even necessary? Those go to another car altogether," Jordan asked.

"Yeah, but when they start looking for this van, they're gonna hopefully keep an eye out for the old plates that will be left here. Different state. Different plates. Should give us a small bit of help."

"Shane, did you grab my charger out of the car before we left?" Tyler asked.

"I thought so. You don't have it?"

"If I had it, I wouldn't have asked you if you grabbed it."

"Whatever, it should be in there somewhere. Look around. I'm in the middle of something."

"Dammit," Tyler said. "I'm running low on battery. Guys help me out."

"What the fuck are you doing on that thing anyway?" Jordan asked.

"I told you. Working. Caitlin check the glove box."

She pulled her feet down from resting on the dash and looked in the glove compartment.

"Oh, shit!" she said.

"You find a charger?"

"Yeah. Here," she said tossing it back at Tyler. "Also, this."

Caitlin removed a black Glock 19 from the glove box and

showed it off to the others. She released the magazine, inspected it, and slid it back in.

"Full clip," she said.

"Beautiful," Shane said. "And we're all set. Let's go."

He fired the van back up and they pulled away, jumping back on the highway.

They drove all day without incident. Clean highway, decent weather, and for the most part, total silence. Dusk crept in to abate the beautiful day, even though the long nonstop driving made time not real. Shane drove as the sun descended behind the mountainous Tennessee skyline. Caitlin rode shotgun fast asleep. Jordan, who sat right behind her, also had been nodding off. Tyler sat alert, locked in on his laptop.

Shane half paid attention to the road and half lost himself in the landscape painted on the horizon.

"I did it!" Tyler screamed.

The van swerved back and forth between lanes before Shane regained control. Jordan and Caitlin both gasped for air after being ripped from their peaceful comfort.

"What the fuck?" Jordan asked smacking Tyler's shoulder. "You're gonna kill us."

"Holy shit! I think we did it!" Tyler said. "Pull over."

"Where? We're on the express way."

"Just pull over!"

"OK!" Shane said, matching his energy.

Shane pulled over to the shoulder and threw the van into park.

"Now what?" Shane said.

"Ok, I think I've got it. It took a lot of digging and working with other people trying to cross reference information."

Tyler's explanation came off more as a verbal train of thought than an answer.

"Tyler," Shane said.

"We took some shit from the FBI, but they surprisingly weren't even looking that hard. I heard we had some people on the inside, so maybe that's it. But then, the info we did get-"

"Tyler," Jordan said. "What the hell did we take from the FBI?"

"What? No, not we," Tyler said making a big circular motion between the four of them. "Like, we." He waved his hand over the computer and his own chest. "But I triple checked and I… I don't think we made a mistake!"

"Tyler, what the fuck are you talking about!?" Caitlin asked.

"We need to make a detour," he said.

CHAPTER FIFTY-TWO

Seth tried to answer the pounding door, but it shoved open as soon as he turned the knob.

"If you're gonna keep coming in this way, we're gonna have to get you a catchphrase or something," Seth said.

"What the hell was that?" Craig said.

"That's horrible. We'll work on it."

"I'm serious. You can't even come out and say how vile of an action murder is?"

"What? Really? I did! Why are we yelling? I said it was irredeemable. I condemned the whole thing. Just, you know, without shitting on the *entire* thing."

"No, you sidestepped the fucking problem," Craig said.

"I don't think so. Look, dude, there's no instruction manual for this. No self-help book for what to do if you started a God damned revolution."

"You tackle it head on."

Seth threw his hands up in the air.

"Look, I didn't ask for this!" Seth said. "Any of it. I was trying to help myself. Sort out my own shit. How was I supposed to know that so many people were just as fucked up as I am? If you think this is so easy, you do it. You put on the mask and make the video," Seth said.

He extended the mask out to Craig. Not really offering. More of a demand. A recruitment.

"You can't walk away from this. At this point, there's no

more acting like you can't control it. That was your chance, and it should have been easy. You're actively manipulating it, now. You don't just speak to the good guys. You get to everyone. That's how all this shit works. So, own your shit," Craig said.

He turned to head out, but turned back around and addressed Seth again. "You know what's really messed up? You really can't go all in on anything. You tiptoe around it all. You don't want to have people look up to you, but their admiration boosts your ego. You act like no one wants to get to know you, but you don't let anybody get close enough to do so anyway. You push everyone away, but you don't want to be alone."

Craig ran his hands through his beard a couple of times while he compiled his next words.

"Do you realize the only time you've had an actual conversation with me is when you were drunk that night at Kasady's?" Craig said. "Of all the times we've talked and hung out. That is the only time you've actually been open and honest without being backed into a corner or me ripping it out of you. Sure, you act like you're getting shit out. But it's all the same. Just fucking hiding behind something. And for what? Who is this even for? Because the way I see it, you still wallow in your own pity. So, it isn't for you. And you can separate yourself from the violence, and the attacks, but you still take pride in the whole God dammed thing. I can see it in your face. Not enough for everyone to know that it's you, of course. You want to be more than a man? Bigger than one person can be? Let the people decide. Put a stop to it. Like, really speak out against it. Because I'm sorry it went sour, dude, but the whole thing is fucked now."

"Oh, so I wallow? You know I never asked you to come over so much. You're just always around. Why? You just sort of appeared. I was doing fine."

"Fine?! Oh bullshit. You were spiraling. You gonna push me away now, too? You think I didn't notice you avoiding me for weeks when I first moved in here? We live down the hall from each other."

"Yeah, well why don't you just get the hell out and head back down the hall then? I don't need your help," Seth said.

"Don't be like this, Seth. Really."

"I don't need your fucking pity either. Is that what this is? Help the broken sad man?"

"That's what it sure feels like sometimes. Holding your hand all the time. Trying to be there for you. People don't leave just you, man. You claim to be so alone, but you're the one pushing every God damn person away. But newsflash, asshole! For some reason people like being around you! So, what do you want? What are you so angry at the world for? Listen, you left a job that you hated, and your girlfriend dumped you. It happens to everyone at some point. Jesus Christ. But what you're doing now is fucking dangerous. You want me to just go? Fine. I'm out. Text me when you realize you're acting like a prick."

Craig left, using his stocky stature to slam the door behind him extra hard upon exit.

"I'm a prick?" Seth yelled. "You marched down here just to yell at me. We were supposed to go see a movie!"

He stared angrily at the door afterward as if there were someone else in the apartment to put on a show for. But there was no one. Once again, it was him and the truths that whisper in the dark corners of solitude. And in a flash, the panicked realization set in. How had he cast out the only person there for him when no one else had been? He unplugged his phone and slipped it into his back pocket, before walking into the kitchen. He would let Craig cool down, and apologize. Then he would fix everything.

While he rehearsed in his head exactly what to say, a gentle tap at the door came from the hall. Three distinct rapid knocks, not with excessive might, but more of a calm reluctance.

Thank God, Seth thought to himself. *Maybe Craig will make this easy on me.*

He turned the knob and swiftly pulled it toward him, before standing stunned. At his door was a small, skinny, teenage boy with dark shaggy hair, and a larger athletic guy with a short fade. They both stood wide eyed as if they were as surprised as Seth that someone unrecognizable stood on the other side of the threshold. Their gaze shifted down toward the mask still held tightly in Seth's hand.

"Holy shit. It's really you." the muscular one said.

CHAPTER FIFTY-THREE

Before Seth had a chance to respond, they forced themselves into the apartment. His attempt to block them from entering proved futile as he was knocked back onto the floor, crashing against the wall. The door thudded upon impact. As it swung back the smaller intruder gave it a good shove to close it behind him. Seth wrestled as best he could to climb back to his feet and regain his balance, but they held him down. His pleas for help instantly suppressed by the washrag one pulled from his jeans pocket and shoved into Seth's mouth. They flipped Seth over onto his stomach. He thrashed, but quickly lost control of both wrists as they were held behind him, and a knee pressed down on his back.

Shane looked up at Jordan.

"You got the rope?" he asked.

Jordan repeatedly slapped the pockets of his pants and jacket.

"Shit, I must have left it in the van."

"God dammit, well do something."

Jordan frantically looked for something to restrain Seth. From the counter, he grabbed a black coffee mug displaying a yellow smiley face. A small amount of coffee with a few loose grounds floated aimlessly inside.

"Jordan!"

As if that were the trigger pull he waited for, Jordan swung the mug and collided against Seth's head. The mug fractured into chunks and Seth's muffled screams amplified. The side of his head bled, sprinkled with shards of ceramic fixed to his ear and scalp. Jordan held nothing but the handle, with the rest lying in fragments on the carpet. Blood splashed across the yellow smiley face as coffee soaked into the carpet at their feet.

"What the fuck was that?" Shane asked.

"I thought it would knock him out."

"Why would you think that?"

"That's what they do in the movies," Jordan said.

He looked around again. He grabbed a phone charger from the wall outlet nearby and used it to tie Seth's hands behind his back.

"That should hold. OK put him in the chair," Jordan said to Shane.

With Seth in the chair still trying to escape, Shane and Jordan collectively shoved him. Seth fell into the chair, sending the recliner rocking backward on its back two feet, before gaining its balance.

"Shh," Jordan hushed him over and over. "Listen, listen, listen. We heard you. We solved your puzzle. You're an inspiration! We are… disciples of yours. We understand what you're asking from us. It's powerful. And brave. We get you need to struggle through this, but we don't want to hurt you too much. We just need you to come with us. This is going to be huge. It's all for effect, but we aren't even recording this part. So, you can either walk out with us, or my friend here can carry you out. I'd prefer the option that doesn't attract so much attention."

Seth shot his eyes from Jordan, back to Shane, and then down. He nodded and his whole body dropped and sank further into the chair. Shane and Jordan picked him back up to his feet.

"Good idea," Shane said. "Now we aren't going to untie you, but if you promise not to freak out, we will pull the rag from your mouth."

Seth nodded again, and Shane removed the rag.

"What do you want from me?" Seth asked.

"What do you mean?" Jordan said. "We're here to answer your call."

They walked down the hall, and down the back stairwell Seth knew all too well. In the alley exiting the side door of the apartment complex, Caitlin and Tyler waited, masked up and ready to open the back of the van door. They tossed Seth inside, slammed it shut, and drove away.

Seth laid on his back on the metal floor. Something sharp dug into his backside as he used any remaining energy to sit up. He tried to shift and slide away from it, when he realized it wasn't from the van. It was in his pocket. His phone. He still had it in his back pocket. He sat motionless and faced silently forward, making sure not to attract attention. He pulled the phone out, gripping it as best he could between his index and thumb. With his phone in hand, he slid back to the corner of the van.

"What are you doing?" Tyler asked him.

Seth froze.

"I thought it would be OK if I sat up, no?" he said.

"Of course," Tyler said. He stared at him; his gaze unwavering as Seth sat with his legs crossed.

He'd been caught. He took a deep breath and sat exposed. The phone pinched behind his back by his tied-up hands.

"I just can't. I mean... wow," Tyler said. "I can't believe it's really you. Sitting right here in this van with us. You're a fucking rock star. Everything you've built. Seth, right? Can I call you Seth? Or is it 'Sir', or 'The Founder'? I can't believe you're here with us. You've changed people. You've changed the world. And we figured out your message. We followed your breadcrumbs. We understand what we need to do!"

"Seth is fine," is all that he could muster to reply. "What do you mean followed my breadcrumbs?"

"I mean, it took some digging, of course. But all the videos were uploaded from the same IP address. It was only a matter of time before we picked up on that hint. From there it was simply pulling a bit more information to find the rest. It worked. You got strangers from all over working together on this common goal, just like you wanted."

Seth's hands shook violently as he tried not to drop the phone onto the metal van floor. He prayed that today of all days wasn't when somebody decided to reach out to him. Now was the time to rely on muscle memory. Who was in his phone? Who had he last texted? Or called? Who was on speed dial? He stared at this thing most of the day. Surely, he could remember where a few buttons were.

He successfully unlocked the screen easily enough with his thumb, and from what he could recall hopefully guided his selections to the phone, then the keypad, then held on the 1. As the phone softly vibrated in recognition, the van wheel below him bounced off of a pothole, upending Seth. The phone knocked loose from his pinched fingertips.

"Oh, man! You OK back there?" Caitlin hollered back to Seth who, without being able to catch his fall, laid on his chest, his hands behind his back. One leg extended on the floor, and another leaned against the wall.

Seth darted his eyes around the back of the van and searched frenziedly for the phone which dislodged from his grip. He spotted it, face down still nestled in the corner. He scooted back and on top of the phone, covering it with his leg.

He casually looked back behind him as he flipped the phone over to show the face, which had not yet gone back to black. It never dialed. It was his text message screen showing.

Not even close, he thought to himself.

He looked back up to the group that took him. The girl drove. The one who tied him up and bludgeoned him rode in the passenger seat. The bench row behind them sat the other apartment intruder, who was preparing something inside of a gym bag with another guy. Seth couldn't see inside the bag, but he didn't feel good about it.

With no one paying attention to him, he wanted desperately to call Lauryn. But if this headed how he imagined, he didn't want her to have to hear his demise. Why would he put that on her? Would Craig even answer? He was undoubtedly still in his apartment pissed off. Hopefully, he would pick up expecting to hear an apology. And fuck, if he picked up Seth would owe his life to him. Literally.

He clicked on the text string with Craig and hit the phone icon from there to call out. He took a deep breath, and looked ahead again at his kidnappers. His followers. His disciples. His potential murderers? It was odd how calm he was right now. Somewhere between disbelief and acceptance. Maybe a slight concussion. Of course, this was how it would end. How else could it?

"What?" was how the phone was answered.

"Stop. Listen," Seth said aloud looking forward, resulting in all of them to look back at him. "If this van is taking us to our destiny. Hopefully, you four prepared well."

"Se-" Craig said before getting interrupted.

"Just listen," Seth said again. "Where is this happening? I assume you have a plan."

"Oh, we're prepared. It'll be glorious. You'll be rightfully honored. That news bitch deserves none of the accolades. You will get your due," Shane said.

"We're headed to the memorial? In a work van?" Seth asked clearly. He annunciated each word carefully.

"I hope you understand the way we're traveling. It's all for show," Caitlin said. "To fully make your point, you need the whole treatment. People think of you as the second coming of Jesus. And this is part of the trials."

"Is it just the four of you?"

Seth looked back at the phone. Nothing. No call ongoing. No connection. A home screen. This was all for nothing.

"We heard loud and clear," Caitlin said. "First you suffer. Then you die. Then they listen. Right? Your heroes either sacrifice themselves or get sacrificed by the devoted."

Seth laid down and stared at the ceiling until the van slowed to a crawl. Through the front windshield, the only window that showed Seth the outside world still existed, dimly lit overhead streetlamps guided them down the desolate roadway. Rows of trucking docks and giant metal warehouse doors extended as far out as he could see. They rolled by slowly, as Caitlin looked out the window searching.

"Should be this one," Tyler said, breaking the long-standing silence.

From the warehouse overhead dock door, they pulled off a keyed lock which had already been cut in preparation. The giant door slid upward in a metallic clanging rattle. Inside was wide-open warehouse space, aside from some manufacturing equipment and random boxes. Some of them contained chewed out holes leading way to piles of the discarded cardboard shreds in the corners of the room. No windows on the walls. The only light shambled in from the exterior lights peeking through the double side doors and the giant hole where the overhead door would close. Between exposed rafters, sparse overhead light gave a dull amber hue after Jordan flicked on the light switch attached to the wall. Tyler grabbed a chair from against the wall and slid it to the middle of the open room.

Alone, in the back of the van, Seth used his feet to slide his phone across the floor under the bench seat of the van.

"OK, you guys know what to do," Caitlin said.

They pulled Seth from the back of the van. He had no fight left in him. Somehow, he accepted his fate. Is this what he deserved? After the harm he caused. People killed in his name. They sat him down in the chair and bound his hands and feet.

Tyler and Caitlin jumped back into the van and drove off, leaving Jordan and Shane to deal with Seth.

CHAPTER FIFTY-FOUR

It took no time at all to construct the Chelsea Winters Memorial Garden. The recently vacant plot of land right in downtown Fort Wayne was quickly landscaped and renamed Oakshade Park. The walking path weaved through perfectly placed trees and two separate ponds filled with koi. It all led to the centerpiece. A thick flower bed surrounding a commemorative memorial plaque which would stand in remembrance of Chelsea Winters. The hero. The angel. The prophet.

The quick turnaround left little room for clean up, so as the media stayed fixed to the ceremony, just out of frame laid the landscaping tools and construction equipment still needing collected.

To raise money for the fresh oasis, tax dollars along with charitable donations paid for the lot of it. No expense spared. The mayor assumed even after tonight, this would evolve into quite the tourist destination for the area and bring in a good revenue stream. Who knew what the future held for this moment in journalism history.

Equal amounts of public monetary donations piled in as toxic emails from those against it. Tonight would be the candlelight vigil and the unveiling of the memorial plaque. People showed up by the dozens and prayed and sang. They left poems and teddy bears and flowers and wreathes at the base of the, still covered, shrine. Handwritten notes flooded the base about how much Chelsea meant to them and how she was an inspiration to women all over the world. That all took place inside the gate. The volume of the songs being sung grew increasingly louder to drown out the screaming of the protesters right outside the barricades. Beyond the gates, Instant Karma showed up in droves.

After seemingly going dark for weeks, the death of Chelsea Winters brought Instant Karma back into the forefront. They protested the media outlets. They flooded the message boards. Instant Karma would make their presence known at the vigil. This was their moment. They recorded their own reaction videos to the announcement of the memorial and candlelight vigil. National news heavily covered the event. Let them think they have their moment. All they did was offer a reason to bring Instant Karma together en masse.

Protesters peppered themselves along the outskirts of the garden perimeter. Masked up. Letting their anger be known. They wanted zero part in honoring this woman. Their signs called out the hypocrisy of honoring Chelsea in the first place. They called her manipulative. They called her a fearmonger. They called her the Antichrist.

The cushion between the service and the protests was much of the fleet of the Fort Wayne Police Department. They kept the protesters at bay as they screamed and chanted and raised their signs to make their discontent known. At 8:00 PM sharp, as the sun began to set, Fort Wayne's decorated mayor took the stage. Flickering candles lit the shrine in a glowing golden embrace. People held each other and wept. More were in attendance than the station expected. The mayor stepped up to the covered memorial with his microphone.

"Ladies and gentlemen, good evening. We gather tonight to pay our respects to Chelsea Winters. A rising star in our community, and a shining light for everyone that had the opportunity to chat with her. Please join me in celebrating the life of this incredible woman. As we gather tonight in remembrance of our own Chelsea Winters, who was brutally-"

He choked to a stop as his voice cracked and he regained composure.

"Who was brutally murdered at the hands of Instant Karma. Chelsea sought to make sure that everyone knew the truth. Her integrity and resourcefulness will live on in the hearts and minds of us all. Please lower our heads as we take a moment of silence for our beloved hero."

Mayor Christopher Best pulled back the cover to show off the shrine to the world. The square pillar base adorned with carefully placed river stones met a marble slab, engraved with an intricate floral pattern border and a passage reading,

"Your life was a blessing, your memory a treasure.
You are loved beyond words, and missed beyond measure.
In Memory of Chelsea Winters
Gone Far Too Soon"

The crowd fell still and silent as everyone lowered their heads. Not a word could be heard other than a few sobs and whimpers amongst the crowd.

Just beyond the barricades, however, the protesters grew louder. They knew they spoke on behalf of Instant Karma everywhere. They began shaking the metal gates. They screamed at the police, making it known they were satiated by the entire ordeal. They made a concerted point not to attack the police but grew pointed. They threatened to storm inside the service and poked and prodded and instigated just enough. During the moment of silence, when they had the full attention of the entire police force, Instant Karma dug at the dirt beneath their feet and launched it. Chunks of sod and small stones sailed over the heads of the Fort Wayne Police, into the garden. Pieces traveled far enough to hit the mourners inside.

"OK, that will do it," one officer said.

"Yup," said another. "Time to shut it down."

As they began detaining protesters. The unrest grew.

"We have a right to protest!"

"You don't have a right to disturb the peace and assault the people in mourning. Get on your knees."

They rounded up many of the protesters, going down the line and securing their wrists behind their backs, then flipping the masks off their faces. As seamless as it was unsettling the protesters all cooperated fully. Equally unsettling, all of the members not only had their faces painted mimicking the mask overtop, but the majority of them seemed to be smiling as the whole operation progressed.

After the plaque introduction, music began to play. All eyes were on Jade Armstrong as she walked on the stage and hit her mark. The spotlight focused on her. As Jade hit the long "A" to begin Amazing Grace, she cut out, interrupted by a woman with a megaphone.

"We are here to honor someone today!" Caitlin said. Her voice boomed out into the crowd. "But I'm afraid you've been mourning the wrong person. I present to you the one who brought us all together. He keeps saying that our mission is bigger than one person, but you don't listen. You cry for this bitch like she's some sort of icon, but what did she do other than promote fear and division? She fanned the flames and spread smoke over your eyes. The Founder warned us about idolizing the flawed, but nobody listened. So, he has taken it upon himself to shed his humanity.

"He says we must transcend! He says if this is what it takes to finally get his message through, then so be it. Making the ultimate sacrifice in the name of the cause. He will live on! He will be here through his message alone. He knows. He's repeated it time and time again. The human skin is nothing to be put on a pedestal. So, tear them down. This whole thing is a joke!" Caitlin turned and spit toward the shrine. "It does nothing but make you feel better. We have lost people, too. People a hell of a lot better than her. True warriors. Remember, we are one voice! And we do not need you!"

As she finished her speech, she pulled white costume makeup from her jacket pocket, and smeared it across her face, except for around her mouth. With her teeth, she ripped open a fake blood pack and pooled it on her eyelids, until it ran down each cheek like bloody tears. Around the ceremony, pockets of mourners pulled Instant Karma masks from their jackets and pulled them over their faces. They grabbed the discarded tools from Oakshade Park's construction, along with additional provisions saved and overlooked.

Explosions of glass and fire burst upon impact of the memorial. The flowers and poems left before it quickly melted and burned away. Caitlin chuckled as the bystanders ran immediately following the explosions. Scared to death, but in no danger. Instant Karma were not murderers, she thought, but merely the scale balancers society needed. Whether they wanted to realize it or not. The blind could run if they wanted. The strong would fight the wars for the weak. They always have.

She ran to Tyler, who continued to work setting up the projector. The screen, already provided by the ceremony, still displayed a slide show of Chelsea's pictures. Both taken from her personal social media pages, as well as publicity photographs from the news station. The screen had been knocked crooked, but remained in operation.

"What the hell is taking so long? Your cue was supposed to be the end of my speech."

"Just give me a minute. I'm working with garbage here. There! Got it," Tyler said.

Chelsea Winter's photo slide show cut out and a live feed to a warehouse took its place. A man with his face covered by an Instant Karma mask sat helplessly in a metal folding chair. He barely moved. His wrists were bound, and a noose tied snugly around his neck. Tyler sent the go-ahead message to Shane and Jordan, before he and Caitlin watched with heart-pounding anticipation. Nothing happened. Caitlin looked on in confusion that Seth still sat, almost at peace, even after the cue was given. What the fuck were they doing?

"Did it go through?" She said.

"I sent it."

"Send it again. I knew I was gonna regret not doing everything myself."

"Hey, fuck you," Tyler said.

He sent another message, more urgent this time. Caitlin turned and ran away.

"Where are you going?" Tyler yelled.

"To go see what the holdup is," she said. "You handle shit here."

Instant Karma took turns with sledgehammers and pickaxes swinging cracks at the memorial plaque. The first few did little to the structure, but as the swings continued to connect, bits of stone and marble chipped away. Before long, large chunks flew airborne and landed haphazardly around. The vigil participants who ran at the sight of danger fortuitously slowed the remaining police from rushing in. The fires which started at the memorial base had traveled throughout the grass and swallowed up the trees scattered around the garden. Glass shards, stone pieces, and discarded skull masks laid littered throughout the area. The police officers, whose numbers whittled down after many left to take in the exterior protesters, finally made their way to the bedlam.

"Put the weapons down, or we will shoot!"

Officers approached and put a stop to the pandemonium, as futile as the effort was. The garden burned. The shrine laid in crumbles.

Tyler, who had gone to the stage and attempted to fix the projector screen, stopped and took cover behind the podium at the sight of the incoming police. When it felt safe, he darted to the projector itself, which had his phone plugged in feeding the video. Midway, he let out a painful cry and toppled to the ground. His body seized and fell immobile as the cop who tased him approached.

"Do not resist us! It's in your best interest," the officer warned him.

He laid face down as the handcuffs closed tightly, pinching his wrists. The officer picked up Tyler's phone and watched for a few seconds before rolling Tyler over with his boot.

"Where is this?"

CHAPTER FIFTY-FIVE

Because of how proud they were for deciphering the riddle Seth didn't know he sent out, they talked openly in front of him. Seth sat bound as a fly on the wall as they reviewed the agenda. Shane and Jordan periodically looked his way as if eerily seeking some kind of approval. Shane was to lift him off the chair by the neck. Jordan was to shoot him as he struggled. That was the plan. That was the video. You struggle until you die. Then you're free. Then they care what you have to say.

As Seth sat nervously in the chair, the rope dug into his throat under the jaw. The fibers rubbed taught against his skin, allowing few options for escape. Above him, the rope draped over the rafter, ready to be pulled from the other end. Seth knew he was going to die here. Alone. Despite everything. All the videos, and supporters, and followers. He would die, anonymously, with no one to mourn him.

"Your message will live on forever. Just like you wanted," Shane said.

"Listen, that isn't what this is about. No one else has to die," Seth said.

"You're testing us. It's not going to work. We are loyal. You don't have to worry."

"I'm worried about fucking dying!" Seth said. "That's what this is. It's murder."

Shane stopped what he was doing and looked at Seth.

"You don't have to worry about me, sir."

"God dammit. You're fucking with me, right? These aren't some Tyler Durden mind games. Why are you acting like that? Talk to me like a God damned human being!"

Shane smiled and walked away, securing the rope to a fire extinguisher bracket on the wall.

Seth turned his attention to the other guy in the room with them, who did not seem as sure handed. Jordan paced nervously around the warehouse floor. He mumbled something to himself, stopped, shook his head in disgust, and began reciting again.

"Hey, Jordan is it? Come here. I need to talk to you."

"Yes, sir."

"Jordan, you don't have to do this. Let me go. In what world do you think this is what I wanted? This is insane."

"I have to do this. Everything will make sense after we do this. Can't you see? It's all been building to this."

"No. Jordan!"

"It's almost time," Shane said as he looked at his phone. "Masks on."

"You too, sir," he said as he walked up and slipped the mask over Seth's face.

Jordan walked over to the tripod and started the video feed. He pulled Shane aside and leaned in, talking just above a whisper.

"Do I need to shoot him? Wouldn't the hanging get the job done? Seems a little much, now that I think about it."

"There's no struggle if we just kick the chair out from under him. It will break his neck. He may die too quickly."

"So, lift him up. Keep him dangling."

"That takes too long. We talked about this. It's all part of the plan. Jordan, look at me, man. You got this. It's just pre-game jitters. Deep breaths, bud. We all have our parts to play."

Shane put his hands on Jordan's shoulders for reassurance, then walked over to Seth.

"You know, people started to believe you were abandoning us. Idiots. I can tell you we never faltered. We read through the lines. You needed to be sure we could continue without your guidance."

"No, no, no," Seth said. "Listen to me. It is not something you need to read between the lines about. I'm talking to you. Right now. This is not a test. It is not a challenge. We can stop now. It's over. Before it's too late."

Jordan stopped what he was doing and looked up at Seth.

"We can't stop now. We've gone so far. All of this, we've done with you. *For* you. We have already sacrificed so much to get here." Jordan took the barrel of the gun and moved Seth's chin up and looked him in his painted red eyes. "We've lost good people along the way. You can't tell me it all was for nothing."

Shane laughed. "Jordan, he is testing your loyalty, man. This is all premeditated. It's all going according to plan. Don't worry. Tyler is going to give the cue here any minute. Get in position."

Shane's phone chimed and he nodded toward Jordan, who still attempted to talk to Seth.

"No. Wait a second. I don't think it is going according to plan." Jordan's nervous demeanor melted away into disgust. "It can't be over. You get that right? Do you know how much I've sacrificed?! What I've had to do to get here!? You telling me it was all for nothing?"

"Not for nothing!" Seth said. "At some point it has to stop spiraling though."

"Spiraling?" Shane said. "Sir, I don't think you even understand what we've accomplished tonight."

He showed Seth the status of the Chelsea Winters Memorial. The plaque being smashed by hammers. The trees and garden on fire. Police fighting with the Instant Karma members.

"Beautiful, isn't it?" Shane said. "It's time."

"I'm sorry. I'm sorry if I led you astray. It was never supposed to be like this. I'm sorry if you felt abandoned. I'm sorry but this is not what needs to happen. This is not going to help anything. No one else has to die."

Jordan took a deep breath, swallowed hard, and exhaled

slowly. He nodded at Shane.

"Wait a se-" Seth began before being cut off by the sudden inability to speak. His body ascended straight upward off the chair. With his hands still bound together, he clawed at the rope, but only managed to dig his nails into his skin. He kicked and kicked but got nowhere. He tried to reach the back of the chair with the tip of his swinging foot for support, but only kicked it over. His eyes and tongue swelled. His energy to fight slowly drained. Seth's peripheral closed smaller and smaller before him. He had little choice but to slowly lose consciousness and listen to Jordan address the world.

"A person is fallible. It's the ideas and the message that are important. We need to transcend, and the words will carry meaning. The flesh and blood behind them mean nothing. He says in this form he can't be the leader that we need. This man before you, our founder, is making the ultimate sacrifice. As our crusade carries on without him, you'll see it's the message and beliefs that will live on. One day you will learn to open your eyes and your ears. See and listen to us as we say… what the fuck?!"

Like an anchor dropping into the ocean, Seth plummeted back first onto the tipped over chair below him. A sharp pain shot through his midsection. The wind was knocked out of him like his soul escaping his body. As he cried out in pain, Jordan cried out in confusion.

"Who the fuck are you?" Jordan yelled.

Seth's throat remained imprinted and burned from the noose, but it no longer was trying to kill him. He winced as he rolled over to see Shane wrestling on the floor with a chubby man, whose beard could not be contained by the white skull mask covering his face.

"Craig?! Fuck yeah! How?"

Seth successfully kicked his feet free and vaulted up.

Jordan held the Glock in two hands. With one eye closed and both index fingers on the trigger, he aimed shakily at the two grappling on the floor. Seth, with his wrists still tied together, impulsively grabbed him, and wrestled the gun away. They both fell to the ground, and the gun slid across the concrete floor until it met with the wall. They darted to the pistol. Jordan reached it first, snatching the weapon up and whirling around. As he turned to point the gun at Seth, it trembled in his hands.

The warehouse doors flew open as Lauryn, also donning a plastic skull mask, rolled across the floor followed closely by Caitlin storming in behind her.

"I saw the fat fuck sneak in. I figured this bitch would want to join too. Who the fuck are you two and why are you ruining this? If you wanted to join, you're finding a weird way to do it."

Lauryn stood up and before Caitlin could ask what she wanted, Lauryn rammed her forehead into the bridge of Caitlin's nose, busting it open. Real blood ran down blending in with the fake blood and white paint already covering her face. Caitlin reeled back as Lauryn hit her twice more, this time with her fists. Caitlin lunged toward Lauryn and grabbed the back of her head. She slammed Lauryn's face into the cement floor, and Lauryn let out a wounded yell. Caitlin lifted her by her thick hair and slammed her face again. Seth sprinted over and lowered his shoulder into Caitlin, tackling her.

Seth turned to help Lauryn, but his entire body wrenched backward as Shane yanked the noose still tied around Seth's neck. He choked and once again struggled to slip his fingers between the rope and his skin. He was dragged on his back across the floor as Shane reeled Seth in toward him. Craig attacked Shane again, and the noose's grip gave way once more while they traded blows.

Lauryn ran to Seth and loosened the rope around his neck. As she slipped it over his head, he drew in as much air at once as possible. They paused, and silently looked at each other for a split second before she moved to free his wrists. The mask Lauryn wore was cracked above the eye, and Seth could see the blood pooling up as it squeezed between her face and the cheap plastic.

As she reached up to remove the mask entirely, everyone froze to the echoing boom of the gun firing. The bullet drilled into the wall and buried itself in the cement behind them. Seth wasn't sure if it was a warning shot or a missed shot. He wasn't sure if Jordan even knew.

"Stop it! You two! Over there into the corner," he said pointing to Craig and Lauryn. "It wasn't supposed to go down this way. This is a ceremony. You guys ruined it."

"Whoa, whoa, whoa! Let them go. They aren't a part of this," Seth said.

"Sure they are. Apparently, they want to sacrifice themselves along with The Founder. This is gonna be great! You will be remembered as martyrs for the movement! Despite what happened here tonight. Shed the flesh and blood and live on through your brothers and sisters as well as our message," Caitlin said.

"Jordan. Set them free," Shane said.

"They can't just leave."

"Right, they can't leave. Set them free from this world. Every sacrifice for Instant Karma makes our whole mission that much stronger. It resonates deep with those still on the front lines."

Seth interjected, "Jordan, stop. Listen to me. Don't do this. I get it. I was in a bad place. Instant Karma helped me just as much as it helped all of you. That feeling of support and encouragement got me through when nothing else could."

He slowly inched forward toward Jordan. He crept one hand up in an attempt to lower the gun pointed at him. With the other, he pulled off the mask he had worn since seated in a chair with a rope around his neck.

"Jordan, look at me. I'm not a figure. I'm not a prophet. I'm scared, and I want to go home. We can stop this, now. The police are on their way. You can hear the sirens. Can't you?"

Jordan perked up upon the sudden realization of the sirens. Seth couldn't see his facial expressions hidden behind the mask, but his whole body nervously twitched and he ran his hands through his hair.

"If you pull that trigger, there's no going back," Seth said.

Jordan mumbled, "There's already no going back."

The sirens grew louder and louder as the police encroached

on their position.

"The sacrifices must be made now," Caitlin said. "It's how we expand. How we show the world Instant Karma is committed to our word. That we stand by our statement that we are all one and nobody is above the cause."

"That's not true. This isn't how things were supposed to go," Seth said.

"It's all I've got!" Jordan screamed as he shifted the pistol from the others up to his own temple. "I'm nothing without it!"

"That's not true. Look at me. I see you. I get you. I've felt like there was no place for me in this world. It's not true. Don't do this!"

The side doors boomed and swung open as police swarmed in with guns drawn.

"Everyone get on the ground!" they yelled.

"I am Instant Karma!" Jordan screamed.

The shot rang out and Jordan twisted and fell limply to the ground.

"No!" Seth called out. "God dammit!"

Seth's ears rang in a high-pitched squeal.

"I said everyone get on the ground. Hands behind your back!" The officer said again.

Shane, Craig, and Lauryn all complied. Seth's stare stayed fixed to Jordan's still body on the ground as he dropped to his knees before putting his hands behind his head and lowering the rest of the way. Caitlin spotted the loose gun lying next to Jordan and sprinted for it, quickly getting shot by a taser and restrained by the officers.

Seth laid on the ground with his forehead resting on the cold concrete floor. His ears still rang, but he heard the muffled sound of Jordan crying in agony next to him. He looked up at the sound, then over to his friends being picked up and led outside by the officers. He closed his eyes and exhaled. Despite everything, he couldn't stop a relieved smile from growing across his face.

"Stop moving," the officer said to Seth as they restrained him. "If you don't hold still, we will use force."

"Yeah, yeah," Seth said. "I'm sorry."

One officer used her boot to slide the gun a safe distance away. Another rolled Jordan over onto his stomach and removed his mask. His shoulder was soaked in blood. Jordan wailed as the officer positioned his wrists behind his back to apply the handcuffs.

"Do you have any other weapons on you? What am I going to find?" The officer asked while they patted him down.

"Noth... nothing," Jordan stammered.

"C'mon let's get you up. We'll get you stitched up before taking you in. We arrested a lot of you fucks tonight, so we may have to ask you all some questions right outside. That work for you?"

Jordan bellowed in pain again as they lifted him to his feet.

They all were taken out and put into separate squad cars while the police sorted out what transpired. As Seth sat alone in the back seat, it didn't feel all that different from sitting alone in his apartment. Just him and his thoughts. The main difference was realizing he caused Craig and Lauryn to fall in danger. But they were here. Here for him. As dumb and selfish as it sounded.

When questioned, Seth was forward about everything. Luckily for him, the camera continued to broadcast the entire ordeal and backed up the stories of Seth, Lauryn, and Craig. Unbeknownst to him at the time, millions of people had already watched him attempt to talk down Jordan.

One of the Fort Wayne Police Officers opened the squad car door and moved aside to let Seth slide out.

"Well, you're free to go. I need to verify contact information first, because I'm sure there will be follow up. Either from us or someone further up the chain later."

"Up the chain?"

"Yes, sir. This was a national event at this point, meaning FBI will take over. But we have nothing to hold you on at this point in time."

Seth walked up to Craig and Lauryn, who sat in the back of an EMT wagon, and collapsed into the two of them.

"You saved my life!" he said, holding back tears.

"Of course. You owe me two now," Craig said.

"I'm so sorry, but also, oh my God I'm so happy to see you here. But how?"

"Your big ass avatar head showed me right where you were," Craig said as he handed Seth's phone back over to him.

He looked at Lauryn. Her eye was cut, but already cleaned and stitched up. Her cheek, red and swollen. He opened his mouth to say something, but she cut him off.

"Man, if this is what you have in mind for us hanging out again, count me out," Lauryn said.

She looked at him sternly for a moment, before her face beamed and she threw her arms around him, pulling him in close.

The news stations, who had swarmed into action while the group had been detained, were in rare form. Lights and cameras shoved into Seth's face and asked questions in rapid-fire succession.

"Are you the leader of Instant Karma?"

"Why did you remain silent for so long?"

"Did you know the individuals who held you captive?"

"Why did they take you? Was this a suicide pact gone wrong?"

"Hi! I'm Crispin Sanders from Fox55. Is it true you ordered the hit on Chelsea Winters?"

Lauryn slipped in front of Seth before he had the chance to stumble through any answers.

"I'm sorry. We have no comment at this time. We've been through a lot and need to regroup. Mr Roberts will make a statement when he is ready."

Seth, Lauryn, and Craig all walked back to Craig's car and climbed inside.

"And there you have it. More questions than answers tonight, as we look further into the events that transpired at both the memorial service as well as here in Fort Wayne's Industrial District. I can tell you though that with the arrests made here tonight, police believe they have made connections to multiple recent bombings around the country, as well as an open murder investigation in Gainesville, Florida. With Fox55, I'm Crispin Sanders."

CHAPTER FIFTY-SIX

Audrey hit submit on her final assignment of the semester. No fanfare. No applause. No congratulations. Just silence.

She picked up the summer classes after falling behind and failing the entirety of her schedule following Ethan's death. Those closest to her suggested she take a break, but she needed the routine. And the distraction.

She closed the laptop and crept down the hall to check on Hayden. Still asleep. He still dreamed pleasantly. Unaware of what he had lost. She was equally envious as she was sympathetic.

She closed the door and entered the spare bedroom. In what seemed like another life, this was her office. Since then, it had shifted into the only place she could decompress. She sat in the tattoo chair, which was covered by a flat sheet with dust and generously speckled in all different colors of paint. She would sit in the chair and release. Her actions were however she felt at the time. Some days she simply wept quietly. Other days she screamed. Other days she threw things against the wall.

In a dish resting on a black floating shelf, she kept some of Ethan's belongings. She slipped his rings over her index and middle fingers and spun them around. She held a red Under Armour hat close to her face and breathed in deeply.

Inside the solace of the empty throne room the world momentarily sat just as still as her. Outside, everything moved swiftly around her. Her eyes absorbed her surroundings with a sickening case of motion blur. She lived life encapsulated inside a breathing long-exposure photograph.

On the day she identified Ethan's body, she thought it would be the hardest thing she'd ever have to do. The way he lay there, lifeless and cold, on the steel slab. She didn't even speak. Gwen gave the confirmation, as Audrey fell just as pale and immobile as he.

She thought the same thing at the wake.

Then again the morning she buried him.

What she didn't expect, or have a plan for, was what came after. After the guests. After the condolences and the casseroles, and the around-the-clock companionship of friends and family checking in or staying over to help with Hayden while she grieved and isolated herself. After everyone else continued living their lives while hers remained shattered.

What then?

She was commended by countless supporters for how well she had been keeping it together. In response, she would chuckle nervously and struggle to maintain eye contact. What a stupid fucking thing to say. What choice did she have?

She clicked on the video baby monitor, and then turned up her music. Killswitch Engage's My Curse rang as she began whipping paint around.

She painted. She painted often and painted angry. Angry at God. Angry at Instant Karma. Angry at Caitlin and Tyler and Shane. But mostly, angry at Jordan.

She didn't paint so much as throw her strokes sharp and spastic and tense. She started with canvases. Everything was jagged abstract lines and scribbles. When she ran out of canvases, she moved on to decorating the walls themselves.

She grabbed a wide brush and approached the wall on which she'd been working. The backdrop before her, once a solid navy blue, now displayed a mural of a man, woman, and baby. They huddled together with terrified faces sprawled across all three while cowering below a massive skull. As big as the three combined, the skull's jaws opened wide, ready to devour the family whole. Its bright red eyes pierced the lot of them. Audrey zoned out as she put the final additions on a storm of wide chaotic patterns to surround them. Blacks and reds burst and splintered around the family being eaten in fear.

A knock came on the door, as the knob turned and slowly opened.

"Hey, how you doing today?" Gwen asked as she peeked her head in the door. "It OK if I come in?"

"Yeah. And I'm doing OK today. Thanks," Audrey said.

"I just wanted to let you know I'm here. Take your time. Have you eaten?"

"Yeah, I had a yogurt earlier."

"I'm gonna make you some eggs before you go," Gwen said.

While she picked at the food, alternating between taking small bites and moving the food around with her fork, Audrey informed Gwen on when to feed Hayden and how long he'd been down.

Multiple times per week, Gwen sat with Hayden while Audrey visited Ethan's grave. She hadn't taken Hayden since the day of the funeral, and wasn't sure of the right age to bring him along. But not yet. He had no idea what was going on, and she needed to be able to process without the distraction of a fussy child.

Birds chirped from trees lining the paved path. Cars honked and revved as they whipped by on State Route 14, running along the south side of the cemetery. Otherwise, the world around her was silent. She approached the grave, placed flowers on top of the tombstone, and sat with her legs crossed at the base. As she spoke, she looked down and plucked blades of grass one by one.

"Hayden took his first steps the other day," she said. "His fat wobbly little legs got him from the coffee table all the way to me on the couch. Five steps. It was the cutest thing. And he was so happy and so was I and I picked him up and twirled him. He let out that belly laugh you love so much. But then... then I immediately started crying. I held him so close and sobbed all over that poor baby. Because this is just the beginning, you know? There's gonna be so many other firsts. His birthday is coming up soon. His first haircut. His first day of school. And I just thought of all the things he'd have to do without you. That I'll have to do without you." She stopped picking at the grass and looked straight ahead at the tombstone. She focused on the born and died dates before her. "It's not fucking fair. All the people out there who do all these shitty things, why you? Why did you get taken from me? God, this is going to sound stupid. But I came here for you to wish me luck." She sniffled and wiped her nose and mouth. "I'm headed to the trial tomorrow. It's crazy. Trial of the decade, they say. I don't know. The whole thing is haunting me. Jordan is being talked about everywhere. They love discussing him. I couldn't help but watch that interview with his parents. I lost it when they suggested he's a God damn victim. It's fucking sickening. They're playing the sympathy card, trying to say he was just mixed up and shouldn't be held accountable. But he knows what he did. So, I need to go and make sure that motherfucker burns."

CHAPTER FIFTY-SEVEN

Well, today is the big day. My mind is racing. Might have to come back and do some more later, but needed to get my head clear early, so here I am.

Seth wrote frantically in his notebook.

After multiple rounds of questioning from the FBI, no charges were ultimately filed against him. He was heavily advised to cease uploading videos of any kind and keep his nose out of trouble. He didn't take this lightly. After the courts compiled hard copies of all Instant Karma videos, he deleted them from the internet. Other versions and duplicate videos were out of his control, but the originals tied to him were gone, at least. He deactivated all of his social media accounts, and moved to journaling in written form.

On my way to testify today. I still can't wrap my head around all of this. But luckily, I have good people supporting me. I'll be so happy when this whole thing is over. Today is just the first. Who knows when the rest will be. The others I need to show up for have way more charges or something, so the whole thing is held up for that. I haven't even been officially summoned yet for those. But was told more or less that I would be. Whatever. Check one off the list, I guess. I'm terrified. I'm overwhelmed. God, I hope this isn't hanging over me for years.

I'm happy now. Which is weird to admit with all this shit going on. But, yeah. I don't know what's going on with me and Lauryn. I'm not even worried. I'm just glad we're spending time together again. I'm sure when all this inevitably gets turned into some Hollywood blockbuster, artistic license will prevail, and movie Seth and Lauryn will ride off into the sunset. I'd like that. Who'd play us, I wonder.

Seth flipped the pen onto the desk and closed the notebook. He slipped it into the top drawer of the desk. On his way out of the bedroom, he grabbed his suit jacket from the bed.

"Feel mentally prepared to tackle the day now?" Lauryn said, as Seth joined them in the living room.

"Eh," he said as he shrugged his shoulders.

"I still can't believe you won't just come work at the bar with me. It's basically the same as being a therapist. Plus, less school and more alcohol," Craig said.

"Yeah, sure. Strangers and small talk. All the things I love," Seth said. "Besides, I want to work with kids. If I'm doing that at Kasady's, people are gonna start asking questions."

Craig flipped through the pamphlets and brochures sitting on Seth's kitchen table.

"Don't worry," Seth said. "They're just the sign-up information. It's all online classes. I'm still not going to be leaving the apartment."

"Well, that's good. I wouldn't want your body to totally go into shock or anything."

"Are you ready for this?" Lauryn asked.

Seth bounced his head back and forth on his shoulders before stretching out his arms.

"Ready as I'll ever be."

He tightened his navy blue tie and slipped on his suit jacket.

"Aww, look at our boy all grown up," Craig said.

"I hate you," Seth said.

"Yeah, I know."

"Hey, try and hold back the urge to yell, 'You can't handle the truth!'" Lauryn said.

"I make no promises."

"You know when you're getting called up?" Craig asked.

"Not sure exactly. But they said I'm the first one."

The drive from Torwood to Fort Wayne remained fairly quiet. Lauryn drove, with Seth riding shotgun. Craig sat in the back seat and watched videos on his phone.

"You think the memorial riot really happened? It's all fake. Look at this video from a bar in Torwood, Ohio. Same guy. It's how they control you. Kind of convenient, don't you think, that it's the only time he supposedly has been seen without a mask on. It's all a damn hoax. They're all actors."

"Oh, shit, dude. You're nothing but a hoax," Craig said.

"God dammit. Turn that shit off. I'm nervous enough as it is," Seth said.

"I don't take orders from false flags."

Seth laughed and threw his crumpled Egg McMuffin wrapper at him.

***

Outside the courthouse was as much of a circus as expected. The major news outlets were all in attendance. But gathered around, standing shoulder to shoulder, onlookers came to view the action. Some recorded the entrances and posted online. Some held signs and chanted. Others simply observed. It had been clearly warned prior to the court proceedings, anyone wearing an Instant Karma mask would be arrested and held for disturbing the peace.

Jordan Tillman, wearing a gray suit which fit slightly oversized, exited the car. One arm still in a sling, he used the other to hide his face from the camera flashes and sun all the same. He walked side by side with another man whispering into his ear, and was followed closely by his mother and father. Reporters screamed inaudible questions all at once as the four quickly ushered themselves inside the giant glass doors of the courthouse.

Jordan looked out into the crowd just long enough to see a massive amount of people. He heard this was one of the most publicized trials of the decade, but he didn't believe it. For him? People took time out of their day to see him and be supportive.

They carried signs that read *Free Jordan!*, and *Jordan have my babies*, and the already classic *I am Instant Karma*. In unison, a pocket from the crowd yelled, "Jordan, you're my hero!" as he was finally pulled inside by his attorney. The way they cheered for him, he couldn't help but smile as he made his way to the defendant table.

"All rise!" the bailiff called as the judge entered and took a seat.

"Day number one of 'The State of Indiana vs Jordan Tillman.' You may all be seated."

After the initial introductions were complete, and opening speeches made, the prosecutor called his first witness.

"Your Honor, the state calls Seth Roberts to the stand."

Made in the USA
Middletown, DE
30 August 2024